John T.

John Trenhaile lives in Ashdown Forest with his wife and two children. His bestselling novels – which are all available from HarperCollins – include *The Man Called Kyril*, *The Mahjong Spies*, *Krysalis*, *Acts of Betrayal*, *Blood Rules* and *The Tiger of Desire*. He has recently published his twelfth novel, *Against All Reason*.

THE TIGER OF DESIRE

'A powerful novel . . . takes the reader through every twist and turn, yet manages to conceal the shattering truth right to the very end.' *Sunday Mail*

BLOOD RULES

'Taut suspense . . . horribly convincing.' *Daily Telegraph*

ACTS OF BETRAYAL

'Shocking . . . the suspense, woven by a British writer hailed as the heir apparent to le Carré, is killing.' *Today*

KRYSALIS

'Tense . . . moves forward smartly all the way. Most impressive.' *Independent*

THE MAHJONG SPIES

'Powerful thriller . . . a grim, tense and violent slice of the action.' *Liverpool Daily Post*

THE MAN CALLED KYRIL

'A wonderfully tough and fascinating story that kept me guessing to the very end.' *New York Newsday*

JOHN TRENHAILE

A MEANS TO EVIL

HarperCollins*Publishers*

HarperCollins*Publishers*
77–85 Fulham Palace Road,
Hammersmith, London W6 8JB

This paperback edition 1994
1 3 5 7 9 8 6 4 2

First published in Great Britain by
HarperCollins*Publishers* 1993

ISBN 0 00 647973 1

Set in Meridien

Printed in Great Britain by
HarperCollinsManufacturing Glasgow

For Richard Vuylsteke.

Guide, philosopher, but most of all, friend.
With love.

AUTHOR'S NOTE

The lines that appear on page 444 are taken from
Part VI of *The Rime of the Ancient Mariner*,
by S. T. Coleridge

Odi et amo: quare id faciam, fortasse requiris.
Nescio, sed fieri sentio et excrucior

Love-hate. Why? God knows!
All *I* know is that it's true.
And it's ripping me apart.

GAIUS VALERIUS CATULLUS

'What's wrong?'

'I know the worst now. The Flying Dutchman: a man doomed to roam the earth for all eternity until he finds a woman who loves him enough to die for him and set his soul free.'

'So?'

'So Tobes just found his saviour in Johnny. And he's just ten years old. Daniel, where's the nearest phone?'

PART ONE

Every cliché you ever read or heard about Southern California is true. The atmosphere is laid-back, the climate warm, the people tolerant. Life has slowed to an almost manageable pace. There are earthquakes, sure, and the occasional Pacific tempest, but even the first garden had a snake, and most of the time this is a benign and beautiful place to be.

My name is Diane Cheung. Being Chinese and a woman (and young), there are parts of the United States where I might feel disadvantaged. But when I walk out on my patio overlooking the ocean and smell the sage, or sit harbourside in Morro Bay eating clams and drinking iced Chardonnay; when hiking over emerald-green hills to Jalama Beach, or riding my bicycle through olive groves; when I am among friends . . . at those times I know what home means, and where it is for me.

Outsiders view us Southern Californians with a mix of amusement and irritation. We have become something of a legend, rather more of a joke. The state has only its fair share of the insane, but half the people you meet here are odd. They rarely die, they scarcely seem to grow old – New Age therapies see to that – and for the most part they're well off. So nobody gives a damn. Especially doctors, and I am one.

For a long time, Southern California seemed the perfect place to practise clinical psychology.

Then the young men began to die. And I met Tobes.

Ray Douggan had Tim Sanchez drop him off at the end of the street, happy to walk the few remaining yards to his house. It was the last Sunday in April, and as Tim did a three-point to get his Mazda around the right way he re-set the dash clock to Summer Time. The police loved him for that, because it meant he'd registered the exact moment of dropping off Ray, two twenty-one a.m., and Tim was the last person to see Ray Douggan alive.

The cops pieced most of it together. What happened was this.

Ray had almost reached the house when he saw a girl leaning up against a lamp standard. There was nobody else about. Not a light showed anywhere along the street. Ray, groggy from too much beer and a joint he'd smoked up at Harley's Diner, gave her a wave; she waved back.

All of which Tim Sanchez vaguely saw in his rear mirror: vaguely being the operative word, because he'd had a few too many at Harley's also and couldn't even swear the figure under the light was female, it was just that she *seemed* kind of female, y'know . . . ?

Now Ray was only eighteen, and slow at school, and he'd had troubles enough with his family, but he knew a good thing when he was on to one. He made his way over to the standard, none too steadily, and said, 'Hi!'

She didn't answer. She just turned away, and Ray knew he was meant to follow. She took him to a car (an insomniac neighbour vouched for the sound of an engine firing at, say, half past two) and she drove him to Court Ridge Cemetery, on a bluff overlooking the town of Paradise Bay.

Now a lot of freaks frequent Court Ridge Cemetery. It's more of a jungle than a graveyard. Druggies, perverts, muggers, homeless: Court Ridge Cemetery holds them all. It is to crack what Amsterdam is to diamonds. Numerous nocturnal activities take place in Court Ridge which decent folks don't want to hear about.

There is a road running through the cemetery. This person, the one under the lamp, took Ray Douggan down that road, off to one side where the land rises sharply towards the ridge that gives the place its name, and the undergrowth is hard to penetrate. They didn't make love, according to forensic, and Ray didn't put up much of a struggle. Anyway, the medical examiner's report contained a lot of detail, and from it we know things must have gone pretty much like this . . .

*

'Hey, come on, this is far enough . . . sweet-*heart* . . .'

The torch-beam played over his face and Ray held up a hand to ward off the light. He was starting to wonder if this was such a good idea. He hadn't even seen her face yet, she was wearing a floppy black hat, and she'd said hardly anything. Now she giggled.

'So . . . we're here?' Ray ventured. With one hand he fumbled in his hip-pocket for a rubber, with the other he unhitched his belt.

The girl dropped the flashlight. It lay in the long grass, still casting its beam. Ray sensed her approaching

16

him. He felt a hand on his shoulder. He poked around with his head, seeking her lips, but boy, was it dark!

He felt her mouth nibble his ear-lobe, perhaps knew a spasm of joy as her hand closed around his erection. Then the knife went in, more or less vertically, through the scrotum and up, up, on and up.

He ran around a bit, must have been howling his head off, but Court Ridge is not a place the Paradise Bay police department habitually trawls for witnesses, and certainly none ever came forward. He was castrated while still alive, though he could have been unconscious from shock coupled with loss of blood. Hard to say. Nobody knows if Ray heard the hissing of the blowtorch as it burst into life and began to eat away at what was left of him.

At some point the perpetrator shot him twice in the torso. The second slug entered his left ventricle, and if he was alive before that he sure as all get out wasn't alive after.

So that's how Ray Douggan died, more or less. He was the second, only at that time nobody knew about the first.

*　　　*　　　*

Diane Cheung had had ample experience of dealing with dreams: other people's. Dreams were both a useful tool of analysis and a way of coping with fears too deep to be expressed. But she was no better at handling her own dreams than anyone else.

For example . . .

The plane is on fire, and falling. Diane fights her way forward along the aisle, striving to reach the cockpit.

Coils of poisonous black smoke slither inside her lungs, making her retch. 'Mother,' she cries, 'Mother, help me!' She has to fight her way uphill (strange, because the plane is diving), every inch feels like a mile, her heart pounds, her eyes dim. The flight-deck door opens. Someone is coming out, someone scary. She falls on her back. The someone comes to stand over her. She – definitely a she – is Diane's end and her beginning. Her mother, Cheung Mei-ru.

Then suddenly Diane is outside herself, looking down. Her body is naked and pure white, arms crossed over her breast like a figure on a medieval tomb. Her eyes are closed. She sits up, that dreadful, dead face, *her* face, coming closer and closer, coming upright, coming upright . . .

And she awakes. Screaming, usually.

That Monday morning, the day it began, she wasn't so much screaming as forcing air out of her throat, 'Ugh!' A protest only, nothing too primeval. Sitting up in bed, the sheets fallen away, Diane felt cold and clammy.

Her bedroom overlooked the Pacific, though today the ocean was shrouded in grey mist and the sound of a ship's siren resonated her groan. Drizzle coated the window. Her clock said seven thirty, time to get up. The clock was white, like everything else in this plain, perhaps cell-like, room, and indeed throughout the house. Diane saw herself as an artist preparing to paint on a vast, unsullied canvas, but she had not yet chosen a theme for her house, a personality. American Native, perhaps, with Rifat Ozbek embroideries? Or a replica of the beautiful mansion her parents had occupied before fleeing to Hong Kong, and thence to America, in 1949? East? West?

She thought about the recurring dream. What to make of it? Which element was more important: the flying imagery, perhaps? The fire? The transference of consciousness outside of herself; the knowledge that she was dead, yet looking down on her own corpse; the presence of her mother as a symbol of threat, her mother who never even learned how to drive a car, piloting an Airbus?

Diane used to tell this nice little story about her mother. In California they designate the places where pedestrians have right of way over traffic by painting, in the highway, 'Ped. Xing'. As in: X-ing, crossing . . . Well, when Diane's mother first arrived in this country from Shanghai she thought America was pretty terrible except for a few things, and one of the things she liked was the way they used Chinese to give pedestrians priority. Because in Mandarin the word for 'go', or 'walk', sounds like this: *sying*. And the Chinese authorities Romanize the sound thus: *xing*. Xing. Diane Cheung's mother thought they'd painted 'Ped. Xing' in the road to make her feel welcome. She never got over that completely, never learned to drive, never ventured out unless she had to.

But in Diane's dream she was always piloting a plane to destruction.

Diane's parents had been wonderful people. She'd loved them deeply, respectfully, with passion. *Ba-ba* had died when Diane was four. She was thirty-five now, so you'd think she might have gotten over it. Mostly she had, not entirely. She remembered him, and there were many photographs, many. *Ma-ma* had raised Diane. She was the kindest woman in the world, and the shrewdest. She'd died two months ago. For Diane, it still seemed like yesterday.

She jumped out of bed and pulled on a robe, because her mind had started its daily yak, *Ma-ma* this, *Ma-ma* that, and she used to tell her patients to keep busy, mind and body, all the time, as a way of blotting out fear.

She showered quickly, dressed and ran downstairs, thinking that although the pine floorboards felt warm to the feet they weren't 'her'. She wanted white everywhere, and pine simply wasn't white enough. In the kitchen her glass cafetière generated black coffee, although somehow that was okay: sand in the oyster.

Diane drank coffee, staring through the double sliding glass doors into the mist. Decisions, decisions. What would transform this wooden house, perched on a bluff five miles north of Paradise Bay, windswept and desolate, into the mansion of a wealthy Chinese-American doctor? How could she put anything into it until she knew? How to find out? Introducing colour would narrow her options. Instead of a billion choices staring her in the face, there would only be millions. Dreadful.

The Channel Islands were out there, on the other side of the fog. Probably. Did they exist even though they were invisible? she wondered. Also, an ugly oil-derrick. She'd arrange the furniture in the big downstairs room so that wherever you were sitting you wouldn't be able to see that damn derrick unless you stood up and looked for it.

Strange, about the islands. Come spring – it was nearly May now – great clouds rolled in, often obscuring them behind a mauve curtain two thousand feet and more high, but leaving the channel clear and glinting in the sun. Yet sometimes, towards day's end, there was this trick of haze and light: the islands stood out, as if carved in bas-relief, while the sea between vanished and the oil-rig was no more. Lovely, lovely.

Ma-ma would never see this house.

Diane's hand was shaking. Although she had not finished her coffee she ran to the sink and rinsed the cup before her hands could weaken further. Time to go: court-referral clinic started at nine.

But she couldn't resist taking a quick turn around her garden, because she was so proud of her home. *Mama* had left her very considerable estate to Diane, an only child, and it would all go into the house. It stood a hundred feet above the Pacific, with a wooden stairway built like a stack of 'Z's angling down to a smooth, sandy beach where not many people came, because they'd have to trek up from Jalama, and that was eight miles away. The house had four bedrooms, a big downstairs room the previous owner had knocked through, a huge kitchen, a patio-deck, a garden where so far all that grew was sage and ice-plants. Diane meant to have California poppies and masses of bleeding heart, perhaps branching out into oranges and avocados once she'd got the hang of things.

The house was shielded from the road by a long driveway (which she knew would cost her, over the years), a hedge of white oleander, and a grove of pine and eucalyptus: the latter her favourite tree, because it reminded her of China. On the side farthest from the road there was also a fence, brand new: Diane's first major owner-expenditure.

The previous owner of her house had quarrelled with Heddy-May, an old woman who counted as the nearest neighbour, although 'near' was a quarter of a mile away. They'd wrangled for years over the precise location of the south-eastern boundary, were still wrangling when Diane bought. She'd settled this potential lawsuit in an afternoon, with flowers and tea and home-baked cookies and the purchase of a sturdy fence, so that now Heddy-May didn't just count as a neighbour, she had become a friend. There was one down side. Heddy-May kept goats. She'd given Diane some of their milk, Diane had pronounced it 'interesting', and ever since then she'd found a quart of the stuff on her porch each Friday afternoon when she returned from work. She bathed her face in it.

Diane got into her car, a Toyota Camry, bright red and gleaming-new. She was doing well, and her book helped; royalties came in every six months to supplement her fees and her University Hospital salary, Mother's estate . . . how to spend all that money? It bewildered her. A friend had suggested she should buy a Porsche. That would be a terrifying experience. Several of her patients drove Porsches. The Porsche was symptomatic of narcissism. A Camry was peppy enough while making Diane feel safe. She'd cycle everywhere if she could, but St Joseph's (the hospital where she was based) sat five twisting, mountainous miles away. The morning ride would be fine, the road was mostly downhill, but evenings! . . . and the hours she worked were long.

So today she reversed her Camry out of the garage and closed the double doors, making a mental note to call the contractor who was supposed to be fitting her house with an alarm system. (Diane was not a timorous woman, but neither had her parents raised her to be foolhardy, and this was a remote location.) Between the house and the road was a meadow, mown for her by one of the local farm-boys; it had stopped raining and rays of sun scythed through the cloud, showing up oxeye daisies, promising the onset of summer, so that soon Diane didn't think about *Ma-ma* any more.

At the road was a gate, although because it didn't hang quite right it often got left open. Diane stopped and reached inside the tube for her copy of the *Paradise Bay Bee*, but it wasn't there. Bobby Dell had forgotten to deliver her newspaper. This was a minor nuisance, Diane somehow couldn't get mad at Bobby Dell. Child psychologists always dread the Bobbys of this world, knowing that one day they will walk out of court having gotten away with murder.

On the other side of the road, which bent at this point, slightly lower than the highway, stood a grove of olive and her beloved eucalyptus; beyond that lay farmland, the ploughed earth just showing coffee-ground rich brown through the foliage. A thin twist of smoke rose out of the hollow. The smoker stood back from the road, face hidden, but his jeans were visible, a sickly shade of green splashed with black, like camou-flage pants.

Although the thicket was shady and leaves obscured the man, Diane could just make out how he was hold-ing a rolled-up newspaper under his arm. A *Paradise Bay Bee*, perhaps? She briefly thought about a cheery hail – 'Hi! Lovely day!' – before deciding against it. As she drove on, her heart beating faster than usual, and feeling vaguely cheated by her own cowardice, Diane made a mental note to ask Heddy-May if she'd seen any strangers around recently.

A mile down the road she joined Route 1. Traffic was light; too far south for Hearst Castle, safely north of Lompoc, her morning drive was normally a swift one. Today, however, she detoured and stopped off at Mr Chadwick's. Mr Chadwick ran an all-purpose store in a tiny burg called Heartness that contained (in addition to Mr C) one Wells Fargo bank, the Harbor Gun Shop, a grey, single-storey cinema, a Pizza Port, a pop. of 94 and an el. of 115 feet. Inside Mr Chadwick's, Diane found Class A consternation.

Bobby Dell the paper-boy, four feet nothing, was standing on tiptoe the better to harangue Mr C.

'Aw, come on, Sam, give me a break! It's income I'm losing here.'

'Better lose income than lose your life. Morning, Diane.'

Diane could see at a glance how distressed the boy was. She put an arm around Bobby and gave him a hug, letting him feel sympathy as a physical sensation. This was only a variant on what she did all day. She was good at it, she got well paid for it; but she cuddled Bobby Dell because she liked him, and it was not in her nature to pass suffering by.

'What's up?' she asked.

'Sam says I can't deliver newspapers any more.' Bobby twisted around to look up at Diane. 'Says it's too dangerous.'

Sam Chadwick caught her eye and sidled down the counter, drawing Diane with him. He must have been about sixty years old, his lawyerly face distinguished by round, silver-rimmed spectacles. 'I'm sorry for the boy,' he confessed, 'but we already have one missing teenager to worry about, and then after what they discovered this morning . . .'

'What did they discover this morning?'

'You haven't heard?'

'I haven't turned on the TV or anything. And my paper's missing, that's why – '

'We had ourselves a murder, down at Court Ridge.'

24

'The boy who was missing? Hal Lawson?'

'No. Ray Douggan, his name was. Early hours of Sunday, they reckon. Pretty gruesome.' Sam's eyes strayed to Bobby; he obviously didn't want to say too much in front of the boy. 'Horrific injuries, you know what I mean?' He lowered his voice. 'Whoever did it took a blowtorch to the body afterwards. Should ask the funeral parlour for a discount, if you ask me. Not enough left to rate a full burial.'

'How sickening.'

'I'm going to have to let Bobby go. This used to be a peaceful place. Not any more.'

Bobby Dell, distraught though he was, had been listening with half an ear. Now he interjected, 'Only one! I mean, come on, *one*! Down in LA they wipe out that many each half-hour. One's the quota out here, right? Whoever iced Douggan doesn't need a pair. Betcha.'

'Well, I don't think your parents would agree with you,' Diane said.

'But Court Ridge is *miles* away . . .'

'That's true, Sam,' Diane said quietly. 'Court Ridge must be all of seven miles south of here.'

'In a car, that's nothing.' Sam shook his head decisively. 'It's not you as would have to telephone Rita and John Dell if something happened, Diane. I can't risk it. The delivery boys go out early, it's dark. They're vulnerable on bicycles.' He took off his glasses and breathed on the lenses. 'It didn't always used to be so,' he said.

'What about me?' Bobby wailed. 'How am I supposed to live on my pocket-money? Huh? Sam, have you no sense of decency?'

Sam merely shrugged and moved up the counter.

'So at least I know why I didn't get my paper this morning,' Diane said brightly, making the most of this lull in hostilities.

Bobby puffed out his chest. 'Whaddya mean? I delivered it six o'clock, on the button. Stupid . . . '

'All right, that's enough.' Mr Chadwick's voice had upped a note or two, turning fierce on the way. 'Bobby, time you went home. Off you go, now.'

The boy left, dragging his feet and with many an appealing backward glance. Sam and Diane half smiled at each other, but both were uneasy. Sam would have to find a way of delivering if he was not to lose custom; Diane was left with the knowledge that somebody – no, not 'somebody', the smoker in the woods – had stolen her newspaper, the first and only time such a thing had happened since she'd moved into the house two months ago.

'Tell me I'm right,' Sam said. 'You're a psychologist, you work with kids all the time. I can't let boys like him roam around in the dark. Can I?'

'You most certainly can't. Well . . . God. I mean, how awful!'

They talked a while longer, but it was getting late. Sam gave Diane another newspaper, compliments of the house. She went out to her car, time only to scan the front page and take in the headline: 'Cemetery Talks Deadlocked; Developer: "We'll Proceed" angers City Hall'. On the car-radio, they were talking about the same thing.

For the past two years, a consortium of developers had been trying to get zoning permission to develop five acres of the mini-hell known as Court Ridge Cemetery. There were objections of a religious nature. But there were also religious people of an objectionable nature. And then there were a whole lot of ordinary citizens who believed, deep down, that Court Ridge Cemetery was a necessary evil because that's where all the trash congregated instead of coming into town and bothering decent folk.

As Diane drove south the radio debate continued, but the terrain here was hilly and the station faded quickly. The San Rafael, Sierra Madre and Santa Ynez ranges conspired to protect Paradise Bay from the worst of the weather, so it was a terrific fruit-growing area, but another consequence was that its FM radio stations had limited range. Diane tuned to one-oh-five, and Mozart beamed up from Los Angeles to soothe her cares away.

By the time she reached St Joseph's Hospital Diane's mind was already deep into her schedule, but today, as always, she couldn't resist pausing by the hospital's main doors to savour the magnificent view.

St Joe's was perched high on a cliff overlooking Paradise Bay to the south. The town was little sister to Santa Barbara, down the coast: smaller, warmer, kinder (if such a thing be possible), but built to the same scheme, though less lovely. The Spanish fathers had by-passed Paradise Bay, leaving it missionless, and in summer this cut the number of tourists to an acceptable level. It might have doubled for a Mediterranean coastal town somewhere in Piedmont.

Spread out below Diane this morning was a broad expanse of greenery, flecked with palms and red-tile roofs, white walls and Spanish grille-work and broad avenues extending as far south as she could see, where the coast weaved inland and Washington Avenue, Paradise Bay's main drag, joined up with Highway 1. Many miles to her left, the San Rafael mountains reared up to saw-tooth peaks from which sunshine was just burning off the last of the cloud.

As Diane's eyes swept down from the mountains, past the foothills that provided such good farming soil, with big, well-organized spreads of maize and corn and vegetables, they encountered a sight that caused her smile to fade.

Between the mountains and the city boundary stood a curious freak of nature: a hump, that was the best word, a hump some four or five hundred feet high and maybe a mile long, with a sharp drop at the northern end but tapering away to ranchland on the south. In the old days there'd been a garrison there, with a court-house and a gallows – hence the name: Court Ridge. As time went by, wealthy people still sought the protection of the high ground, even though the garrison had faded into history: the best, most sought-after houses in Paradise Bay were to be found atop Court Ridge.

On the inland side, nearest the mountain range, the earliest occupants of the garrison had laid out a cemetery. Diane couldn't see it from her vantage point at the top of St Joe's driveway, but she knew it was there. Everyone knew Court Ridge Cemetery. Knew it . . . hated it.

On her way in, Diane passed the florist's stall and sweet peas caught her eye. She could not resist buying them; flowers were one of the few things that had kept her going since *Ma-ma*'s death. While unlocking her office, Diane knew that familiar moment of silly pride as she read the plaque: Dr Diane Cheung PhD, Director of Psychological Services. She gave herself permission to exult a little, to renew her self-respect. She was Chinese, a woman, thirty-five years old, author of a textbook on disturbed adolescents that had stayed on the *New York Times Book Review* bestseller list for eight months. She'd had her failures, but did not lack success.

The office was modern, equipped with a powerful PC, the latest fax-cum-answering-machine, and sleek designer furniture. On her desk, however, Diane kept an inscribed plate that was far from new. Strategically placed so that she could see it wherever she was sitting, it contained some legendary words of an even more legendary therapist, Donald Winnicott: *'The "good-enough analyst" – one who is reliably there, on time, alive, breathing; who keeps awake and preoccupied with the patient, remaining free from temper tantrums and compulsive falling in love.'*

While Diane was flicking imaginary dust off her plaque, Julia Page came in. Julia was doing a residency programme in the hope of obtaining hands-on experience of forensic child psychiatry through Diane's connections with the local court clinic. The Paradise Bay court of common pleas, as in most towns of similar size across the US, had a section dedicated to young criminals, known as the Juvenile Court. Attached to this court was a clinic, staffed by psychiatrists and psychologists, who assisted the judge in determining who was mad and who was sane, who would benefit from correctional training and who should fry in the chair. (Notionally speaking.) Often, in the case of disturbed juvenile offenders, they recommended a session with Auntie Diane, the adolescent's friend, as an alternative to two years in jail.

Diane had put Julia in charge of managing her court-referrals on a rotational basis. She liked her. Julia had lots of fluffy blonde hair that refused to lie down, generous lips, dimples, lovely skin. If only she wouldn't wear big, round glasses in the mistaken belief that they made her look scholarly, she'd have been a beauty. She thought boys should respect her for what she was, but then she was a Valley Girl, so what could anyone do?

Today, however, Julia appeared subdued. 'Did you hear about the slaying?' she asked.

Slaying – such an emotive word, Diane thought. 'Yes. Court Ridge.'

'Do you feel safe?'

'At my place? Sure.' Diane hesitated. 'Where is safe, these days?'

'Here used to be pretty okay.'

Diane gave her a smile, trying to inject a little 'Oh-come-on!' into it, although she knew in her heart Julia was right.

Julia said, 'They're waiting.'

She handed Diane four files, along with her own notes. Diane scanned the names. She had met these four boys before, but not often. They seemed to make a convincing group, they related. One of them interested her tremendously. His name was Tobes Gascoign and he was the most seamless liar she'd ever encountered in professional practice. He was also extremely well and widely read: a self-taught Renaissance Man.

The two women walked along the corridor to the playroom.

This had been constructed to Diane Cheung's design. It faced south, and the outer one-third section was all tinted glass, like a conservatory, with plants and tanks full of tropical fish. The playroom looked out over the hospital lawn to a rise, beyond which was the ocean. The temperature was strictly controlled by some sophisticated sensory equipment that had cost a lot of money, but her textbook had been riding high then, taking her hospital's reputation up with it, and so budget hadn't entered into it.

A comfortable, padded banquette lined the rest of the room. On the walls were paintings, many of them done by clients. The floor was littered with toys and she'd been careful to include several from China – dragons, puppets, decorated spears, face-masks. 'Be different,' she used to tell the children; 'Imagine!' There were bean-bag seats, and soft chairs, there were tables for drawing and Lego and paints, crayons galore. No TV, although music could be piped in. Along one side-wall was a mirror. A two-way mirror. Julia and Diane used to stand behind it and spy on what happened in the playroom.

Sometimes at parties people asked her what she did and she would say, 'I'm a secret agent.' Then she'd come clean, and laugh . . .

Today she saw at once that the configuration was interesting, and new. The four youths were sitting around a table. Two of them were smoking. There was a businesslike atmosphere; maybe they were union officials working out the next set of demands. Maybe she had been cast in the role of employer. But this table thing was new; normally they stood, or slouched, or slumped on bean-bags.

Julia, too, sensed new departures. She sat on the banquette with her feet up, notebook in her lap, and waited. Diane approved. By acting thus, Julia counter-balanced the aura of formality the boys had set out to construct.

Diane did the opposite of what they expected. Instead of sitting in the chair at one end of their table, she plumped herself down on a cushion and spent a minute in the lotus position with her eyes closed. When she opened them again she found the boys glaring at her. She'd spoiled their plan.

She looked from face to face, reviewing what she knew about them.

None of them were juveniles, that was the first thing. Strange? Well, yes. Three of them had first come to her from the Juvenile Court, via the clinic, and then reoffended once they'd passed eighteen. Diane had persuaded the judge to hand down community service orders and give her babies back to her.

Gascoign was different.

Tobes Gascoign was twenty years old. He had lived in New York state and then in LA, which was where he'd first been busted, for larceny. He was a compulsive shoplifter. He was good at it, but not so good as to escape all the time. A drifter with no parents, no home, he worked as a vegetable-cook in one of Paradise Bay's two good restaurants. His record had followed him; when first he'd come to the attention of the court here, Ventura County had sent up the papers and they were an inch thick. 'Incorrigible.' That word was a red rag to Diane's bull.

Although Tobes was not a juvenile when he came before the Paradise Bay court of common pleas, he was sufficiently odd to warrant psychological assessment. A friend of Diane's at the court clinic ran a Minnesota Multiphasic Personality Inventory, a Likert scaling, and a Jesness Inventory – standard personality and social attitude tests. He showed her the results and asked, 'Diane, is this guy for real?'

As an experienced clinician, Diane knew the test results had to be wrong. Nothing human was that consistent.

She'd badgered the judge into giving her Tobes. Judge Cyril DeMesne was one of the good guys, he *believed* in her brand of black magic. Tobes had to attend her group if he wanted to stay out of jail. He fascinated her, not least because in him she sensed an intelligence almost on a par with her own. She'd made him a member of this group thinking the others might provoke him into revealing his true nature.

Ramon, the would-be bank robber, was first to speak. 'We're gonna talk about Jesse's sister.'

Billy-the-Kid, whose hobby was stealing cars in order to drive them at high speed before wrecking them, nodded agreement. Billy was addicted to nitrous oxide, which he called 'hippie crack', but today he seemed reasonably on top of things. Jesse stared at Diane, willing her intervention. There was a long silence. Tobes smiled neutrally at the table-top.

'Listen,' Ramon says. 'We have had it up to here, see, with Jesse and his sister. We want to clear his ass out of here. He won't say nothing about what happened. The rest of us, we came clean.'

Here he broke off to look from face to face, waving his hand in an arc that embraced his buddies. Diane was aware of Julia writing and wished she would stop. Covertly she made a sign, the one that meant: Desist.

'Tobes came clean. Didn't you, Tobes?'

Tobes appeared to be only half listening. He sucked in his lips, raised his eyebrows, and nodded. Today he was wearing soiled blue jeans and a pristine white shirt; the contrast seemed intentional. He had not pressed the shirt but otherwise it looked good; stolen, maybe? Tobes had a preppy face, betrayed by a weedy frame. His thick gold hair, almost white, formed natural waves. He looked at you through piercing blue eyes of transparent honesty. Diane often felt he was on the point of calling her 'M'am'.

'Tobes stole, we know all about it. I tried to rob a bank.'

Billy-the-Kid laughed. Everyone joined in, even Diane. Ramon's efforts at bank-robbery would have graced a Buster Keaton movie.

'And Jesse . . . Jesse tried to screw his kid sister.'

For the first time, Jesse reacted. 'You're just an asshole.'

'Look – '

Jesse stood up. The boys' reactions showed they thought he was going to hit Ramon, but Diane knew he would not do that. He walked towards the door. Ramon called after him, 'Chicken-shit. Come back here and face it.'

The door was locked. Jesse stopped there, defeated, not knowing what to do. He turned. 'I don't need this,' he said quietly.

Jesse was black, the group's only person of colour, with hair styled in a High Top Fade as a means of ID-with-attitude. He did, of course, need this. He'd made a clumsy attempt to rape his fourteen-year-old sister, backing off the minute she screamed, but then hitting her across the mouth. She had lost a tooth. The court clinic physicians cluck-clucked at Diane, saying he should be in a sexual offenders' group, but Jesse was not a sexual offender, nor was he habitually violent. Jesse was nineteen, a mixed-up kid in need of peers who could give him some self-respect. Having him here could be stigmatized as a risky experiment, but that was the Diane Cheung special-of-the-day. (Her favourite cuisine was Sichuan; she used a lot of chili.)

'Jesse,' she said, 'why not sit down? I have a question I want to ask you.'

He came back. It took time, but he came. 'Why are you so hard on yourself,' Diane said, 'when no one else is?'

Tobes smiled. *Why?* she wondered.

'I don' wan talkbout it,' Jesse said.

Ramon thumped the table with his fist, embarking on a spectacular Spanish tirade; and so the morning wore on. The group passed through many modes, some of them new; on the whole Diane was pleased with them, because even if they took unsatisfactory directions at least they were not static.

At last it turned five minutes to ten; she knew by following Tobes's eyes as they strayed to the clock. Suddenly Tobes leaned forward to rest one forearm on the table, his other hand thrust into the pocket of his jeans. Jesse sat immediately to his left. He waited for silence. Then he said, 'Amy loves you, Jess.' (Amy being the name of Jesse's sister, the one he'd tried to rape.)

'How do *you* know?'

'You're here, aren't you?'

'So what?'

'That's thanks to her. She could have pressed for a jail sentence. The judge would have listened. Am I right, or what?'

Jesse said nothing. Diane sat up. Tobes was, of course, quite right. This young man was capable of empathy and imagination, of deductive reasoning, and now at last he was shedding his chosen role of cipher. Only one thing was wrong: the way he'd looked at the clock before deciding to intervene.

Who's in charge here? she thought. *Now just a minute . . .*

But before she could snatch the initiative back from Tobes he laid a hand on top of Jesse's and gave it a squeeze. For a moment Jesse sat there, stony-faced. Then he shook off Tobes, but only so that he could wipe his eyes. 'Shit,' he said. Tobes held out his palm and Jesse gave him five, hard, *bang*, like that.

Diane rose; so did they. Jesse was the last to file out. Diane, too, held out her hand; Jesse hit it, but gently, and she knew she'd had less effect on him than Tobes. The door closed. Diane leaned against it. She said to Julia, 'Given the choice between two-to-five upstate and forty sessions with Diane Cheung, what would your choice be?'

'I don't know how to break this to you, but . . . '

Diane longed for the restorative comfort of chrysanthemum tea, but there was no time. She and Julia flew along corridors, trying to make sense of the day's schedule.

'Tobes Gascoign,' Diane said. 'Have his school records shown up?'

'No response from the county director of education; you have to go to state now.'

'Okay. Remind me to run through his contribution to today's session with you.'

'Fascinating.'

'Agreed. Next, Johannsen. I read the papers and last week I interviewed him again. I'm convinced he's insane within the meaning of the ruling in People versus Drew, and that the County Medical Health office are wrong. Call his lawyer, say I believe Johannsen killed while the balance of his mind was disturbed, but he'll need to back me with two whiz psychiatrists in court.'

'Guilty but insane: great.'

'Not guilty by reason of insanity. Be precise! Be accurate! Better yet, be compassionate. What time is the car supposed to be here?'

'Ten fifteen.'

'I'm late, I'm late . . .'

When Diane arrived at the studios of PBCR, Dick Jacobson, the presenter of West Coast Crimewaves, was already in the studio, talking with someone seated at the table. She raced in and said, 'Hi, Dick, long time no see!'

'Hello, Diane. Do you know Ed Hersey, of the third precinct?'

Dick moved aside, allowing Diane to see the man who was now rising to greet her. For an instant she felt sick. Only a last, lingering trace of self-preservation prevented her sliding to the floor. 'Oh,' she said, and that single word cost her more stamina than she would normally burn in a day. 'Yes. Sort of.' In the same instant Ed said 'Sort of' too, so that the words coalesced.

Diane made herself look Ed Hersey full in the face. His stocky, energetic body (he reminded her of a terrier) was encased in the same grey suit she remembered so well, creased around the crotch. His shirt strained a little with the effort of keeping his manly chest in check. The tie was loose, his shoes, as ever, spotlessly clean and polished; Diane knew, without looking, that he still hadn't had the heels fixed. He was much the same as she remembered, although there were bags under his eyes and his curly chestnut hair could have used a trim. For a man one year her senior he seemed in pretty good shape.

Ed had one of those faces that exude honest simplicity. He is simple, he is honest, she'd told herself when she'd become his lover. Then a third precinct clerk she used to play tennis with had taken her aside and said, Look, honey, I don't like to see my friends get hurt . . .

They didn't play tennis any more after that.

Ed's face creased into a dozen smiles – eyes, mouth, dimpled cheeks, even his ears rode up his skull – and he said, 'Diane, you look the picture of summer.'

His voice was deep, gruff, but also musical. (He could even sing. He liked Gilbert and Sullivan.) Diane heard it and tingled in dangerous zones. One thing kept her flying straight and level: Ed was half an inch shorter than she was. The ten in her five-ten enabled her to look down on him, ever so slightly. Impossible to throw yourself at the feet of a man whose heart is nearer those feet than you are.

'You look kind of autumny,' she riposted blithely. 'Winter not far off, I guess?' She greeted Dick with a peck on the cheek and didn't even mind when he put an arm around her waist. Hell, why should Dick have taken the trouble to tell her who her fellow guest would be? He wasn't to know they'd conducted an adulterous affair.

West Coast Crimewaves was a half-hour, once-a-week slot, bringing news and updates on crime and law enforcement to anyone within a fifty-mile radius of Paradise Bay Community Radio's studios on the corner of Washington and A. It solved crime, it worked; which didn't stop the sponsors once a year trying to axe it in favour of something more easily broken up by commercials. Dick was fifty-eight, stolid, not easily ruffled. Diane reckoned he'd go on presenting West Coast Crimewaves until he retired, after which he wouldn't care, but he'd go on till then.

'Okay, people,' he said. 'This morning's murder of Ray Douggan: can you take it in somehow?'

Diane looked at Ed; both nodded. 'Wing it,' Diane said.

While Dick adjusted the mike and set levels, Diane got her heartbeat down to a manageable level. She fluffed up a brightness she didn't feel and asked Ed, 'So how are things? Got any kids yet?' Oh, she felt evil. *Yao-ren*, the Chinese say: sorceress.

Ed shook his head. 'No. I – '

Dick said, 'Ten seconds.'

'I have some news for you,' Ed whispered. 'About that stuff you had stolen. You remember – '

The On-Air light illuminated and Dick went in off the high-board.

'This is West Coast Crimewaves, I'm Dick Jacobson. Today we welcome Detective Edwin Hersey, of the Paradise Bay police department, and Dr Diane Cheung, head psychologist at St Joseph's Hospital, up the coast from here at Bel Cove; she specializes in disturbed children and what makes them that way. These two busy people have been good enough to give up their time to come and share some information, maybe some thoughts as well, about the recent disappearance of teenager Hal Lawson, which has been attracting a lot of media attention. And, of course, we'll be talking about Ray Douggan, whose savagely mutilated body was found in Court Ridge Cemetery earlier today. Diane, if I can turn to you first: I believe you've written what many folk consider to be the leading textbook on the disturbed teenage mind, *To the Dance of a Different Drum*, have I got that right?'

Dick was looking at her with an expectant smile, one eyebrow raised. Be cool, be calm, she told herself; you are a professional.

She'd never known that Ed was short for Edwin . . .

* * *

A lot of people heard that broadcast. Down on the waterfront, where the fishermen and yachtsmen were painting hulls, stitching nets, that kind of thing, about one in four radios was tuned to PBCR because there would be a full weather report on the hour. Many of the oceanside cafés and bars had it on too, while the owners cleaned up after last night, or sat peeling potatoes in the sun, or checked stock. Down at the gas-station on the turn-off from Highway 1, where Diane usually filled up, the cashier, Tony Deer, was listening, because whenever she drove in for gas he asked when she next planned to do the media and so he'd known she was going to be on today. Tony was an actor 'between jobs', had been for three and a half years now, and he liked to keep in touch with the industry. Mothers were listening while they changed diapers or fixed coffee. In trendy Fountainside, boutique- and store-keepers kept a portable on as background solace for their recession-driven pain. Alarm-radios jerked people back to life with the sound of Diane explaining why she'd written *To the Dance of a Different Drum: Disturbed Children and What Makes Them That Way*. All sorts and conditions of men and women and children heard Ed talking about violent crime statistics and how Paradise Bay, for a Californian town that size, was still relatively peaceful. Bernie Dinh, the bar steward out at Tarrant Country Club, between Court Ridge and the mountains, polished a row of glasses and learned how when they last released reliable figures there had been a violent crime every twenty seconds, a rape every six minutes and a murder every twenty-five minutes, and this year Paradise Bay had notified two murders if you counted Ray Douggan, and already it was the last week of April; and Bernie, who had smuggled himself out of

Vietnam in 1975 along with five members of his family, smiled, because today was a nice day, a *fine* day.

Of course, some of the people listening paid more attention than others.

In the Anderson house, high up on Court Ridge, with its overgrown tennis court, and balconies, and gravel driveway, and its panoramic view of the ocean, domestic tension clogged the airwaves. Reception, great in one sense, was poor in terms of audience appreciation.

Nicole Anderson and her ten-year-old stepson Johnny were in the kitchen. Outside the sun was shining. It was almost May, the Andersons thought it hot, but then they'd just moved from Mansfield, Ohio. Nicole was fixing breakfast. She'd turned on the radio. Johnny was trying to listen while he pushed wheaties around in the bowl. Every time he pushed, milk spilled over. His game-plan was to end up with all the milk on the table, none in the bowl, none in him, no way! He knew how much this would annoy Nicole. She would smile in that meaningless way she had but he would look into her eyes and see the fear. Great.

He could hear this woman with a soft voice and endearing accent talking over the radio. She was on about a poor little rich boy who'd gone missing from his home, and another one who had been killed. There was a cop with her. Johnny longed to watch TV but the set hadn't been unpacked yet.

'Isn't it sad?' Nicole said, unwrapping a cup. 'Somewhere out there, mothers are weeping.'

Johnny sniffed, but said nothing.

'Why does that presenter have to be so tough with the detective?' Nicole went on. 'He's got a difficult row to hoe.'

'Because the PD here stinks,' Mike Anderson said, coming in from the back yard. He was dressed for golf: red T-shirt, tartan trousers, white golf shoes. Johnny surveyed his father covertly. Not a hair out of place, he could even see the tiny flecks of dried gel. 'It stinks because it's inefficient and overmanned,' Mike went on. 'Do we have eggs?'

To Johnny's huge joy, Nicole panicked. Where were the skillets? Mike unfolded the paper and started to read. Then he remembered his son. He winked. 'Hi, J-Boy, how are you doing?'

''Kay.'

'School today?'

'Not 'til Monday.'

Johnny felt tight inside. It was a kind of pain, kind of not that bad. Mike knew damn well school didn't start until next week. His eyes hadn't left the paper during this exchange; Johnny wanted to scream at his father, 'Look at me!' But he wasn't sure what would happen if he did. So he didn't.

The woman on the radio was saying, 'The missing boy will be confused, he'll be frightened, he could well be feeling guilty.'

And because Johnny was feeling all that, too, he started to concentrate.

' . . . Hal was carrying a lot of money. He came from a rich background, he knew the combination to his father's safe and he used it to take with him in excess of one thousand dollars. People notice things like that. Kids with money attract attention. Someone, somewhere must have . . . '

Mike started rooting around the kitchen. Nicole asked him what he wanted. Mike said it didn't matter, but he went right on looking. Johnny gazed at his

42

father, wondering what would happen if he said, as he longed to say, 'Will you just sit down and be quiet!'

' . . . This kid will not be behaving normally,' said the radio-woman. 'I beg all of you out there to keep an eye open for him, and not to hesitate to approach him with sympathy and a smile if you should see him. He is not dangerous, he is sad. And if he is alive, he is certainly going to be a very frightened young man.'

Johnny thought: That's wonderful. That's me. I am not dangerous, I am sad. I am frightened. Of what's inside. Of the animal that's in my body and won't come out. Because the animal's afraid, too.

Mike Anderson sat down again and said, 'Where are those eggs, honey, I don't have a lot of time.'

Nicole found the pan, cooked his eggs the way he liked them, which was sunny-side-up and a drizzle of melted butter on top. (Those kind of eggs made Johnny feel sick.) She poured a cup of coffee for herself and the grown-ups talked like Johnny wasn't there.

They were talking about how worried they were. At least, that's not what they were saying, but it's what Johnny actually *heard*. Like: they didn't want to be here. They'd loved it in Mansfield. But Mike Anderson worked for a huge construction company and Johnny knew it was struggling, although that was one of the things his father was busy not saying. The owners had heard about this project to build some place in California, and gotten a toe-hold. They'd sent Mike over to the west coast to make sure the regional set-up didn't screw up.

So now Nicole asked (politely, she didn't care to upset Mike) why he had to go play golf when there was all this unpacking still to do. And Mike Anderson went on about the importance of signing the contract soon, and his inter-personal skills being so important to the company, and Johnny didn't know what else. He was a wonderful man. Johnny didn't know any kid who'd got a father like his. So powerful and strong and who could speak so well.

Johnny had this feeling, coiled deep inside him like a sleeping snake, that Mike hated him. Just a feeling . . .

Mike and Nicole went out. The house was quiet, except for the presenter giving the cop a hard time over something called the Juvenile Crimes Unit. Seemed like the woman had started it and things weren't going well. The radio guy said it was a gimmick, dreamed up to get the heat off the police chief. The woman didn't buy that.

Nicole came back in the house, her face tenser than ever. She turned off the radio. Johnny said, 'I was listening.'

'Well, if you're through eating, I think you should go tidy your room, young man.'

'Don't patronize me.'

'I am not patronizing you, Johnny, I am asking you to tidy your room.'

'Don't call me young man, then.'

'Well, what *should* I call you? Because let's face it, your father and I've been married two years now, and you still won't tell me what I should call you, and you won't call me anything.'

Wrong. Johnny called her the Wicked Witch of the West. The Fat Bitch. The Old Whore. Lots of things he called her.

She ran a hand through her hair. The tense lines in her face rearranged themselves; she was about to cry. Johnny knew better than to spoil things by answering her. He kept quiet and stared at Nicole, until she looked away. Hardness burned a hole in his stomach. She should help him, she was his stepmother, she ought to try and love him.

'I don't want to go to school next week,' he heard himself say.

'You'll meet new friends, you'll have things to do, there'll be sports.'

No reply.

'What you need is something to occupy your mind.'

'What I need is a proper mother.'

She stared at him. They had been here before, the territory was familiar to both of them. Nicole hated it but Johnny loved it, because if he went on long enough it would bring back his real mother and this witch could take a hike. Until now, he'd always given in early. Not this time. This time he'd see it through.

'Johnny, we've discussed all this.'

'So?'

'Your mother is . . . is dead.' Nicole's voice dropped, out of fake reverence (Johnny guessed). 'Now maybe I'm not a very good substitute, but I'm here, and I'm trying.' She paused. 'God knows, I'm trying.'

'I didn't ask you to try.'

'But your father did.'

'Mike Anderson doesn't know you the way I do.'

'What's that meant to mean?'

But Johnny shrugged. Hell, *he* didn't know. It was something to say, that's all. Anyway, Nicole got a grip on herself. 'Tell you what,' she said brightly. 'Why don't we take a ride into town and see what's in the shops?'

Johnny shook his head.

'Bet we can find an ice-cream or two.'

'You'll get fat – ' Johnny decided to go one more notch: 'Fatter.'

The boy got up and made for the door. Nicole shrieked, 'Sit down right this minute!'

But he felt bored. This wasn't a good time for going the distance, after all. His back was to her. Chair legs scraped on the floor. She was going to make a grab for him. Run! Johnny fled through the back door. Noises behind him meant she'd tripped and fallen. Great!

Keeping low, he crept back to the kitchen window and listened. Nicole was sobbing quietly; the elastic band in Johnny's gut wound another couple of turns. He felt good and bad at the same time. Then she was phoning. Who? Mike Anderson . . .? No, he'd gone golfing. But he had his mobile with him . . .

It wasn't Mike, it was the hospital: Nicole wanted to make an appointment. Oh-oh. Johnny knew what *that* meant. Dr Baggeley Mark Two.

Dr Baggeley had been his therapist in Mansfield. Now there was one ignorant man. He knew nothing. He cared nothing. But he'd been masterful in his ignorance: determined to prove, very forcefully and clearly, how little he knew, or cared, about Johnny. So Johnny had showed him a tiny slice of what he felt and kept the rest to himself, like grown-ups did. Johnny was pretty grown up, in some ways.

Nicole couldn't even remember who she was supposed to ask for. Johnny heard her fumbling around, looking for the referral letter. Then she must have found it, for she said, 'Dr Diane Cheung, it says here.'

The boy thought: What a weird name. Chee Ung. (Which was how the Wicked Witch of the West had pronounced it.) Sounded like a kind of monkey.

Johnny skipped.

Down the lawn, out through the back gate, into the

path that backed onto all the Court Ridge houses. What a beautiful day! Sun, green trees, grass. Mansfield was never like this. In Mansfield, the only kind of grass they had was the cut kind – flat, with lines where the mower had run over it. Here, the grass came in patches and clumps, the trees grew where *they* wanted. The sun shone through leaves and there was a breeze – piles of diamonds littered the path, all constantly moving. The air smelled sweet, but the scent was somehow heavy. It hung around. And there were too many flowers for Johnny to take in all at once.

He turned right, because that way the path went down. Through the trees on the left side of the path he could see rolling hills, not too high. They were green, there were many more trees. Suddenly he saw a smaller path leading off to the left, away from Court Ridge, towards the hills. There the grass grew high as Johnny's belt. He took the small path because it went down more steeply, into a hollow, and looked the easy way.

The trees grew more thickly here. Wherever you had two trees on either side, they leaned towards each other and their branches meshed. So it got darker. Also a lot colder, and damp. Johnny was wearing only a T-shirt. Goose-bumps rose on his arms. He shivered.

The little path was a mess. His trainers were soon splattered with mud: another task for stepmommy-birdbrain when he got back. Suddenly his eye latched onto this stone, to one side of the path.

A gravestone.

He was in the cemetery.

For a moment, Johnny felt scared, really and truly scared. He'd realized the cemetery must be out here somewhere, but . . .

A butterfly perched on top of the gravestone. It was

red and black; its wings moved slowly up and down. Johnny wanted to see the butterfly, so he moved closer. His feet snared in something. There was a smell. Dog-shit! He laughed, thinking what Nicole would say. Then he looked down and saw the turd was crawling with slugs and stuff. There was a funny pink thing alongside the turd: clear plastic, long, with a nipple at the end. It looked kind of dead. Also disgusting. Suddenly he lost interest. Home beckoned. *Now*.

So he turned around. And there was this dog.

Johnny liked dogs. He'd always wanted his dad to buy one, but Mike wouldn't. A Labrador, maybe, or German Shepherd. Now this dog wasn't one Johnny would have had Mike Anderson buy. Its legs were tan-coloured, the rest of it was black. No collar, no tag. Teeth, it had teeth. All of them were on display like trophies in a case. Six feet away, maybe. From where Johnny was standing they seemed closer.

The dog was panting. Every time breath came out of its mouth, there was this moan. Maybe it was in pain. The dog lowered its head, teeth still out. Its lips curled back and up. Johnny couldn't move. He stood there, looking at this animal, and he knew it was going to bite him and that would hurt. Hurt a lot. So he stood there like a statue, because he wanted to put off being bitten. There was nobody for miles. He began to cry.

The tears weren't only terror. The air was thick with pollen and Johnny suffered from hay-fever. His eyes were running so that he couldn't even see the damn dog so well now. And worse – something had begun to rise up his nose. He was going to sneeze.

The sneeze came out as a hail of snot. The dog crouched lower, whimpered . . . and ran off.

The sneeze had scared it.

But Johnny wasn't thinking that, he wasn't thinking anything except how fast could he run. He'd never run so fast in his life, not even when Al Vasili and his gang were after him for splitting on them the time they tied a fire-cracker to a cat's tail. Next thing he knew he was haring through the garden gate, he slammed it shut, he had his back against it.

So that was his first visit to the cemetery. Took him a long time to get over it. Weeks later, he still felt scared whenever he thought of that bright sunny morning, with the smell of grass, and flowers, and shit.

Once, in school, Johnny had overheard these two eighth-graders talk, cool dudes both, and one of them had said, 'First time it happens, you know, you feel so, like, dirty. Guilty.'

And the other guy had laughed. 'But you – '

And the first guy had laughed too; then he'd said, 'Yeah, you do it again the next night. And it ain't so bad.'

Johnny hadn't been sure what they were talking about. But it could have been Court Ridge Cemetery. Because that morning he swore he'd never go back.

He went back in the house and the Wicked Witch was doing her ignoral thing. Wouldn't talk to him, wouldn't look at him. She sat at the table shelling peas, giving them her face.

As Johnny went through into the hallway she spoke. Quietly.

'Just remember one thing,' she said. 'It wasn't me killed your mother.'

The kid waited. Like he'd waited for the dog to bite him, yes? Knowing what was coming.

'Your father did that.'

*　　　*　　　*

49

Diane and Ed dawdled through reception, as if not quite ready to *fen shou*, Chinese for 'part hands', which was a softer way of saying 'split' that Diane used a lot.

'With friends like that . . . ' Ed said, and Diane nodded wearily.

Halfway through the interview Dick Jacobson had matured into a son-of-a-bitch without warning, and who did he think he was – some adolescent, or what? The Juvenile Crime Unit had been all Diane's idea and a lovely one, too: a team that would complement but not eliminate the court clinic, a group of psychologists working fulltime with the police department on crimes where either the perp or the victim was under eighteen years old, with special reference to sexual abuse. She'd planned it so that the team's primary aim would be to educate the police in how teenagers react and feel when under stress; but therapists would also be available (see how devious a negotiator she could be) to counsel policemen who needed it. Dick Jacobson (may he live in interesting times, Diane cursed bitterly) had just told her to her face, on air, that this was a gimmick dreamed up by Peter Symes, Paradise Bay's chief of police.

'Maybe I made a mistake,' Ed said. 'Applying for the transfer.'

It took a moment to sink in. 'You're . . . you're joining my unit?'

'If you'll have me.'

Joke! No way was she working with this man on a regular basis. Yet . . . 'Why?' Diane asked weakly.

'Because we should be targeting the kids. Like the Jesuits, you know – "Give us the first seven years and we'll keep him for ever"? Religion isn't an answer these days, but at least they can be taught to be civic . . .'

Ethics from Ed somehow sounded strange in Diane's ear. Yet she was not unmoved. He had a point.

'. . . Because I'm one of five kids myself,' he went on, 'and I can still remember the pressures. Because last week I had to book a thirteen-year-old boy for raping a seven-year-old girl and when I came to read him his rights the kid told me if I screwed up my Miranda-Escobedo spiel he'd bust my ass. Not his lawyer: the kid.'

Did she want this detective, this – 'Are you still a Second Grade detective?' Diane asked him, and he nodded – did she want some Second Grader on her team? *This* Second Grader . . . ? But the question never received an answer, because Ed was speaking again.

'How about the *good* news?' Edwin (damn, Diane couldn't stop thinking of him as that now) leaned against the receptionist's desk, looking smug. 'We found a lot of the stuff that was stolen from your old apartment.'

'The *shen pai*? Oh, Ed!'

She so wanted to go on, but she couldn't force out one more word. Thieves had broken into her apartment overnight while she was moving out of there, into the new house. They'd stolen the family's ancestral tablet, the rectangle of polished wood that Chinese use to record domestic ancestry, standing them on family altars. Diane's tablet began and ended with *Ba-ba*, her father. Cheung Chang-hsien, citizen of Shandong province: the only man she'd ever loved, even though she'd scarcely known him. Diane used to light incense-sticks before his tablet, and pray to him, each day. When his *shen pai* was stolen, it was as if the

51

thieves had taken him away, too. The joss-sticks went out. So did another part of the light, her light, already a bare, smoking wick after *Ma-ma*'s death.

'The *shen pai*, yes; down in the Quadrant. Some blues found it on a crack raid. Inside the apartment were your stereo and TV, purse with two hundred-thirty dollars and the ring. But no gun, that's still missing.'

Diane got a grip on herself. 'You'd think they'd have the sense to junk the *shen pai* someplace else,' she said in a choky little voice.

'The criminal mind, Doctor, the criminal mind. Any time you're passing headquarters, step in and sign for the stuff. Ask for Sergeant Mellow. How about dinner Saturday?'

For a moment Diane, still overwhelmed with emotion, couldn't take in what he'd said. The words drifted through her mind, not making contact with anything. Then they smacked her right between the eyes.

'Oh, sure,' she said. 'Bring Rowena, why don't you?'

'Diane – '

'See you, Edwin.'

After taking three steps Diane stopped and looked back, lips curled in amusement. She knew it for a cheap shot, but – 'Edwin? *Really?*'

Ed said nothing.

'All that time together and I didn't know your real name. All those evenings you said you were on duty and went home to your wife, the one you never happened to mention.' Suddenly Diane's ire spilled over. 'You have some nerve, asking me to dinner.'

She marched out into the sunshine and climbed into the cab Dick had ordered. Despite its air-conditioning she was boiling. Poisoned memories flooded up: of their many failures in bed, of Ed's treachery out of it, of lies and betrayals . . .

When Diane got back to the hospital she was glad to find that Julia had gone to lunch. She made herself some tea and drew up a list of people to telephone. First on the list was an outfit called The Safety Net.

These guys were under contract to fit Diane's house with a sophisticated electronic alarm system, and had been for the past two months. Their working week ran always from 'tomorrow' and consisted of five tomorrows, none of them apparently consecutive. They irritated the heck out of her, but they were renowned for being the best. None of the participants (they did not believe in directors, partners, and the like) was over twenty-four, all but one had dropped out of school and they knew electronics like Diane knew psychology.

This afternoon Diane got The Safety Net's answering-machine, as usual, and left her usual message. 'Get over, start work, today.' But by now the cloud was riding high in a pale blue sky, the sun had turned hot, somewhere along the coast there would be surf . . . Well. Tomorrow, maybe.

As Diane put down the phone Julia came back from lunch. Seeing Diane, her eyes lit up. 'New patient,' she cried gleefully. 'And *boy*, does he sound yummy.'

'Court?' Diane sighed.

'Uh-uh. Private. This woman, Nicole Anderson, called to make an appointment for her ten-year-old, Johnny. I squeezed them in late afternoon, is that okay?'

It was not. Diane's private list was bursting at the seams. She had explained this before and now she did it again.

'But I checked the referral,' Julia said, producing a sheet of paper from her clipboard. 'Francis Baggeley, he's your co-alumnus, right?'

The letter was dated April 5. Diane must have received it, presumably read it, too, but she had no memory of that. Overwork, her mother's death . . .

'I can't do this.'

Julia's look said: Too late, this letter is nearly a month old. But – 'See if you can raise Francis on the phone,' Diane said.

Julia flicked open the Rolodex. 'I knew he was an old friend of yours,' she said defensively. 'And he did ask you to take the boy as a favour, so I assumed it would be okay to give a short appointment for prelim assessment.'

'Just find the number, Julia.'

Frank came on the line very quickly, thus dashing Diane's hopes that he'd be in mid-consultation, or at court, or pony-trekking in Bhutan.

'Johnny Anderson,' he said, straight to the point as ever.

'Right. Frank, I really can't handle any more patients right now.'

'But he needs you, Diane. He's a pleasant, confused little boy who cries out for time with the author of *To the Dance of a Different Drum*.'

'He's ten. Too young.'

'Mature, in many ways.'

'But disruptive.' Diane scanned the letter. 'Learning difficulties.'

'Slight dyslexia. Hyperkinetic child syndrome. He suffered a lot from bullies at his last school.'

'Can be foul-mouthed and obstreperous. Failure to bond with stepmother . . . '

'His mother's dead.'

'How?'

'The father was driving; mother in the passenger seat. A truck drove into her side. Death was instantaneous. Father walked away from the wreck without a scratch.'

'And the boy blames him, right?'

'Got it in one.'

'With justification?'

'Yes and no.'

'Oh, Frank!'

'There was never any question of Mike – the father's name is Mike – being prosecuted. But the insurance people got busy and stuck him with ten per cent liability.'

'Does the boy know that?'

'Yes. He's a wonderful eavesdropper. If I was to career-counsel him, I'd be pointing him towards the CIA.'

'But he was never told properly, by his father?'

'Correct.'

'Ye-ow!'

'Correct again. The second marriage followed on pretty fast. I have to warn you that the father is a difficult customer.'

'Did you ever consider a career in sales?'

'Diane, I really like the little guy, was sorry to see him go. I'm not about to pass him down the line to any hick operator with a bottle of snake-oil in one pocket and a board-eligible cert in the other.'

'Thanks for the compliment.'

'Oh, come on! You know what a typical therapist would recommend: several big fat doses of Methylphenidate and radical reindoctrination. Anyway, will you do it? For me? Please?'

Of course they both knew by then that she would, but the question remained: How? Her list really was full. By making time for Johnny she'd be paring somebody else to the bone, spreading herself thinner than the gold leaf on those rings the Cambodian gangsters wear in Long Beach's Little Phnom Penh.

'I may have an opening Sunday mornings between two and three a.m.,' she told Frank.

'Thank you, Doctor.' He spoke quietly; he meant it.

As Diane put down the phone she realized that it was when he'd said, 'I really like the little guy,' in a certain tone of admiration, and frustration, and sneaky affection, that she'd fallen for it. She'd always trusted Frank. For two years of post-grad he'd been poised to go to bed with her and she sometimes still regretted holding him off.

Julia came in, saw from Diane's face that they had another little client, and beamed.

'Fax just in from police HQ,' she said, handing over a sheaf of paper. 'You asked for Ramon Porras's rap sheet, remember?'

Diane skimmed through it. 'Grievous harm . . . robbery . . . assault first degree, Class-C felony . . . divorce. *Divorce?*'

The last sheet was headed Orange County Family Court. A divorce decree. Edwin Hersey versus Rowena Linda Hersey.

After a long pause Diane said, 'Julia?'

'Mm?'

'Am I doing anything Saturday night?'

'Not with me, honey.'

Another long pause. 'Boil water,' Diane commanded. '*Pu-erh* tea. And make sure the water really does boil this time.'

'I tremble and obey.'

'You can forgo the tremble. Bring me Rachel Lyne's file and get ready to think.'

But there was no opportunity to think, or even for tea, because ten-year-old Rachel and her mother were already waiting in the playroom, and the few seconds it took Diane to walk along the corridor were all the time she had to review everything she knew about bed-wetting.

*   *   *

Hi there!

I'm Tobes.

My given name is Tobias, but you may call me Tobes. Everyone does. And you've heard a lot about me from Diane, I bet. She'll have told you what she knows, only she doesn't know me very well, not yet. She'll come to know me better.

So will you. Even though I don't yet know who 'you' are.

Listen up: Dr Diane gets all her patients to keep a diary. She told me and Ramon and Billy and Jesse to spill it on paper. They did; I had more sense. I know why she wants us to do that, you see. It's for *you*. The person she reports to. You're cops, I guess.

I refused to keep a diary. So what made me change my mind?

It's a long story.

Even if you're cops, we're going to be friends. I can always sense these things. You're educated, you're intelligent; you have to be, or you wouldn't be reading this, my will and my testament.

Johnny Anderson keeps a *memoir*, too. That's why I

changed my mind. (Not that I'm going to show these musings to anyone just yet. Not even him.)

Nice thing about a *memoir* is this: you can write down just exactly what you want to and no more. You can tell things. And you can withhold.

Dr Diane told Johnny to write *everything* down. She gave him these yellow pads, like the ones lawyers use (I've had a lot to do with lawyers). He has to write in them every day. He told me. He doesn't understand that a *memoir* should serve only the writer's purpose, no one else's.

I'm dying to read Johnny's notebooks. I want to know what he thinks about *me*.

Dr Diane never gave me a notebook. I didn't have to buy one, though; I can steal one whenever I want. Stealing is easy, as I'm sure you know. Stealing's fun. *Stealing's against the law.*

Puzzled? Why, heavens to Betsy, so you should be! How come a nice young man like me came to be involved with little Johnny-fruitcake-Anderson?

Here's how.

It began a while back. (In future I'm going to keep contemporaneous records, but this first bit is a recon-struction. Don't worry: my memory for anything that affects Johnny is shining-immaculate.)

So. Let us go back in time and set this thing up properly.

The room where I mostly sleep is slime. South-west of the city-centre, fourth-floor tenement, one block from the railroad station, over a greasy-spoon diner and a laundromat, the latter of which has metal grilles padlocked to the windows and the former of which you can't see into on account of the fliers stuck on the glass, mostly written in some gobbledegook foreign tongue.

Mixed neighbourhood: crooked Koreans, crooked Jamaicans, crooked Blacks. Mixed, but consistent! Only honest man among them is True Tobes Gascoign, yes sirree. If you ever visit my room (and I bet you will, but bring warrants) . . . don't inhale. Rock fumes come up through the floorboards. (Rock is the name they give crack in this town. Did you know that Irish people call good conversation 'the crack'? I'm an educated fellow.)

So I don't spend much time in my room. No, my place is in the cemetery. Deep inside. Takes me twenty minutes, good, from the main gate on Winchester. First you follow the north-south road, then branch off, keeping Court Ridge up above on your left, with all its fine, big houses. At first there's a path. Then there are signs known only to me.

Don't go alone.

This cemetery is haunted.

There are some pretty funny people around, also; types you're probably not familiar with. I am referring to:

Drug peddlers.

Homeless.

Mental incompetents.

Teenagers screwing in the undergrowth.

Other teenagers shooting up.

Queers.

Perverts.

Homos.

Murderers.

Me.

(I am starting to enjoy this; I can see why Dr Diane encourages it.)

I'm the only person who can find my place in the

cemetery, and I can find it blindfold. It's a clearing, in the middle of a clump of trees, and vines, and creepers, and poison ivy. And that clump itself is in the middle of the oldest part of the graveyard. This is where the place originated. It's wet here, because there are hidden springs. When it rains the springs come to life. The earth claws your feet. You sink where it looks firmest. At those times, you really have to know your way around.

Or you don't get out.

In my clearing – it's only a clearing because I cleared it – is a tombstone. It belongs to the first person who was ever buried here. You can just make out her name if you peer close: Alice Mornay.

I went down to City Hall and checked through the archives. Sure enough, there was an Alice Mornay and she was the first person to be buried in Court Ridge Cemetery, in AD 1854. She was twenty-three, which is three years older than me. M~ybe she had an early case of AIDS. Maybe she was just consumptive. Or *maybe* her father beat her to death. We do not know. History does not relate.

I am sorry. We have allowed ourselves to be led astray. You want to know how I met Johnny, my friend, my *best* friend.

So picture this. I'm in my place, the clearing. It's late, the sun is high in the sky: I've spent the night here, engaged in this and that until I grew tired, whereupon I laid me down to sleep. I wake, cold and stiff. I stretch, I yawn, I take a leak over Alice Mornay and while I'm doing that I talk to her.

'Good morning, Alice,' I say. 'Looks like it's going to be a good one.'

Alice does not reply, which on account of her being dead these one hundred forty years is hardly surprising.

'Did you have a good night?' I ask her. We chat in desultory vein. I improvise answers for her. And then, not wishing to neglect the inner man, I eat a Snickers bar and spend a little time listening to music. My Sony compact-disc player is excellent; it cost nothing. My taste in music . . . well, I don't feel quite ready to talk about that yet. Now is not the time or the place. Bad *feng-shui*. You know about that stuff? No, nor did I – until I met Dr Diane Cheung. Since when I have acquired detailed knowledge of many things Chinese, knowledge we shall share. One day. For now the important point to notice is that bad *feng-shui* (pronounced 'fong-shway-ee') = Bad Vibes.

Not that *you* give me bad vibes. Nothing to do with you at all. Relax.

I collect my Trek Bike from its hiding place, close to my clearing, and I take off along the path beneath Court Ridge. I need to return to my room and wash up before my weekly appointment with Dr Diane: new briefs (in case she tries to seduce me, even though I'm not yet sure if I'm ready to share myself with her), deodorant under the arms and in the crack of my ass. Because you never know. So I ride hard, because I fear to be late.

She's a very interesting person, something you may already have picked up on. Actually, I realize full well that Diane Cheung won't want to sleep with me, now or ever. I merely put that in to conceal my nervousness, Arf! Arf! Ha! Ha! Laugh, clown, laugh. (*Pagliacci* is a trifle too melo-d' for my taste though if you like it don't let me undermine you.) She unsettles me, as you can see. Her *feng-shui* is unknowable: dangerous but superb. (People don't actually have *feng-shui*, only places, but stretch your imagination.)

61

I clean up and make my way to the hospital. I chain my Trekkie to the railings and sneak a final cigarette. It's two o'clock, usual time. The nurse on duty directs me to wait in the playroom.

This is a big, airy room with glass at one end and a mirror running along one wall. Diane stands behind this and observes us. Well, of course – oh, come *on*! She's only doing her duty. There are toys here (other than the patients, I mean, arf! arf!) and the toys are interesting. Apart from paints, wax pencils, paper, etc, there are trucks and cars, dolls, building-blocks and *dragons*.

Diane is not afraid of her cultural background. She puts it to good use; I have observed this on several occasions. We have dragons, we have spinning tops, toy spears decorated with ribbons, masks (I love the masks) and Chinese picture books. Most of these concern themselves with legends of no little tedium.

I debate: to play or not to play? Diane is watching. Now, I have to sell myself to Diane as someone who intends to change. (Diversion: How many psychologists does it take to change a light-bulb? Answer: Ten; one to do the physicals and nine to establish that the bulb *really wants to change!*)

Pausing only to assume an expression of thoughtful seriousness, I move to the bookshelf and thumb through what's on offer. Ah yes, *Journey To The West*. Child's version, of course, and a far cry from what Wu Ch'êng-ên actually wrote, but by choosing it I indicate a desire to improve my mind and broaden my experience, plus I demonstrate to my Chinese doctor a liking for Chinese stuff.

Holding the book in such a way as to let its title be shown in the mirror, I return to my seat, cross my legs and allow a faint frown to crease my brow, counteracting

62

it with a pursed-lip kind of smile. Message to Diane: Should I allow my high purposes to be diverted by this literary humoresque, albeit one with an educative dimension? I am still working on my facial lines when the door opens and . . .

. . . and

and . . .

I look up, catch sight of the woman and lower my gaze. The woman is dressed as if for lunch, in a cream pleated skirt, green cutaway jacket, gold necklace, diamond brooch. She looks lost. A patient, presumably. But as I return my gaze to the page, another movement flits across my line of sight and casually I look up again. And.

And.

It is as if I race around a corner and there is the Mona Lisa, easelled just for me.

This slender little boy slouches into the room. Part of me knows he's with the woman but he's working on that: he doesn't want anyone to guess. His hands are thrust deep into his pockets. He refuses to look at anything but the floor. Note: it's not that he's nervous, or timid: he is *refusing* the chance to see the world because that way he doesn't have to accept it. To acknowledge. To face the fact that things are never, never going to move his way . . .

Oh, I know. Johnny, I *do* know.

He's wearing these bleached-blue jeans that cover his protuberant little butt as if hand-tailored. (A jut-butt.) He's wearing a football shirt three sizes too big for him, the chest marked off in four quadrants, each a different colour. The skin at the neck, visible between the white collar-cuffs, is white, pure white. Alabaster. His face . . .

His face.

HIS FACE!

Is lightly sautéed, not perfectly white like his chest, but mini-tanned. There are freckles. One or two. His eyes, what colour are his eyes . . . ? Too far away.

Fix that.

He has the narrowing, slightly impure face of Pan's favourite. Does he realize how lovely he is? On a scale of self-awareness, one to a zillion, where does this little boy stand?

The woman sits on the edge of a hard chair, hands clasping her purse, and stares at the big windows. She looks around, doesn't acknowledge me. She gets up, goes over to the bookshelf, selects a magazine, sits down in another chair, begins to leaf through it. She ignores the boy.

Now isn't that interesting?

What colour are his eyes?

Wait.

The boy leans against the wall. After a while he catches me eyeballing him. *And he doesn't look away.* His expression tells me he's fed up. Locked in a role he wrote and directed himself, leads nowhere. Can't admit that, though, or the lost-looking woman will win. Tough one, kid.

Only one way out. Kid knows it. I know it.

Yup. He raises his head, looks around, and slouches over to the toys. Trucks. He's interested in toy trucks.

Diane is behind the mirror, watching. Any second now, any moment, she will summon me. Or the boy. Or the . . . no, the woman has nothing to do with this, she's not Dr Diane's client, don't ask me how I know.

I concentrate on the page in front of me. My mind is working well today. I see a way forward. But the kid has to help me.

As the thought enters my brain, he *does* help. It's as if he knew.

He knew.

*   *   *

Next door, Diane concentrated on Johnny. He was playing with toy trucks. Diane's lips twitched, she felt roguish. A nod towards Johnny. 'Julia, describe what you see.'

Julia folded her arms and stared through those big specs of hers and for a long time was silent. Then this.

'Well . . . he's smashing the two trucks together . . . building bricks over them now . . . arranging several trucks side by side . . . now in a line.'

'Interpret, please.'

'When he smashes the two trucks together, he's representing his parents in the act of sexual intercourse, the primal scene. When he forms them into a line he's really saying he wants to engage in intercourse with the parents, too. The bricks signify guilt, rage, anal sadism: a desire to bury, destroy, annihilate these feelings of lust.' Julia hesitated. 'When he picks up crayons, like now, and rubs them together, he's unconsciously acting out homosexual masturbatory fantasies in a fairly overt manner; perhaps you should concentrate on school experiences, with a view to uncovering a specific trauma.'

Julia, intimidated by Diane's silence, stuttered into a silence of her own. After a while she asked, 'What do *you* see?'

'A little boy playing. Let's go and – wait a minute. Now this is interesting.'

Concentrating on Johnny, Diane had been only

half aware of the other male in the room. Of course, Monday: Tobes Gascoign had an appointment at two. Now Tobes laid down his book and approached Johnny. The boy smiled up at him, not at all perturbed. They talked, though Diane and Julia could not hear what they were saying. Tobes sat cross-legged on the floor next to Johnny. He picked up a toy truck.

Nicole Anderson continued to study her newspaper.

'Shall I break it up?' Julia sounded uneasy.

'Why? This may be the way into Tobes we've been looking for.'

'But I've just remembered, he shouldn't be here. I sent him a letter cancelling, because we weren't sure how long the radio-show would take . . .'

'Break it up,' Diane told her. 'Now.'

*   *   *

The kid helped me, he knew what we both wanted. He sat on the floor and began to play. Smart. Obvious, but smart.

'Hi!' I say. 'Is it okay . . . ?'

'Sure.'

I sit on the floor next to him, close enough to know he smells of soap, close enough to see the droplets of sweat on his neck, and I say, 'Hot today.'

He nods, not looking up from the car in his hands. But – 'Do you work here?' he says suddenly.

'No, I'm a client of Dr Cheung.'

His mischievous faun's face turns rigid at that. 'Me, too,' he mutters. 'I guess.'

'Don't you know?'

'It'll be our first meeting.'

'That's your mom?'

'Her? That's Nicole. My stepmother.' He speaks softly, to the car, not to me. Ah-*hah*!

I pick up a toy truck and run it along the floor, pull it back, roll it again. When I've done this several times, and its wheels are racing around, I let it go. The truck shoots almost to the wall and stops. The kid grins. He does the same with the car he's holding; his bangs into the skirting-board. We both laugh.

'What's your name?'

'Johnny Anderson. You?'

'Tobes Gascoign.'

For a moment, no reaction. Then his lips form a smile and I break up too, I mean, I mean, *man*, that's . . . that's there aren't the words stuff, you know? Light, let there be light, and there was light, flash, bang.

'Gascoign,' he says, in an awestruck kind of way. 'What a neat name.' And he repeats it, slowly, treasuring it on the tongue like a delicacy. My insides curl and shrivel, I am dying, slowly, by inches.

'Where do you live?' I ask.

'Court Ridge. Number Fifteen.'

Those houses have fancy balconies and french windows and lawns. Never did it occur to me that one day I would get to meet a native, or that he would cup my heart in his hands like this. Court Ridge, overlooking the cemetery, oh my! So close to all I hold dear.

'Johnny,' says the woman, the lost-looking woman, the stepmother; 'Come here,' says Nicole.

Johnny does nothing, makes no reply. Then he looks up at me, slyly, from under his eyebrows and I note sleek lashes, ticklish and fine. *Blue*. His eyes are pale blue; they go with his pale, pale hair. His face, I now perceive, is not a child's face. Not rounded, padded with soon-to-be obsolete flesh, but narrow and lean. Tense, this boy is tense. Worry has burned the fat off him. He holds my gaze with his own, while making little movements of the head: those blue eyes must be fixed on gimbals. He is telling me something through those eyes. First, that he isn't going to obey Nicole. Second . . .

He picks up a face-mask, leaving me wondering what other messages are to be left in my box, leaving me frustrated as hell. The mask is a Beijing opera prop, mostly black and white, but with red around the eyes and a long trail of artificial hair, which tells me it is a villain's mask.

Johnny was never a name that appealed, until recently. Five minutes ago. Now it is the only name.

His attention wanders. I mean, dammit, away from me. How to re-ensnare him . . . ?

Behind me, Julia says, 'Hello, Johnny, it's time to meet Diane. Tobes, didn't you get my letter?'

I stand up and turn, preparing a smile for the mirror, for the intern too.

'What letter?'

'The one I sent you postponing your appointment to tomorrow?'

I shake my head.

'Oh, I'm sorry, your journey's been wasted.'

Not at all.

'Is tomorrow all right?' Diane's gofer asks. 'Same time, okay?'

'Take no heed for the morrow, for tomorrow we die.'

Johnny laughs. I stagger. Well, perhaps I do not stagger; a metaphorical lurch only. His laugh is musical and sweet, but there is something unexpected back of it, something reminiscent of the mad scene from *Lucia di Lammermoor*.

'Tomorrow,' I say; but I'm looking at Johnny. And – 'See you,' I say.

I go out, somehow. It may be raining for all I know, or possibly that earthquake they're always talking about is in full flow, it doesn't matter. My personal earthquake predominates, coupled with my internal volcano. Quite a little freak of nature we have here. Tidal waves next. Whoosh.

I hang around the parking-lot, not risking a smoke because Dr Diane might see me, and if I split somewhere out of sight I'll miss him. Johnny, I mean. (When I talk about 'him', 'he', etc, from now on, you'll get the referent.)

Eventually they come out, he and the woman. They get into a car and drive away. I jump on my Trek Bike and follow.

At first this is easy: the woman drives real slow, and the road's level. My legs are powerful because I take care of myself and I ride a lot. Besides, the Trekkie has a comfortable gel saddle and excellent gears, a Shimano 300 LX groupset. The road runs straight alongside the state beach. It's sunny and hot; I start to wish I'd not dressed up so much for Dr Diane.

Shame I forgot about the cancellation.

Shame I *said* I'd forgotten.

Had I really forgotten?

I don't know. Remember, this is a diary: I can give or I can withhold.

The woman makes a right and starts to head uptown, still keeping it nice and slow. Good neighbourhood, this: shaved lawns, swings on porches, one-car-in-the-drive, one-blocking-the-sidewalk kind of families. Fences, no: they would look unfriendly. But thick clumps of flowers and small-growth trees do a good job of keeping people to themselves. A quarter of a mile behind the car, a tan Infiniti J30, I cannot see what's going on inside. I pedal faster, gain a snitch.

Then, disaster.

Instead of continuing towards the freeway, the woman makes a left. She's going into town along Nicosia Drive. Now, shit! Wait a minute . . .

Instinctively I am starting to know this woman, a process that began the minute I logged how much he hates her. She will speed up now, because she's heading towards the ghetto. She's afraid to drive on the freeway, because of all those nasty would-be rapists who cut her up, but she will take the ghetto route as long as she can take it fast.

What about stop-lights, lady? Or is red simply not your colour?

My thesis proves correct. She's piling on the gas. The space between us opens up. My legs twinkle around and around, to no avail. Despair gives me an extra ten per cent. It's not enough.

The lights are on her side. Ahead of me, far away to the horizon, bright emeralds diminish into the distance, the heat haze causing them to ripple. We're on a wide, four-lane highway. The buildings are mostly single-storey; some are burned out, many have been boarded up. Souvlaki joints vie with dentists offering 'drilling at rock-bottom prices you can afford', with dirty bars, with pawn-shops, for a dollar that here is spread mighty thin. Power-lines and their thick, intrusive poles dominate the landscape. People are scarce. Some black numbers stand around on intersections, having not much to do and doing it in a way that's kind of sinister.

We leave black territory and pass through two Viet blocks. The street is cleaner; the enterprises are the same; the language differs vastly. My legs are exhausted, their muscles threatening me with cramp.

A red light.

All the way to the horizon, down a slight decline and up again to where the city of Paradise Bay takes over, with its carrot-coloured roofs and tower-blocks, and Spanish-style façades, fuzzy rubies shimmer in place of the emeralds. She has broken the smooth, onward flow. Bad *feng-shui*. It is just.

I pant up to the intersection, changing down a gear. For a moment I am tempted to insert myself alongside the Infiniti and rest my weary hand upon its roof. Sanity prevails. I keep three cars back, resting my weary hand on the back of a pick-up instead.

Some hoodlums who have been standing around now approach.

'Nice bike.'

The head honcho and group spokesman is about twenty-five, dressed in jeans, jeans with a *crease*, for God's sake, and a suede shirt with bootlace tie. Vietnamese, scarred, angry about something – his eyes tell that story. I raise my hinged shades the better to examine what we have here. He has a gang of so-so *hombres* with him: lesser fry, but available in quantity.

'I'd like to borrow your bike.'

The light remains red. Even if it changed I have this problem: accelerating on a bike is not like powering a Tomcat to take-off speed, it takes time and during that time you remain vulnerable to goons on foot like these.

He is already reaching out for me. Not the bike, me.

'Sure,' I say. Brace thighs . . . 'I don't want it. Here – take it.'

71

Two feet between us. But by the time I hit him the bike has all my weight behind it and my targeting is perfect: the front wheel lands between his legs. I twist through ninety degrees, ram forward one more time and back off. He goes down flailing. The noise he makes is beautiful; reminiscent of Liu's death in Puccini's *Turandot*. Before his allies can come to the rescue I am away like the wind in pursuit of the Infiniti. I do not look back. (Bad aerodynamics.)

Now the thing about the ghetto is this. Ghettos are circumscribed in area. By definition, right? So what you do is, you take two helicopters. The front chopper sprays the ghetto with petrol. Then the guy riding observer on the second drops a match.

You think I am mad, don't you?

But consider. Have you never entertained a similar thought? Been caught in an ugly trap, with bad *hombres* bearing down on you and the Hill Street blues nowhere in sight? Never been mugged? Had your house burgled? Never shaken a fist in the face of God and screamed, 'It's all so damned unfair!'?

I no more believe they should torch the Paradise Bay ghetto than you do. But that was how I felt then.

It doesn't mean I'm mad.

*   *   *

Throughout the car journey into Paradise Bay Johnny knew rage and didn't understand why. It was the not knowing why that bugged him most. The visit with Dr Cheung hadn't been so terrible. She'd spoken kindly, seemed interested in him, was nice enough: just as nice as she'd sounded on the radio, in fact – he recognized her voice straight off. But still he bobbed on a sea of tempestuous rage, unable to glimpse land or light. If he'd been a few years older he might have looked back over his session with Diane and recognized the symptoms that signal a stranger coming in below the radar, fast and clever and going straight for the heart; might even, if the circumstances were right, have called it Love. But this wasn't love. This morning Johnny hated the world and everything within it.

Nicole drove under the freeway spur and turned right, into Main, cutting diagonally across the business district. Then she made another right, into Fourteenth this time, and saw their destination ahead: Brunsekka and O.

Brunsekka and O was Paradise Bay's biggest department store. It occupied one whole block, which was no big deal, because Paradise Bay wasn't New York, but still, a block. Six storeys high, on the roof there was a café-bar-restaurant called Bistingo's, where people could sit out in summer and watch the yachts tie up in the marina, less than half a mile away. Bistingo's' clientele was on the select side. There were those who said that three dollars fifty for a small cappuccino, even with choice of cinnamon or chocolate, bordered on the realm of federal offence.

Nicole swung onto the ramp leading down to the underground lot and found a space for the Infiniti. She and Johnny got out, their quarrel preceding them like a fanfare. She half dragged him to the elevator.

'I want a soda!'

'We'll have time for that later.'

'Now!'

As the elevator car-door slid shut Johnny caught a glimpse of a face he knew. Down at the far end, by the ramp, a guy was chaining his bicycle to a yellow water-pipe. Where'd he seen him before . . . ?

Johnny and Nicole rose through household and domestic appliances, linens, perfumes, furnishings, fashions – ladies', fashions – men's, to Books'n'Things, at the pinnacle.

Brunsekka's bookstore was huge, and always crowded. To Nicole's alarm, Johnny broke away from her and headed straight for a pile of books by the cashier's desk. She ran to catch up, and grabbed him by the upper arm. He clutched a book to his chest with his free hand, while other shoppers made a wide berth around the squabbling couple.

'Buy it for me! You gotta buy this book!'

Nicole glanced at the cover, saw the picture of a ghoul rising out of its coffin, and smartly said, 'No.'

'I want it!' Johnny yelled. *'I want it!'*

*   *   *

I am a long-standing patron of this store. Brunsekka's (people mostly drop the 'O', largely on account of nobody knows what it means; is it an Indian name, or some guy's initial, or what?) boasts an excellent music section. I pick up my CDs there. Free of charge. Security's radical.

It is no hard task to track Johnny to the top floor by watching the elevator lights in the basement. I rise after them. The doors of my own elevator slide open like stage-curtains, to reveal high drama.

Man, is Johnny excited! I sidle out of the elevator-car and immerse myself in Latest Fiction. The store designer has arranged books in spiral staircases, pyramids, towers; there is plenty of cover.

Johnny is hugging a book to his chest with his free hand. On the jacket is a picture of a ghost. Another jolt of excitement surges through me: *he likes ghosts!*

He's the one!

The words come into my mind. The novel I am holding slithers from my fingers, which suddenly have lost their strength. My breathing stills. The store dims for a second, as when electricity surges then fails and the lights die, all in the space of a heartbeat.

He is the one who is most like me.

By the time I recover, they have disappeared.

How can he abandon me this way?!!! I stride towards the Metaphysics section, which is where I last saw him. He's gone, vanished, like a ghost himself. My head twists this way and that. Desperate now. Then, far away down the aisle, I catch sight of a blonde head above a blue jacket. The wicked stepmother! Go!!

I pad after them. They are making for Audio-Visuals. This slots in with my own wishes, because a guy's CD collection can always use supplementing. The woman goes to stand by the service-counter, trying to attract a clerk's attention. Johnny folds his arms on the counter and rests his head on them.

Now here is a funny thing. Johnny has been wriggling; suddenly he becomes still. He half raises his head, but does not turn. I watch, fascinated; what has got him going? Then he *does* turn, and I know, I just know, that he has sensed my presence. So what do I do?

I hide.

Yes, that's right, I hide; even though I think, I believe, I KNOW this is The One I've been waiting for all these years, The Twin, The True Friend Who Will Understand Me. I am all-of-a-sudden shy. Gauche. And so I slip behind a rack of CDs.

But then fear reawakens, fear of losing him, and I risk a peep around the stack. Johnny's standing with his back against the counter now, staring at the floor. His mouth is half open; is he moronic, I wonder? *Don't be ridiculous!*

He's about to look up again. I withdraw my head.

I am up with the classical 'B's. Bach JS, Bach CPE, Bach JC. Beethoven, the late piano sonatas, played by Brendel: a re-release. My fingers stray of their own accord. This is wrong, for I should be concentrating on him. And yet . . .

I know the security guard is three stacks away, because after a while these things become second nature: walk into a store, check out the guard. Harley taught me that. Harley Rivera is my best friend, a connoisseur of fine music and petty larceny. He pointed out to me that there are no ceiling-mounted cameras in Brunsekka's. What they do instead is fix this thin metal gizmo to the back of the CD's plastic container-case; in order to get out you have to walk between two pillars, Scylla and Charybdis, and if you're carrying something with the gizmo still on it, a bell rings and the sky falls in.

Admit it – that reference to Scylla and Charybdis took you aback. You weren't expecting it from this quarter. Well, you think it's only CDs I steal? You are wrong. My book collection is a large one. Although on account of space (lack of) I have to keep it revolving. I steal a book and read it, I put it in a box; when the box is full, I leave it outside the charity store two blocks down from my place. (Place = my room, not the cemetery. There are no charity stores in the cemetery.)

Property is theft, remember that.

Now, I intend to take charge of this Alfred Brendel re-release. It is to become, for the sake of argument, 'mine'. How to effect this, given the electronic Scylla and Charybdis hereinbefore mentioned? Easy: you prise it off. Not that just anyone can do this; you couldn't, for example. You need an implement like the one the salespersons use. I have such an implement; Harley gave it me.

Must check out the scene first, though . . .

*   *   *

Johnny turned away from the week's pop-chart to see Tobes Gascoign standing at the far end of the nearest stack, and his eyes widened. He was about to go up to him when Tobes replaced a CD on the rack and meandered down to the cross-aisle furthest from the counter. A security guard stood there, talking with some guy-in-suit. Tobes studied the guard for a moment before going back to where Johnny had first seen him, nice and slow. He lifted a CD down and pretended to study the sleeve-notes. His right hand dipped into his pants pocket and emerged holding a curious metal instrument. Tobes looked to the left, looked to the right. Johnny followed his glance. Down the other end of the stack, an old woman was browsing. Two teenagers stood side by side, casing Light Classics. None of them took any notice of Tobes.

There was a flurry of action. Tobes applied the thing in his hand to the back of the CD cover. He glanced up, trying to keep his movements casual, and that was when his eyes met Johnny's.

By now the boy was standing midway between the counter and Tobes's stack. He had his arms folded across his chest and one corner of his mouth was screwed up, the way a cop looks at a public gathering:

contemptuous, assessing. He looked into Tobes's eyes and read their appeal for clemency. It was a good feeling, a *great* feeling. *Power!* He had the power to make this guy like him. Johnny could see Tobes knew that, too.

They stood there for what felt like a day. Then Johnny's face broke into a smile, he unfolded his arms and stuck up his thumb. Tobes's face flickered in a brief smile. He pocketed the CD. Then he turned and walked towards swing-doors marked 'Exit'.

Nicole asked, 'Oh, while I'm here, do you have *Miss Saigon* on tape?'

Johnny snuck a glance at her. She was going to be tied up for quite a while. He eased away from the counter.

The stairway on the other side of the swing-doors marked 'Exit' was broad and empty. He climbed, slowly. After a second or two, other footsteps began to echo his own. Someone was climbing the stairs ahead of him, someone who had waited to make sure Johnny was there before proceeding upwards.

There were fifteen treads in the first flight. Johnny reached the landing. Another flight ascended to his right, heading back in the direction he'd just come, only upwards. The air was warm and stale, the light dim, protective . . . friendly. He did not pause, but he slowed, and looked up. Deep gloom prevented him from seeing anyone. A shiver of excitement ran from the crown of his head to the soles of his feet. Keeping one hand on the rail, the other in his pocket, Johnny rounded the corner of the landing and started to ascend the last flight.

*   *   *

Ahead of me is a door. It is marked with a sign: 'Emergency Use Only This Door is Armed'. The roof. Johnny and I have nowhere else to go.

I am almost at the top.

The light here has turned sickly-poor. Underneath the emergency exit a thin white line shows, telling me the sun is shining. I am on the last step. I begin to turn. Heavy silence overlays everything, for no one uses stairs when they can ride the elevators: only those with an ulterior purpose choose the stairway's privacy.

He advances, half in shadow and half in dim light cast up from the floor below. I want him to join me and yet, inexplicably, I do not.

Johnny comes to a halt four steps from the top. He raises his left foot to the next step up, but that is all. He keeps one hand on the rail, the other he rests on his left thigh. His face is invisible. We do not speak.

Maybe a tiny part of me is starting to hate this kid. I need to dominate. I am an active personality. I had him down as passive, he is not. He is dangerously sharp. And I think he knows it.

The seconds tick by. This moment is finite. Soon the woman will come in search of him. I must make use of my opportunity. But I have a problem. My bladder is full to bursting. Nerves, I guess. The pain is getting out of hand.

One of us has to speak. To advance this thing, speed it along tracks that were laid years before, leading straight and true to a horizon where the sun will set.

Johnny says, 'I thought there was a toilet here.'

He is trying to sound casual, but his voice catches, and his face tells me his need is as great as mine; my bladder contracts in sympathy. Seconds tick away. The risk is great. I take it. (This is degenerating into a medical emergency.) I turn to face the white line beneath the emergency door. Slowly I unzip my fly. He can hear the sound of the metal fastener snagging down. If the roof-door were to open right now, and a cop walk through it, I'd be safe. Borderline, but still safe.

I make arrangements.

Johnny hears the first splash of slash, and laughs. There is admiration in his tone and something else, too, something simpler: delight. He is a rebel, one without method. (I can give him method.) He comes to stand on the top step next to me so silently that when I do become aware of him my skull seems to lift off my neck.

Another zipper on the way down. His movements, unlike mine, are brisk and to the point. He bends slightly to make his own arrangements: through the gloom I can just perceive that jut-butt of his jolt backward and, immediately after, forward again. I keep my eyes turned down. Now there are two streams playing against the door.

He directs his jet at mine, mingling the waters. *He* did that, not me. It's important for the future that we get this straight, *he made the first move*.

I look over my shoulder. The stairway is empty. No sounds echo from below. I turn my head towards the boy. He looks up at me, grinning. My own lips mould themselves to match his. Another glance behind. No one.

I lean towards him, my twin . . .

The swing-doors slam, two landings below. 'Johnny! *Johnny!*'

Come on, we had it lucky: she could have broken in on us any time, we did what we had to do, we got things moving.

80

'Johnny, can you hear me? Answer me! Where are you?'

I zip up quickly. But piss smells; if the woman comes, there'll be no talking my way out of this one. What will Johnny do?

What will he do?

He looks at me with an angelic smile. He sprays a last few drops against the door and zips up his fly before turning to face down the stairs. I hold a finger to my lips and he nods.

'So long,' he whispers. 'See yah!'

And he is gone, racing down the steps so lightly that he scarcely makes a sound, leaving me weak and helpless to the point where I have to lean against the door to stop myself falling over. Already I hear the Anderson Civil War recommence: she accuses Johnny of being a selfish brat, he counters by calling her stupid. The doors swing to and fro, that is the last I hear of them.

I slide down to sit on the uppermost step, barely conscious of the puddle of pee, and I lean against the wall. My hands are shaking. My mouth is caked with foul-tasting crud. I have never known such sensuous happiness.

*   *   *

It was only five o'clock, but Mike Anderson already had a vodka martini on the go. He stood staring out of the big downstairs window, alternately drinking and looking at his watch. 'What time did that shrink say she was coming?' he grumbled. (To Johnny, trying to concentrate on a Roald Dahl book, it sounded more like 'damn shrink'.)

'Five,' Nicole said. She folded up her magazine and threw it on one side. 'Dr Cheung said she'd come by at five.'

'Why does she have to come here?'

'To assess Johnny's needs in a structured home environment. To see if family therapy or one-on-one would suit him best.'

'*Family* therapy.' Now Mike Anderson was angry. 'You mean she thinks *we* are in need of help *too*?'

'She didn't say that, sweetheart.'

Johnny tried to focus on his Roald Dahl but with half an ear continued to monitor the talk, in case stepmommy-dearest began to misrepresent their big scene in Brunsekka and O. But before Mike could think of a come-back, the doorbell chimed.

Nicole and Mike went out to the hallway. Johnny heard the usual melodies: greetings, polite phrases, laughter. His stomach went hurly-burly. He hated meeting new people, and Diane Cheung was still new enough to rank.

Should I tell you about the weirdo in the store, Diane Cheung? he asked himself. *Somehow I feel I should; he's important. But also, he's mine. No sharing. Not yet.*

'So where do you come from, Diane?' Mike asked as he led the way into the living-room and offered her a chair.

'I was raised in Seattle . . . Thank you.'

Johnny took a good look at Diane as she sat down and wondered if Mike Anderson had really meant that. Perhaps it was a polite way of saying, You are a foreigner and before I let you anywhere near my kid I want to check you out. Chinese people ran each other over in tanks: Johnny'd seen that on TV one time.

'If you'll forgive me for saying so,' Mike went on, 'you scarcely look old enough to be qualified.'

Diane laughed, as if her tummy was tickling like when you hear something *really* funny.

'Well thank you, sir,' she said. 'That's the nicest thing anyone's said to me in a while.' She turned away from Mike and smiled at Nicole. 'Moving is such a strain, isn't it? I've moved three times in my life, and each time it's taken me seven years to get things straight.'

Everyone laughed, except Mike Anderson.

'And you have such a charming garden,' Diane said, swivelling in her chair. 'Will you mow it yourself? It's on a slope; that can be tiring.'

'Oh, I'll hire a man to clean it up,' Mike growled. 'Take a while.'

Then he went on to ask Diane about her qualifications and she began to talk, but Johnny had heard enough. All this time he'd been sitting half in the group and half out of it, with his chair turned towards the wall so that although Diane could see a chunk of him she couldn't see the rest. Now he rose and carried his book up to his room. Nicole tried to call him back, but he kept on climbing the stairs.

Once in his bedroom he lay on the top bunk and stared out of the window. He could see the path from there. The evening light was fading now. Cigarettes glowed in the shadows of the trees; men walked up and down, up and down the path. Johnny glanced at his book, read a few pages, looked out again.

One of the men had long hair, a bit like Tobes Gascoign's. That funny guy who'd followed him to the store . . . What a weirdo!

Johnny didn't know why he thought Tobes had followed him. Maybe he had, maybe he hadn't. He was neat, anyway. Johnny liked him. Kind of. He continued to gaze out of the window. Where was Tobes now? What did a guy like that do with his time . . . ?

*　　　*　　　*

By the time I return to Brunsekka's parking-lot the Infiniti has gone. I walk to stand for a moment in the space it occupied, closing my eyes and breathing deeply. The stale smell of gas and leaked oil does not repel: it is part of *his* smell. I feel no sadness at his departure. I have his address, but more than that, I have his cooperation. His assent.

Court Ridge Cemetery is the place I want to be. I jump on my bike and race up the ramps, going against the flow. Startled ladies honk their car-horns, annoyed with me for rattling their composure, ruffling their coifs. I wave apologies, eager to share my well-being and show what a nice young man I am.

Once on the street I turn left. At the intersection of Fourteenth and Van Ness there is an excavation in progress. I cut down a narrow street, meaning to make a right back onto Van Ness one block nearer the harbour.

I have penetrated an upcoming quarter of the city. In the past known simply as West Central, among the cognoscenti it is now acquiring a soubriquet: Fountainside, named for a stone head spouting water sculpted out of an old church wall. The head is reputedly a Gorgon's; the snakes I regard as the giveaway. This church bounds one side of a small square. One day some bright young entrepreneur dumped two chairs, a marble-topped table and a Martini umbrella in the square, and a passer-by had to go order an espresso, and before we knew it this section of our proud city was the Fountainside Quarter (if you are a real-estate agent), or Fountainside for short.

It's not my scene. My carry-phone is with the repairers, y'know? As are the Gucci loafers and my Dunhill handbag, whereas the Armani slacks need cleaning and I've yet to get around to paying the garage for that last set of repairs to the Ferrari. It's full of trendy shops, restaurants, bars and cafés, most of which close within a month of Grand Opening Night, but that doesn't matter because there's always another sucker standing in line ready to lose his dough on the same location. A few – a very few – make the grade. Venezia, the original marble-topped table and espresso outfit, has been around for over a year now. L'Ancien Régime got a write-up in the *LA Times*, largely on account of its decor; now the line extends around the block and they've made their reservations number ex-directory. *Can you believe that – a restaurant with an ex-directory phone number?* Only in California . . .

I whiz along, wondering where this maze of little streets will take me, when suddenly there is an explosion and I fall off my bike.

Ho, boy! Guilty of a little exaggeration there. What I mean to convey is that *somethinghappened*. This afternoon too much has happened already. Now this. Whoo!

A blaze of colour is what happens. Brakes! My bicycle tyres shed an unwanted skin on the roadway as I skid to a halt outside a shop. One-third of its frontage is a door with a brass knocker and knob. The other two-thirds consists of a bow window, y'know, like those illustrations Phiz did for Charles Dickens, *The Old Curiosity Shop*, that stuff. *And it is all painted pink!* The pink of strawberry ice-cream melting down the side of the bowl. Above the bow window is a fascia and on it is written, in curly letters of exquisite orderliness, 'MAXINE'S'. Beneath that we have the following: 'Theatrical Costumier's'. The letters are gold, picked out with black to give them depth. And I think to myself, I think: WOW! Because this is some experience.

Oh, I left out the best bit. (Silly me.) In the bow window stands a female mannequin, dressed after the style of the eighteenth-century French court. Think 'Let them eat cake' and you'll get the picture. There is a small sign: Marie Antoinette. On top of her head is one of these beehive white wigs, topped by a ridiculously out-of-place hat. In her hand she holds a single rose. The woman is fake. The rose is real.

I stand on the sidewalk, transfixed. My bike clatters to the ground, it goes unheeded. Pink is my colour; I've always loved it. This is shockingly pink pink, the essence of pinkitude. And recently – since first meeting Dr Diane, in fact – I have developed a passion for cut flowers, like that blood-red rose. The shop has the effect on me of a Siren's song: it lures me inside like a soft, fleshy . . .

I don't think I'll write that. It would be artificial.

I push on the door and it yields to my touch. A bell rings; not an electric buzzer, but a real bell on a spring, with a clapper.

The place is otherwise quiet, except for the slow tick-tock of an old grandfather clock. Everywhere I look I see natural wood. Hearing strange sounds behind me, I turn. A Persian cat sits inside the bow window, paws tucked up under his breast. He surveys me coolly through big yellow eyes that do not blink quite shut. Evidently he does not object to my presence, however, for he is purring. Now that the bell has died away to silence, the cat and the clock vie for supremacy in the noise department.

On my left hangs a rack of costumes. I mooch along it, fascinated. Littered around on the floor are boxes containing grease-paints. At the back is a counter, behind that a curtained doorway. No one comes. I turn back to the window. Reverently I lay a hand on the mannequin's just above the rose. The cat's mouth parts in a silent hiss.

'Can I help you?'

I swing around, startled. 'Excuse me, where does that rose come from?' The words blurt out minus conscious input from me.

A girl in her mid-twenties, wearing a dirndl dress, headscarf, long ear-rings and a dreamy expression, wafts into view. There are sandals on her feet; they scrape the wooden floor, calimph, calumph.

'Rose,' she says, 'what rose? Oh . . .' (She sees my hand by the rose.) 'There's this magic flower shop two blocks south, down an alley. Kind of hard to find, but I can direct you.'

We examine each other. The clock ticks; the cat views us approvingly. Shafts of sunlight pick out the dust. I sense Maxine's attracts few customers.

'This shop, it's yours?'

'Yuh. My name's Maxine Walterton. Hi.'

'Hi.'

She's pretty. That creamy skin, so smooth and yielding, one of those skins you know, without having to touch it, will yield thus far and no further. Lovely green eyes, narrow, almost almond-shaped. Almost oriental; does she perchance have Chinese blood? Instinctively I run hooked fingers through my hair. 'This place . . . it's great.'

'You like it?'

'It's beautiful. No other shop the same. No way.' (I am really talking about *her*. She knows this.)

'I'm so glad you like it, but . . . ' She looks around dolefully, a smile for the cat, ' . . . why?'

'Why?'

She is a little afraid of me. 'Yes. Why?'

''Cause here, every man can get to become some-body else.'

I mean, I thought she would know, but even now I've told her she still doesn't quite understand the reason this place is strong for me. She says, 'Oh, you can buy the rose at that place I told you about, you go out of here and go left down the alley – '

'I'll find it.'

'You're sure?' she ventures.

'I found you, I'll find it.'

At the door I turn and blow her a kiss. Maxine laughs. I've delighted her. (Stupid phrase: in truth, I've *lighted* her. Lighted up her face.) But no, this girl is genuine; I cannot leave without offering a word of advice. I close the door and say, 'Would you be offended if I told you something about the dress in the window?'

'Marie Antoinette?'

'The very same. You see, she was married to a French king, right?'

Maxine nods.

'And you have her in your window wearing a *robe à la française*, which is perfect for her, but . . . '

'Yes?'

88

'She shouldn't be wearing that hat. It's a Gainsborough hat. They only had that kind of *chapeau* in England, it was never a continental style.'

'Oh.' For a moment Maxine looks blank. Then her face dissolves into a broad smile and she says, 'Are you a designer, or something?'

'No, no. I just happen to know, that's all.'

'That's . . . well, that's fantastic. Thank you.'

And so, having embarrassed the shit out of myself, I make my escape. As I exit the bell clangs once more. Miracle of miracles: nobody has stolen the Trekkie, despite the fact that in my excitement I forgot to immobilize it. I ride away, mulling over the events of the past ten minutes.

Maxine disturbed me. In consequence, I handled our encounter badly. Think of the primeval swamp: suddenly there is a loud 'gollop', the mud bubbles, sinks, falls silent. Maybe it is a freak air-pocket. Maybe a monster. We do not know what lives in those slimy depths. Maxine was such a gollop.

I reach into a pocket of my jacket and take out one of her make-up crayons. I ride off slowly, painting my face as I go. She will not miss it. By the time I reach the florist's my face sports cat's whiskers and devil's eyebrows: not bad, I see in the shop-mirror. I buy a red rose, restraining the assistant when she wants to shake off the water droplets, and head north, the bloom clamped between my be-whiskered lips.

Alice Mornay is going to love this.

When I arrive in my secret clearing, I lay the rose on Alice's tomb, saying, 'This is for you. A flower to make you beautiful, Alice. I'll never neglect you, you do know that, right? And Johnny will be here soon. He's going to love you, Alice. Both of us.'

I fall to musing about Johnny. Does he like flowers? I'll get some for him. That's what you do for your lover: you buy him flowers.

Does he love me? Is he *really* The One?

Now, at last, and I'm sorry to have kept you waiting, you know why I have decided to compose a *memoir*.

My watch tells me I still have four hours before I need to go to work. (I chop vegetables for a living.) I set my CD player, tune into the beloved 'Dutchman'.

Senta sings.

> *'Er sucht mich auf! Ich muss ihn sehn!*
> *Ich muss mit ihm zugrunde gehn!'*

It's conceivable, excuse me, that you do not share my familiarity with the German language. Senta sings:

> *'I'm who he seeks! I must go to him!*
> *His fate shall be mine!'*

*   *   *

Mike Anderson's voice grated on downstairs. Johnny covered his ears and stretched out on the top bunk, eyes closed. He could imagine what was going on: Mike Anderson laying down the law, Nicole chewing her hands, Diane all sweetness and care. But then an unexpectedly close voice said, 'Hi, Johnny, mind if I come in?'

Johnny raised his head. Dr Cheung had come to stand on the threshold of his bedroom without making a sound. She was smiling. At that moment he didn't like her at all, because her smile was one of triumph. She had high cheekbones and upwardly slanting brows, and she seemed ugly to him, like a demon-woman from out of his Japanese-inspired comic-books. She'd invaded, got him beat.

Then he noticed that Dr Cheung was still on the landing. She needed his permission to enter. Perhaps she was a vampire?

'Sure, come in,' he said. Why not be gracious? He'd always hoped to meet a vampire. Besides, she was wearing this cute sailor's jacket, with rings on the arms and little anchors on the collar: he wanted a closer look at that.

'You can see the cemetery from here,' Dr Cheung said, walking over to the window. 'Peaceful.'

She leaned against the frame, half looking out, half turned towards him, with arms folded. Johnny saw how her eyes darted from object to object: his model Space Shuttle suspended on a string, the kites, the toy Uzi (what did *that* tell you, Vampire?), the duvet with its cotton crossword cover, black and white squares – and purple where he'd used a marker-pen to fill in some of the clues. Indelible purple. She examined the collection of shit on the bottom bunk. What was Dr Vampire looking for?

She sauntered across the room, dipping below his vision, and surfaced again, this time holding a book called *Spirit Lore.*

'He looks a friendly fellow,' she said, pointing to the cover. There was a smiling ghost, arms extended over gravestones, on the front. Johnny was about to explain all that, when she said, 'The guardian ghost, right?'

Johnny jumped off the bunk and said, 'Yes!' before he could stop himself. Because that was actually very cool of the doctor. Only a few people knew the legend of how the first person to be buried in any cemetery

91

became its guardian ghost, whose duty it was to protect the place and keep out evil spirits throughout eternity and offer welfare to the other ghosts. Johnny knew. And Dr Cheung knew.

'We have them in China,' Dr Cheung said. 'Supposedly.'

After a pause – 'Do you believe in ghosts?' Johnny asked. It was terribly important, this. He needed her validation, either way.

'I'm not sure.' She frowned. 'But I've always liked the story of the guardian. It appeals to my romantic nature.'

'You're romantic?'

'I surely am. You?'

Johnny shook his head, although suddenly he wanted, *really* wanted, to tell her about Tobes, and it was all because she'd used the word 'romantic'.

'I don't believe in ghosts,' he said. And then he had this strange feeling: he could trust Dr Cheung. 'I've visited the cemetery, you know.' Johnny could see from her face that she was interested. 'And I . . . I was scared to death.'

'Did you go at night?' Dr Cheung sounded mighty impressed.

'No. Daytime. But even so, it was scary. There's dogs. But don't tell my dad and don't tell *her*.'

'I won't. They'd be afraid for you, Johnny, and they'd be right. The cemetery isn't a good place to go.'

'Why not?'

'Because some of the people you meet there go to shoot up drugs, or drink, or even to steal money from the visitors.'

Johnny's heart was beating fast. Dad had bought a house next door to a *snake pit*? 'But not everyone,' he pleaded.

'Not everyone,' Diane agreed. 'And maybe I'm the wrong person to ask. I'm not comfortable in cemeteries, perhaps because I believe in living my life, not brooding about death.'

Her face was somehow different from when she'd come in. She didn't stare at Johnny any more, her eyes flickered away. Her voice sounded lower. She was a softy, after all.

'I should go visit my parents' graves more often,' Dr Cheung said.

'They're buried near here?'

'Down at Yorba.'

'Hey! Did you ever see the pink lady?'

'The what?'

'You must have heard the story. Must have! The pink lady was a woman who got herself killed young in a buggy accident, and she appears at Yorba Cemetery on June 15 every even-numbered year. Did you see her? Did you?'

'Sorry, no.'

'Oh.' Johnny deflated very quickly. There was a long silence. 'Anyway . . . my mom was cremated.' A longer silence. 'We scattered her ashes, we . . . '

Suddenly he was crying. Dr Cheung wiped his eyes, gave him a little hug. 'Why don't we go for a walk in the cemetery now?' she said gently; and when Johnny looked at her like she was some kind of nut she burst out laughing, and he did, too.

'Come on,' she said, 'we won't go far.'

'But it's not a nice place; you just told me!'

'It's fine if you're with a grown-up and it's daytime. What do you say?'

Johnny thought, *They will hate it downstairs*. 'Let's go,' he said.

Sure enough, Mike wasn't happy about Diane's suggestion of 'a nice walk in the fresh air'. (Her words.) But then this crazy thing happened: the Wicked Witch rode in on her broomstick and said yes, they should go.

'I feel gruzzled,' Johnny said as they set off, beating down the long grass that lay between them and the gate.

'What's gruzzled?' Dr Cheung asked, taking his hand.

'When you have this tight feeling 'cos something's wrong and you don't know what it is.'

'Great word. When did this feeling start?'

'Just now. When *she* said we could go.'

Dr Cheung walked in silence for a while. 'Maybe you're old enough not to need Nicole's approval of everything you do,' she ventured.

'Yeah. What business is it of hers?'

At the gate they turned right, down the hill, as Johnny had done the time before. It was twilight now, but there were people about, with dogs on leashes, some of them arm in arm, and he could hear laughter far off.

Dr Cheung said, 'Still gruzzled?'

The boy shook his head.

'Now tell me . . . who lives there?'

Johnny saw her looking at the house next door. 'That's the Keeton place. They've got two kids. Not bad. And up the hill from us, that's where old Miss Grant lives, with her dogs. Somebody comes to walk them for her every day, she pays 'em and maybe I could do that, what do you think?'

'Perhaps, if your folks agree and you don't go alone. Who lives next to the Keetons?'

'Mr Sage and his brother. His brother's insane. I think. He doesn't go out, ever; that's what I heard Mrs Keeton saying to Ni . . . to *her*. Mr Sage owns a ship. A big ship that carries oil and those containers. Maybe more than one.'

'Does he have dogs, too?'

'Yeah, a pit-bull. And a burglar-alarm and lights that come on if you blink. That's what Mrs Keeton says, I've never seen these people. Well, Miss Grant, I've seen her. That's all. Her Pomeranian peed on our gate-post.'

They walked for a bit. Dr Cheung's hand felt great, Johnny decided: dry but not too dry. She smelled terrific. Not that yukky stuff 'Poison' the Witch wore, all heavy and . . . well, poisonous. Dr Cheung smelled of flowers.

She was nice.

'Can you help me?' Johnny blurted out.

'Yes.'

'How?'

'By setting you free from the prison you've built.'

*   *   *

I nap for a while – it's been an exhausting day, what with meeting the Love of my Life, and Maxine's shop and roses and things – but at five o'clock I have to go make a little bread. Even though I'm a good thief, I need a reliable source of income with which to feed and house myself; such solid, middle-class values as I possess are not unlike yours.

So I am pushing my Trekkie out of the bushes when it occurs to me to ride past Court Ridge, suss it out. Maybe the boy will be playing in the garden. I see myself sitting on my bicycle, resting one arm on the fence, talking with him. Perhaps he would like a ride. He can perch on my lap, his hands overlying mine on the bars. We will freewheel. Oh *yes!*

I start to cycle up the path, nodding in friendly fashion to the courting couples, to a man trying to pretend that the German Shepherd on the other end of his leash is not shitting. Maples line the cemetery side of the path at this point; on my left are fences belonging to the houses on top of the Ridge. Back gardens slope up and away from me; odd how people differ in their approach to Nature. Here, a beautifully tidy garden; next door, jungle. The sun is setting behind the Ridge. Each house has become a black shape against a pale blue sky with a golden halo. They are solid constructions, these houses: made for large families, built for balls, dinners, parties.

Things start to go awry.

Johnny is coming down the path towards me. I know at once it is Johnny; he's wearing the same clothes he had on earlier, but even without that clue I would recognize him anywhere. You know, like auto-zoom focus. But he's with a woman. Stepmother . . . ? And then I see it's Dr Diane.

I dismount and thrust self and Trekkie behind the nearest maple. Bushes cluster around its trunk. There's plenty of cover. My heart is beating fast: did they see me? Your voice, high-pitched and musical, dear little Johnny, injects my ears with honey. Dr Diane is looking particularly fine today. She's not tall, but she's thin and has graceful hips that swing when she walks: I have this fantasy vision of her in a white woolknit dress, and often wish I had the courage to ask her if she owns one. (Or would like one . . .) Her hair, molasses-black, is luscious and thick, but why must she re-style it so often? Long, short, flowing, French plait – from one session to the next, I never know what to expect. She has such a pretty face! A *sweet* face, brimming over with kindness, with a little pointy chin. She looks very Chinese, very oriental: pronounced cheeks, almond eyes, seagull-shaped, well-plucked brows; her face has this kind of squashed expression, making her everyone's big sister, favourite auntie. Her mouth is nearly always smiling, like her eyes. However, Dr Diane's best feature is undoubtedly her skin. It is without fault or flaw: not so much yellow as creamy. Dark cream. When she tans, I bet the cream thickens.

Naked, on a white bed, she'd be irresistible . . .

'Tell me what's it like in China!' Johnny pipes.

Diane says something I can't catch.

'The graveyards, then; tell me about them. And guardian ghosts.'

What is it about the supernatural that obsesses you so, dearest Johnny?

'The graveyards . . . well, usually you find them in hilly areas, with water nearby. The graves are like little houses, sometimes; but the best ones are built within a low, rounded wall. There are paths, like here, but they zig-zag.'

As the two of you pass out of earshot, she embarks on an explanation of why Chinese ghosts hop instead of walking. I, too, am interested to know, but your voices fade.

I wait until you are no longer audible, even as faint echoes. I wheel my bike onto the path. As shadows lengthen and the light begins to yield, I follow, yes I do.

*　　*　　*

This little boy interested Diane more than any patient she'd seen since the death of her beloved *Ma-ma*. There were many disturbed children in America; lots of them passed through her door; few of them stuck in her mind. She knew right away, this would be one of the stickers. She liked Johnny. Since he had no reason to be afraid of Diane he would soon learn to trust her, and then the liking could begin on his side, too.

The book she'd written, *To the Dance of a Different Drum: Disturbed Children and What Makes Them That Way*, was one long celebration of the bold stroke. Because children admired the unexpected, always craving something new, 'Take risks,' she preached; 'dare!' But taking him for a walk in the cemetery, against the wishes of his father (whom he plainly adored) was bold even by her standards. At least the tactic had served to flush out the stepmother: a capable woman, stronger than she knew, who'd instinctively backed Diane against the father.

The father was part of the problem, Diane thought. Unfortunately, like most fathers she met, he thought of himself as all of the solution.

As they walked through the gate together a ramble in Court Ridge Cemetery seemed like the most wonderful departure, fully in line with her treasured theses. Only when they had gone some quarter of a mile did she begin to question the wisdom of it.

There was a well-trodden path, with mature trees on their left and the back gardens of other houses on their right: a reassuringly artificial environment. But just beyond the treeline lurked the cemetery, and through the trees Diane could see how unkempt it looked. The light had turned the dark, rich, coppery tone of a fine evening in late spring. The shadows were velvet, but very dark; and suddenly there seemed to be many of them.

A breeze had sprung up, bringing goose-bumps to her arms. Johnny didn't seem cold, so she said nothing. He was animated, waving his arms around and talking nineteen to the dozen. Diane worked on listening to his every word, trying to forget her unease; for they were descending into a deeper pit of shadow now, and strollers with their dogs had become less frequent. They came upon a man beneath a tree, smoking. He wore leather pants, leather jacket, a leather cap like a Nazi SS officer's, and a chain dangled from his waist. Time to go home.

They went on.

They went on because Johnny had noticed nothing amiss, was still talking, and if she cut him off she'd cut off his burgeoning confidence, too. But her arms felt chilled to the bone, and a dry, sulphuric taste infected her mouth.

Suddenly Johnny stopped and pointed. 'That's where I got scared.'

A path led off to the left, descending more steeply into the undergrowth. Here and there were scattered gravestones, many of them on the tilt. Diane bent to inspect the nearest one.

'Look,' she said, 'a child is buried here.' Johnny came over; she could almost hear him subtracting one of the dates carved in the stone from the other.

'Ten,' he said dolefully. 'Same age as me.'

Diane remembered the grave at Yorba where *Ma-ma* and *Ba-ba* lay within the earth. How long had it been since she went to lay flowers?

'When did your mother die?' she asked Johnny.

'Eighteen months ago. Nineteen.' Johnny paused. 'November 12, year before last.'

'Do you have a photograph of her you'd like to show me?'

'No. I mean . . . I do have photos, but they're mine, okay?'

'Sure.' The two of them stood in silence for a while. 'Car-crash, right?'

Johnny nodded, but continued to stare at the child's grave.

'And your father was driving?'

'But it wasn't his *fault*!'

'Did anyone say it was?'

Johnny kicked the gravestone a couple of times. 'No.'

'Want to talk about it?'

He shook his head. Diane was about to change the subject when he added, 'Not yet.'

'Shall we go home?' Diane said. Her voice was bright, though she did not feel it: the walk home lay uphill, and by now shadows had left the twilight scant leeway. Would the leather-clad man have gone? she wondered. Or had he stayed, to be joined by other creatures of the night . . . ?

Johnny took Diane's hand; they started to walk back the way they'd come. 'What was *your* mother like?' he asked.

'Oh . . . wonderful. She's been dead so long now . . .' Diane should have stopped there, but some inner compulsion drove her on. 'I still miss her, though.'

'Did your dad remarry?'

'He died long before she did. *Ma-ma* remarried.'

Johnny grunted. Diane wanted to explain that remarrying after the death of a spouse was often a sign of good mental health: the survivor had mourned his way through the grief and come out the other side, ready to start anew. But dark eddies were swirling in her mind now; she couldn't give him what she herself most needed, because *Ma-ma*'s remarriage had not been a success.

'You were happy as a child,' Johnny said. 'Weren't you?'

Yes, Johnny, I was happy. Surrounded by love, protected from all outside interference, I floated through early childhood on a magic carpet. Ba-ba died when I was four. The magic carpet crashed to earth. It never flew again.

'My mother and I were very close,' Diane said, surprising herself. Perhaps this was her defence against demons: the ones hiding behind every tree as they wended their way up the path, now deserted. 'So close that when she died, I thought I'd die, too.'

Johnny's hand gave hers a squeeze.

'I loved her,' Diane blurted out, 'so . . . so . . . *much*.'

And suddenly, without any warning, she was standing in the middle of the path and crying her eyes out. Not just her eyes: *everything* came out: the leaden sorrow, loneliness, resentment – all the desperate paraphernalia of which she had been incapable since her mother's death.

The boy stared at Diane through wide, unblinking eyes. He took both her hands between his own and rubbed them, awkwardly, as if not sure whether this gave her comfort. It did, oh how it did!

She liked this boy very much.

'I shouldn't let you see me cry,' she sniffed. 'Not professional.'

'You're nice,' Johnny said.

For a few moments longer they stood there, not sure how to break this up. Then Johnny said, 'Let's run!' And next thing Diane knew, he was pulling her up the path and she was shrieking protests, but he was stronger than her . . . *And how I've longed for that, Ma-ma, since you left: to be able to hand over the struggle to someone stronger than me.*

They reached the gate panting, protesting, full of laughter. As Diane put an arm around Johnny's shoulders and guided him inside, she decided not only to take the case, but to write Frank Baggeley and thank him for the referral. Also, she'd definitely phone Ed when she got home and accept that dinner invitation. The sun had yet to set, the sky seemed lighter than a moment ago, the twilight less cold.

'Johnny,' Diane said, 'listen carefully to what I'm going to say. I want you to start keeping a diary.'

*　　　*　　　*

I thought that Johnny was perfect, when I met him. The One True Friend I'd been waiting for all my life. My dreams lasted less than a day.

For a long time I couldn't move. Couldn't cycle, couldn't walk, could not even think. She had cried in front of him and he had taken her hands in his. 'You're nice,' he had said. *For Christ's fucking sake, nice!*

It's hard to capture a rage like mine on paper.

Inside my brain was all purple thunderstorms, with vivid streaks of lightning. Blood filled my head until I thought it would burst. My whole body was trembling, and it hurt.

Johnny isn't for me: that's what I thought, then. I despaired. But amidst all the anger and despair was mixed up a lot of hate, too. Hatred of Dr Diane, because she'd become a rival. And worse, much worse . . . hatred of Johnny. For being imperfect.

102

Sins can only be redeemed through suffering, Johnny. Strait is the gate.

*   *   *

Next day Johnny tried to read, but couldn't. Lying on his bed he felt hot. His forehead was damp. Maybe he'd run a fever; then he wouldn't be able to go to school Monday, hooray.

He lay on the top bunk, staring out of the window, wondering what his new school would be like. Johnny was afraid of kids his own age. They picked on him. No reason, they just did. Teachers the same. He was in fifth grade, and struggling. It wasn't his fault he had trouble with spelling. Reading was great, Johnny loved that. Did it really matter he couldn't spell good? Miss Harvey, at his last school, said some of the greatest writers in history never could spell.

Dad helped him over math. Trouble was, he got impatient when Johnny didn't see things as fast as he should, so most times he just pretended to understand, even when he didn't. Less hassle.

The afternoon was warm and cloudy. A day for sitting quietly and sipping lemonade: that kind of day. The house was quiet. Nicole must be asleep: she usually napped, this time of the afternoon. Anyway, his worries were none of her business. Dr Cheung, yes, Johnny could have talked to her, but she wasn't around.

Johnny had spent the morning writing his new diary. Felt weird. Dr Cheung had asked him if he had a photo of Mom. He'd got lots. He'd been looking at them earlier. One was his favourite. He was going to carry it in his shirt-pocket, next to his heart. Before, it had hurt too much to look at it. Now he wanted this photo where he could see it whenever he wanted.

Johnny was still staring out of the window, at where the overgrown lawn sloped down to the fence. A figure appeared on the other side of it, stopped and waved up at Johnny.

For a moment the boy just lay there, propped up on his elbow, and nothing registered. Then he realized that this man was waving at *him*. So he jumped off the bunk and went to the window, curious, because how could the guy have seen him?

Tobes.

Radical! Tobes was funny, like in funny-weird; which suited Johnny fine, because he was nice-weird, too. Now he felt inside the pockets of his jacket and brought out some things and juggled them. (Johnny had never known anyone who could juggle.) After he'd been juggling for a while he stopped, unwrapped one of the things and started to eat it. A candy bar! If Johnny squinted he could see the wrapper was brown and white. Snickers. His favourite.

Tobes beckoned. Johnny didn't feel sick any more, he felt hungry. So he held a finger to his lips and he nodded and went to take a look in on Nicole. She was lying on the bed with airline shades over her eyes. She was snoring. Well, not really snoring, but breathing real ugly.

Still, Johnny's heart was going chug-a-lug, kind of. This could turn into quite serious shit if she woke up and found him gone. Nicole wasn't into funny-weird, she wasn't even into funny-ha-ha.

Johnny went down. Because he was worried about his diary – shucks, only a notebook, really – he took it with him.

As the boy came through the gate Tobes tossed him a candy bar. Without a word they started walking up past Miss Grant's house. They came upon this bench, underneath one of the trees on the other side of the path. The bench was in a circle, all around the tree. Tobes led them to the back of the tree-trunk, away from the path. They sat. The birds were noisy today, maybe they'd seen the chocolate bars.

'What's that?' Tobes said, pointing to Johnny's yellow pad.

'It's a diary. Private.'

'A diary, huh? You always keep one?'

'No. Dr Cheung said I must.'

'Let me see.'

'*No!*' Johnny clutched the pad to his chest, turning away.

'Okay, okay, don't get mad.'

Tobes was cross, but Johnny didn't care. After a while, Tobes seemed to get over his sulk. He took out some more candy bars and juggled again. He tried to teach Johnny how, but the boy kept dropping them. Tobes said, 'Take a rest now, or you'll get bored, and then you won't want to try again.' Which seemed like sense to Johnny.

'Don't you have any work to do?' he asked Tobes.

'What makes you think I work?'

'Well, you're old enough to.'

'How old do you think I am?'

Johnny studied his new friend's face. He was wearing a check shirt today, open at the neck, and black jeans. Young people's clothes, and yet . . . 'Thirty, I guess.'

Tobes burst out laughing; but then he ran his hand through the boy's hair and gave his shoulder a squeeze. (*Feels good*, Johnny thought.)

'Thanks,' Tobes said. 'I'm twenty.'

'Oh. Sorry.'

'Don't apologize. At least you think I'm mature.'

Johnny hated that word. *Hated* it. He knew *he* was immature. Mike said so. 'Where do you work, then?' he asked.

'It doesn't matter.'

Wrong question, huh? Did that make Johnny a klutz, or what? Why wasn't there a book on what questions kids could ask? But then Tobes said something strange: 'You're too young to understand,' he said.

Now Johnny knew he was immature, and all that, but the notion of being too young to understand what work Tobes did struck him as downright silly. Come on, what could he be? An executioner? Drug-trafficker?

'Do you believe in ghosts?' Tobes asked suddenly.

'No.' The question gruzzled Johnny, he didn't know why. Because he wished Mom would come back, maybe he believed in ghosts at that.

'Me neither.' Tobes stuck his hands in the pockets of his jeans, and spread his legs wide. He looked right and left, as if checking for enemies. Then he said, 'Funny things happen here at night.'

'You come here at *night*?' There was an excellent word Johnny had learned from Miss Harvey: blasé. He spent a lot of his time trying to sound blasé, and sometimes he succeeded, but when he said, 'You come here at night?', that wasn't such a time, 'cause Tobes had rocked him right off of his seat.

'Mm-hm.'

'Jesus,' Johnny breathed. 'Aren't you, I mean . . . aren't you *terrified*?'

Tobes stopped looking from side to side and focused on the boy. 'You would be.'

'No, I wouldn't.'

Tobes laughed. Then he gazed straight into Johnny's eyes, and maybe he wanted to convince him how tough he was, but his eyelids were twitching the way Johnny's did when he was afraid he was going to cry. He said, 'My place, my room . . . it's not so great. Not anywhere I'd want to take you. And this, well, it's fresh air, y'know?'

And he laughed again, but Johnny wasn't laughing, because he sensed how unhappy Tobes felt. His wasn't much of a life, but this cemetery mattered a lot to him.

'I'd like to come here at night,' Johnny said at last.

'Still say you don't believe in ghosts?'

Johnny nodded. But Tobes was making him think of Mom too much.

'Well, if I believed in ghosts, I'd say I'd seen a few, right here.'

Tobes's eyes were beautiful and kind. His smile was gentle. But his left leg had begun to fidget up and down, up and down, and this made Johnny nervous. 'You're full of shit,' he said, and then was horrified: how could he talk to a decent guy that way? But a moment ago he'd seemed so sad, so nice, and now he was . . . not scary, not threatening, but . . . Johnny didn't know the word.

Tobes burst out laughing. 'Knew you wouldn't believe me,' he said, tousling the boy's hair again. His hand felt comfortable, kind of. After a while he used his nails to massage Johnny's scalp, ever so gently: really soothing, though his nails were awful long. His hand dropped to Johnny's shoulder and as it brushed his cheek the boy flinched at it's ice cold touch.

'Look,' said Johnny, hastily taking a photograph out of his top-pocket. 'That's my mom. Was my mom. She's dead now.'

They stared at the photo. Mom looked so good in it, dressed up for skiing, in her big, thick yellow parka and bobble-hat. Her face was beautiful. Her eyes shone, her skin had this lovely tan. She was smiling, *Oh God . . .*

Tobes pulled the boy towards him. For a while Johnny was content to rest his wet face against the other's shoulder, which was soft and tough, and he knew deep down Tobes was feeling for Mom, along with him. But after a bit Johnny pulled away. You should never let a stranger touch you, they told you that in school and Nicole and Mike Anderson had both rubbed it in, but this guy was hardly a stranger, now was he? No, what made Johnny pull away was the smell. Not like when you don't wash, or at least, a bit like that, but like when your waterproof gets soaked in the rain and you hang it up to dry somewhere not too warm and then, a day or too later, it smells.

'I don't have a mom and dad,' Tobes said suddenly. 'They got divorced, and I hated both of them, so I came to live here.'

Johnny pocketed his mom's photograph. 'All by yourself?' (This was far-out stuff for him.)

'All by myself. I like it. I'm not the lonely type.'

'I am.'

'I know. That's why you need a grown-up friend like me. You're not happy, are you?'

Somebody who understood! Johnny shook his head, afraid that if he spoke he'd cry again.

'So we'll be friends. I'll teach you how to juggle. I can show you another world, a magic world. One you've never even dreamed of. And it's right here.' Tobes waved his arm. 'All around us.'

Johnny looked. 'I don't see anything.'

'You have to come at night. With me to guide you there'll be no problem. They're afraid of me.'

'Who?'

But Tobes said nothing. Time to be getting back, Johnny told himself nervously. If Nicole woke up and found him gone . . .

'Gotta go,' he said, standing up. And what if Tobes replied, No, you're not going anyplace, what if he made a snatch for the diary . . . ?

'Sure,' Tobes said. He didn't get up, just lifted a hand. 'See you soon, yeah?'

By now Johnny was several paces away from Tobes, and already missing him. This guy made him feel so darn *confused*. He looked back to see Tobes spread his arms along the back of the circular bench, grinning farewell. To think he'd imagined he might hurt him, for heaven's sake!

'Tell you what,' Tobes said. 'Look out of your bedroom window just before you go to sleep. Maybe you'll see me. Then it's adventure time.'

'When?' Johnny could have sworn to God he hadn't meant to say that; it just came out. 'Tonight? To-morrow night?'

Tobes didn't answer for a while. 'When I'm ready,' he said at last.

'What time?'

'What time do you go to bed?'

'Aw . . . nine o'clock. Sometimes later.' (Sometimes earlier, to escape.)

'Nine thirty, then. That's our time, from now on: nine thirty p.m.'

This was meaningless stuff, of course; wouldn't ever happen. But Johnny felt grateful to Tobes for jazzing up his life a little. *Our time!* He took a few more steps, stopped and looked back. 'How did you know that was my bedroom window?' he asked.

'What?'

'When you beckoned me earlier, how did you know that was my window? How did you know I'd be in?'

'Just luck.'

Tobes's eyes didn't blink. He stood up, and although he made no move towards Johnny the boy felt his feet taking him back to the tree; it was as if they didn't belong to him, as if he were two eyes floating without a body. Tobes laid his hands on Johnny's shoulders and bent to place his lips on the boy's forehead. Then Tobes pushed him away, but that was wrong; he didn't want to be pushed, he wanted Tobes to hug him, like Mike Anderson sometimes did, and he wanted another kiss on his head. But Tobes was rejecting him: play-acting the grown-up when really he was just an older, funnier, better child than Johnny.

As the boy went in the gate he turned to wave, but Tobes had vanished and Johnny realized he'd been walking in a kind of dream. He'd been in the cemetery again, and found a friend, and come home all alone, and he felt good.

Got to keep Tobes a secret from *them*, though.

Would he really come one night, like Peter Pan? *Will he take me to the land of the Lost Boys?*

Will he?

*   *   *

110

It took a while for Ed and Diane to set up their dinner-date. She was busy, he was busy . . . and perhaps at the back of everything was a perfectly understandable mutual fear. Of renewed failure, of seeing a second chance whirl down the plughole. Whatever the reason, Diane was content to wait. She worked all the hours God sent. On those rare occasions when she had leisure she either pottered in her new garden, or practised Chinese scroll-painting with the help of Dr Leong in St Joe's paediatrics department. She'd been doing this for ten years, on and off, and it was as frustrating as hell because Diane still could not master perspective. It irritated her, sometimes to the point where she'd put her brush aside for months at a time. She always came back, though. She wasn't going to let a little thing like perspective beat her.

There came a day in early June when Ed's calls became more persistent. Diane didn't really have time for a date, but . . .

They sat by the water's edge at sunset, watching the Moks' boat cream into the pier while they sipped chilled Belvedere Reserve Chardonnay, and all around them the fishing fraternity bustled in preparation for their night's work.

The Moks were heavily into theatre. Their trawler tied up. Mok The Youngest – he was about fifteen – lammed along the pier on bare feet, carrying a basket of lobster. Mrs Mok had charge of things on the deck outside their restaurant. As Mok The Youngest neared her station, she upped the lid from a pan of boiling water. Next second the contents of the basket were flying through the air, into the pot, down went the lid, slam!

No one cooked lobster like *Ma-ma* Mok of Bel Cove. Diane sighed, thinking of the poor beast's last moments, and met Ed's eyes. Tonight that simple, honest gaze seemed even more direct than usual. He oozed sincerity. Diane should be on her guard. She should.

Although this was a Wednesday evening the open-air restaurant was crowded. Actually, there were several restaurants along the waterfront by Bel Cove pier, but they had a tendency to blend into one another. At the start of summer, like now, first week of June, the waterfront got crowded with in- and out-of-towners; there was always plenty of noise, lots going on. This suited Diane well, because those wide-open, integrity-filled eyes opposite were starting to drag her down; the crowds gave her a good excuse to ogle without seeming to snub Ed.

'So where is my stolen property, Detective?' she said at last.

'That can wait. You haven't heard my news yet. Promotion.' He picked up his glass. 'Detective, First Grade, as of June 1.'

They drank. She was about to say 'Congratulations', when Ed broke in: 'I'm assigned to your new unit, also as of June 1, as principal liaison officer. *If*... you'll have me.'

Diane had told Peter Symes that one of his people would have to act as main linkage between the police and her; she'd asked for a woman.

'Oh.'

'Give it a try?'

So he feared rejection, did he? Diane, too, feared rejection, but that hadn't stopped Ed concealing the existence of his wife from her. Before she had to produce an answer, however, assorted Moks rushed to her rescue. The lobster was served amid great fandango, but what it came down to was utterly fresh seafood boiled in herbed water and served with a tomato-garlic-and-mayonnaise

112

sauce for which Mrs Mok was famous along the Pacific seaboard. There was rice, cooked chewy as Diane liked it, and there were bowls of highly spiced oriental salad. A plastic orange washing-up tub doubled as a finger-bowl, but there was a solitary lotus floating in it.

'Everything all right?' enquired father Mok, rather spoiling the effect by saying 'Good' and racing off before either of them could think of a superlative.

For a while they wielded their chopsticks in silence, while the sun sank over the horizon and the water began to silver. It was as if some invisible signal had been transmitted down the coast: Bel Cove, empty a week ago, tonight was packed. People squeezed past their table; one lady apologized when she knocked Diane's jacket to the ground. A Mok switched on the rows of coloured lanterns that swung crazily around their terrain; some people clapped and soon everybody was joining in. Diane tried to recall when she had last felt so quietly happy, but failed.

'Okay,' she said.

'Uh?'

'The unit. You're in. On appro, mind. Now prove you're a good cop by giving me my things back.'

Ed retrieved a tote-bag from under the table and opened it. He handed over Diane's leather wallet, stained and smelly, with no money but the charge-cards intact (why had the thief not used them, she wondered?), plus a few odds and ends. And the *shen pai*.

It wasn't much to look at – wooden, one foot high, five inches wide, set in a plain base, with Chinese lettering on it – but as Diane took it from Ed her hands trembled a little.

'What does it mean?' Ed's eyes said he was curious, not just making chat.

113

'Oh . . . this character is his . . . my father's name. And where he was born, his piece of "earth", that one means "earth".'

Diane placed the ancestral tablet in her purse, slung over the back of her chair along with the jacket the woman had dislodged earlier. Ed produced a form and got her to sign it: a receipt.

'Still no gun?' Diane said.

'Sorry, no. You'd better get yourself a new one.'

'So where did you find my things?'

'Like I told you, on a raid.' Ed wiped his mouth with a paper tissue and dunked his hands in the plastic bowl. He was a messy eater, always had been, eating too fast for his digestion's good. Then – 'Duty calls,' he'd used to say, in that light, joking tone of his, before going back home to his wife Rowena and explaining to her that he was home late because duty had called.

Change track, Diane told herself. 'Ed, please thank the squad who found my stuff.'

'Of course.' For a while they ate, and watched the boats, and failed to meet each other's eyes. 'We need to talk about the unit,' Ed said at last.

She nodded.

'Peter Symes is gung-ho,' Ed said. 'I mean, really. He sees this as a great opportunity to show the caring face of police work.'

'So he should.'

'But he needs to be able to sell it. All big police departments employ psychologists now. We need a unique angle.'

There were many things for Diane to swallow there, none of them as palatable as lobster à la Mok. Psychology should not be something that required

114

marketing, like a new brand of popcorn. Symes, however, was a self-publicist with aspirations; he did not intend always to be police chief of a smallish city. Diane was well aware that her proposal for a special liaison juvenile crimes unit would look good on CVs other than hers. But . . .

'That kind of psychologist is on the pay-roll,' she said. 'Oh, I know who you mean: Marcia Long down at headquarters, Jules Campion at court clinic. But I'm not on Peter's pay-roll. And the counsellors you're thinking of are employed by Internal Affairs to take care of personnel problems, men who've witnessed one shooting too many.'

Ed could not handle lobster on the shell. He looked so vulnerable as he wrestled with his chopsticks that Diane's heart started out towards him, drifting on a dangerous current. It was time for a firm hand on the tiller. She wrenched her mind back to politics.

'That kind of psychologist is employed to serve the interests of the department,' she told him. 'My unit will serve truth, in the abstract.'

'Diane.' Ed laid down his chopsticks. 'Can we step back in the real world?'

She was a professional among professionals; counsellors were traditionally courteous, respectful of one another. She had forgotten how irritating, and how stimulating, direct speech could be. But . . . 'No,' she said firmly. 'This is *my* world; I'm creating it, according to my notions of what is decent and right. Peter's already bought that.'

She wished others had bought it, too. The unit was encountering more opposition at grass-roots level than she'd anticipated. The men attended her lectures only under protest, or because they wanted the extra money.

115

'Okay, try this,' Ed said. 'A kid complains her father raped her. You counsel the kid, you counsel the officers on the case. Then we come around to the view that the kid is wasting police time and resources by faking a case against a parent she can't relate to. Is the kid your client, or what?'

'It would depend – '

'Could we subpoena you to testify in court about what the kid had said?'

'Probably yes, because – '

' "Probably"?'

'Come on, Ed, this isn't – '

'This isn't very well thought out, is what I'm saying.'

Edwin gave her another of those long, hard looks; then he smiled and went back to messing up his lobster. Diane longed to retaliate, swiftly, cleanly . . . 'Need any help?' she drawled, unable to stand a moment more of his ineptitude with those damn chopsticks.

'I thought you'd never ask.'

Diane used the lobster-pick to prise out the flesh for Ed; it was like feeding a baby. He sat there looking down at her busy hands with a look of wonderment on his face; he might actually have *been* an outsized infant.

'There,' she said, pushing the plate back towards him. 'Eat. And listen.' She straightened out her thinking, took a deep breath, and pitched. 'You know as well as I do, there's going to be further preparation, with a huge amount still to do. But we can win, as long as everyone's pulling on the same team. Now, do I have that?'

He gazed across the table at her. 'Will it actually help anyone?'

'Yes. Right from day one, it will benefit the kids on the block your men caution and counsel without arresting, because cops will be more able to distinguish between helpless cases on the one hand, and children who've just gone a bit wild. Joe Blow in his squad car will feel less vulnerable when faced with a juvenile situation. And that's just for starters. Afterwards, lower juvenile crime statistics, less time spent in Juvenile Court – '

But Ed held up his hands. He was laughing. For a moment Diane felt fazed; then she started to laugh, too. She was suddenly aware of a great need to have this man on her side; as her liaison officer, his influence was going to be profound and for that reason if no other they should be friends. She reached back for her purse and took out her name-card case, realizing he didn't even have her new address yet.

Give a person your name, give him power over you: old Chinese belief. So this was a symbolic gesture. Did Ed know that? Now where . . . ?

'What's up?' Ed said.

Diane's eyebrows had risen, telling him something was wrong. 'I thought I had more name-cards,' she said, handing one over.

'Maybe the thief took them and we didn't recover them?'

'No, at the time of the theft I hadn't even had these printed. Oh, dear. Memory failure in ageing spinsters; there's a big literature on that.'

'You never age. And you don't have to be a spinster.'

'I don't?' *Wow! Careful, Doctor . . .*

'Sounds a lonely location,' Ed said as he turned the name-card over, smiling at the Chinese version of her name on the back.

'It is.'

'So don't forget to buy that replacement gun.' Ed drank some wine, caressing Diane with those dark grey eyes and she knew then how much he wanted her. 'Or a live-in protector.'

'Fat chance!' she scoffed. 'The big problem facing modern American womanhood isn't the menopause or combining babies with a career; it's the statistic that says all handsome men are either attached or gay.'

'I thought women only found a man handsome if they *knew* he was married or gay.' Diane's laugh encouraged Ed to continue, 'I gather you and I can work together, then?'

'You certainly seem to have read your Amateur Psychologist Monthly. We'll get you on to solid fare soon enough.'

Ed had finished his lobster. Diane waited for him to light a cigarette, not minding, not too much; but when he didn't she felt puzzled and asked, 'Not smoking tonight?'

'I quit. Two months ago. By the way, something came up on that missing kid we did the broadcast on.'

'Hal Lawson?'

Ed nodded. 'There was fantastic feedback. The studio had forty-eight people call in that special number they gave out, and we had another eighty or so calls at HQ. By following up the leads we got from that, we've managed to pin down where and when he was last seen. Second week in April, at a place called Harley's Diner. Know it?'

'No.'

'That's good, because you'd have gone down in my estimation if you did. Harley, the guy who owns the place, is into all kinds of mayhem. It's on the beach, up Point Sal way.'

'Who goes there?'

'Local kids, bikers. There's drugs, but we never managed to bust anybody.'

118

'That doesn't sound like Hal's kind of place.'

'Maybe. Anyway, no progress. Couple of the guys went up there and tried. Zilch.'

'Went up there with warrants and cars with red lights on the roof?'

'I guess.'

'Smart cookies, your colleagues. Talking of which . . .'

Right on cue, Mr Mok brought the basket of fortune cookies, plus two oranges sliced into eighths.

'So what happens now? About Harley's, I mean.'

Ed shook his head. 'We went, we interviewed, we tried.'

'And we failed,' Diane said. 'Right, why don't we bike up there ourselves, one Saturday, and check it out?' Ed reached for a slice of orange, but Diane smacked his hand before it could take the fruit. 'Ed, you don't get it, do you?'

He looked down at her hand, and the orange. 'It seems not.'

'Oh, you . . . ! You're not taking this seriously. As a psychologist, I have a lot to teach about interview technique; it's one of the things I plan to make big in the unit. We'll go to Harley's, you watch, you listen.'

'Diane, you're not a cop.'

'Nor do I want to be. But I can help and that's what Symes wants. Come on, Ed, it's a simple enough request. What harm can it do?'

'It's against police procedures.'

'You solve crimes only according to the rule-book? And there I was, thinking you employed imaginative lateral thinking.'

'We don't just throw the rule-book out of the window, Diane. It has a purpose. For one thing, it protects us when things go wrong.'

'*Protects* you? Who the hell cares about *you*? You're there to be shot at.'

The wine was working inside Diane, that and Ed's smile. She kept remembering times they'd had together. The camping weekend at Lake Zaca, when they'd walked so far along a mountain-trail that they'd damn near fallen down exhausted in the sun and gone to sleep, and when they'd woken up her left leg had been red with sunburn, and she'd hobbled back to the campsite on Ed's arm, miles and miles, with the evening getting chillier . . .

What had he told his wife that weekend? That he was working? *Oh you miserable bastard,* Diane thought; *how I hate you. And how resourceful you are, how strong, kind, caring . . .*

'Diane, I'm not going to do what amounts to an undercover operation with you for all kinds of reasons, the first being that *you* need protecting, too. Your unit hasn't got off the ground yet. Can you imagine what would happen if we talked to people at Harley's and evidence started coming out and we couldn't use it?

'All right, try this. The rule-book doesn't prevent two friends going out one weekend just because they happen to be working together, right?'

'Like that time at Zaca, you mean?'

Lying there beneath the stars, the world had seemed harmonious, and good: that's what he was deliberately reminding her of as he smiled into her eyes: So cruel. So unfair.

'I guess,' he went on slowly, 'there's nothing to prevent us dating just because I happen to be attached to your unit.'

'We're not dating.'

Ed didn't answer directly. He looked around the waterfront at all the other happy couples, eyebrows raised, taking his time over it before once more concentrating on Diane with an ironical grin; and she thought about killing him, and how it would feel pretty good, actually.

Ed had picked up one of the chopsticks and was toying with it, which somehow enraged Diane still further.

'We are not dating,' she said, forcefully enough to make heads turn. And – Boom! Her world exploded into chaos, all in the blink of an eye. Ed threw himself across the table. Diane fell back, chair buckling beneath her. As she went down she saw Ed stab viciously at her hand with the chopstick; no, not *her* hand, but a man's hand. Her purse, its strap broken, was lying on the ground next to her. Voices, many, cried out in panic as the table shuddered, overturned and landed on Diane's chest.

Mrs Mok hauled the table away and helped Diane to her feet, cooing Cantonese expressions of dismay. Diane shook and shivered, but she was alive. The storm had passed. Everyone around was standing, looking her way: 'What happened?' 'Did you see that?' 'The other guy got him, I saw.'

Then Ed was making his way through the press. 'Police. Excuse me. Relax, folks, all over now. Police. Everything's history. Relax.'

He put his badge back inside his shirt-pocket and ran both hands through his tousled hair. Mrs Mok helped Diane into a chair while her husband sprinted along the waterside with two tumblers full of Scotch, as if Diane's life depended on him getting her to swallow whisky in time.

'What happened?' she asked Ed, though her voice was husky and it shook like her body.

'A thief. I'd been watching him cruise the tables, looking for a mark. Your bag was over the chair-back. When he made his move I went for him with the chopstick.'

He held the chopstick out to her. There was blood on the end of it. 'Ugh!' Diane recoiled. He wiped it with a napkin and handed it to her again. 'Memento of a golden evening,' he said. 'You keep one, I'll keep the other.'

Diane didn't want it, but she couldn't say no to Ed right then so she slipped it inside her bag.

'Better than a can of mace any day,' Ed smiled.

'I owe you,' Diane said, 'and your reward is, you get to go to Harley's Diner with me. Just for the hell of it. Afterwards, we can swim.'

He thought she was still in shock, whereas she was proving something to him, and to herself: that she could make a comeback. Even from Lake Zaca, and what had followed: it was the Tuesday after their romantic weekend that Diane's friend-turned-informer had proposed a game of tennis, 'so we can talk, quietly'.

'Why don't we go to LA next Saturday instead?' Ed countered. 'There's *Pirates of Penzance* and *HMS Pinafore* playing at this little – '

'Because there's only one deal and this is it. And I'm busy next Saturday; make it the Saturday after that.'

He grunted. Then he said, 'Okay.' And her whole body sagged, like a beach-ball with a slow puncture. 'But I'm the boss,' he warned her. 'We go to Harley's, we look, we drink a cola.'

Ed paid the check. Originally Diane had intended to insist on going Dutch, but she, who spent her life caring for others, in desperation and secrecy longed to be taken care of; when this strong, masterful man took charge, he provoked no contest from her.

They'd come in separate cars. As they parted, she tried to find words that would express the muddle inside: hope, liking, gratitude, respect, suspicion, fear. Short of the Lord's Prayer, Diane could think of nothing that embraced all of that, and Ed never had been religious.

'Well . . .' Her voice faltered. 'Thank you.'

'No big deal.'

For some reason, righteous wrath surged through her. 'It was!' she told him fiercely. 'Oh, but it *was*. I've been out of things. Too long.'

She kissed his cheek. Before she could back away, he'd kissed her on the lips. Diane's body clenched from scalp to toenails, darkness came down over her like a shroud. She quivered within seconds of screaming: '*No!*'

But then he released her. Diane got into her Camry. She started the engine. She drove away without looking in the mirror.

*   *   *

It's good to have this project. At first, I thought the whole idea was dumb: you know, writing down what happened/happens. Now I'm hooked. Everything sharpens up when you have to tell it to another person. If you have to write it, you sharpen it some more.

Also, it helps keep me awake.

It's mid-summer now. June 16.

Johnny sucked his Pentel. Often things just came out, but sometimes he felt a bit constipated, like today.

When Dr Cheung had walked with him in the cemetery all those weeks ago and agreed to take him as her patient, he'd felt elated. He'd been afraid she'd turn him down, when she spoke to Dad and the WW later, and when he heard the Yes it seemed like the start of something good. Then she'd asked him to come out to her car, see her off, so Johnny had known she wanted to talk without *them* hearing, and that was out-of-sight wonderful. He could work with this woman.

She'd given him a yellow pad from the trunk of her car. Last thing she'd said before leaving was, 'I want you to write down everything you think is important about your day. Start with when you first moved in here, Court Ridge. Write what happens, what you feel, what you want, your dreams. No one will ever see what goes into this pad, unless you show them.'

'Not even you?'

'Not even me; though I hope you'll let me review the books from time to time. Remember: it doesn't have to be wonderful, grammatical English, don't worry about spelling, don't get formal. When the things you write feel too sad, or difficult, just turn the page and start anew. Be real.' And here she'd made a fist and banged on the top of Johnny's head with it, playful like. 'Always be real. You can write the word "shit" as much as you like, but no shitting.'

That had made him laugh.

So here he was, nine twenty-five pee-em, and him feeling tired, but he ought to write in his diary.

Today was a good day at school. My home-room teacher is Miss O'Shea. Still don't know what I feel about her. She's got red hair and dangly ear-rings that make her look kooky. Been there six weeks and no one's beaten me up yet. Ben comes around, we hang out sometimes. Kind of friendly. Travis Lomax still doesn't like me being called Johnny, says it was stoo-pid.

I'm waiting for Tobes to show.

Johnny slowly crossed through the last sentence. Maybe Dr Cheung would still be able to read what he'd written? Better tear out the page.

What Tobes had said was: look out of your bedroom window at nine thirty and maybe you'll see me, and it'll be adventure time. So now Johnny put away his pad (he kept it under the mattress) and went into his nocturnal routine. Tobes sure wasn't in any hurry about keeping this appointment, Johnny had been watching out of his window for weeks. If Tobes came he'd slip down the back staircase, out through the kitchen door. *They'd* be watching TV. To stop him they'd have to come out, cross the hallway (which was big), chase him down this corridor, turn left by the dining-room, down more corridor and into the kitchen. It was a huge house. As you came in, there was the main stairway, and upstairs all the bedrooms were arranged around the landing, a full square. Mike and Nicole slept on the opposite side to Johnny, the ocean-view side. They were not exactly thrown together in this family. He could run outside butt-naked and they'd never know . . .

Nine twenty-eight . . .

The lawn sloped down to the path. The path was dark. But the next-door neighbours had lamps in their garden. At night, their pool was lit up. Beside their wicket-gate, the one that led to the path, they had this old lamp on a column, with a glass thing. Lantern, that's the word: a lantern. And underneath the lantern, at nine forty, Tobes was waiting.

Johnny's bunk lay right by the window, where he'd pulled it (Nicole hadn't liked that), so he had a perfect view. Tobes stood there in the light. He wasn't smiling. He didn't wave. He seemed awful pale.

Johnny rubbed his eyes and sat up. Huh? Surely it couldn't have been a dream . . . ? But now there was no one there. The lantern still shed its pool of light, but it illuminated nothing. He slid off the bunk and went over to the window. And then he saw Tobes's head. Just that. A white face floating through the light. But nothing around it. Nothing *underneath* it.

Next came the hand. A white hand that beckoned, slowly. Johnny knew he was calling him, that he was the vampire's chosen one. With each drawn-out movement of that white hand, he felt himself lean further out of the window, further . . .

A laugh echoed through his head. Horrible, horrible. Like the cuc-cuc-cuc of a nasty bird, picking over prey. Tobes's laugh. It grew louder. And then suddenly Johnny jolted out of his trance to the knowledge that this was real. He slammed the window shut and jumped back onto his bunk. He pulled the blanket over his head. He cried, but quietly, because he didn't want Mike Anderson to know he was crying.

After a while he reached for his notepad . . .

Shit, shit, SHIT!!!
Okay. It's ten fifteen. Same night.

126

New page, new page, new page.

I was looking out of my window. Dream? Can't have been . . . Face it. I'm scared of Tobes. I thought I could play with him, but I don't like his games. He's weird. He scares me. Really.

I'm not going to see him again.

I want my mommy. She's dead. I just cry and cry.

*   *   *

Randy Delmar was number three. By this time, what with Hal Lawson still not showing up, maybe folks were beginning to have him down *as* number three, even though he was only the second corpse to be found so far.

Randy, just turned nineteen, had a terminal fight with his family. He slept on a friend's floor till the friend's parents threw him out, and for the next few days he bedded down where he could. Someone tipped him off about this derelict warehouse down by the old railroad station and he spent a couple of nights in there, along with rats animal and rats human, but Randy was not much of a fighter and he reckoned he wouldn't survive a third night there, so he moved on.

After a week he'd pretty well run out of money, but he wasn't ready to go home and sue for peace. Wasn't even sure if they'd let him do that, because the fight had been a heavy number involving a misunderstanding between him and his pretty little thirteen-year-old cousin.

He felt faint with hunger. He'd last eaten the day before: the remains of a hamburger some dude had dropped in a bin close to where Randy lay slumped in a doorway. He sat on the rocks at the south end of

Paradise Bay Beach. Ahead of him the sun was setting in a halo of orange and fiery reds. On his right, the beach curved away up to Bel Cove, with St Joseph's Hospital on the spur. Weren't many people about at this time of the evening. None of them exactly looked a soft touch. Besides, Randy was afraid of approaching anyone in case the cops had put out his description.

No help for it: he'd have to go home.

It was a four-mile hike to the house where he lived with his folks, in Causeway, on the east of Paradise Bay: a low-quality housing area between Highway 1 and the start of the city proper, bordering flat farmland. The journey took Randy a long time; he had to stop, often, while he got his head straight again. But the third hour after he'd left the beach saw him turning into his road, nearly home. He reckoned he'd been lucky not to be picked up by the cops. And yet . . . his eyes narrowed. Maybe his luck had run out. A black car sat parked just a few yards down from his house. As Randy hove into sight, the car came to life. Headlights on, engine running, signal-light twinkling.

Randy leaned against a tree for support and looked around. Nearly dark now. Was this a cop-car, come for him . . . ?

The car drew up alongside Randy Delmar. The window lowered. Inside was no cop, just this cool dude wearing black: black leather jacket with fur collar, short black hair, black aviator shades, black cap. Randy didn't get much of a sight of him. Just saw the wad on the passenger seat. Must have been two hundred dollars there, more.

Dreams come true, but where was the catch? Police HQ had never marked Causeway down as a cruising area, or a drugs depot; it was just your typical, seedy residential dump.

Now the driver leaned across to open the offside door. His hand, wearing a black leather glove, beckoned. Randy considered it. He sure as hell didn't want to go home, but this stank.

'Whaddya want?' he said thickly.

No answer.

'I ain't goin' to let you do nothin'. See?'

The driver's left hand rested on the passenger seat, its fingers lightly caressing the wad of bills. Randy licked dry lips.

'I'll let you suck my cock and I don't come in your mouth, deal?'

The driver patted the wad, then flicked it off the passenger seat. Randy took a quick look up and down the street, saw no one about. He jumped in and shut the door. The car roared off.

Randy tried to study the guy, but the collar of his leather jacket was up, concealing most of his face. Marlon Brando clone, into leather. Shit, those guys could be rough.

It didn't occur to Randy to ask himself *why* this dude happened to be parked near his house, *why* he thought that might be a good place to pick up trade, *why* he, Randy, didn't just turn his back on the whole stinking deal and go home. Randy was a high school drop-out, not a professor of logic.

He decided he wasn't going to let this weirdo suck his cock, so he'd better start making plans.

'Where we goin'?'

No answer.

'I said: where are we *goin'*?'

By now the car was travelling fast along straight roads, heading back into the city. Darkness stifled Paradise Bay. Randy was starting to get a bad feeling about this. The dude smelled funny. Leathery smell, but more than that. Unnatural.

'What day is it?' Randy asked blearily. His stomach was eating itself away, or that's what it felt like; how long since he'd eaten? Ahead of him, a fancy dashboard clock glowed pale green. He tried to focus on the numbers as they floated in and out of his vision. June 16.

The car made a left and began to climb. Randy knew where they were, now. 'Court Ridge?' he said incredulously. 'You live here?'

Now *that* changed things. Court Ridge was for the high and mighty. This guy must be loaded. Suppose he lived in one of those grand old houses overlooking the ocean? Randy could beat the shit out of him and no one would ever know. And there'd be things worth stealing, too.

But then the car turned off the highway and stopped. The driver got out, taking the keys with him, and set off down a track. Randy blinked. He felt around but there was no money where he could find it. He could just see the shape of the driver, ten yards away. With a quick glance over his shoulder, Randy followed. No lights anywhere, hell, which part of Court Ridge was this?

The driver set a good pace. He seemed to know these woods, for he avoided all the twigs and overhanging branches that snagged and scratched his companion. Randy was panting, he was scared, and before long he was determined to make the guy pay for all of this.

'Hey!' he cried. 'Wait for me!'

As he spoke the last word, he cannoned into something soft and yet solid: the driver. Randy hastily backed off. Everywhere he looked was dark as pitch.

He heard a hissing, and was aware of light. The driver stood with his back to him, legs apart, holding the light-source so that Randy couldn't see it. A match? Helluva big one. Then he saw the driver reach into his pocket with one hand and remove something. Something pale, that rustled. Money!

The driver threw it over his shoulder onto the ground. Randy nearly toppled over, he felt so weak. If he didn't get food soon he was going to die. He had to take a chance, *had to*! The wad still lay on the ground behind the driver's back. Guy seemed preoccupied with his flashlight, his whatever – maybe it was his cock, glowing in the dark, Randy didn't care shit. He'd had enough. If this weirdo chased him, it should be easy to lose him in the woods . . .

As Randy made a dive for the wad on the ground, the driver turned, holding a live blowtorch, right hand coming forward in a dead straight line, aiming for the boy's eyes.

Randy screamed. Over the next half-hour or so, he screamed a *lot*. Nobody heard him through the gag, though.

*   *   *

Nothing works. I fall in love for the first time, I go to the library and raid it for every book I can find about this supposedly energizing experience, the books are useless. I rearrange my job schedule, taking days when I should be working nights, so that now I owe favours to everyone, and the boy does not show. I may be mad about the boy, but there is something of the cad about the boy, tra-la. Yeah, definitely.

(About that job: time to quit. I am a conscientious worker, but there are limits to how many potatoes a man can peel and retain his sanity. I am not, nor have I

131

ever been, the kind of person who takes pleasure in jerking off into the *mousse à l'orange* while the commis is taking a break, although believe me when I say I have worked alongside many who did, and further believe me when I say that I have jerked off in numerous situations and places and at times that would surprise you: I have nothing against jerking off.)

Sadness is a new thing to me. I go to the library and ask for poetry, love stories, psychology, anything. Lots of it's above my head, anyway. But there's this strange theme running through what I read, like those little golden stars in the Hollywood pavement, leading me on, and it's this: love is sad.

In my life I have known rage, fear, hatred, depression and suicidal despair. Never sadness. When I first met Johnny I discovered what joy meant, and that was the easy part. He left and I felt something else, but didn't know what. We met a second time, the same thing happened, only the feeling when we parted was worse. But I couldn't find a name for it. Heaviness, fatigue, a lack of desire to go on with what's left of the day. A lump in the stomach, grit in the heart.

The odd thing was, I could see colours like never before, and the air was sweeter than I remembered, and in the cemetery birds sang. Were they part of this new thing called sadness? I felt beautiful, too, as if someone had clothed me in lights. Then I saw him with Dr Diane and the lights all went out at once. She wants him as much as I do, any idiot could see that. Well, she shan't have him! He's mine, MINEITELLYOU . . . Igor, prepare the electrodes . . .

Everybody's laughing at me. I'm just a joke, I guess.

To resume. After a while, anger and jealousy faded. That's the strange thing: they just went away. Even the

132

sadness left me, to be replaced by desire for the Loved
One that nothing but his presence could quiet. Hence
my manifestation at Court Ridge on the night of June
16. And he chooses this moment, the moment of my
total self-discovery, to reject me.

I stand beneath the neighbour's lamp and I wave
and I'm sure he's seen me, so I laugh and wave again:
Come on down! But – he doesn't! He bangs the
window shut and next minute his light's out, and I'm
standing there feeling stupid.

I wait for him to open the window again. Then I
think: maybe he's coming down, any second now he'll
be out. (Of course, it's obvious from the way he didn't
wave and slammed the window that this wasn't the
case, but love is sad, remember.) Then: maybe his
parents have nabbed him. Then . . . nothing.

As my steps drag me through the long grass, away
from the Anderson house, deeper into the graves, my
mind summons up that particular kind of unpleasant-
ness to which it is prone. Maybe it has something to do
with my surroundings; are you sensitive to ambience?
There are many dogs here, some brought on leashes by
devoted owners, most of them wild. All of them,
however, shit. Suddenly there's this unmistakable
smell. I have trodden in dog doo-dah.

Soft shit.

No, I don't think we are ready for *soft shit* yet. We
will come to that.

Now what occurs to me, as I wipe my shoe on grass,
is that there appears to be a lack of discipline in Johnny
Anderson. My little boy needs a firm hand to guide him
through life's joys and sorrows, its highs and pitfalls.
Tenderly but firmly, I must admonish him. Counsel
him. Steer him away from rocks that threaten his

frailty. I am not going to do him any favours by letting him run wild, like the dogs in Court Ridge Cemetery. It is never in a child's best interests to let him roam entirely free, I remember my own father saying that, and ohmigawdbutweareback . . . with soft shit, and I don't. Want. That. Yet.

I want a photograph of Johnny.

The cemetery teems with moving shadows; there is no moon, but I know my way. My eyes spend a lot of time piercing dark crannies. I tend to eschew light. (Isn't ESCHEW an *excellent* word?) This part here is where the addicts shoot up, chase the Dragon, do whatever.

Now I am starting to climb again. This is one nasty bit of graveyard, let me tell you: thorns on every side. But it's a short-cut to the civilized sector, where people still get buried sometimes, and relatives come to lay flowers of a Sunday. There, a wide road runs straight and true from the main gates on Winchester to the back exit at Seymour. At night, this road is a lively place. There are streetlights there, some of them working. Faggots cruise up and down, their cigarettes burning red as devils' eyes. This is somewhere I must take Johnny. He is not going to grow up like the demons beneath the trees, with their cigarettes, and poppers, and filthy bodies to match their minds. He must see how I treat those people; then he will learn, and understand.

There is so much I can do for that darling child.

My thoughts are aflame as I push my way through the last thorn-thicket, on to the cemetery's main drag. The dull embers of sadness have been fanned into a blaze of rage. Sure enough, there's quite a crowd tonight. One of them stops and turns my way. No

134

doubt he thinks I've been enjoying myself, enjoying another man. Or he wonders if I've *been enjoyed* I stand where he can see me in the light from the nearest standard. I am young, muscular, blond, tall, lovely.

Slowly he comes towards me. I thrust my right hand into the pocket of my jeans, where I finger the switchblade. My smile is welcoming. Let him touch me. Let him try.

Maybe he sees something in my eyes, perhaps he has a sixth sense that preserves him, who knows? He falters. Then he shuffles away at an angle to me. I swivel. I keep my eyes on him and he knows that. Every so often he casts a fretful glance back over his shoulder, until at last he disappears.

What happens to them when they go beyond the pool of light? Do they sink into the slime, or what? You never see them in daylight.

I lope along the driveway almost to Winchester, where I have left the Trekkie chained to railings set around a miniature mausoleum. This is a real curiosity: some child's grave with a little house built on top, not a Greek temple thing, but a toy gingerbread house, the whole being enclosed by iron railings. Makes me shriek each time I see it. The bike's still there, so I unhitch and am on my way, riding straight at a man coming in off Winchester, forcing him to take a dive to one side where there are nettles. This will take his mind off sex and that is good.

There is someone else who knows about sadness: Dr Diane. I need to take this problem to her. But I do not have an appointment.

Now, oh reader, it may have pricked your consciousness, as you plough this my furrow, that I have conceived a great interest in Dr Diane.* I worship her, albeit from afar. At the moment, from afar, although tonight I feel in the mood for research.

It's a long way to Dr Diane's house by the sea, but my legs are sturdy and pedalling massages away my sadness. Her place is lonely, but then she is a good witch, and where does any witch frequent except lofty mountains, secret bays, deep groves? The night air is filled with beguiling scents. Only once is the magic mood shattered, when I hear a car and before I know what is happening its headlights sweep over me, ensnaring me in their gleam like a missile's lock-on guidance system. Then the car, a red Camry, is ahead of me, a thing of the past; but I recognize it as Dr Diane's and the knowledge that she will soon be home soothes my mind.

By the time I pedal up to her gate, only a single light is burning, on the upper floor to landward. Her bedroom? No, she'll sleep with a view of the ocean. The light is extinguished. I leave my bike in the usual place, deep in a clump of maples opposite her gate, and light a Marlboro. (I do not fear the big C; to die of cancer is not my destiny. Dr Diane doesn't know I smoke, however; that is my secret and the knowledge would diminish me in her eyes, for sure.)

The house towers above me. A lane skirts the house and goes on up the coast, north, for a little way, but there is only one other property at that end of it: a farm. So what you do is, you follow the lane a few yards before cutting through an overgrown field (beware of the ditch in the middle) and so on down to the beach. There are dunes here, not very high, and

*Maybe it is you, Dr D, who are even now reading this . . .

paths between the dunes, where spiky grass and ice-plants grow. This place is lonelier than the moon.

I walk along the beach until I am directly beneath the house. No lights. It stands out against the cloudless sky, charcoal on grey. She is there. All by herself. Asleep.

I lie on my back so that I can keep an eye on the house. The beach shelves gently; all the blood within me drains down along my body, towards the sea. Tonight, everything is peaceful. A few stars pin-prick the dark cavern above. The ocean stirs weakly, almost too tired to bother but needing to prove it's still alive.

What am I going to do about Dr Diane? She is wonderful, yes; but she knows too much and is finding out more, all the time. The slope is slippery, the gradient steepening, no end in sight. Unless action is taken I shall be in the shit, even (God forbid) the *soft shit*; and *that*, as the broker said when Mike Milken offered him a junk bond, is not an option.

So what's a boy to do?

The question preoccupies me for ages, until at last I drift into this spooky state: half conscious and half asleep. Suddenly I awake with a start. Light has done that. Dawn is coming. It's almost too late to do what must be done.

*   *   *

Diane finished writing up her dream book, closed it and put it away in the bedside drawer. She took a shower. Outside her window birds sang and, as she dressed, Diane sang with them. Once downstairs she turned on the TV: Ray Douggan's murder still occupied space, but its allure was fading. Peter Symes came into shot, well tailored, hair immaculate, voice confident. 'We *will* find the sick individual behind this loathsome crime, we *will* find Hal Lawson and Randy Delmar . . . ' A protest-group of parents broke in, but this was old news. 'And now, what weather can we expect today, Malcolm?'

The day's going to be just fine, said Malcolm; it will be hot. Even so, Diane phoned The Safety Net, and – a miracle! Someone, a *person*, picked up. Her project had not been overlooked; they were awaiting delivery of components from Chicago, next week had been mentioned as likely ETA, soon her house would be protected by a fully-functional electronic alarm system. Diane did not necessarily believe any of this, but was content to live in hope.

She collected her purse and started out for the integral garage. She opened the connecting-door, took a step inside. Then a blob of coffee-flavoured bile erupted somewhere in her gut and she stopped dead, for she could smell cigarette-smoke in the garage and her heart was pounding fast.

In those first seconds all that occurred to her was that the intruder must still be here, in her car or underneath it. Or in the house . . . no, she'd just this minute unlocked the connecting-door, he couldn't have penetrated further than the garage. Diane bent to look beneath the car: nothing except some oil spills. Inside the car, no one. Thank God, thank God.

Slowly she approached the garage's double-doors. They were the old-fashioned kind: no up-and-over, no radio-operated switch, just solid wooden doors on hinges, secured by two bolts. Last night, she must have forgotten to fasten the bolts, for they were drawn back. How stupid of her.

Standing by the doors, she looked down and saw a cigarette-butt on the garage floor. She bent to pick it up; it had been crushed, by somebody's foot, she guessed, but she could just make out the word 'Marlboro'.

Diane did not actually know anyone who smoked Marlboro, but a whole lot of people did, and it was perfectly possible that one of her acquaintances or patients did without her realizing. Now wait a minute: why think in terms of acquaintances and patients? What was wrong with a nice, old-fashioned intruder, chancing by and trying his luck?

Well, a nice old-fashioned intruder would have smashed the window and raped Diane before slitting her throat and making off with her purse. (Probably the man who'd stood smoking in the hollow the morning Douggan was murdered – Jesus, how she hated the Safety Net people.) No, this was the kind of thing that happened to film-stars and therapists: someone with a fixation began to haunt them.

Haunt: such a dreadful word. Diane shivered. Maybe she should call the Santa Barbara County Sheriff. Maybe this house was not such a great idea and she should sell it. *(What? Before going to work, you mean?)* Or perhaps she should just get the hell out and stop being so childish.

The last option had appeal. She threw open the garage doors and with a rueful smile on her lips went back to the car, groping in her purse for the keys. As she unlocked, her eyes came level with the Camry's rain-gutter above the driver's door. There was something in there: a white card. She swept it up and found herself holding one of her own name-cards.

Something impelled her to turn it over. On the back, just above her Chinese name, was written, in bold script, 'Love you . . . XXX' and her heart turned cold as her skin.

Diane's mind raced back to when she'd offered Ed Hersey one of her name-cards and found far fewer than she'd expected. Somebody had stolen the others because he had something specific in mind and this was just the start of it.

Ed's name inspired weak, unrealistic hope. Perhaps this was some kinky joke of his, perhaps he'd called by last night, while she was out, and when he found she hadn't locked the outer doors he'd left the card as a tactful way of saying, 'Look, I know you're an adult, but you should take more care.' How sweet!

Once Diane hit the road to Bel Cove, however, her mood hardened. It was wrong of Ed to act this way. All the evidence pointed to a prowler and a competent cop should have realized it would, before staging some kind of object-lesson. And hadn't Ed said he'd quit smoking? Did he use to smoke Marlboro? Diane couldn't remember.

The first thing she did on reaching her office was call him. She chided him, gently. He listened in silence. Then he said, 'It wasn't me.' Movement rustled down the phone. 'I'm looking at the card you gave me, right this minute.'

A blinding flash of light illuminated the landscape; Diane did not like what she saw. There *had* been a prowler who'd gained entrance to her sanctum, her womb; he smoked, as did the man in green-and-black jeans who'd stolen her newspaper; he had her name-cards; *he loved her*. Such 'hauntings' were well documented; some of them had lasted years.

'Diane?' Ed said. 'Diane, are you still there?'

'Yes, I'm here.'

'Did you really think I'd stoop to such a thing? Come on, what kind of a peace officer would do that?'

'Sorry. I should have realized it wasn't you. As long as I thought it might be you, everything seemed okay. But now . . . '

'What about the alarm system? Didn't it activate?'

'It hasn't been fitted yet.'

Ed's silence was quite outspoken, for silence.

'I'm having one fitted. Soon.'

'Good. And you should definitely replace that gun that was stolen.'

'I will. Promise.'

There was another silence, kinder this time. 'Are we going to fix up something?' he asked.

'Harley's, Saturday . . . remember?'

'Oh. Yuh. I guess.'

'We can take my car.'

'Great.'

'You want me to pick you up?'

'That would be good. Say noon, at headquarters?'

'You've got it.'

Diane put down the phone feeling warm towards him again – that stuff about 'did you think I'd stoop?' she found particularly enchanting – but in a perplexed frame of mind. Julia chose this moment to enter, a sheaf of reports under her arm.

'Julia, did you ever take away any of my name-cards?'

'No.'

'Well, someone did; I'm way short.'

'Patients pick them up, sometimes.'

'No, no. I mean my personal name-cards, with my home address.'

Diane explained what had happened.

'Probably a court-referral,' Julia suggested when she was done.

'Why do you say that?'

Julia shrugged. 'They're just a bunch of crooks, aren't they?' she said with a brazen smile; and even Diane had to laugh.

'Now,' she said, 'let's get serious, let's talk about Johnny Anderson.' She unlocked her briefcase and took out a yellow notepad. 'This is his first effort. It covers the second week of May. Scan; tell me what it reveals. Pay particular attention to what he's written about his father. He refers to him by name, sometimes first and last name both, and I want to find out why.'

Julia took the pad. But before she started reading she said, 'You know, I've been thinking about Johnny. His first visit, when Tobes got his appointments mixed up.'

'Yes?'

'You remember how Tobes played with trucks, and things? Don't you think he was a little old for that?'

Diane frowned. 'You're right,' she said slowly. 'Yet he's so intelligent. Funny, he's been on my mind a lot lately . . .'

She stood up and motioned Julia to an easy chair by the conference table, going across to join her.

'Johnny Anderson,' Julia mused aloud. 'I can't figure why, but Tobes only did that stuff on account of *him*.'

Diane frowned. 'Maybe. Listen, I want to run something past you,' she said, sitting down. 'It's been bugging me, and it's important.'

'Shoot.'

'You know how Tobes loves to flaunt his reading, his intelligence?'

'Right.'

'And it's not all bragging, as it would be with so many kids his age; there's substance to it.'

'A lot of substance.'

'So now close your eyes and visualize for me. How did Tobes come by that store of knowledge?'

Julia gazed expectantly at Diane, but then she realized that her mentor was perfectly serious, so she shut her eyes and concentrated.

'What do you see?' Diane asked after a while.

'I see . . . Tobes sitting at a table. With books. Propped up in bed, surrounded by books. Lying in a field, reading.'

'What's his body language telling you?'

After a long silence Julia responded, 'He's got his hands over his ears. He's staring at the page and reading very fast.'

Diane banged the table, delighted. 'My vision, too!' she exclaimed. '*He is shutting out a world he cannot cope with!*'

Julia opened her eyes and they grew wide with excitement. 'Because he can't bear his childhood environment, he escapes from it into a mystical world where things go better.'

'Precisely. And because his environment was *absolutely intolerable* – it must have been, there's no other explanation – he pours his whole heart and soul into that other world, to the exclusion of all else. All that knowledge is just so much by-product.'

Julia's face was troubled. 'Yes, but . . . he's never suggested his childhood was anything like as bad as that.'

'No. Why do you think that is?'

Julia stared at her, stuck for an answer. Diane was anxious to continue, but then the phone rang, announcing the arrival of her first patient, Gary Gilbert, a seven-year-old boy who'd reacted badly to his parents' messy, ongoing divorce. It was a case requiring extreme sensitivity and much thought, but as Diane walked the few yards along the corridor to the playroom her mind kept reverting to something Julia had said earlier: *Tobes only did that stuff on account of Johnny*. If she was right, Tobes's conduct that day was part of a pattern Diane couldn't yet begin to discern.

Diane went in, nodded pleasantly at Gary's mother, and – 'Good morning, Gary,' she said brightly. 'So what have you been writing in your diary for me this week?'

*   *   *

I am starting to know the Anderson domain well. There's a place from which most of their house is open to my inspection: an oak tree near their back gate. It's possible to climb into the first major fork and not be seen on account of the leaves. I can see Johnny's bedroom window from there. Also, the back garden, which truly is a mess. The grass has grown taller than Johnny, the beds are full of weeds, the back fence is rusty and, in places, holed. Somebody is going to have to do a ton of work and, with summer here in force, I don't envy him. Only I do. I'd give one eye to work there.

Come Saturday morning, I am sitting in my tree. It's early. The sun is still pale yellow, and there is a breeze cool enough to raise bumps on my exposed flesh. Experience has already taught the need for a pillow if I am not to suffer extreme pain up here; how do birds cope? I listen to the Dutchman on my phones, and wait for Johnny to appear.

Movement.

Two people walk around the side of the house from where I now know the kitchen to be. Dr Diane and Johnny. She has a hand on his shoulder. By an act of extreme will I quell my fury and concentrate on her other hand, which holds some books. I would give my last eye (the one left over after I'd used the other to buy my way into the Anderson household, remember?) to know what they are saying.

*   *   *

When handing over her gifts that bright Saturday morning Diane watched Johnny narrowly, to gauge his reaction. The Chinese Opera book bagged his attention at once, as well it might: the author, writing especially for children, set out half a dozen plots, with copious illustrations and photographs, plus notes on the facial make-up that distinguished hero from villain, scholar from soldier. What Diane wanted to get across to the boy was how values indicated by fairy stories and ghost tales could not only hold their worth to the present day, but also become an art form: her first, cautious step towards weaning him from ghosts and ghouls.

He liked the book. He turned it over and over, then flipped through, stopping whenever a picture caught his eye, but because Diane was deliberately talking to him all the while he could not become too engrossed. She quickly turned his attention to *Fun with Chinese Characters*; but it was the third book, the one on Chinese customs, that intrigued him the most. He wanted to read it all at once, now, while she waited. He made her hold the others and set to work on the index. Glancing over his shoulder, she saw he had fixed on 'death-houses', and felt a little less sure of her plan.

'Did they really just lie down and wait to die?' he asked in awe.

'Yes. There were special streets for death-houses; when you knew your time was near you went there and waited for the end.'

'But how did they know when it was time?'

Diane mulled that one over. Mei-ru, her mother, had known. She had started wearing those high-collared *sam-fus* more often, and taken to visiting people she hadn't seen in ages. She'd became increasingly vague. In her role as clinician Diane had diagnosed BSF, or benign senescent forgetfulness, thanking the gods that Alzheimer's had passed *Ma-ma* by. Once she'd caught her giving a lock of hair to her oldest friend, a woman she'd fled the Mainland with in nineteen forty-nine: for Chinese, a sure sign that death was near. Then, a week before *Ma-ma* had fallen asleep for ever, she'd made over her wedding-ring to Diane, saying she didn't want to be buried with it on her finger: the most shocking thing she'd ever done and one Diane still wasn't sure she understood.

'Some people seem to know when they're dying,' she said. 'Doctors can't explain it.'

'Doctors know shit.'

How true! Diane thought. Also, how interesting that Johnny should grant himself permission to say that in front of his therapist. Progress! 'The trouble is,' she said, 'doctors know a lot, but never about the things *we* want to know.'

'Right,' Johnny agreed.

Doctors are father-figures; doctors and fathers know shit about the important things; that's what he's saying. Hm . . .

They'd been walking up and down beside the house; now Johnny took off at a tangent, heading for the fence at the bottom of where one day a proper lawn might be. Diane followed, looking at her watch. The purpose of this visit was two-fold: to catch Johnny in a home-context again, and to investigate Mike Anderson. But Mike was 'busy' (didn't want to see her, in other words), and she was due to pick up Ed for their expedition to Harley's in less than three hours' time.

'Want to show you something,' Johnny said over his shoulder. He stopped, and took something from the hip-pocket of his jeans. It was a Polaroid photo of a pretty woman wearing a bright yellow skiing jacket and wool hat.

'Your mother?'

'Mm-hm.'

'She's beautiful.'

'I got a new friend,' Johnny said as they walked on, now side by side.

'Oh, yes? At school?'

'No.' He pointed. 'There.' He indicated the pathway that led down into the cemetery.

'You went again? Alone?'

'No. Like you said, it could be dangerous. I met him on the path.'

'Who?'

'A ghost.'

Johnny walked on, staring ahead as if he didn't want her to read his eyes.

'You're sure it was a ghost?'

'Mm-hm.'

Was that a yes or a no? 'Friendly ghost?'

'Very. Y'want to see if we can find him?'

They had reached the gate; she was on the grid, it scorched the soles of her feet, but – 'Sure,' she heard herself say. *Dare!*

147

Then Nicole called from a downstairs window, 'Can I interest anyone in some lemonade?'

'I'm thirsty,' Diane said gratefully. The boy looked up at her; impossible to tell from his expression whether he regarded that as a betrayal, a cop-out, a welcome relief. As they turned back to the house they heard cars in the driveway. Johnny scowled. 'That'll be Dad's friends,' he said, putting unwonted emphasis on the last word.

'Your father's a builder, right?'

'Yeah. Mike works for this company. Project Director, they call him. He's been sent here to work out some big deal. These guys are coming to meet with him about it.'

'Why do you call your father by his name? You do it in the diary a lot, too. Most boys would just say "Dad".'

Johnny shrugged. From around the front of the house wafted the sound of greetings. They reached the corner by the kitchen window and as Diane and Johnny were about to turn it, a boy came running down the passage. After they'd sorted themselves out Diane had a good look at him. He was tall and skinny, with sparse, dull black hair hanging in rats' tails. His clothes – bleached blue jeans, a Lakers T-shirt, red sneakers – all seemed too large for him. His tanned face was freckled, but this was not a winsome child: his eyes, narrow and savvy, regarded them with a hostility which perhaps derived from his being bad-mouthed at school about his jug-ears. Diane had never seen such big ears on a boy his age – which she took to be twelve.

'Hi,' he drawled. 'I'm Arnie Krantz. You must be the Anderson kid, my dad told me to come find you.'

'Hi,' Johnny said. He did not introduce Diane and that was fine because she didn't want to inhibit the forging of new bonds, although instinct whispered that nothing good could come of this. As she walked into the kitchen she heard Arnie Krantz say, 'Which school you go to?' with all the charm of a Grand Inquisitor waiting for the irons to heat up.

Nicole saw Diane enter and rolled her eyes in sympathy. 'I'm afraid you've missed Mike,' she murmured. 'They're all going out for an on-site meeting. There's sub-contractors, and surveyors, and the zoning expert's just arrived, and I don't know who else.'

She laughed, hoping to pass off ignorance as insouciant femininity, but she was trying too hard, a trait Diane had observed in her before. Today she wore straw sandals, a button-through flower-print dress and no make-up. She looked young, in her twenties, although Diane knew she was thirty-four. She wondered if Mike had a thing about round-featured blondes; the first wife had looked like this.

'Maybe we could talk,' Diane said, accepting a glass of lemonade. 'You can help with my main problem.'

They sat themselves at the pine table. The lemonade was excellent, not over-sweet, but just the way Diane liked it.

'What problem is that?'

'Whether to opt for family therapy, or keep Johnny one-on-one.'

Nicole's gaze slithered away from Diane, who sensed she was obeying an auto-reflex to seek Mike's reaction, even though he wasn't present. 'I'm afraid I don't . . .'

'I'll explain. Families duplicate themselves, generation by generation. You and Mike chose each other as life-partners because you have similar families – oh, you may not think so, but it's true. You're screening off

149

the same problems from each other, and from Johnny. You do have problems, don't you, in your marriage?'

Nicole looked shocked; this was no way for a guest to talk in her Poggenpohl kitchen! After a long, uneasy silence, however, she nodded. 'We . . . find it a little tough-going. At times.'

'So you feel guilty, inadequate – sometimes towards Mike, sometimes Johnny. And I'm afraid of Johnny being made the scapegoat. If we're going to off-load all this stuff from his back, it is essential to off-load it from yours, too.'

'Oh, but we would *never* blame Johnny!'

'Consciously, no. But this whole thing is about the unconscious – yours and his.'

Diane used to have ways of softening this stuff, of leading into it gently; but when her mother died the gentleness had ebbed away, too. *Ma-ma*'s death had brought home to her the need to be more direct about everything. Now Nicole's face told Diane what she was thinking: Mike would make trouble.

Mike *was* the trouble. As if to underline Diane's thought, his voice floated in through the open window: ' . . . enough time on those dumb books, Johnny, you and Arnie come with us, and don't get lost.'

Nicole's eyes briefly met Diane's; they contained less of the conspiratorial goodwill Diane had noticed earlier. *Who threatens my husband threatens me . . .*

'Mike's worried because they're not bonding the way they should,' Nicole said in a low tone. 'He likes to do basketball and all that stuff; Johnny hates it. He's a timid child, am I right? Mike, well . . . '

'Is not timid. But the principal thing wrong right now is the child's failure to relate to you, his stepmother.'

'I've tried everything I know, Diane.'

'Maybe you've tried too much. Perhaps it's time to lay down a few ground rules, give him the security of knowing when he's out of line.'

'Maybe.' Nicole sighed. 'So many problems . . . Johnny loved his mother, he worships his father, and can't see why Mike's wasting his time with me. Then there was the car-crash, when Lesley was killed.'

'Lesley . . . the first wife, Johnny's mother?'

'Right.'

Diane leaned forward to emphasize her words. 'She dead.'

'Tell that to Johnny.' A long pause. 'Tell Mike.'

*　　　*　　　*

Tell you a funny thing: went down to the library yesterday, took out some Charlotte Bronte. 'Gentle Reader,' all that crap. Maybe I'll model my style on hers. Because you see for the first time it occurs to me there's a story in this, a story that one day must be told. Perhaps it's *important* that I'm writing all this down. At first I thought it was simple therapy: getting it all off the chest. Now, I'm starting to wonder.

'Reader, I married him.'

Famous last words.

Yes.

So I'm up my tree, like a gorilla in the mist, right? And suddenly there's this snake-oil convention marching down the path from *chez* Anderson (romantic language, French), unfolding plans and wielding tape measures and heavens! I dunno what else. Now my script does not contain this passage, Mr De Mille. I mean, who *are* these people?!

151

They wend their way down the path like a procession to the scaffold, with my lamb in the middle, a sacrificial victim who today looks at his most victimish.

He is not alone.

Side by side with my Johnny there walks a slimeball. I am an expert in these perceptions, I do not need to hear a sneaky voice or touch a wet palm. A boy about Johnny's age, having a vicious look; someone with designs.

I slip down and begin to follow at a distance. Snatches of conversation drift back to me. I overhear talk of City Hall, fixing the zoning authorities, somebody knows a cardinal who might be persuaded to help with the deconsecration in exchange for a gift to church funds. Mike Anderson is working hard to qualify as Good Ole Boy, assuming we have such things here in California which really I wouldn't know.

The first group is approaching the path that leads to my and Alice Mornay's special place. Thank God, they ignore it, filing on down the main track, which must eventually bring them out at Winchester.

Slimeball, however, catches sight of that side-path. He grabs Johnny by the arm and hustles him down it, into the mess of undergrowth. Johnny resists but Slimeball laughs; 'Just kidding,' I hear him say; 'C'mon, John-boy, let's find out where the wild things are.' Mike Anderson, walking ahead with some of the other men, doesn't see.

Joy arises within me. Meting out justice to Slimeball is going to be a pleasure. If he lays hands on my beloved again, I'll take him apart.

He does. *He fucking does!*

What happens is – this dickhead, this turd, he puts both hands to Johnny's waist and squeezes. Johnny's elbows come down hard, a reflex I remember well from my own happiest-days-of-your-life, and he wriggles away. Or *tries* to, because Slimeball doesn't let up. Johnny flails with his elbows, twisting from side to side. Slimeball, of course, is stronger.

By now they are fifty yards down the path. I follow, keeping within the trees. My feet make no noise; the children do not know an angel is upon them.

Johnny at last breaks free. He runs straight ahead, heedless young fool that he is. There are fallen branches, rotten logs, to contend with. Grass, ferns, brackens snag his feet. The trees become ever more dense, the smell is dank and foul: Johnny sinks up to his ankles in black mud.

'Johnny!' sings the slimeball. 'Come play with Arnie, now.'

Arnie.

Ar-nie.

Arnie!

'Arnie,' I say.

Slimeball hears. He stops. He looks over his shoulder. He does not know it but he is looking straight at me, my face concealed behind a bough thick with leaves. He's frowning. He is alarmed, and I am glad.

I want Arnie, and I shall have him.

By the time Arnie has turned around again, Johnny's disappeared.

My own heart skips a beat. Nobody finds their way out of this corner of the cemetery without help. No one.

Arnie begins to follow. There is a tangle of fallen willow in front of him; he picks his way through it, only to end up in the same pond of mud as Johnny. He staggers and then, in a comical slow-mo, sinks down to one side.

Two dogs appear from nowhere, growling. One barks furiously. Slimy Arnie leaps out of his mud-bath like a human cannon-ball. By advancing a few paces I give myself a ring-side view. Arnie's ass is disappearing through a clump of white birch. The dogs chase him for a while: one is red, with short stumpy legs and long hair. He's an old friend, he means no (great) harm. The other I've not seen before. Looks like a Doberman. Once he had a gold-and-black tail; there's still three inches of it left, ending in a greyish lump of ooze where it was bitten off and hasn't healed.

Things don't heal well here.

The dogs stop this side of the birches, red one in front, still growling. My knife springs open, but then I skirt around the problem, not wanting to mess my hands with blood. Yet. I snap the blade shut. The dogs have gone, anyway; back to whatever tasty mess Arnie nearly landed in when he fell.

I don't think I could kill a dog. Not really. Not unless the dilemma came down to the wire as Pluto or *moi*, in which case it would be *moi* who walked away.

Now I notice something interesting: Johnny, as if attached to a homing device, has drawn near my lair. There is no path, scarcely any daylight. He is blundering through a forest of thorns; soon he'll run out of breath and energy and the will to live. Arnie will come upon him hanging, arms outstretched, caught up in a monstrous spider's web.

Do you know that wonderful picture-card (you find them all over) of the guy leaning forward towards the camera to rest his folded arms on a rail and his head on his arms, so that you can't see his face? He wears nothing but a towel. I often wonder if that guy is really crying, and why. Maybe that's how Arnie will find Johnny . . .

I make a wide detour until I can enter my secret space without either boy knowing, though I can hear them both. 'Johnny,' Slimeball coos. 'Johnny, where *are* you?' His voice is mocking and high-pitched. I will pitch it higher still, just you wait and see.

Alice is well, her ancient, moss-green gravestone undisturbed since last time. Most of the litter here is mine, I check. Not surprising: to get here, you have to crawl on your hands and knees for about ten yards. Not that I am the *only* person who knows about this place; others sometimes use it. Today, for example, there is a big mound of earth beside Alice's stone. Looks new, the earth freshly turned. Good rich clay soil lurks beneath the tangle of greenery, so this mound is almost red, almost the colour of that paint they use to keep out rust. I detest these wanton invasions of my territory.

Johnny's voice sobs nearby. 'No, no,' he pleads; 'shit, shit, *shit*!' Starting to crack now. I pivot, listening hard. Yes – *that* way . . .

When I materialize at his elbow the effect is not what I thought it would be. He does not jump, or whimper. He turns, ever so slowly, until he's looking me full in the face, and then he says, 'It's you.'

His face is white and blotchy; also, there are scratch marks from the thorns. His pants have torn. He stinks: the mud-traps here are foul, and the dogs, well . . . there are so many dogs, and they all shit. But when he leans into me, and I put my arms around his little body, none of that matters. We find peace together in the haunted forest, and although there be wolves circling all around, they cannot harm us.

Voices rise and fall, barely pricking the fetid, dead air. 'Johnny, Johnny!' Not slimy, smarmy-Arnie this time, but adult voices, a long way off. Johnny yanks away from me. 'I'm lost,' he says in a trembling voice. 'Gee, Tobes, what am I going to *do*?'

I reach out for him again, but he brushes me aside. 'You're so cold,' he says, with a shiver. 'You could be dead, you're so cold.'

'Johnny,' a man's voice calls, further off now; the hunt is drifting in the wrong direction.

'He'll kill me when I get back,' Johnny mutters.

'Who, Arnie?'

'My dad.'

'Don't worry, I'll take you home.' I hesitate. I intend him to see my clearing, of course I do, but this is a serious moment in our relationship: once we cross the Great Divide . . .

Okay, here goes. 'Want to meet Alice? This way . . .'

I turn at once, leaving Johnny no time for questions, and sure enough, he follows. Soon we have to crawl in single file, until suddenly the trees and rotten logs and fallen branches yield. We rise to our feet, he looks around, and I see my clearing as if for the first time, only through his eyes. The tamped earth; Alice's stone, bevelled with time; the new mound; the trash; saplings and trees so dense here that they form an impenetrable, ugly wall – ugly, because so many of them are stunted by their overbearing neighbours that they have twisted into strange, distorted shapes that trouble the mind. Here are sickness and decay and deformity. He senses that. I see it in his eyes.

'Say hello to Alice,' I say, gesturing at her grave.

He can never get out, unless I help him.

He's trapped.

If I killed him, and buried his body, no one would ever know.

That's what I read in his eyes.

'I want to go home,' he bleats.

I say nothing, nor do I move. My eyes stray to the mysterious mound of earth next to Alice's tomb. The soil is still crumbly. This is because rain cannot penetrate here, the overhead canopy of branches is too thick. The mound's surface has not melted into a smooth skin. When the really heavy rains come, and ancient springs stir in the bowels of the earth, it will be a different story. The mound will slowly disappear, along with what's underneath. The ground will swallow it. Digest it.

'Please,' Johnny wails.

I walk towards him. He backs away. But the tree wall is implacable. His eyes flicker around, looking for the place where we crawled in. I advance until I can put my hands on his shoulders. He is shaking. I squeeze. Hard.

'Johnny,' I whisper. 'Johnny . . .'

And then, very close, just the other side of the trees in fact, Slimeball says, 'Ah-*hah*. So that's where you are, you little creep.'

Arnie can see us! No, can't, *no*! *He must not see this place.*

My heart steadies to a regular thunder-roll. He's bluffing. He can't see anything.

Where is he?

Say something, Slimeball; let me hear you.

Johnny's eyes meet mine. I smile, laying a finger to his lips.

'Come on, Johnny,' Arnie yells, 'come out of there.'

I shake my head. Johnny's lips twitch in a half-smile.

'Your *dad*-dy wants you, creep. Can't you hear him calling?'

Feet rustle the undergrowth, giving me a fix. He's close, but not as close as I feared. Suddenly Johnny

157

presses his mouth to my ear; he says, 'Don't let Arnie get me.'

Leading him by the hand, I tiptoe to the tunnel through which we entered and indicate that he's to follow me. He nods; we crawl. At last the green morass thins and we are out. I have no plan, except to take Johnny back to the main path, close to his house, and leave him there. Then Fate takes a hand.

The enemy is delivered unto me.

Arnie is on the side of the clearing furthest from where we are. I take Johnny's hand again, and start to make off away from Arnie, towards the path that backs on to Court Ridge. The going is tough until we hit a patch of freeway, a place where for some reason trees have never rooted and gravestones are visible all over, tilting at wild angles like dinosaurs' teeth in a field of grass. We break into a run. But behind us we hear another person crashing through the undergrowth.

Nobody must see us together. That's important, for the future.

I deviate twenty degrees off course, into the nearest trees, and glance back. Sure enough, Arnie bursts into sight. He stops, surrounded by all those gravestones, and looks around, shading his eyes against the sunlight.

'He's going to beat me up,' Johnny whimpers.

No, he isn't.

I shush Johnny and plant him behind a plot of willow. Satisfied that he can't be seen, I go hunting.

It doesn't take me long to find what I want. Grass snakes are plentiful here, in this open patch, especially on hot days. I pick up one of my little friends by neck and tail, coil him up, stick him in my pocket, where he moves fretfully. Today everyone is fretful, for some reason.

Arnie still hasn't seen me. He's starting to come my way, though. I select my tree, not far from Johnny's hiding place, and swing up. My feet scrape the bark, making too much noise; by the time I'm on my perch, Arnie has located its source and is coming closer.

'Johnny,' I call, not caring if Arnie hears. 'Walk out, let him see you, then move off into the trees, the way we were going.'

Arnie doesn't take a second to notice him. He breaks into a run.

Johnny flees.

Arnie gains fast. Twenty yards. Ten. Five . . .

'Hello,' I say, 'Arnie.'

He skids to a halt and glowers up at me. I drop the snake on his eye.

My, what a to-do! Now Arnie making a fuss I can understand, and even the grass snake, because reptiles have an excellent sense of who's good and who's bad, but what upsets me is Johnny's reaction . . .

I jump down from the tree. Arnie's writhing on the ground, screaming. I mean, you know . . . *really* screaming. Like he's going to choke and die, right there. No sign of the snake, of course; got better things to do, take a hike, man. I like disappearing evidence. I am tempted to piss on Arnie, cool him down, decide against it. I laugh.

'Don't *do* that!'

Johnny is staring at me with horror back of his eyes. 'Do what?' I ask, truly non-comprendo.

'L–laugh.'

'What's wrong with my laugh?'

But this is no time for a philosophical dissection of my personal idiosyncrasies, because men are crashing through the jungle, seconds from now they will be here, which means that we must not be. I pull Johnny away, but he keeps looking over his shoulder to where Arnie shimmers on the ground like a blob of hysterical jelly. 'That was h–*horrible*,' Johnny says. 'What if someone did that to you?'

No one would ever do such a thing to me. That phase is history. Nowadays, I am the doer. 'You should be grateful,' I sulk. 'Thought you hated the little runt.' We are already back in the thickets, but the ground is rising steadily and the main path cannot be far away. 'Nearly home,' I mutter, placing a fatherly arm around his shoulder in an attempt to give comfort.

'Take your hand off of me.' He wrenches away. 'You're so cold. I don't like it when you touch me. And I don't like it when you laugh. It makes you sound mad.'

I stop, downcast; he continues up the hill. Eventually I summon up the energy to go after him. The woods are thinning out, here the mud has dried, the going is easy. 'Come on,' I say, as I catch up. 'I'll take you home.'

'Don't *want* to go home.'

'So come live with me.'

We walk on in silence for a while. Then he laughs, his cloudy face dissolves into sunshine, the bad magic is broken. I laugh too. I mean, if he thinks it was a joke, why not?

'Okay,' I say. 'But I'm always here for you.'

'Thanks.' He keeps his eyes fixed on the ground, though. Then he stops. He looks at me. He says, 'What do you want from me?'

'Want?'

'Yes. You show up wherever I go. You act strange. You scare me.'

I look at him and see that joking won't get me out of this. I know what I have to say (the truth) but it sticks in my throat. I mean, how is this kid going to under-stand/believe me?

'I want to be your friend,' I say. (Doesn't come out too well. There's an impediment.) 'Sincerely. 'Cause I don't . . . don't have too many of them.'

'You're older than me. Get a friend your own age.'

'But I like you!'

'You don't know me.'

'I know you enough to like you.'

He stops staring at me and trudges on. When I catch up with him I see he's smiling, but far away, as if he's got a secret to cherish.

'Soon you could know this place as well as I do,' I implore. 'Every inch. Would you like that?'

He shakes his head, then nods. 'Yeah, maybe.'

'If you're good, that is.'

He looks up at me with hatred in his eyes; boo-boo, Tobias! *If you're good, Daddy will* . . . Shut up. Shut UP.

SHUT that up, or we will be in the (soft) shit.

'I'll take you to another world,' I tell him. And then, because the hatred in his eyes changes to wonder, and pleading, I am committed and have no choice but to continue. Only trouble is, I don't know where the hell I'm going; I say, 'The world of Alice Mornay.'

He stops again, and faces me again. Behind us the commotion is settling down, but I feel uneasy, because soon now somebody is going to have the bright idea of coming after us. I want to move on. Johnny stands his ground. 'She's dead,' he retorts.

'Yes. She was the first person ever to be buried here. I checked.'

Nudge 'n' Hold: I have hit jackpot. 'You mean, she's the guardian ghost?' he cries. Funny: when he was walking with Dr Diane in the cemetery that day, he used the same kooky phrase . . . 'Do you believe that?'

I nod, hoping it's the right thing to do.

'*Really?*'

'*Really.*' I pause, trying to see my way ahead. And then it comes. 'But you have to pass tests first, before I can take you in there.'

'What kind of tests?'

My improvisational skills scoot into overdrive. 'To prove you're not a coward. Like the other night, when I called you and you wouldn't come down.'

His eyes slide away from mine. 'You looked . . . scary,' he mutters. 'I could only see your head. Like, you know? – it had been cut off.'

What is he talking about? I cast my mind back to that fateful night. And then it hits me: my leather jacket! I was all in black. I am about to explain this to him when it occurs to me, better not. The role of headless corpse appeals not a little.

We are pushing through the last of the trees that separate us from the main path running alongside Court Ridge.

'You don't believe in ghosts,' I say. 'Do you?'

'No.'

'What if I show you the ghost of Alice Mornay? The guardian. What then?'

He glances up at me; there is something sly about his expression. 'Do it,' he says. 'Then we'll see.'

'You mean it?'

'Next time you call me down, I'll come.' Surprisingly, he takes my hand. My heart beats wildly. He shall be mine, this boy; the precious moment approaches apace.

162

My whole body is trembling. I light a cigarette, not wanting to but robbed of choice. The lighter-flame will not hold steady.

'Oh my God,' Johnny says, not in his usual voice. 'But I *do* so apologize, sir, for the state of our garden.'

Through a haze of soothing smoke I see his house looming up. Two women stand at the gate: Dr Diane and the wicked stepmother. I twig: Johnny was aping the stepmother. Quickly I stub out my cigarette, hoping Dr Diane hasn't noticed.

'You really will *have* to forgive us . . . ' He breaks away and runs towards the two women. His stepmother, the dreaded Nicole, reaches out a hand, but he ignores her, making instead for Diane. He embraces her and buries his head in her waist. As I make my slow way up the path, I intuit that Dr D's embarrassed by this overtly treasonable behaviour on the part of the kid, his stepmother standing there and all. But she can handle it.

Try handling this, Dr Diane.

'Quite a mess,' I say casually, nodding at the overgrown garden. 'Morning.'

'Good morning, Tobes,' Dr Diane says, cool as watered silk. 'What brings you here?'

'I often walk in the cemetery first thing. Clears my head.'

'He's my friend,' Johnny pipes to her belt.

''S'right,' I confirm. 'We met at clinic. He told me he lived on Court Ridge. Got lost today, didn't you, Johnny?'

'Yup.' He releases Diane and looks up at her face. 'Tobes rescued me.'

Nicole says, 'Where's your father and the rest of them? You mean, they let you get *separated*?'

'Uh-huh.'

'But I told . . . ' Nicole glances at me and shuts her mouth with a snap. 'Johnny, go inside and get cleaned up.'

'No.'

There will be tears momentarily, and tantrums, and I'm not in the mood; besides, I have my own agenda to consider. I say, with another nod at the garden, 'Want some help clearing that? I'm very reasonable, I think you'll find.'

Johnny squeaks with undisguised delight. 'Can he? Say he can. *Please.*'

'Well, I . . . ' Nicole can't think what to do. She looks at Diane. 'Do you know this person?'

Dr Diane hesitates. 'To a point.'

'So what do you think?'

Tough one to call, right? Here I am, a patient, a court-referred patient, doing time on the couch in lieu of time in the classical sense. I am mad, I am bad, and I sure as hell am dangerous to know.

'Could you fit it in with your other job?' Dr Diane asks me.

'Oh, sure. If I work three afternoons a week, how would that be? Seven dollars fifty an hour: believe me, that's cheap. Three hours a day, how's that?'

Nicole knows this is a steal; she's been reading the Work Wanted ads. But there are other factors to consider, one of which is trundling up the path behind me: I've been aware of his approach for some time.

'Johnny, where in heck have you been?' Mike shouts.

I swivel. We are all of us looking along the track at Mike and the other men: hot, red-faced, sweaty and bad-tempered, fathers to a man. Arnie sulks a long way

164

behind. I wonder if he caught a glimpse of me before the snake landed in his eye. If so, he shows no sign. Arnie has been quelled.

'I got lost,' Johnny says calmly. 'Arnie dragged me into the cemetery. I didn't want to go but he made me.'

Mike wipes his neck with a handkerchief. He is a good-looking man, handsome as an Ancient Roman general might have been handsome: grizzled, Ross Perot haircut, gaunt, overflowing with character. But this is beyond even him. Arnie belongs to one of his camp-followers, perhaps an important member of this motley team, and Mike is torn.

'I'll speak to you later,' he says to Johnny, 'about telling tales. Go in.'

There is an awkward pause. Johnny slopes inside, not looking at any of us.

'Mike,' Nicole says, 'this young man rescued Johnny from the cemetery.'

I nod agreeably. Mike frowns, then he, too, nods. 'Thanks.'

'He's a gardener,' Nicole goes on. 'He's offering to clear our place up. Seven-fifty an hour.'

Mike knows this is a steal, too. His eyebrows ride up his handsome face, his lips purse: 'What's the catch?' is written in letters a mile high. 'Got any experience?' he asks.

'Yessir. When I lived down in LA I took care of a lot of places. I know how to use a power trimmer, hedge-cutter, mower . . .'

'Okay, okay.'

Out of the corner of my eye I see Dr Diane open her mouth, ready to speak. Every inch of skin constricts. I am doomed, I am done for.

'Perhaps you . . . ' she begins, and then she falters. Mike looks at her. Doesn't like her, that's for sure. 'Oh?' he says. 'Yes?'

'This young man is my patient, Mr Anderson, and I – '

'Then I'm sure that makes his credentials admirable.' Mike stares her down; I could grow to love this guy. He turns back to me, slowly, like he's still making his point. 'When could you start?' he asks.

'This afternoon.'

He considers it further. Time ceases its relentless forward roll. I hold my breath without realizing it and bombard Dr Diane telepathically. *Dr Diane, DO NOT SPEAK!*

''Kay,' Mike says. 'Give it a trial. Come by this afternoon at three, suit you?'

'Surely. Thank you, sir.'

'I must go,' Dr Diane murmurs to Nicole. 'Give my best to Johnny, say I'm looking forward to next Tuesday.'

Jealousy spikes my heart. Tuesday is his day, then. With her.

'Have a good weekend,' I say.

'I will. I'm going to the beach.'

'That's nice.' I lift my hand and wave; she nods pleasantly. I start to lope off down the path, thoughtlessly lighting a cigarette. But before I've gone very far I hear Dr Diane call my name, and realize with a start that she has been following me; indeed, when I turn she's almost on my back.

'I didn't know you smoked,' she says.

'Well, I'm kind of embarrassed by it.' My voice is all croaky, and I stutter. 'Weakness, you know?'

'All the time you've been coming to me, you never once smoked.'

What is this thing about smoking? Did somebody blow smoke up her fanny when she was a baby, or what?

'Is Marlboro your favourite brand?' she asks, and I see she's shifted her stare to the pack in my hand. I'm pissed off by now; what's it to her? So I just nod, and stub out the cigarette.

'Don't take liberties here,' she says quietly. 'This is a quiet, respectable family home. Behave.'

'I will,' I reply, equally quietly. 'And thank you for backing me.'

'I didn't back you.'

She continues to examine me through those shrewd eyes, as if I am a rare specimen of uncertain disposition, possibly dangerous.

'You see,' I go on (I know I should shut up, but I can't help myself), 'this is a big opportunity for me. Open-air work. Nice people, nice family.'

Diane's gaze does not waver.

'My chance of a lifetime.'

After what seems an endless age, she says, with a sigh, 'Let me tell you what I believe, okay?'

I grind my nails into my palms and say, 'Sure.'

'You are so full of shit.'

Her anger rocks me on my heels, but I know enough to wait.

'You fill me with despair. Why? Because you are engaging, even charming on occasion. You are well-read, literate; more so than some of my friends. And you are throwing yourself away.'

It should not hurt, but it does hurt.

'You have potential, Tobes. So *use it*!'

She turns away without saying goodbye. I watch her go. Only when she is almost out of sight do I light another cigarette. My fingers tremble again, the flame will not hold steady. With the first deep draught of smoke comes release, and its companion: the laughter that I've been holding pent up inside me ever since Mike gave me a job right next to his boy.

My boy, too.

*   *   *

Tobes's laughter sounded to Diane the way a film does when it splits in mid-showing: the broken end flickers and clicks to a rhythm that's not quite regular. It troubled her.

What was he laughing at?

Diane had been hoping for a talk with the father, but it was obvious he'd be tied up for the rest of the morning and anyway, she wanted to interview Mike calm and he was too upset by Johnny getting lost in the cemetery to give her useful input now. So instead of driving straight down to collect Ed from headquarters she was left with a couple of hours to kill, and went home, trying to make sense of a situation that didn't appeal.

Should she have blocked Tobes's bid to work for the Andersons? Her clinician's experience told her he was harmless: zonked by whatever bad experiences he'd had as a child (and she must chase those high school records); over-fond of his place in the cemetery, the one he was always harping on about in therapy; but sincere at base, and capable of reform. He was good for Johnny, she could see that, and Johnny seemed good for Tobes, too. Anyway, it was obvious that Mike would have done the opposite of whatever she'd suggested, so no point in getting spaced out about it.

Tobes had no history of violence or sexual perversion, as far as police records went, no homosexual tendencies manifest anywhere. He had talked to her about his experiences with girls: what he said rang true and was perfectly normal for somebody of his age.

Tobes could be useful to Diane in a variety of ways. Perhaps he could do something with *her* garden, too?

So, now – how to dispose of these unwanted two hours? She garaged the car and went inside her house. The boxes were still there in the hallway, accusing and sullen.

These boxes were yesterday's acquisition. She'd at last felt ready for music. Letty, an admissions clerk at St Joseph's, had a son, Nick, in the hi-fi business; she seemed dubious whether he and Diane would get on, but promised her a discount and said, Try anyway. So Diane went. Nick turned out to be one of those long men with a pony-tail who stand up to greet you and somehow seem to go on standing up and standing up for ever. The shop was down by the harbour, back of A and near the corner with Seventh: a quiet location. Diane had been expecting to have her ears beaten out with hip-hop or heavy metal; all she got was this young man uncoiling himself in an empty emporium and some beautiful music, played very softly in the background.

'What *is* that?' she asked him.

'Dame Kiri. Puccini: "*O mio babbino caro*".' His expression was stony, conveying, You should know that. Then his face cracked into a smile and he asked, 'Did you catch the movie *A Room With A View*?' And it clicked: of course, that wonderful song.

She saw why his mother thought *they* might not click. Within seconds Nick was dazzling her with woof factors and speaker mega-hertzes and flutters and wattages. It all passed over her head. What she wanted was boxes: things she could unpack and strip out of their plastic covers and join up with the help of a screwdriver and a manual that hadn't been composed in Japanese. Nick got the message. He sold her a lot of boxes, surprisingly cheap. When he offered to come up and tie everything together, she said no. He seemed a nice guy, but if her house was ready for music, it still wasn't ready for guys. Besides, Diane was capable of doing these things for herself.

Although not this Saturday, not in less than two hours. In the kitchen, humming Elton John's 'Your Song', she packed munchies for herself and Ed. She still needed to buy cutlery, among so many other things. All she had in one drawer was a knife and fork and the single chopstick Ed had given her that night when he'd rescued the *shen pai* a second time. She tried a drum-riff with it, failing miserably, and tossed it aside.

What was she going to do about Ed?

'Mother,' she said aloud, 'what am I going to do about him?'

'Who is this Ed anyway?'

The mist had rolled back to reveal the islands, far away on a crystal horizon, beneath a pink-white strip of cloud. The oil-rig stood out black and forbidding, like some prehistoric bird of prey.

'He's a cop. A friend. I came close to falling in love with him, once.'

'And you never told me?'

'No. I was going to. Then I found out he was married, you see.'

The prehistoric bird of prey lifted off its perch. It began to fly towards the coast.

170

'Married . . .' *Ma-ma*'s voice sounded in Diane's inner ear. Like being inside a recording-studio – the heavy door swings shut with a little whoosh of expelled air, and afterwards whatever you say sounds dead, without vibrancy – that was how her mother sounded. *Ma-ma* stood very close to Diane's body, with her lips (Diane could not feel them) pressed against her ear, and then she spoke again. 'What were you doing, wasting your time with a married man? Was that any way to carry on?'

'Oh, Mother . . .'

'Please don't lecture me about this being the twentieth century.'

The prehistoric bird approached. Its shadow moved across the face of the water, coming her way. Diane stared, unable to blink, unable to run.

'It's not just that,' she said.

'Then what is it?'

'Work.'

The kitchen grew darker. All the sun had gone now. The bird opened its wings, a vast cloak of night that snuffed out Diane's vision. Her body quaked with cold. She felt herself stagger, and reached out to the stove for support.

'But mostly Ed,' *Ma-ma* said.

'Mostly Ed.'

'That's bad. Bad.'

'He's divorced now.'

'He says.'

'He *is*!'

'Do you love him?'

Diane burst into tears. She held her hands before her face to block out the hideous bird, the beating of its wings loud in her ears now. 'Don't kn . . . kn . . . know,' she wailed.

She broke down.

Consciousness returned much later, or maybe seconds afterwards: she didn't know anything, except that the bird had gone back to its perch in the bay, the beating of its monstrous wings no more than the rhythm of her over-stretched heart; the sun was out, her kitchen filled with whiteness and light.

She got up off the floor, where she must have fallen, and did a forlorn damage check. No bruises, no cuts; she'd been lucky.

It couldn't go on like this.

Today wasn't the first time.

Well, well, well. Let's achieve some perspective, Doctor.

Diane had read pretty much everything worth reading about grief and the mourning process. She still could not mourn her mother properly, because there'd been unfinished business between them the day *Ma-ma* died. So these hallucinations occurred. They were born of wishful thinking, an unwillingness to face the harsher aspects of reality; they could lead to rejection, denial, and, ultimately, severe neurosis or even schizophrenia.

This morning Diane handled it as she had done before: with humour. 'Mother,' she said, 'I'm sorry, but I cannot go on talking to a dead person. Do you hear, Mother?'

'I hear.'

But that time Diane had conjured up *Ma-ma*'s voice deliberately.

She trotted up the steps to police headquarters, a horrible, high old building on the sunless side of Fourth Avenue, and by the muster desk she ran into Leo Sanders.

Leo, who was an airhead, had already crossed swords with Diane in one of her preliminary psychology

172

classes. His game-plan was to be genial towards her while he got the guys on his side: Leo prided himself on a good manner with women. He did not lack chivalry, but his was a twisted chivalry. Women must be stepped on and then helped up, because that was how things had always been, for ever and ever, amen.

'Hi, Diane,' he greeted her. 'Now see if I remember lesson one . . . Nothing wrong with those kids a father couldn't beat outa them. Am I right or am I right?'

'You should play the halls, Leo.'

Diane found him hard to dislike. He was overweight and jowly, and a man in his fifties shouldn't smoke so many stoogies each day, but there was a twinkle in his eye that appealed to her. Something about the way he moved – very gracefully, considering his body weight – suggested he'd be good company in a bare knuckle fight. Diane wished he would buy a dandruff shampoo and stick with it, or that his wife would at least make him take a clothes-brush to his jacket in the mornings; she wished he would just sometimes knot his tie right; but Leo Sanders (an Americanization of Saarnski) and she were not going to fall out overmuch, and if ever he did go to play the halls she just might tag along.

'Diane,' he said, spreading his arms wide, 'gimme a hug. You're driving me crazy.'

'Not so far to drive, that's one good thing. Hey, Ed . . .'

Ed came down the stairs two at a time and Diane felt her face relax into a smile. It made her happy when he hustled her outside and away before Leo could think up another one-liner, and she told him so.

'He's a great detective with a long record and pension in sight. He's not about to change his world for you, sweetheart.'

'Nor do I want him to. But how a man like that can get on my unit, without my say-so . . . ?'

'It's political, Diane. It's that, or back to the good old days.'

Ed was referring obliquely to the incident of 1989, when Paradise Bay had lost its police chief to Haiti. There'd been a scandal involving the then chief and money not his own; no extradition treaty subsists between the USA and Haiti; Peter Symes was brought in to clear away the mess, with his fancy MBA, fast-track record from the LA police department, youth and good looks. Paradise Bay snapped him up, he did what was necessary and now Paradise Bay was stuck with him. Morale in his force remained low, however, and Peter, a quick results man, had a fondness for gimmicks. Diane, along with many of those who listened to West Coast Crimewaves, feared she might be merely his latest gimmick. Hence Ed Hersey as her liaison officer; hence Leo Sanders on the team: all thanks to Peter Symes, who reasoned that if he could only win around the Leos of this world he'd have got morale licked.

It would take more than Diane and her fancy new unit to get it licked for Peter. He had two teen disappearances and a murder on his hands, and not all the spin-doctored sound-bites in the world were about to alter that.

As they pulled away, Ed wordlessly handed Diane the name-card she'd given him over dinner at Bel Cove.

'Keep it,' she said. 'And you didn't need to prove anything. Your word's good enough.'

Ed began flicking through the airwaves on Diane's car-radio, reminding her how much that had used to irritate her. Ed was a fidget. He flashed through half a dozen stations in so many seconds and at last found something to his taste: light classic. Then he made a long arm around the back of Diane's seat and came up with a plastic wallet.

'This is for you.'

'Thanks. What is it?'

'Family album. No, seriously: it's photographs of Lawson and Delmar, the missing kids, plus statements: what we've managed to find out so far. Not much.'

Diane glanced sideways at the wallet. On top lay a couple of big glossies, overlapping, but with enough visible to reveal two very different types: a thoughtful-looking, handsome teenager, everybody's number one choice for the school prom, and a sulky fat slob with zits and an attitude problem that came shining through.

'Hal and Randy?'

'Right. Randy's the dweeb.'

'Did you interview the parents yourself?'

'Hal's mother is nice. Homely, anxious I didn't have enough creamer in my coffee: you can imagine. Father het up because the police aren't *doing* anything, and what do we pay taxes for.'

'Familiar mix.'

'Right. To them, their boy was just a Mister Average. Only fault he had was addiction to Metallica and Mötley Crüe.'

'Ouch. What did you smell in the house, apart from yesterday's broccoli?'

'Hard to say. There were photographs dotted around and I homed in on what turned out to be a sister. Grown, married. When I talked about interviewing her, there was a moment of . . . I don't know.'

'What are you saying?'

But Ed's face tightened, he needed help. 'The big "I" word?' Diane prompted. 'Incest?'

'I really don't know,' he said after a pause. 'I went up there with a man called Green I hadn't worked with before, water dripping off his ears: in the car he'd kind of implied that the best thing most kids can do is run away, and so what? Why weren't we out there dealing with rapists and robbers?'

'It's precisely that attitude I'm trying to change. *We* are trying to change. What about Randy?'

'I didn't see his family. Thanks for the "we", by the way. There's a statement, but it's short: come to think of it, Green did that one, so no wonder it's short. No enemies, no depressions, no friends who'd be likely to know where he'd gone. Tell you a funny thing: Hal had no friends, either.'

'Good-looking boy like that, and no friends?'

'Strange, isn't it? And it wasn't just parental bullshit: if those two had friends, we can't find 'em. There was a guy from school Randy stayed over with a couple of times, and he told us he'd seen Randy after he'd had a bust-up at home, but that was all.'

'Bust-up?'

'Yeah. Randy's parents claimed it was just the usual teenage thing. Hal was just the same; there'd been a row, it was over, forgotten.'

'How much is being turned over to this in the way of resources?'

'More than was allocated a fortnight ago, let's say. Peter's feeling the heat since Douggan's murder.'

'Good. Do you have a suspect?'

'On Douggan? Several. I'll tell you the problem with suspects, Diane. Paradise Bay has a population of some fifty thousand, right? Approximately half of them are male, and males are much more likely to have committed this sort of crime than females. Take out the women and kids, weed out the old men, and how many have you still got left? Add in the tourists, the business-travellers passing through . . . everyone's a suspect and they run to tens of thousands.'

'So what are you going to do?'

'Profiling, of course. Plus we have a dozen or so leads. You and I are following one of them right now. Against my better judgement, today we're going in search of a guy name of Besto.'

'Is that a first name?'

'Who knows? How much did I tell you about Harley and his diner?'

'Enough to put me off phoning for a reservation.'

'Right. Well, Harley depends on casual labour: wetbacks, drop-outs.'

'And Besto is a pseudonym for one of them?'

'Yes. No social security record, no federal withholding tax. Ray Douggan was last seen at Harley's the night he died. That same night, Besto took off.'

'You think there's a connection?'

'Could be. Randy Delmar went to Harley's a couple of times, too, so let's just say we'd like to talk to Mr Besto, soon. Now the officers who interviewed Harley Rivera didn't get anywhere, so what we want today is a quiet talk with *monsieur le* proprietor, and a look over his clientele, see if we can't start putting together a list of regulars.'

'Without upsetting Harley so that he goes to headquarters with a complaint.'

'You said it! If Peter Symes finds out about this he'll go apeshit.'

Ed reached out for the channel selector-button, but Diane was ahead of him. Her smack hurt her almost as much as Ed.

'Ow! What did you do that for?'

'I like this music. Relax. It's the weekend, remember?'

'Oh, yeah. I remember those from when I was a kid.'

Diane turned off the road south of Orcutt and they started to twist and turn upwards, through Forestry Department land. Here the hills were a rich, mint green. The road-surface was rough with potholes; in places they caught sight of a burst tyre, a discarded hubcap. The sky had turned overcast, giving the light a strange, sickly quality. Fine dust blew in the window and Diane closed it. Two or three spots of rain flopped onto the windshield, but there was no downpour and soon the droplets dried, leaving smudges on the glass. Diane drove on, the road growing ever steeper, until the Camry rounded a corner and there, ahead of them, lay their goal.

They were a couple of miles south of Point Sal, overlooking an outlandish stretch of coast. Where Diane lived was hilly, with a gentle cliff: soft countryside. But within a few miles you could find windswept desolations of blown sand and scrub, moorland sloping down to a sullen sea where terns nested and salt lakes formed in summer. Vandenberg Base, the missile launch centre, was one such place. Here was another.

Diane pulled off the road and for a while she and Ed sat staring at the view. Below them, about a mile away, was the beach. Today the sand had a grey tinge, reflected off a sullen sky. Nothing moved, except the odd clump of larkspur wavering in the wind. Wild sage coated the nearby hills like a layer of cigarette-smoke.

The beach was invested with a derelict wooden pier, on the landward side of which stood a shack: single-storey, colourless against the horizon, dilapidated.

'Harley's?'

Ed nodded. Five or six more rain-drops fell, followed by a tattoo. Big splodges of water filled in the wind-shield until there was no more bare glass. The car inter-mittently shivered and shook as a particularly strong gust came batting off the ocean. Far out to sea, a long, steely gleam of light burnished the water, the only sign that this was daytime.

'You want to go down?' Ed asked.

'I guess.'

The road twisted some more before depositing the red Camry on a pebble parking-lot outside the diner. Diane applied the parking-brake. 'Well,' she said with artificial brightness, 'here we are.'

Harley's was part brick-built, part corrugated iron, part wooden: it looked as though it had been con-structed haphazardly over the years. Bottle-crates stood piled by the back door. Around the front were rusting metal tables and chairs. One table lay on its side: some-body'd left an umbrella in its centre-hole, the wind had blown both of them over. Maybe the season hadn't started yet. Maybe Harley's was always like this. Certainly the place offered no welcome to the tired trav-eller. Once-bright-red paint hung from the walls in maroon strips. The windows were fastened tight shut, its door stayed closed, the Coke sign quietly rusted away.

'Ed,' Diane said, 'it's now or never. Either you take me in there right this minute, or . . .'

They approached the entrance hand in hand, like Hansel and Gretel penetrating the blackest part of the forest. The door, iron-heavy, lacked a window but boasted a powerful spring: they entered, it crashed to behind them and now there was only gloom and a howl of raucous sound.

Diane knew they were in a bar-diner and that it contained people, yet she could see nothing. Panic flapped around her head like a nervy bat. Then, as her ears accustomed themselves to the heavy metal soundtrack, objects started to come at her out of the darkness, like an old black-and-white TV warming up.

They were in a bare-board room about fifty feet by forty, its few windows obscured by blown sand and sea-spray. A juke-box stood in one corner, source of the discordant music. Tables and chairs were scattered around, as in any bar, with a small open space in the middle for dancing. The place smelled of old dust and ocean wet-rot, of last month's cigarettes and yesterday's beer.

Diane followed Ed over to the bar, aware of many dark human shapes slumped in one corner around a table littered with bottles. They watched her appraisingly, but did not speak. For the first time she registered photographs . . .

Ed was saying to the bar-tender, 'Mr Rivera? I wonder if I might ask you a few questions?' His hand moved to his hip-pocket and Diane knew he was about to magic that old blue-and-gold police badge into sight. But she did not catch Harley's reply, because by now all her attention was focused on the photographs.

There were hundreds, thousands of them. Every square inch of wall was covered with photos: monochrome, colour, sepia, faded, new, large, small. Many overlapped. Some were framed. Hugging the circle of light from a wall-lamp she approached the nearest montage, curious. A big colour photograph caught her

eye. Wooden beams, rope, a doll, what was this . . . ?
Then things sharpened around the edges, she caught
her breath . . .

'Cambodia. Tuol Sleng.'

Startled, she turned towards the table from where
the voice had come. The pool of rancid yellow light
revealed a pork-bellied Hell's Angel and he was smiling. His voice sounded growly, not hostile.

'Khmer Rouge torture camp,' he said, apparently
keen to educate her. 'Meticulous people ran that joint.
Photographed everything.'

He laughed softly; Diane saw his beard shiver; she,
too, shivered. For the photograph that had been gripping her attention when he spoke was of a teenage girl
hanging from a gallows. Diane hugged the wall, fascinated and sick to her stomach. Without exception, she
now saw, the photographs portrayed obscenities. Death
in all its manifold forms was here, and there were so
many children: burned, mutilated, shot, knifed, decap-
itated, eviscerated.

'Genocide,' her Angelic friend interposed, 'should be
recorded.'

'Yes,' she whispered.

'We got copies here. Not all, but most. You want all,
you go to Tuol Sleng.' He paused to light a cigarette.
'Used to be a school.'

'You've been there?' Diane could not bring herself to
look at him.

'Couple of times.'

He shifted in his chair. *If he gets up, I'll scream*. He
remained seated.

Diane dragged her gaze away from the wall of all-
enveloping death and eased over to the bar. Ed asked,
'Want something to drink, Diane?'

'Beer.'

Harley stared at her before breaking open a Bud and pushing it along the bar. Ed said, 'Make that two,' and got out his wallet.

'Thought you were a cop,' Harley said sourly.

'Off duty. This is just an informal chat, Mr Rivera. Be frank with you: we're not making much headway with Ray's murder.'

Diane took her first proper look at Harley. He wore black: black jeans, black short-sleeve shirt, black band around his forehead. He was a tall, thickset man with muscular arms and a beard: one of those shaven jobs that just edge the chin and jaw, with a pencil-line moustache. His skimpy hair had been clawed straight back from a low forehead. Diane put him at about thirty-five years old, one-ninety pounds, six feet nothing. His face looked gaunt and pale, with tight, narrow lips. His eyebrows were plucked into elegant tildes: they, and the moustache, made her think of him as an artist. Such a face might float above a guitar on a candlelit terrace in Seville. And yet somehow he belonged here.

'You a cop?' he said to Diane.

'No. Just a friend of Ed's.'

Harley's eyes slid sideways. 'I told them all I know already,' he said. 'You can't make me say anything I don't know.'

His voice sounded soft yet strong, with a slight overlay of Mexican accent, very slight.

'Sure,' Ed said, 'I appreciate that, Mr Rivera. I'm not interested in where your employees come from. So some of them are Mexican, so you didn't always pay your taxes on time. I'm not from the Internal Revenue. I'm a detective and we have on our hands a particularly repulsive, gruesome murder of a young man, who was mutilated.'

Diane thought of the photographs on the wall. Torture, death . . . *genocide should be recorded.*

'There was this guy called Besto.' Harley started to speak, but Ed cut across him: 'He never had any other name, I *accept* that. I do. I just want to talk with him, that's all.'

'He used to work here. Lots of people used to work here.'

'And you don't know where he went after he left?'

'No.'

Diane sensed that her presence was not helping and she moved away, penetrating further into the diner as if in search of more photographs. Someone shouted out an order for burgers. Harley came down the bar in the direction Diane had taken. He opened a door, letting her catch a glimpse of the kitchen and a man hunched over a griddle. At first Diane thought he was an oriental, like herself, but then she saw he was suffering from Down's syndrome. Harley spoke to the man, who nodded, reaching up to the shelf above his head. His lower forearm was one big frenzied lump of scar tissue. He had been savagely burned.

Diane's head hurt. The music was grinding her into rough-edged little pieces. Her eyes picked out more photos. To her surprise, however, these were genuine snaps. Happy young people with their arms around one another made faces at the camera, blew kisses, did silly things with surfboards.

Diane drifted along the wall. Suddenly she encountered a gap: a door ajar. She glanced over her shoulder; Ed and Harley were deep in conversation. She pushed on the door to reveal a spooky office: papers scattered across a desk, bills spiked on nails banged into one wall, a phone. And a cassette-player, with a light glowing on its face. Diane looked back again. No one had noticed her. She darted inside the office and bent down to listen to the machine.

Its volume control had been set so low that she could scarcely hear anything, just enough to realize that this was Beethoven. Even Diane, no classical music buff, could recognize the famous Fifth Symphony.

She edged back into the bar, relieved to find that nobody seemed to have remarked her absence; but then, to her consternation, Harley flung open a flap in the counter and stormed over to the wall, close to where she was standing. Desperately she tried to think of an excuse for having trespassed inside his office, but – 'There,' he said, hitting a photograph with his thumb. 'You want a physical description, it's there, okay?'

Ed joined Harley. 'Who are the others?' he asked.

'Employees. Customers. We were having a party, is that now a crime?'

Diane crept up behind them and peered at the photograph. There was just enough light to see six grinning faces: Harley stood in front of his diner along with the Down's syndrome short-order chef, three girls and one other. They were happy, Diane could see.

Diane was not happy.

'That's Besto, Mr Policeman,' Harley said. He jabbed a finger at the face on the extreme right of the picture and he said, 'There's your fucking suspect.'

'When did he start working for you?' Diane asked.

'February this year.' Harley shot an exasperated glance her way. 'What the hell does that matter?'

184

It mattered because the young man known to Harley as Besto had never told Diane he'd worked in a diner; because he'd started working here one month after the date of Judge Cyril DeMesne's referral; because his real name was Tobes Gascoign, he was one short step away from being a murder suspect, and Diane had just stood by and let him get a job at the Anderson place, and she really didn't know him at all.

PART TWO

The sun came out, and with it Diane's desire for razzmatazz. She'd had enough of louring skies, menacing Hell's Angels, Tuol Sleng, and yearned instead for happy kids, the smell of barbecue, radios played loudly without thought for others.

'Let's hit Jalama,' she said.

Ed looked at her as if she'd gone crazy, but it was Diane's day. She let him drive. On the way south her mind toyed with the American Medical Association's Principles of Medical Ethics. The relevant part ran thus: 'A physician shall respect the rights of patients, of colleagues, and of other health professionals, and shall safeguard patient confidences within the constraints of the Law.' Or something like that – with the Law sitting beside her, full of constraint, Diane found it hard to remember exactly.

'You knew the guy in the photograph,' the Law said. 'Didn't you?'

'Mm-hm.'

'You know him, and you're going to tell me where to find him. Right?'

'Wrong. He's a patient, and as such entitled to my silence concerning his affairs.'

'And is that it?'

'That's it.'

They had reached her country now: rolling sward interspersed with rocky outcrops and clumps of hardwood. The road wound between green hills dotted with cattle, and a clean blue sky above. When on her European grand tour Diane had visited Wales, which reminded her of here, but with more rain in a day than fell on Southern California in a year. Now, everywhere she looked she saw her beloved, emerald landscape, and no way out.

'How come you have this guy as a client?' Ed asked.

'He was a court-referral.'

'Did he seem violent to you?'

'No. He's just a harmless fantasist who can benefit from counselling.'

'So look how well your new unit is working already: we started off trying to trace Besto, now he's turned into someone else, and where does he live, by the way?'

'It's not meant to work like that, me giving away clients' secrets.'

'Well, hey, maybe it's not such a bad idea. This PD is on the skids, we need a break.'

'With people like Leo on the force, I can see why. Drive, Ed.'

He banged the wheel in frustration. 'Why do you insist on making problems?'

'Leave it with me, and I'll find out all you need to know from . . . from my client.'

'Oh, Diane, come on! I've told you before, you're not a cop, you're a doctor.'

'And I've told *you* before, I'm a better cop than you. I'll prove it.'

'How?'

'Psychology has immense value in solving crime, my unit will work, wait and see the results I get.'

'You're pissing in the wind.'

'So don't stand leeward – and don't hit those cyclists!'

Ed swerved.

'Diane,' he said. 'You've put me in an impossible position. How am I going to face them down at head-quarters?'

'Refer them to me, I'll explain about ethics and how, unlike policemen, I have some.'

Before he could reply, Diane reached over to the back seat and hauled out the file of photographs. The faces of the two missing boys gazed up at her, serenely uninformative. 'Have you read anything about child abuse?' she asked Ed.

'Some.'

'Did you know that people who were themselves molested tend to be those who abuse children later in life?'

'Yes.' He frowned. 'Are you trying to tell me something about Besto?'

'No, forget him.'

'Then why mention molesters?'

'They suffer extraordinary depth of damage when young. Mostly.'

'So?'

'So sometimes they become dangerous. Lethal.'

He grunted impatiently. 'I wish you'd say what you mean.'

Diane tried to think how she might convey her innermost fears to Ed, but the gulf between them extended way beyond her Camry's gear-shift.

Jalama was not as crowded as they'd expected. Because the weather had started out wet people had left it late to come from the cities; the car-park was still less than half full. The ocean turned sprightly and, in contrast to the grey hostility of an hour ago, shiny sapphire. Ed at last went to change into something more appropriate than his work-suit; Diane stood in line for a couple of burgers from the shop. While they were broiling she went through her Jalama rituals, patting the stuffed rattlesnake in its glass case and, for the hundredth time, letting herself become absorbed in the pictorial history of America's worst maritime disaster, which had occurred just down the coast at Point Conception. Jalama Beach never changed, Jalama Beach was fun.

They jogged through the surf, and were happy. Ed moved to push her in the sea, then rescued her at the last moment. Diane clung to him, her body no longer going into spasm at his touch. The bad memories had faded, to be replaced by new hope.

A mile up the beach, where the coast begins its curve out to the west, they flopped onto the sand and took a breather. Diane folded her arms around her legs and stared out to sea. Salt coated her lips, sand grains danced over her feet, dry-white with exposure to sun and wind. She thought of all the unhappy, starving people in the world who could not enjoy this precious day with a likeable fellow by their side. The Down's syndrome chef would perhaps be cooking up a storm in Harley's now, ignorant even of the sun's emergence.

She must have looked solemn, for Ed patted her knees and said, 'Penny for them?'

'Oh . . . I was just thinking about that poor man I saw in Harley's kitchen.'

'The Mongol?' (Diane hadn't heard that expression in a while.) 'He's not unhappy.'

'How do you know?'

'Because my youngest brother's one.'

She sat up straight and looked at him. Ed, too, was staring out to sea, oblivious of her astonishment. They'd dated for six months before that fateful tennis-game; she knew that Ed's father was an army colonel, retired, that his siblings were over-achievers to a man, that his upbringing had been strict, conventional, loving – an ideal combination, in her view. No mention of a Down's syndrome brother.

'You never told me,' she said.

'Kenny?' He turned to look at her, eyebrows raised. 'No, I guess I didn't.'

'Is he institutionalized?'

'Lord, no. He lives at home, with the folks. They love him to death.' He picked at a sprig of spike grass between his feet. 'So do I.'

His voice was unexpectedly fierce, as if he'd suddenly been called upon to take the oath of allegiance. Suddenly Diane wanted to share his memories. All of them. She reached out her hand and gave his forearm a squeeze. His skin was dried out, showing tiny hair-wrinkles. He should take an oil-bath now and then. She could recommend a good one.

'You know something?' Ed asked. 'At Christmas, he makes presents for everyone. Home-made presents. And they're the best kind.'

Without looking at Diane, he put an arm around her shoulders. She snuggled against him. The tenderness in his voice was gently flushing away the scummy memories that clogged her system: of quarrels they'd had in the past, and, worse, of cool, distant, ultra-polite exchanges after yet another failure in bed . . .

When he kissed her it was frightening at first; then she felt something come untied in her stomach, all the way up to her throat.

'Don't rush me,' she murmured, pulling away.

'I won't. Not as long as you can give me a little hope.'

It was a curiously old-fashioned sentiment. More and more chains were coming undone within Diane; time to go. But she was reluctant to stand up and leave this tranquil spot, blown clean by a wind that had travelled thousands of miles to find her.

In the end they walked slowly back to the car, arms around each other's waists. Her heart was brimming with things to say to Ed, so it came as all the more of a shock when he had to go and declare, 'This is the last time we mix personal with professional, right?'

He was sitting on the Camry's front seat, dusting sand from his toes. She stared at him, trying to relate these words to what had been going through *her* mind this past half-hour: Hi there, stranger!

'We've both got careers to lose,' he went on. 'With Symes hovering . . .'

Then she realized that, like women since the dawn of history, it was her destiny to be stronger than the male and not let him know. With that revelation her ideas tempered into resolve. She would be a better cop than Ed, but he must never see that. She would demonstrate who had killed Ray Douggan and do it in a way that would enable her to keep this man, his pride intact. She felt immense dignity and strength within herself. There was a future; it was noble; she'd turned a corner. But then God chose to remind her that she was still vulnerable.

They were driving home, the sun on their left was sinking into this soft pink and mauve array of clouds above a Pacific of silver and gold. Ed turned on the radio and flicked through the airwaves. Suddenly she reached out to check his hand. Tears began to roll down her cheeks. She could not stop crying, although she cried in silence.

Ketty Lester was singing 'Going Home'. Haunting, beautiful, ineffably sad, the music filled the car and her heart, too. Came the phrase, 'Mother's there, 'specting me; Father's waiting, too', and the sun set; why Diane's heart didn't break she'd never know.

*   *   *

I really need to keep a record now. Because later, when I'm old, I'm going to think back over this and say, Nah! You weren't really that clever, Gascoign, come on, you're kidding yourself. So I'm going to write a little each day from now on; that way there's no danger I'll forget.

Not that I forget much.

Not that I have to include everything. Only what interests me.

Took a phone call at work, from Harley. (Decided to stick with the day job, after all. If I'm to stay alive without stealing I need a legal source of income. Can't afford to risk rejection by Dr Diane, you see – another essential part of my plan – and there'll be presents to buy for Johnny.) Harley wanted to talk, wouldn't say why, and in any case, the owner of Café Pesquod (my boss) doesn't like staff taking calls during hours, y'know what I mean? So after Harley promised to stop by my place and pick me up I cut it short and said to myself, Instead of staying in with Maxine tonight, why not take her to Harley's?

Ah, sorry, need to catch you up. Maxine and I have been seeing each other. She likes me on account of I

195

don't try to rape her two minutes after I walk in the door; she says I'm a gentleman. Whereas actually, consensual sexual relations hold no fascination for me. Either I have passed through that phase or I am waiting for it to occur. Probably the latter. I had an unhappy childhood. My father beat me a lot. He could be cruel.

Anyway. Maxine and I spend time together. Mostly in her shop, which I adore. Dressing up is such fun, and besides, she lives at home with her parents and I'm hardly into that kind of structured environment. So this evening Harley comes by the shop in his pick-up and as soon as they clap eyes on each other I know it's trouble.

We squeeze into the front seat. Harley doesn't drive off at once. He looks across me (I'm in the middle) at Maxine and she looks at him; they're smiling like a couple of idiots. I have not seen Harley operate in this mode before. I effect introductions, thinking maybe this will break up the heavy atmosphere. It doesn't.

Harley drives off. Knowing how hard this man finds it to chew a straight line and walk in gum, I rest easy until we're headed west, out of Orcutt, and then I say, 'Why did you call me at work?'

'The cops have been around, asking about you.'

Now this is a jolt. I sit up. 'What are they on to me for? If it's about CDs . . . '

'More like murder.'

Thusways does the sky fall in.

Maxine has been staring out the window. Now she jerks her head around to stare at me. She moves her leg so it's not touching mine, or is that my imagination? Surely she can't think . . . So when did this girl ever think, don't panic, just get at the facts, m'am.

'Whose murder?'

'That guy Ray Douggan. A man and a woman came by couple of Saturdays ago, asking questions about you. When did you work for me, why did you leave, that kind of stuff.'

'They knew my name?'

'No, and I didn't tell them anything.'

That, at least, is a relief. But it wears off fast. 'Why do they think I'd got anything to do with Douggan?' I ask.

'You know those two kids who went missing? Seems you left around the time one of them was last seen. And he was last seen at the diner, wouldn't you know it?'

'You didn't tell them where I live?'

'Right.'

This is frightening shit. When we get to the diner I help Harley clean up and get ready to open, but all the time I'm thinking, Where did I go wrong? What's Douggan to me? Why do they want to connect me to a murder?

Eventually my brain gets tired, I guess. I come back to reality. The place is humming, even though it's midweek. There are some faces I know. Maxine is up at the bar, sipping Coke through a straw. Harley goes to serve somebody, then comes right back to talk with her. Because of the music, the talking and such like, they have to bend their heads close together. Maxine is wearing a smile I've not noticed before: kind of closed, sleepy. Whatever Harley says seems jake with her.

And I think, Oh-oh . . . If I was the suspicious type I'd suspect them of fixing up a rendezvous, *sans moi*. Which is amusing, because I really don't care (too much) if Harley and Maxine hump all year, just as long as they keep out of my light with Johnny, and for that

I need Maxine's assistance. More precisely, I have need of her stock.

Anyway, we dance and we drink Coke and then we find a couple who are planning on driving back to town and they'll be passing right by Fountainside as they've heard of this place where you can buy the latest designer-labelled recreational drugs, all of which they explained to me in lingering detail, all of which I've forgotten on account of I don't do drugs. But we have a ride into town. On the way (we sitting in the back seat) Maxine asks me a load of questions about Harley, where I met him, who he is; life-story baggage in general. I tell her mostly the truth: which is that Harley and I shared a cell one night in Santa Barbara – he'd got busted for breaking up a bar, me for the usual, with frozen pizzas that time, I seem to recall – and we just kind of hung together for a while, and when he'd scraped up enough dough for the diner I helped him by working there on low (often ='d no) pay. (None of which have I confided in Dr Diane, but that's a different audience in need of another kind of drama altogether.)

Maxine loves all this. She invites me back to the shop, says she's planning to sleep there as it's by now too late to go home. Since Harley has obviously made a dent in her, I feel curious: am I to play surrogate penis, or what? But, by way of a change, this is not a situation I can run away from.

I go in the shop with her. She locks the door, then turns and puts her arms around my neck. I kiss her, knowing this is what's expected of me. Her mouth tastes all squelchy and wet and like a sponge: YUK! Her breasts press against me like foam pillows. When I consider I have done my duty I step away from her and say, 'I want to rent a dress.'

She grins at me, stupid bitch that she is (may her cunt fester with gonorrhea and tainted sperm), thinking I jest. But I persist. (I think I will draw Maxine's hole, later; then I'll be able to compare it with my drawings of Dr Diane's and see if it bears out my theory that all women are the same.) I say, 'I want that nineteenth-century woman's dress, over there.' (Pointing.) (Is that how you spell gonorrhea? One n, two rs . . . ?) She asks me what I want it for, but I refuse to tell her. I am such a tease, but it's all part of my plan, you see.

In the end, she agrees. I only want it for one night, and I pay cash. She gets angry – I seem to remember that, it's all a little vague. Then I am out of her shop, with my new dress under my arm, ready for curtain-up on my first night. With Johnny as an audience of One.

*   *   *

A few weeks passed.

In the big world outside, the media slowly lost interest in Ray Douggan's murder. Peter Symes equably handled a number of press conferences, punctuated with interruptions from Douggan's grieving parents, angry citizens and busybody screwballs. A mothers' group based in the ultra-desirable suburb of Paignton Glen announced that they were hiring buses to ferry kids to and from social events, 'as the police can't be trusted to watch over our young'. Several of Diane's adolescent patients asked her to intervene with their folks against rulings that they must be home before nightfall; she declined. Four more or less mad people walked into Southern Californian police stations and confessed to Douggan's murder; one of them, on being told to get the hell out, set fire to himself in the street; they extinguished him but he died a few hours later. A girl called Meriel Burnett stayed over with her boyfriend one night, forgot to phone her parents, and suddenly this, instead of being probable cause for a smack around the head, was in all the papers next day, with grieving father this and hysterical mother that. Tim Sanchez, the last person to see Douggan alive, became ever more vague each time some reporter asked him to 'go over it again just once more'. There were few clues to the murder and, according to Ed, little chance of ever solving it. 'Every contact leaves a trace,' that's police lore the world over, but whoever contacted Ray Douggan left remarkably few.

Johnny Anderson acquired the habit of showing Diane his diary on an irregular basis. The entries confirmed her impression that he was the most interesting kid she'd had around for some time, but what really grabbed her was the missing days. Pages had been torn from the yellow pad she'd given him. He signalled that these pages related to material he wasn't prepared to share yet. Diane gave him rope.

It was a Tuesday in early July, right after the holiday weekend, bright and sunny. The Safety Net guys were working on Diane's house, to make it secure. She stopped off in the hospital flower shop to buy half a dozen white roses for her office. Julia greeted her with a smile, looking tanned and relaxed.

'Did you have a good time in San Diego?' Diane asked as she unlocked.

'Wonderful. Thank you so much for the trip.'

'My pleasure.'

'Here's the paperwork.'

Julia handed Diane an envelope containing a used ticket-stub and a hotel receipt.

'Thanks,' Diane said. 'I hate to trouble you with this, but the frequent-flier programme audits tickets regularly: no paperwork, no freebies.'

Diane's phone rang. Neither of them was anticipating an emergency. As Julia picked up she began to unwrap the roses' cellophane with her free hand.

'What?'

Diane turned to see Julia holding the phone against her chest. A drop of blood dripped onto a white rose; she'd pricked her finger. 'What is it?' she cried.

'It's the police. They're – '

They were here. A perfunctory knock on Diane's door preceded Leo Sanders, Ed a step behind him, both their faces grey with fatigue and strain. While Leo spoke, Ed leaned against her filing-cabinet.

'We found the body of a young, Caucasian male called Carl Jensen this morning. His body was buried in a shallow grave, up at Court Ridge Cemetery.' Leo made a stab at a grin. 'Appropriate, no?'

Diane sat down, not from choice; Julia likewise.

'Diane . . . ' Ed eased himself away from the cabinet. 'We think we've got a serial on our hands. That's how Leo and I got the case, we're what's called "the first men up", because we took care of Douggan. Jensen was shot, last Saturday night, according to forensic; the corpse had been mutilated and burned, just the way Douggan's was; he'd been tortured before he died.'

'Tortured?' Diane breathed.

'We didn't spill that to the press, about Douggan,' Leo replied. 'But yes, both of them had been tortured before they died.'

'Diane,' said Ed, 'we found one of your name-cards beside Jensen's body.'

After a long silence Diane stuttered, 'What did you say?'

'You remember the name-card you gave me,' Ed said, 'the personal one? The same. Six feet away from the corpse, covered in mud. Just like the perp had dropped it in his hurry.'

They were looking for her reaction, Diane realized. She ought to say something. 'Surely you don't think that I – '

'Oh, for Christ's . . . ' Leo laughed at Ed, as if to say, Jeez! What a cookie! 'No, we don't think you spend your nights practising carving on a live audience. We think you must know the perpetrator, though.'

'What? But, why? I mean . . . '

'Diane,' Ed said, 'I know that Besto's real name is Tobes Gascoign.' Her expression caused him to smile briefly before he went on, 'We traced him through one of the diner's regulars.'

'Lucky you.'

'Not luck: we just waited until we saw a familiar face at Harley's, someone with prior, then we leaned. Skill, Diane: professional, regular, police technique. But now we do need to talk to you, fast, about all your court-referrals, about anyone else who might have had access to your cards.'

'Oh, yes. Yes, I see. When did it happen, the . . . murder?'

'Small hours of Sunday, forensic say.' It was Leo who provided this information, Leo who now said, 'We need a list of all your current court-referred patients, Diane, and we'd like you to come down to the station to make a statement. And after that, we'd welcome whatever input you can give about these two crimes.'

'Input?'

'We're having a profile done by the FBI Behavioral Science Unit at Quantico,' Ed put in. 'We want to identify the kind of person we're looking for. Know anything about profiling?'

'A bit.'

'We have a meeting with the FBI Field Profile Co-Ordinator in an hour's time, when he gets in from LA. Can you be there too?'

Diane looked at Julia. 'What's today?'

'It's your reading day; no appointments until two.'

Diane stood up. 'I'd like to get this over with, please.'

'And your list of referrals?'

She was still debating internally where she stood on the ethics of that when Ed said, 'Diane, I can go in hard on Tobes Gascoign, get the names out of him. Or I can get a court order.'

'Are you so sure?'

'You've heard of the decision in Zürcher versus *Stanford Daily*?'

'Enough to know it stinks. Bully-boy tactics, huh? Nice pair of jackboots you've got there.'

'Diane – '

But she'd decided. 'Tell it to the judge.'

'Diane, if you – '

'Get a court order. And get those tanks off my lawn, Detective.'

Leo and Ed exchanged ironical glances. See, those glances said, told you how it would be . . .

'Okay,' Ed said. 'If that's what you want.'

'And leave Gascoign out of it.'

'You do your job, I'll do mine. I don't want to go

rifling through your files for the sake of it; we can cut it down. When did you have those name-cards printed?'

'When I closed on my new house. Say January. Ah, wait . . .'

'What?'

'After Mother died, I took a sabbatical, in Europe. I reassigned all the court-referrals I had at that time to other clinicians. There was a clean break. Mother died when I was in the course of moving into the house, so . . .'

'Okay, we'll restrict the order to the court-referrals you've had this year, since buying the house. To start with.'

As they went out to the car, Diane ran the names through her mind. Ramon, Jesse, Billy-the-Kid, and Tobes. But there was no need to rush headlong into sacrificing these lambs on the altar of so-called justice. Let Ed persuade the judge if he must, her conscience would be clean.

In the car on the way to headquarters Ed sat next to her and, in a low voice, gave details of this latest slaying. He had photographs; they were bestial. But as they rode downtown, Diane wasn't focused on the fate of Carl Jensen, not exclusively; she was more concerned about the future prospects of Diane Cheung.

She had trusted her court-referrals to reform under her tutelage, to become acceptable members of society. Her reputation was on the line, along with her pride. And in backing herself up to the hilt, she'd taken risks. But of all the risks she'd taken, none, with hindsight, seemed so reckless, so devoid of merit, as her decision not to block Tobes Gascoign getting a job with the Andersons.

No one was subsequently going to understand why she'd done that. But now she stood between the devil and the deep blue sea. If she cut the ground from under

204

Tobes's feet, he would never trust her again and might even request an ethics hearing. But if she did nothing . . .

They arrived at HQ. Bad news travels faster than light. The Fourth Avenue headquarters building was under siege. Demonstrators marched around and around in front of the main entrance, their placards held high: 'STOP THE BUTCHERY NOW!' 'PROTECT OUR CHILDREN.' 'SOFT SOAP, NO — HARD RESULTS, YES!' 'OLD DIRT, NEW BROOMS NEEDED NOW.'

Peter Symes was going to love that last one.

Diane saw a couple of TV cam-corders and a long furry microphone hurriedly being carried up the steps. Three men and a woman pushed through hastily erected crowd-barriers, marching across the open space enforced by blues with night-sticks. Leo sounded his horn, forcing a way with the help of traffic police.

As they went inside Diane had a TV camera thrust in her face, heard many discordant voices shouting questions: 'Detective, is it true about the burn marks?' 'Do you have a suspect?' 'Do you expect to make an arrest this side of Thanksgiving?' And she wondered, inconsequentially, if her hair was straight . . .

The doors slammed behind them. A line of blues stood ranged across the hallway, expecting trouble. The atmosphere fizzled with tension. Men talked in low voices, a buzz punctuated now and then by the 'bleep' of a radio. Diane, Ed and Leo hurried on up the stairs to the first floor, making for the interview rooms, but before they could get there a voice hollered, 'Diane!'

'*Damn!*' Ed muttered, but they stopped and turned around, because the voice behind them was Peter Symes's.

'Glad to see you,' he said laconically, coming down

the corridor towards them, the usual gaggle of heavy dudes in tow. Peter had a liking for Praetorian guards.

Today he was wearing a chalk-stripe dark grey suit with burgundy tie and matching handkerchief in the jacket top-pocket. His tasselled, black, patent leather shoes gleamed as if they'd been oiled. His jaw preceded him, giving solid foundation to an ironclad face, with its thick eyebrows and dark blue eyes beneath a crop of grey-white hair. Peter's hair, rich and full of body, stood up a good inch off his head. He was forty-five, but with the skin of a man fifteen years younger, standing six feet tall and stocky of frame. When he wasn't working (Peter was usually working) he sailed his boat, and it was easy to daydream him into the role of not-so-old sea dog. He had a naval officer's bearing, and a rating's lockerful of obscene jokes.

This was the man who claimed to be glad to see Diane. She scented a trap, and waited.

'Diane,' he said, slipping a hand through the crook of her arm as they walked forward together, 'Diane, we need your help.' His gravelly voice, honed by years of bellowing across vast, choppy distances at fellow yachtsmen, brooked no denials. 'We are facing a crisis,' he told her, 'of inordinate proportions. We hold the pass any which way we can. I've got to put a brake on these people, and I've got to do it today.'

It sounded simply wonderful; already her head was nodding in approbation.

'Psychology,' he said; 'we're going to need more than a little psychology today, Diane. Stay close, now.'

On this last word he wheeled right, in through some swing-doors, and bedlam broke loose.

He had, Diane realized, hijacked her into the mother and father of all press conferences. They found them-

206

selves in a room the size of an airplane hangar, with an acre of floor to cross before they reached the podium where men were quickly putting together a montage of blown-up photographs.

As Diane and Peter marched through the scrum there were people, many people, who tried to check their progress. It was a re-run of the hell outside, but with no avenue of escape. A dozen microphones were poked in Diane's face, as if the holders meant to ram them up her nostrils. Peter held up his free hand and looked to right and left, jaw thrust even further forward: the stance of command.

'Give way,' he barked. 'Give way to the front, there!'

And they did!

Peter steered her into a seat next to his. Someone reached across to tap the microphone in front of him. The racket diminished. There were seats for everyone, but nobody sat, they were too keen to get themselves forward into the front row.

The room might be packed but when Peter stood at that podium there was only one man in it, no question. Diane cast a sideways glance at him, remembering how he approved of marriage in theory but not in practice; at least, that was what he'd once told a CBS interviewer and although he had practised three times with different ladies he was currently back to theorizing.

'Ladies and gentlemen . . . let me introduce the team.' Peter's voice carried easily to the four corners of the cavernous briefing-room. 'On my left, Lieutenant Caplan, homicide; Alfred Terrigo, Chief of Detectives; Dr Michael Frexa, forensic scientist . . . to my right, Chief of Patrol McShea, Assistant District Attorney Salven Thomsen, and next to me, Dr Diane Cheung, head of the Paradise Bay Juvenile Crimes Unit.'

Did you set this up, Ed? – that's what Diane was thinking as she tried to smile and look serious at the same time – *You bastard, did you know about this press conference before you dragooned me down here?*

'Before taking questions,' Peter said, 'I will read to you a statement.'

The room fell quiet. Peter took papers from an inside pocket and unfolded them. He opened his spectacle-case and placed his glasses on his nose, adjusting them with the care of a scholar preparing to analyse a palimpsest. Diane became aware of his cologne radiating out to ensnare her: the heady, pungent, aptly named 'Fahrenheit'.

As he began to read, Diane's mind went to work. Her conclusion: this was indeed a trap. She absolved Edwin of complicity, but he'd been used.

And her reasoning . . . ? Peter realized Paradise Bay's new Juvenile Crimes Unit was a two-edged sword. If it worked, he could use it to scythe down his critics. If it flopped, that would be Diane's fault and he'd take good care to be in another city on the day. So this was her first public test. Questions would be directed at her by the press, and some questions would be re-directed her way by Peter Symes. If she failed in a time of crisis, what hope was there? But if she scintillated, public sympathy would swing behind the unit, which would be well and truly launched.

Diane resolved to scintillate. What did she know about murderers . . . ?

Peter seemed to be winding down. A nervous glance over her shoulder took in blow-ups of the crime-scene with little grisly detail visible, plus shots of the two dead boys, Douggan and Jensen, taken during their lifetimes. No help there, or anywhere.

Peter said, 'And now I know there are questions you'll want – '

The media were fast off the mark. Their first few questions concerned time of death, location of body, state of cadaver. Diane felt herself relax as the heat turned on Frexa. He was a capable, experienced forensic clinician, well used to these people, and he handled their questions with aplomb. Yes, he was quite sure death had occurred some time during the hours of darkness, Saturday-Sunday. The body had been found in overgrown land in Court Ridge Cemetery, not far from the main road. Two bullets had been used. There was nothing he wanted to say about the state of the cadaver at this time.

A woman stood up, holding a microphone. She was wearing a Versace, a goddam Versace dress; Diane had seen it in last month's *California Magazine*. She smiled. This woman had lovely teeth and Diane got to see them all. 'Dr Cheung,' she said, 'what forensic experience do you have?'

Every eye locked on to Diane. She felt as if a cross-wire had been etched across her pupils. She took a deep breath, focused her cross-wire on La Versace's forehead and went to war. 'Fingerprints and bloodstains, none. Since the day I qualified, I've been working on and around the criminal mind, and we are looking for a very special type of mind here.'

'The serial-killer mentality?' Versace counter-attacked.

'It depends how much importance you attach to strict accuracy.' Diane's oh-so charming smile clashed in mid-air with Versace's. 'The FBI define serial killers as murderers who are involved in three or more separate events, with an emotional cooling-off period between each homicide. It's the cooling-off period that distinguishes the serial killer from other varieties. Then we come down to features. A serial killer will target a *type* of victim, and confusion in this case may arise if too much attention is fastened on the fact that both victims were young white males whose bodies had suffered . . .'

There was more, much more, to come. Diane was just starting to enjoy herself when Peter rose and said, 'I don't like to check Dr Cheung, but at this stage of the investigation we can't afford to let rip with too many details of the state of the corpses.'

He smiled, even patted her on the shoulder as he sat down, but Diane could not bring herself to look at the reporter in the Versace number. And she'd thought she was doing so well . . . Then her disappointment yielded to anger: Peter should have briefed her properly before they'd come in.

There was a question to the ADA about charges and likely penalties and did this case highlight the ongoing debate about the legitimacy of capital punishment? Someone asked if any progress had been made tracing the girl Tim Sanchez had seen in his rear-view mirror after dropping off Ray Douggan. (Answer: No.) Diane stared at the table, trying to remember to smile in case some camera picked up on her and she earned prime-time billing as The Look of Despair.

Then a man's voice asked, 'How many does it take to die, Chief Symes, before you and your men wake up?'

Diane raised her head. The questioner was a young, bearded man whose grim look matched his words. Before Peter could answer, a woman rose to back the previous speaker. 'Have you any idea,' she said, 'how *angry* local people are? How *afraid* they are? Can you

210

conceive what it's like to be the parents of adolescent boys in this area?'

There was a loud murmur of assent from the hall; it swelled when a third voice chimed in, 'Is Hal Lawson still alive, do you believe? Is Randy Delmar?'

'It's important not to let this get out of proportion,' Peter said. 'We've had two murders – '

'And that's all – is that what you're saying?' The bearded man had hit the ground running. 'That as long as we stick with two, that's acceptable?'

'What about three?' put in Versace. 'What's your cut-off point, Chief?'

Peter raised his hand for silence; it was a measure of the man that he got it. 'All I'm saying,' he went on quietly, 'is that if you look at the statistics, Paradise Bay stands up well against all other cities of comparable size, nationwide. We have our homicides each year, yes, but the record is a good one compared to, say, Santa Barbara or even San Clemente. You can't put my men on the spot by raising spectres of mad stalkers and Friday the Thirteenth, because you simply haven't got the evidence.'

'Yet,' called a voice from the floor.

'I won't rise to that. We're doing everything humanly possible and we shall continue to do so, but I won't have my people subjected to unfair pressures. Parents are going to take extra care of their kids, whatever I say, and that's good.'

'You believe this will happen again, right?' (Versace.)

'I'll leave the predictions to astrologers and the weather bureau. And now, we all have a mountain of work to do, so if . . .'

Peter moved out from behind the podium to a babble of sound. For a moment it looked as though the press would mob him, but blues cleared a path and when Peter pressed forward Diane made sure she was at his heels.

Versace plucked her arm. 'Nice doing, sweetie,' she said. 'Here, this is my producer's card: call him, we can do a night spot for you . . .'

The rest was lost in the crush. Diane dropped the card. She'd had enough of name-cards for a long time to come.

'Who was that?' she gasped as they emerged into the corridor.

'The woman who grilled you? That was Angela Souvrain, of CBS. Remember her face: you'll be seeing a lot of it.' Peter took Diane by the arm. He gazed into her eyes and he said, 'Diane, you handled that superbly. We are going to work so well together. And please don't worry about me stopping you in mid-flow: I didn't want anyone to know about your name-card being beside the corpse.'

Diane was about to explain she knew enough not to mention that interesting fact to people whose job it was to destroy other people's reputations, when someone thrust a fax into Peter's hand and he turned away.

'Dr Cheung?'

A pale-faced man wearing a smart tweed jacket above inconsistently crumpled, pale chinos had come to stand at her elbow. He was her height, his eyes were crinkly and fun-packed, his sandy-coloured moustache was too thin to be anything but a mistake.

'Daniel Krozgrow,' he said, extending a hand. 'You're *Dance of a Different Drum*, right?'

'Wow! You've actually read it?'

'Working it's way to the top of my bedside-table pile . . . though seeing how you handled that question on serial killers, I plan to promote it.'

'I'm sorry, but I don't – '

'FBI,' said her new friend and admirer, holding up a badge. 'Field Profile Co-Ordinator. Nice to be working alongside someone who knows the biz.'

'Well, I'd hardly lay claim to that. What are your plans?'

'First, I'm going to take a look at that darned cemetery. They're in there, all right.'

'They?'

'All of them. Hal Lawson. Delmar.'

'But we don't even know they're dead!'

'They're dead. And they're in Court Ridge Cemetery. Look, Douggan was found there with certain marks on his body, Jensen was found there, same marks. All my experience and training tell me that that's where the others are as well.'

'Both of them?'

'Why say both? We know of two boys that are missing. There may be more.'

Diane found Daniel Krozgrow's confidence a little chilling: attractive, but chilling. 'Any idea of who did it?'

'Young white male.' Daniel shrugged. 'We'll narrow it.'

'Our only witness says a young woman was the last person seen with Douggan before he died.'

'Sanchez? That guy changes his story every time he opens his mouth. No woman ever went in for systematic torture in circumstances where she might be discovered any moment. Trust me: we're looking for a man, in his mid to late twenties, and he's white.'

Diane wanted to talk some more but she had to make that witness-statement. When she explained,

Krozgrow nodded understandingly and stood aside. At the end of the passage, something made Diane turn. Krozgrow was talking with Peter Symes, but, as if he felt her eyes on his back, he too swivelled until their eyes met, and he smiled.

Leo and Ed were waiting for her in an interview room. A sheet of paper lay on the desk. Leo handed it to her and Diane saw it was a warrant to search the office of Dr Diane Cheung, authenticated by her old friend Judge Cyril DeMesne, and boy but was *he* buying next time she ran into him in Quincy's Bar.

'You've proved your point,' she said dully. 'I'll give you the list.'

'Does this mean we don't get to smash up her office?' Leo asked Ed in an injured tone.

'Shit,' Ed agreed. 'I was going to read all those dirty case-notes. About perverted sex with animals, and stuff.'

'That's why I'm going to give you the list,' Diane said. 'I love my animals too much.'

After she'd given the statement about her name-cards, and phoned to clear it with Julia for when someone came to St Joe's to execute the search warrant, it was time to go sit in on the FBI conference . . . only to find it breaking up. Daniel Krozgrow took her on one side as the others left. 'Can you give me your number?' he said. 'I may want to talk later.'

Diane happily gave him her work number and hoped he'd ring soon (though she didn't tell him that). She looked at her watch. One thirty: if she hurried she could make it back to the hospital in time for her two o'clock. While she drove, Diane was working on a plan. The afternoon dragged endlessly, but eventually she'd seen her last patient and could set off home.

Wayne Ortiz was sitting on her front step, reading Wingrove's *Chung Kuo*. He glanced up, saw her, and leapt to his feet.

'Hi, Wayne,' Diane said. 'All through?'

'Uh . . . no.'

Wayne pocketed the book and adjusted his baseball hat through one-eighty degrees so that the peak was at the back. He looked far too young to be involved in an electronic security company having an annual turnover running into high six figures, but that was the way of it these days, she guessed. His face wore a sheepish look she didn't much like.

'Diane, we have a problem.'

She glared at him. 'What?'

'The switching-board's d.f.'

'*What?*'

'Defective. Whole batch of them came in from Chicago yesterday; can't make a darn one work.'

'You mean, after all this wait, I'm still not protected. Oh, *Wayne* . . .'

'Okay, okay, I'm sorry, truly. Tell you what: we'll talk compensation some other time, okay?'

'I don't want compensation, I want a functional alarm system.'

'You've got it. Just as soon as we get a replacement switching-board.'

'How long will that take?'

'Coupla weeks. This is highly specialized stuff we're talking here.'

They went inside the house. He proudly showed her how everything was in place: rape alarm there, there and there; circuit-breakers on the windows and doors; master panel . . . and defective switching-board. It was lovely, it was just that none of it worked. Diane said a doleful goodbye to Wayne, and wondered if she shouldn't perhaps abandon plans for the rest of this odious day when nothing had gone right.

A hot shower and change of clothes stiffened her resolve. She phoned Julia and had her retrieve Tobes's address from the files. Half an hour later found Diane heading down to Paradise Bay.

The area where Tobes lived didn't inspire confidence. It was close by the old railroad station, a brownstone in a street littered with newspapers, and orange skins, and a furry, four-legged, utterly still lump she didn't want to inspect too closely. Black kids in bright clothes watched her from behind impenetrable expressions as she mounted the stairs to the front door. It was open; she went in. She climbed to the first floor, trying to pretend the smell was of no consequence, and knocked on his door: a scrawled message held in place by a pin told her that this was the place, 'Number Five,' it read. No reply. He must be at work.

Diane scribbled a note, asking him to call urgently, and slipped it under the door, hoping there wasn't a rat waiting for its dinner on the other side. Rather to her surprise, the Camry was still parked where she'd left it, all hub-caps intact. As she drove off she racked her brains for what more she could do, and lo! – the answer came. Perhaps Tobes wasn't at work at all, perhaps he was socializing. Another quarter of an hour found her on the coast road heading out of Orcutt towards Point Sal, and Harley's.

Today Diane's was not the only real car in the diner's lot, there were mountain bikes chained to the fence, several couples sat outside drinking cola and most of them looked at least half human: an improvement on last time. But no sign of Tobes. She went in.

Harley glanced up from washing glasses behind the bar, and did a double-take, obviously not pleased to see her. Today he wore off-white jeans and a vest that displayed more of him than it concealed. He was heavily tattooed, something she'd failed to pick up on last time.

'Can I have a word with you?' Diane said.

'What is it now?'

'I didn't get a chance to explain myself, the other day.'

'What's to explain? Excuse *me* . . .'

Harley sloped off to the other end of the bar, where a teenage hoodlum was yelling for espressos.

'It's about a friend of mine,' she called. 'Tobes Gascoign.'

Harley looked up. He sidled back along the bar. 'Who?'

'You knew him as Besto. Maybe you didn't realize Tobes was his name.' Which couldn't be true, because she'd caught his change of expression when she'd mentioned Tobes's name. However . . . 'I'm a psychologist,' she went on. 'My name's Diane Cheung. Hello.' She held out her hand.

And to her astonishment, Harley's face broke into a smile, he took her hand and he said, 'Hi, Diane. Tobes *said* you were a doll.'

'Well, thank you kindly.'

Diane's heart beat fast. She'd overcome a major obstacle. Harley *did* know Tobes, he just hadn't wanted to admit it to the police. So much for Ed's 'professional, regular techniques'.

'What do you want to drink?' Harley asked. 'On the house.'

'Got a cold Sol?'

217

'Coming right up.'

Harley brought the beer. 'No, but seriously,' he said, leaning across the bar in a burst of confidence, 'Tobes says you are, like, you know, totally far out. Like, brilliant. He called you that several times.' He cupped his hands around his head and expanded them outwards; Diane saw he was describing a super brain, and smiled.

'Then maybe you can help. I need to talk to him, and it's urgent. Have you seen him around, or are you expecting him? I know he doesn't work here any more, but . . .'

'Maybe.' Harley's smile was fading now. 'But why didn't you say who you were that Saturday? You were with a cop.'

'My boyfriend.' It was only stretching the truth a little.

Harley's look said, Some women have no taste. But – 'How can I help?' he asked. 'I don't want to help any cops. You, you're different.'

'Got it. My client, Tobes, Besto, whatever, is in trouble with the Law. The police are going to track him down soon anyway, and I can't stop that, but I need to talk to him, fast.'

Harley subjected her to a long, penetrating look. Then he said, 'Okay. Yeah, he does come around. Sometimes. Only I never know until I see him.'

Diane tried to conceal her disappointment. 'When was the last time he came here?'

'The last time?' Harley sought the answer in the dusty beams above their heads. Following his glance, Diane noticed for the first time a real skeleton hanging from a noose. Someone had clipped a dildo to its pelvis.

'Last Saturday night,' Harley said.

'Thanks. Look, if you see him, *please* tell him . . .' Diane broke off; Harley stared at her. 'Saturday night,' she said hurriedly. 'What time Saturday?'

'Oh, came in about eight, I guess. Stayed till dawn – we had a party. Some guy's birthday.'

He went on to say something about it always being some guy's birthday around here, but Diane wasn't listening, she was calculating. Leo Sanders had said earlier that Carl Jensen was killed in the small hours of Sunday; Frexa had as good as confirmed it at the press conference.

'Did anyone else see Tobes in here Saturday?' she asked excitedly. 'Could you find a few people to say he was here?'

Harley spread his hands expansively. 'Fifty suit you?'

Only with difficulty did Diane repress a cheer. She was a better cop than Edwin.

*   *   *

Getting excited, now. Coming close, vr-vr-vr-VROOOOMMM!!!

Tonight's the night.

It's my p.m. gardening shift. I find this machete in back of the Andersons' garage. It's old and rusty, but a few minutes with my trusty steel soon brings it back into shape. Then, *schwing!!!* It cuts beautifully. I get into a rhythm, build up a sweat. Tall weeds fall to the ground in casual, criss-cross patterns. The sun's hot. By the time I've worked my way along twenty feet of fence, the first weeds are drying white-pepper coloured and I'm planning where to build the fire. Everything'll go up in a trice, whoosh! Won't need any paper, just a match.

I love fires.

Johnny sits on the edge of the patio, watching me work. Swish, swish, swish, goes the blade. Sometimes I bring it down a little too close for comfort. He jerks his body away, his eyelids flutter madly.

This boy is scared of me. No, really: he thinks I might actually bring this blade down on his neck, snicker-snee! Think of all the blood whooshing out. It troubles me, this certainty that he believes I might harm him.

'Want some lemonade?' he calls timidly. 'Great,' I reply.

When he gets up, he leaves his diary notepad on the step. Is that because he *wants* me to read it? Or as a test? Or simply because he forgot? Before I can make up my mind on this issue, he returns, carrying a pitcher of lemonade. He pours me a glass. I lay down my machete and drink; he sits down on the step. Flies hover over a patch of weeds. One of them lands on the step, next to Johnny's foot. I spit an ice-cube at the fly, which floats off; Johnny laughs nervously.

'You've got good aim,' he says.

'Sometimes.'

The ice-cube rolls off the step, onto the ground. The soil turns dark as the ice melts. An earthworm crawls out of the patch of newly moistened soil. It's long, with a pale pink head, a white body and an end that's dark purple, like a hungry cock. It starts to slither away. Casually, I reach for the machete. Up-down, one-two: the worm becomes two worms.

'Here,' I say, ever the genteel host as I offer Johnny a wriggling dose of protein. 'After you.'

He shies away. When I shrug and pop the wriggly-piggly tasty morsel into my own mouth he looks like, you know, he's about to gag, or something.

'You're sure you don't want it?' I say, holding out Part Two. He just moves his butt a couple of steps higher. So I get to eat both bits of the worm, which is delicious. Just as squeamish little Johnny's turning his head away, I say, 'Tonight's the night.'

'What?'

'Tonight. Is. The night.'

'What's happening tonight?'

'Nine thirty. Watch the path. Be ready to slip out when you see me under the light.'

He says nothing. Only his eyes move left-right, left-right, like an anxious rabbit's, and I know that this time he'll show.

The machete rides high up in the air, swish, down it comes, burying itself half an inch in the wood beside Johnny's sandal, and his feet leap off the step like they'd been burned.

'Missed,' I say. 'Damn!'

*　　　*　　　*

'You did *what*?'

Ed's voice carried across the squad room, causing colleagues to look up in surprise. But Diane was unrepentant. 'I went to Harley's and established that Gascoign was at the diner for all of Saturday night. He's not the perp.'

Edwin scowled. 'You're heading for trouble,' he said, 'if you usurp police functions.'

'I'm not – '

'Did you caution Harley that his words might be produced in court as evidence?'

'No.'

'Did you tell him he had the right to have a lawyer present?'

'No. Should I?'

'Well, let's say it's desirable.'

'But not essential?'

Ed breathed hard.

'All you succeeded in doing was frightening Harley,' she told him. 'As a psychologist I was able to communicate with him more effectively. The unit's going to work, Ed. Trust me.'

Ed was still trying to think of a reply when Leo came in carrying a sheaf of papers. 'Ah-*hah*!' he cried. 'Don't tell me: shoot-out at high noon.'

'Very funny,' Ed said.

'It's Tobes Gascoign,' Diane explained to Leo. 'I've just established an alibi for him, and Sherlock Holmes here is miffed.'

'Really?'

'Really. The worst you can say about that poor mixed-up kid is that he smokes too much, and even in Southern California they haven't made that a felony.'

Leo gazed at her. 'Are you sure?'

'Yes.'

'Shit.' Leo mimed picking up a phone. 'Larry, let them go, willya? Yeah, all eight thousand nine hundred and four of 'em.' He put down the imaginary phone and turned to Ed. 'Did Gascoign's alibi check out?'

'Not yet.'

'It will. Betcha!' Leo grinned at Diane. 'So go tell your boy he won't get to fry in the chair. *This* time. He's not to do it again, that's all.' He had gripped Diane's arm and was breathing into her face. 'Did I ever tell you, sometimes when they pull Old Sparky's switch the guy's eyes splatter out, fizz, pop! Like that?'

'No, Leo.'

'And sometimes they have to fry him four times before he's done? You have easy-over executions, see, and sunny-side-ups. Now in a sunny-side-up – '

Diane pushed past this maniac, grinning despite herself. 'Goodbye, Leo.'

But before she could leave the squad room she heard Ed say, 'Do you really have to be so anti-social to my girl?' And Leo replied, 'Sure. Tough bitch like that, you gotta keep your end up.'

She burst out laughing. Sergeant Leroy on the muster desk looked up in surprise, but Diane was out of there.

*   *   *

Welcome. Or as the Chinese say, *Huan-ying guang-lin*. That's what I will say to Dr Diane the day she finally walks through my door: *Huan-ying guang-lin*. She'll probably keel over in a state of terminal shock. You are sophisticated people, reading this; a traditional Chinese greeting does not repel you, I am sure.

The room is another matter.

The room is . . . repulsive.

So, where are we?

This is my home, the place I sometimes sleep, and it's where I hang out when it's raining, too wet for Court Ridge Cemetery and external activities generally. Welcome, welcome. You have not seen this place before, so thrice times welcome.

A little descriptive material may not come amiss.

223

My room is on the first floor of a brownstone building. There is a fire-escape beyond the window, built of rust, arf! arf! (Latest construction methods, folks, no finer rust this side of Pittsburgh.) But since the sash-window is jammed open one inch, short of breaking the glass I am trapped in here anyway.

The door (wooden) is painted brown, like the bare floor and the window-frame and the walls, only they are a paler shade of brown. The door has a split in it, but the lock mostly holds. I do not like my landlord; he is a creep. Sixty if he's a day, and a cripple to boot, Red slithers around spying on me and his other tenants like an evil old stickleback. I have asked him to repair the crack in the door many times: it lets in a draught and is wide enough to let people observe me at my devotions. These requests are ignored. His requests for rent are likewise sometimes ignored, but Red is afraid of me, too afraid to risk upsetting me with talk of eviction. There was an incident between me and Red. Don't ask about that.

The neighbours? Well, this is quick-changeover population we're talking here. There are a dozen rooms to let and I guess there must be sixty or so people sleeping here on a typical evening. Next to me is an old guy who keeps cats – wheeeWWHHH! So much for him. (Mr Willem, that's his name. I think.) Along the landing we find a bunch of Puerto Ricans (I've never seen their door open), next to them Roh, a Korean student doing electronics at University of California Paradise Bay, whose folks never send him any money: hence his residing in this hovel. Told me once he made a living out of translation work, though me, I think he's a pimp. Leastways, there's always a heap of oriental girls passing through his room. Doesn't matter: Roh's an okay guy. Lindy, a young white girl with a brown baby and no husband, completes my stairway. She's on welfare. Upstairs you find assorted nationalities, age-groups and occupations, but you have the flavour already, and, as I say, this is a transient crew. Red has only two rules: no Viet, no Cambodge. That's it.

The room is fifteen feet by twelve: not a palace. You come in, the window is on your right. On the left, tucked into the far corner, is my bed: a foam-rubber mattress with a sheet and two blankets. It will be cold in winter, but we haven't had one of those yet. I'll steal an electric fire, maybe. By the bed is a rickety old cupboard, where I keep my clothes, etc. There are cardboard boxes, many of them. Some of them are neatly labelled, such as the ones wherein I keep papers relating to Dr Diane and Johnny Anderson. My drawings – the pornographic ones, the ones that Dr Diane encourages me to make – are under the mattress, along with my money and anything else of particular importance. You are nice people, reading this; I trust you with these secrets because I am starting to like you and I want you to like me. 'Getting to know you, getting to know all about you . . .' Great movie, did you catch it?

I think I am writing all this down for the police. Don't ask me why, because I don't know.

By the bed is a mirror, propped up against the wall. In the corner next to the window is a wash-basin with one of those stupid electric water-heaters that takes all day to produce an egg-cupful of tepid water. No chairs or tables: just scatter-cushions, without covers. A small refrigerator completes the basic picture, except for the smell, which is a mixture of gas, garbage and the seed I spill upon the ground. (The sheet, actually.) Light comes from a sixty-watt bulb dangling on a cord from the ceiling. There is an electricity meter that gobbles coins, but since I moved in it has been starving.

I have picked up several skills, here and there. I am, for example, a whiz with juice. There is this convenient little wiring arrangement that by-passes the meter. Not for the faint-hearted, folks: don't try it without the supervision of a properly qualified person in attendance. (Such as me.) I have a table-cloth that I throw over the meter when Red comes to call. Since the incident between us, he calls much less frequently.

Tonight is the big night so I am sitting cross-legged in front of the mirror, making up my face in preparation for my greatest-ever performance, all for an under-age audience of one. I use pale foundation, carmine red for the lips, purple mascara. I look a fright. Exactly how a ghost should look, in fact.

As I wield brush and blusher I consider the significance of the note pushed under my door. Dr Diane is starting to find me interesting: seems she wants me to call her, urgently.

I will not be rushed.

Mention of Dr Diane takes me back to a conversation we had some weeks ago, during one of my private sessions with her. I told her I'd always wanted to be an actor. I thought she would laugh, but she didn't. She asked why. And I told her, because when you dress up, and make up, and act, you're somebody else. And ever since then she's been encouraging me to go in for acting. Like it was, you know, like I had a career choice or something.

She's weird.

But tonight, Dr Diane, you would be proud of me.

The dress I rented from Maxine hangs from a hook on the picture-rail between the window and the wash-basin. In the dim light of my single bulb, it is all shadows and mysterious folds, dark as Satan's cloak.

It fits me like a second skin.

My CD player is set up with its mini-speakers next to the bed. The music booming out from it is the overture from *The Flying Dutchman*. Of course: this is Johnny's night, remember? The night of The One.

I survey my handiwork with a critical eye, but it's okay. My face is dreadful. Full of dread, dreadful.

I look like a ghost.

Now one thing is not good: I have mislaid the make-up crayon I stole from Maxine that first day we met. I've turned the place upside down, but cannot find it. It occurs to me that the crayon may have slipped down inside Dr Diane's box. I haul the cardboard container into the middle of the room and up-end it.

My, my, what a collection! Pride of place goes to her book, naturally. It still has the library sticker inside, I should really tear that out. There are newspaper articles about her: the Paradise Bay library computer had quite a little stash of them. Also, her name-cards (which is how I found out where she lives, because she isn't in the phone book).

That was a day, oh man. We were in group session. We'd made an arrangement beforehand about how Jesse would distract her and give Ramon a clear run at her purse, with me blocking Julia Page's line of sight. But it all worked out so much better than we planned. Outside, there was suddenly this terrible scream, see? And a naked woman was streaking across the grass, two interns in hot pursuit. We all stood on our chairs and hollered and clapped, because we knew what that was all about, that was a patient from the psychiatric ward gone bananas. Dr Diane ran to look, with Julia behind her. Piaow! Ramon had that purse stripped in a second.

We weren't after her money; we're none of us that dumb. No, we had a bet: was she on the Pill or not? Billy-the-Kid laid down she had a Dutch cap, he being the only one of our number who knew what that was. Anyway, afterwards Ramon told us, Zilch. Nothing. But he had all these name-cards. We told him he was crazy, but he said, 'Nah! She's never going to miss 'em, and anyway she started to turn around, y'know, and I panicked, because I thought she'd seen me in the window-glass.' So we all grabbed a handful of the cards Ramon had snitched. I keep mine in the box, where they won't get dirty.

Sure enough, underneath the cards, I find the missing make-up crayon. I use it to draw three thin lines across my white forehead. Then I'm ready.

My trusty Trekkie is parked across the doorway – my burglar alarm. I stuff the dress into my saddle-bag, lock up behind me, carry the bike down to the street. I mount my steed and ride off into the darkness.

By the time I reach the cemetery's main gates on Winchester it's fully dark. I chain my Trekkie to the usual set of railings and set off into the jungle, lugging my saddle-bag. A fresh breeze causes the trees to rustle ominously around my head. Apart from the ssh-ssh-ssh of leaves, no sound disturbs the silence. Yet my heart is beating strangely, I no longer feel at ease.

My pace slows to a crawl. What is this?

I know this territory, it is mine, but tonight there's an alien quality to the land which frightens me. Something is in the bushes, there, there, *there*. Something that waits. Something quiet.

I move on, clutching the bag to my chest. I want to run. I know that once I start to run I shall never stop. The quiet thing watches me. I feel its eyes on my back. Not a dog, not a man. Something.

There comes a moment when I need my flashlight to see where I'm going. The thought of turning on the light fills me with dread.

I am afraid. Of the light.

When I was very young, I had a dream. It was pitch dark, except for a huge white moon in the sky. A pillar of light shimmered between the moon and the ground in front of me. Its shimmer was evil, ripe with terror. I knew that if I touched the light I would be sucked up to the moon and die. The light was pulling me towards it. I could not resist the pillar of light. I awoke with a high fever and was ill for days. Mom took care of me. At first.

It is close, now. I cannot see the light. It is there.

When I swallow, my throat clicks; no saliva floods to ease it. The leaves continue their silken rustle. The breeze dies. All around me is black night, I can see nothing. My spine prickles. I do not dare look behind me. If I do not look behind me, there is nothing there. The terrible column of light does not exist, never has. *Believe it.*

Now there is noise. I struggle to identify its source and nature. Only after clumsy seconds of jerking my head about does realization dawn: the whimper I hear is my own.

Somehow I manage to switch on my flashlight. Its beam shakes because my hand shakes also, but it guides me to the clearing. No one, nothing follows me. The mound of earth and Alice's tomb are the same as always. Now comes a touch of soft summer rain, and I complete my transformation to the sound of its pit-pat-pit on leaves.

There is no moon; there is no column of shimmering white light.

I am ready.

Is he?

*   *   *

Nicole said goodnight, and turned off the light. Johnny waited. He counted up to a hundred before looking at his watch. Nine-oh-eight. He turned over so that he could see out of his window. The neighbours' light was on, but the path was empty. Nobody there.

Tobes had told him earlier: tonight's the night. (And eaten a worm first!!) Johnny was feeling calm and good about himself. He counted up to five hundred. Then he got out of bed and dressed, because when Tobes said tonight was the night, Johnny believed him. (Maybe the worm had convinced him.)

Johnny was wearing his watch, just to be sure. At nine twenty-nine he was sitting by the window. The path was empty.

Nine thirty. Still empty.

Nine thirty-one. Empty.

Johnny looked up at the sky. No stars tonight. It was raining a little. A movement outside the house caught his eye, but somehow he didn't want to look because he knew this was it.

Johnny had to look. Yes, someone stood on the path. Not Tobes; a woman. Not an ordinary woman; she was wearing a Red Riding Hood kind of cloak that covered her face.

She was beckoning with her right hand. Beckoning him.

Johnny waved, hoping to see her face. Tobes had said he'd show Johnny the ghost of Alice Mornay, hadn't he? This wasn't a ghost, this was Tobes wearing a cloak. So let's see your face, Mrs Ghost!

Tobes wouldn't wait for ever. Johnny slipped downstairs, silent as a shade. Mike Anderson and the WW were fighting; their voices echoed in the hallway as he passed. WW didn't like this rented house, she wanted a place of her own. It was too big, too inconvenient, too near the cemetery. She was concerned about the effect it was having on the boy: hah!

As Johnny flitted down the passage to the kitchen he heard Mike announce that he *did* like the house. Furthermore, it was time Johnny grew up.

Going into the darkness somehow didn't bother him any more.

He opened the kitchen door. A big patch of black separated him from the neighbours' light. He stepped forward into it, to boldly go, etc etc. He reached the gate. And . . . *no show!*

Johnny turned his head all ways; still nothing. The rain was really beefing up now. He went out onto the path. A gust of wind shivered the branches above his head, sending drips showering down inside his collar.

Hey, (he thought), I'm going back inside. This is ridiculous. This is how kids end up murdered, with their eyes gouged out, lying on trash-heaps with their hearts by their sides . . .

Johnny turned through a half-circle, because that was the way he'd get back to the gate. And as his eyes swung around they connected with a tiny, moving light, down the hill, where the graves began. Say twenty feet away.

A candle. How did a candle stay alight in wind and rain? Maybe it wasn't a real candle. So what was it?

The flame rose slowly. A face swam into view. White, white, UGH UGH UGH . . .

Johnny could not think of that face, even in next day's sunlight, without heaving. It was snow-white, and for eyes it had two black holes and the mouth the same. Yet it was human. Not a skull. A face.

Johnny wanted to scream. He wanted to run. But then a hand came out of the darkness beside the candle, and beckoned him. And suddenly the shock wore off and he felt better. Because this was Tobes and the whole thing just might be fun. Play along. He isn't going to hurt you.

Johnny approached, slowly, giggles fizzing inside his tummy. It was not Tobes. It *was*. Another couple of steps and he'd know. One more step.

The figure slowly, silently turned away from him and set off down the path. For a moment the candle was hidden; then that grisly white hand extended to one side, again sharing its feeble light with the boy.

They'd reached the turn-off, the tangled path leading down into the depths of the cemetery, and that was where Tobes meant to go, Johnny felt sure. The figure was moving faster now; the boy had dropped behind. So he ran to catch up, calling, 'Tobes.' His mouth was dry, the word didn't come out the way it should. He swallowed and tried again. But the figure moved faster. They were flying along now. The ghost floated, it had no feet, it made no sound.

A twig scratched Johnny's face. 'Tobes,' he cried. 'Come on, stop this. It's great, man, but I want to see you.' Another twig got him across the eye; that hurt. Johnny saw what he thought was the ghost, moving up ahead.

Then a voice spoke beside him, up close. He turned straight into that horrible white face, the two black holes moved towards him, he saw a line of blood dripping from the empty mouth, no, not blood, a worm . . .

The candle went out.

Johnny screamed.

Johnny ran.

He could have won any race you cared to name. He didn't look back. He slammed into the kitchen, not caring how much noise he made. There was a little light from the hallway. He sat at the kitchen table with his head in his hands, whimpering. Not crying. Not making much noise at all.

The voices in the living-room continued their argument. It was about money now. Suddenly there was silence. Nicole said, 'What's that noise? Somebody crying? Johnny . . .'

Footsteps. He stood up, but there was nowhere to go. Trapped. The WW came into the kitchen, switching on the light.

Funny, but it seemed almost as if she was his real mother, then. She helped him upstairs. Made him a hot malt, with a cookie. She stood by the bunk, holding his hand, for a long time. She said a lot of things to him, though later he couldn't remember a darned one, just that they'd been sweet.

Mike Anderson was at the door, hands in pockets. Seemed kind of bored. ''Night, Johnny,' he said, when Nicole finally let go the boy's hand and switched off the light. He didn't come in.

'I'll leave the landing light on,' Nicole said from the doorway.

'Nicole.'

'Yes.' She came back quickly. 'What is it, Johnny?'

'I guess I was crazy. Going out like that.'

She looked over her shoulder, to check that Mike wasn't still watching. 'Ssh,' she said, raising a finger to her lips, and then he understood that she'd not told Mike he'd gone out.

Johnny squeezed her hand.

'I told him you'd had a bad dream,' she whispered. 'He thinks you went sleep-walking in the garden. Don't let me down.'

Johnny nodded. 'You won't tell him I went out?'

'Not if you promise not to go again.'

'Promise.'

'There've been two murders near here recently. What you did was . . .'

'Mad.'

Nicole hesitated, then nodded. 'Totally. What made you – '

'I saw a ghost. Out the window. There's no such things as ghosts. Are there?'

Johnny saw he'd shocked Nicole, *really* shocked her.

'Definitely not,' she said, after a pause. 'You must have been dreaming.'

'Must have been. 'Night.'

Johnny rolled over and closed his eyes. He lay there, trying not to think about that white, white face, but he dreamed about it anyway. Just as Tobes had known he would.

Time to let Dr Cheung in on some of this.

*   *   *

CASE-NOTES: *Johnny Anderson, July 8*.

Wechsler Intelligence Scale for Children shows him scoring highly on performance abilities, even higher on verbal skills, unusually potent combination. Reinforces impression of child advanced for his age.

In our fifth session we achieved a minor breakthrough, query more than one?

The boy showed me extracts from his diary, then launched into a vivid description of how he'd gone into the cemetery the night before. He accepted this was wrong. It had caused his parents unnecessary worry and had exposed him to danger. He was alert to the implications.

When I asked him why he'd gone out, he replied, 'I thought I saw a ghost.' Before I could react, he asserted that there were no such things as ghosts, and he must have had a bad dream.

He thinks this episode has brought him closer to the Wicked Witch. She had her good parts, he said. Father still not showing much interest.

I ventured an interpretation of his use of his father's name(s), first and sur-. Was it because J blamed MA for first wife's death and wanted to distance himself from the negative affect this inspired? I gave him some insight into the transference process, which he seemed well able to digest. J claims to worship his father; picked up on overtones of 'worship': God, infallibility, fear. Boy accepted some of this, said he liked to think of father as Mike, made him seem more equal, less of a gap between them. (Less of a threat??)

Generally, not nearly so much talk of him feeling 'out of the real world', of 'not existing'; his in-session drawings no longer suggest a need to be held, embraced, put in context, etc; he was presenting with greater self-esteem.

Made him promise to stay well away from cemetery unless with grown-up. He said, 'Like Tobes?' 'Parent, better. T has a gardening job, you shouldn't distract him. Not fair if he falls down on job and that's due to you.' 'I like Tobes.' 'Good.' (Developing relationship with adult shows he's ready to transit beyond receipt of immediate rewards to permanent bonding; *very* important step along road to individuation.)

At conclusion he threw his arms around me. Quite spontaneous. Both v. moved. Query leave Tobes in the Anderson household, safe . . . ??? (NB: Re-read decision in Tarasoff v. Cal. Univ. Regents. Consult American Psych. Association??)

*　　　*　　　*

I mean, shit, who does he think I am? I rent the fucking dress, I make up my face, I put on a play of which Shakespeare might have been proud. Does the audience clap? Is the Pope a Jew?

Day after my Oscar-winning performance, he comes out on the step after school, carrying the lemonade pitcher and two glasses. I ignore him. He pours drinks and carries one glass over to me.

'Here you are, Mrs Ghost.'

I carry on scything, don't speak.

'Aw, come on, Mrs Ghost, I know you'll like this lemonade. The Wicked Witch made it with finest quality cyanide.'

I want to grin but check myself: no time to display weakness in the face of the enemy.

'She minced up some centipedes and slipped them in, I saw her do it myself. Honest!'

My methodical sweeping-action continues unabated. 'Please!'

I'm tempted to melt, just for an instant. Then my anger resurfaces and I deliberately turn my body so that he can see even less of my face.

You know what the little runt does? He grabs the waistband of my jeans, pulls it back and tips half a glass of lemonade down my ass!

I drop the scythe and rocket upwards. For a second I plan to grab and maul, but he's grinning at me and I can't make a dent in him hard enough to destroy that grin without going over the top. A funny sensation ripples through me – what? *Laughter*, that's what.

I reach out as if to grab his shoulder, knock him gently on the ear instead.

'You want some lemonade?' he asks chirpily.

'Yeah, but in the hole that was designed for it this time.'

'Yuk, you do talk bad. Go wash out your mouth.'

The thought of sitting down is unattractive to me. I lean against the terrace-wall and sip my drink. Nicole makes a mean glass of lemonade, you can say that for her.

'Alice tells me you didn't show,' I say. 'She's sulking.'

'Tough.' He, too, takes a drink. Then he says, 'Tobes . . . it was you, wasn't it?'

This is a cry for reassurance, comfort, release from fear. A great voice, I love it.

'I don't know what you're talking about.'

'Last night. In the cemetery. With the candle.'

'Last night I was up at Harley's place with my girl-friend.'

'Aw, come on . . .'

'Aw, come on,' I mimic. 'Baby doesn't *like* me, baby doesn't *like* me.'

'You're mean.'

'I am that. Tell you what, though: you can come to Harley's too, when you're older. If you're brave enough, that is.'

Johnny turns away in a sudden, violent movement and stares at the ground. 'I'm not going anyplace with you,' he mutters.

'Why? Scared you'll meet a *ghost*?'

'*No!*'

'Why, then?'

'I'm just not. That's all. Anyway, it's all going to be built over soon.'

For a second there I think he's kidding. Then I don't think he's kidding. I think this is very, very serious.

'What did you say about building?'

'My dad's company's going to build houses on the cemetery.'

My mind races back to the day I rescued him from Arnie. Those men in the cemetery, with tape-measures and plans . . . why didn't I twig then? I stare at him. I really feel I *am* a ghost for a moment there. 'No,' I say. 'Not possible.'

'It's gonna happen, I tell you.'

'They can't do that. They can't.'

He looks at me like I am stupid. I feel stupid. *This cannot be happening yet is.*

'Why does it matter?'

Good question. 'It's . . . it's my place. My one good place. Where will I go, where can I . . .'

Why should Johnny care?

'I'm going to stop it,' I say. 'Alice Mornay won't like it. She's going to see the others aren't disturbed.'

'You can't stop it. Nobody can.'

'The people I'm thinking of don't have *bodies*.'

'Come on, there are no ghosts.'

'Which is why you won't come in the cemetery.' I finish my drink and put the glass down on the step. This boy needs controlling. He's not mine, not yet. He will be, though. 'You're a wimp,' I tell him. 'You're no fun. I knew you weren't the moment I set eyes on you.'

'I'm not a wimp!'

'You're chicken.'

'Am not.'

'Are so.'

He scowls at me, his face an ugly mixture of red and pale. His skin is thin, my barbs penetrate like grenade-harpoons puncturing a beautiful young dolphin.

'It's irresponsible to go into the cemetery, especially at night. Dr Cheung explained it to me today. I told her what happened last night.'

So-*ho*. Dr Diane, Dr Diane, what's a boy going to do with you?

'Do you believe everything she says?'

''Course not.'

An alarm bell is ringing inside my head. 'Did you tell her you thought it was me, in the cemetery?' He shakes his head. But the bell refuses to still. 'She'll have me fired if you do.'

'She wouldn't do that. She's nice.'

'She's worried about you. Tell her lies about me, she'll have my ass out of here quicker than . . . '

I am about to say, 'Soft shit.' Johnny looks at me, waiting. My mind is blank. My head aches more than somewhat. The day is hot, and sultry. What was I saying . . . ?

'Don't worry, I won't tell her a thing,' Johnny says. 'You're cuckoo, anyway; she knows that.'

'I'm what?'

'Cuckoo.' He holds a finger just short of his forehead and makes little circles with it. 'Nuts.'

It crosses my mind that his legs are so thin I could cut through them with a single slice of the scythe: the force would sweep him sideways, the upper part of him that is, for there would be two Johnnies then; the blade would sweep him sideways, off his stumps, and he'd fall back to earth before keeling over on his side and bleeding to death . . .

'Got work to do,' I mumble. 'Take a hike, will you?'

Later that night, something drives me out to a phone booth. It's gone two. I dial Dr Diane's home, endlessly, over and over; each time she picks up, I cut off. Five, six times. After that I get the busy signal. But by then it has started to be fun. I dial at random. Maybe an hour I spend in that booth, dialling, dialling. A lot of people get rid of a lot of rage. They vent it over the line at me. Only I'm silent, see? I don't vent a thing.

*   *   *

Diane lay in a deep sleep. She heard the phone ring, and knew it was her mother calling to tell her *Ba-ba* was dead. Then she jerked awake and picked it up. No answer. She said, 'Hello, who is this?' Silence. No clicks, just silence. The line was open, somebody was there, only they didn't want to talk to her. She dropped the phone back on its hook.

The phone rang. Again, silence. This time she said, 'Who is this, do you know what time it is?' No answer.

She left the phone off the hook while she went to the bathroom. When she came back, there was a little grey light filtering through the curtains, so she watched the ocean for a while, mentally planning a flower bed or two, for the lower terrace. Climbing back into bed, a thought occurred to her: she should call Ed. No, selfish – he needed sleep, too. But the idea, once implanted, wouldn't go away.

Diane dialled. He answered quickly. 'Hello?'

'Ed? It's me.'

'Diane . . . what . . . hey, is something wrong?'

It occurred to her that maybe this wasn't such a good idea. What if Ed had someone there . . . ?

'I'm sorry,' she said. 'I got a phantom caller.'

'A what?'

'Someone phoned me half a dozen times, wouldn't answer when I spoke. Made me feel spooked, that's all. And I thought, well, I . . .'

'I'm glad you called. Thank you.'

The sleepiness was back in his voice after that momentary urgency, but it was a nice-sounding sleepiness. She lay back against the pillows. 'So how are things?'

'Not so bad. You?'

'Getting by.'

'No more than that?'

'Uh-uh. Busy days.'

'And the nights?'

'So-so.'

'Mine, too.'

'You're not dating?'

'No.' A pause. 'You?'

'Yeah, I'm dating. Nice guy.'

A long silence tremored on the line.

'Well,' said Edwin, 'that's good.'

'You know him, actually.'

'I do?' *Son-of-a-bitch*, she heard beneath the silent tremor.

'Yes.' She made him wait a while longer. 'You see him every day.'

'You mean he's a *cop*?'

'Detective.'

'In my precinct?'

'In your shaving-mirror.'

Her giggle was not infectious. Edwin took a while making up his mind to laugh. 'Diane,' he said at last, 'you're a tease. Know that?'

'What kind of a tease?'

'It begins with C.'

'I had this feeling it might.'

'You did?'

'This strange feeling . . .'

A long pause . . .

'Where are you feeling it? I mean, right now . . . ?'

'Oh . . . ' Her hand was not entirely within her control. Her hand was astray upon the land. 'Here . . . and here . . . and . . .'

'Need help nailing it down? I could come over.'

And now the silence reverberated from Diane's end of the phone-line. Her hand was back where it ought to be, her mind with it. 'No,' she said quickly, 'I have to get up early tomorrow . . . today.'

'Are you sure?'

'Sure. But . . .'

'Yes?'

'Soon. Very soon.' She made a kissing noise. 'Goodnight, Ed. Thank you.'

He said something as Diane replaced the phone on its rest, but she couldn't make out the words. Didn't matter; they were kind.

*　　　*　　　*

As soon as I set eyes on it I know this is right.

'That uniform,' I say to Maxine; 'it's new.'

'I went to an auction in LA last week. Some of the studios were having a big sell-off, that's where I get a lot of my stuff.'

World War II infantry officer's uniform, captain's rank, side-holster, belt, ammunition-pouches, webbing and cap. This is so me!

'Or you can have a helmet,' Maxine puts in. 'It came with both.'

The helmet is rusty and covered with camouflage net; it's boring. I try on the cap. Perfect fit.

'I'll swap,' I tell Maxine, taking the Alice Mornay dress out of my saddle-bag.

'You want the uniform?'

'I have to have the uniform.'

She gazes at me through those cow-like eyes of hers. She says, 'You're so cute. Know that?'

'Mm-hm.'

'Gimme a kiss.'

'Harley would be jealous.'

'Oh, Harley . . . What do you want with an army uniform?'

'Amateur theatricals.'

'Can I come see?'

'No.'

'Why not?'

When I don't answer, she crosses both hands on my shoulder and kisses me on the neck. I push her away, but without rancour. Maxine's okay, she's just not my type, that's all.

'You know I used to be an actress,' she says coyly. 'I could maybe help improve your technique.' She gives my shoulder a squeeze. One of her hands descends

243

towards my waist. I disengage and unhook the uniform. 'Better try it on,' I tell her.

In the fitting-room I ask myself what to do about Maxine. She used to be an actress, sure, like I used to be an electrician: in the story books. I'm going nowhere with this woman, but I like her and she's useful. As I admire myself, left side, right side, front and back, I have to admit she's useful.

I'm tempted to wear the uniform out of the shop, but it might get soiled. So instead I change back into my own threads and tell Maxine to invoice me. She wants me to go for a hot dog with her, but I'm already late for Dr Diane.

*   *   *

Diane surprised Julia by calling the group to order, saying, 'I have something to say; please listen carefully.'

Ramon, Jesse, Billy-the-Kid and Tobes, scattered around the playroom, displayed varying degrees of attentiveness.

'There's going to be some hassle,' Diane started off, 'with the police.'

'Already hassling me,' Ramon said. 'About the murders, no?'

'Yes. Have any more of you received a visit from the cops yet?'

They shook their heads. Diane turned to Ramon. 'Please tell us about it.'

He was more than ready to blow off steam. While he talked about how the pigs had come in and turned over his room, and upset his mom, and planted grass behind his bed (Diane's heart sank), she glanced occasionally from face to face to see how they were taking this.

(Badly.) Funny, she thought, funny how each of them boasts at least one characteristic of the serial killer.

Ramon, the speaker, had suffered a blow to the head when he was small. He was unconscious for days, and it took him months to recover fully. A statistically remarkable number of serial murderers could say the same.

Jesse liked to inhabit fantasy-land. He never grew up into the real world. Plus he'd tried to rape his sister – maybe. He was capable of violence. His family was a total mess. Of these four, he had most points against him.

Billy-the-Kid had suffered physical cruelty at the hands of first his father, then his stepfather, then a succession of his mother's live-in boyfriends. Something about Billy attracted the aggressor in older men. He'd been beaten, bruised and burned.

Tobes, too, used to suffer at the hands of his drunken father. He'd grown up in extreme poverty, sometimes unsure of where the next meal was coming from. He claimed to have been bullied at school, though his records were still missing and Diane sensed a mystery about that.

All of them were in the frame.

When Ramon had finished speaking Diane said, 'I'm sorry the police gave you so much trouble, but they've got a difficult job to do.'

'Which is why they planted grass, right?'

'Ramon, I don't believe for one minute they planted grass on you. Face reality: a lot of people smoke, some get caught, it's not the worst thing that can happen. It's a set-back, but it's not murder, okay?'

He half smiled. 'Guess I will live.'

'Guess you will too. Now, guys, hear me. You remember what Ramon just said – the police asked him if he'd got any of my name-cards.'

They nodded.

'There's a reason for that. I know what it is, but can't tell you. Trust me when I say they need to know about those cards.'

There was silence.

'Why does it have to be one of us?' Tobes asked indignantly. 'Why does it always have to be us?'

There came a loud murmur of assent.

'You know why,' Diane told them. 'Cops like to make life easy for themselves. You have records, and you're in weekly touch with me. So let's not pretend ignorance, okay?'

After a pause they nodded again.

'Now, is there anything you'd like to tell me?'

In the silence that followed there was a lot of eye-contact between the four young men. Who would break first, Diane wondered?

Ramon raised his hand.

'Yes?' Diane said.

'You remember the naked broad?'

'What naked broad?'

'That day the woman streaked towards the cliff.' He cupped his hands around imaginary breasts and jerked them up and down. 'B'boom, b'boom; remember?'

'What about it?'

Ramon explained how they'd been planning a raid on her purse and the 'naked broad' was the perfect excuse, except that Diane had turned around early, so Ramon got stuck with the cards, which he'd then divvied up among the rest. Her face remained cast in stone, but she longed to laugh out loud with relief. Another mystery solved.

But all of them had taken her name-cards. 'I'd like them back,' Diane said.

'I threw mine away,' Jesse said. 'When I heard how the cops got to Ramon.'

'Where did you throw them?'

'On the beach, up Point Sal way.'

Point Sal was where Harley had his diner. Did Jesse know Harley? Who might have picked up that card . . . ?

'Jesse, when the police talk to you, tell them the truth, exactly as you've told me. Yes?'

'Yes.'

'The rest of you, I want those cards returned. Ramon, you sit tight: no need to contact the police again. But if they ask you any more about the cards, just tell them the truth, please, and explain that you were scared before. Refer them to me if they're suspicious.'

Ramon shrugged, without looking at her.

'I won't disclose what's gone on here today, *unless* . . . I have to in order to take the heat off you.' Diane paused for emphasis. 'Remember: if the police find out about your taking my cards, it won't be from me unless that's the *only* way of helping you. Now have you got that?'

Tobes said, 'I believe you.' No one else spoke.

'All right,' she said. 'Billy, starting with you, tell us one thing you've achieved these past seven days . . . '

*   *   *

I didn't mean to take Dr Diane's life. It wasn't serious, you see. Just a jape that went wrong.

Let me tell you about it from the start.

We, that is the four of us, had a groupie with Dr Diane and Julia Page. Dr Diane led off about the name-cards. Well, I guess we all of us knew she'd latch on one day. Ramon surprised the shit out of me: he came clean. We didn't let him down. Funny, we are all four kind of friends now. So there was Dr Diane, knowing about the name-cards.

She wouldn't tell us what had happened to make those cards so vital. Something had, though. Something very bad, evil and awful. She asked us to trust her, and we said yes. I said yes. I believed her. Still do.

Actually I knew why those cards were important. None of the others did, but *I* knew.

Then it was my turn for a private hour alone with her. It would have turned out differently if she hadn't let me down over timing.

Now, first thing Dr Diane tells a patient is, 'Be on time for me and I will be on time for you.' Lateness isn't just an issue, it's a killer. You have a meeting with her, you're there one minute before, because that's the way it has to be. That's how trust grows. A girl stands you up, your mom promises to fetch you from school and doesn't, one December 25 the chimney stays Santa-less; but Dr Diane starts on time, according to her word.

Except that today she didn't.

We come out of the playroom and I hang back as Julia Page shepherds the other three guys down the passage. Dr Diane's office is next door. I wait while she unlocks, then go inside. She strides around her desk and starts opening drawers while I settle on the couch, for we are into hypnosis now, and I am keen on that, I want to start. So Dr Diane is about to finish whatever she's doing on the desk when there's this ever so light tap on the door, which opens to reveal an apologetic-looking *hombre* with a weedy moustache. He's smiling, and Dr Diane's smiling too, and she stands up, and she says, 'Why, Mr Krozgrow, Daniel . . .'

'I know this is a bad moment.'

'I was about to start with a patient . . .'

'Five minutes.' And the guy turns to me and he says, 'I apologize for intruding on what I know is your time, and I wouldn't do it if it weren't urgent, but I'd like your permission to talk with Dr Cheung for a few moments.'

And I say, Yes, meaning No, shithead, fuck off. But he's not into nuance, this guy, so Dr Diane looks at me and says, 'Perhaps if you were to wait outside,' and the guy says, 'No, it won't take a moment, we can talk in the corridor,' and so Dr Diane gets up and goes out with him, not quite closing the door behind her.

I am alone in her sanctum, surrounded by her womanly secrets. She is outside, talking in a low voice, her hand still on the outer door-handle. Then she lets go the handle, but the door remains ajar. For a few seconds the murmur of voices continues; then it fades and that means they're walking along the passage, away from me.

And I think, so this is Ali Baba's cave. Oh, boy. I mean, what would you have done? Oh, *come on*, for Christ's sake . . .

One drawer is half open. I peer inside to see a dozen lipsticks: gold, silver, black, cheap plastic, pricey platinum. So I pocket the plastic lipstick, 'cause she's never going to miss one, and I could use it.

Still no sign of a return. I flit across to the door to check. They've gone.

What else is there to do?

In another drawer I find an envelope. It's brown, approximately twice as long as it's wide, unsealed. Its back is bare. On the front, 'Diane.' Only that, no surname, nothing else. I dither, but there's still no word from the twilight zone outside, so I don't dither long.

The envelope contains a used airline ticket, LAX-SAN-LAX (Los Angeles–San Diego round trip), dated a few weeks back, name of passenger, D. Cheung. Also, a receipted hotel bill. And a handwritten note, which reads as follows:

> Diane . . .
>> Can't thank you enough! Had a wow time and the hangover proves it!!
>> Owe you one, more, many . . .
>> Love,
>> Julia

Now (I hear you say), does this guy Tobias Gascoign have a good memory for remembering the exact terms of other people's letters, or does he not? And the answer is . . . not. For you see, I have that note before me as I transcribe its contents into my notebook. Which came about as follows: just as I'm trying to decipher the fifth word I hear a quick pit-pat of footsteps in the passage, a hand's rattling the door, and . . . and, well, I am on the couch, Dr Diane is in the office, ticket and hotel reservation are back in the envelope, and Julia's note is in my hip-pocket, where it feels about as comfortable and reassuring as the acid that pierces through seven steel floors in *Alien*.

My heart's making enough noise to wake the whole of Court Ridge Cemetery, my cheeks are flushed, I'm sweating. I close my eyes and heave deep breaths. Dr Diane bangs around her desk, slamming drawers, shuffling pens and generally acting het up. That *hombre* Krozgrow sure put a hex on her.

'So,' Dr Diane says, all brittle. 'How's the art coming along, Tobes?'

'Okay.'

'Anything you want to show me?'

'It's not ready yet.'

She comes to sit beside my head, facing backwards, i.e. away from my feet. I don't like her doing that. She's intimately close, but I can't look into her eyes.

'Is that your way of saying you think I'd be shocked?'

'Maybe.'

An intermezzo here: the good Doctor has suggested I draw dirty pictures. Well, not quite like that. She says I ought to float all that scummy stuff to the top of my subconscious, where it can evaporate into clean air. She wants me to write/draw hard porn, is what it comes down to; she intends to examine it for insights into what's preventing me from linking into society as agoodandusefulmember thereof. I enjoy drawing dirty, but no way am I going to let her see product, right?

'I wouldn't be shocked,' she goes on.

'I'm sure.' My voice trembles, I'm still nervous. Fortunately, the subject-matter of our conversation would naturally make anyone nervous. Dr Diane passes on.

'Done any acting recently?'

'No.'

'Well, you should, you know? There's an amateur dramatics club meets once a week in Orcutt, I know the club secretary. Interested?'

I hesitate. 'Could be.'

Dr Diane makes a note. 'You once mentioned how much you enjoyed dressing up when you were a child. I'd encourage that.'

This is weird. What with my captain's uniform hanging on the rail and so on . . . 'You would?'

'Certainly. As a form of escape it's hard to beat, and it's harmless.'

She makes another note. I do not comment. Then she goes on, 'Do you find the trances beneficial?'

'I do.' Sincerely. They're wonderful. Drug-induced ecstasy, without the drug. And *you*, Mr Taxpayer, are funding this!

'Okay. Let's try another.'

She begins her spiel: I feel my eyelids growing heavy, when they are too heavy to open my finger will automatically lift, etcetcetc. My finger duly lifts. I am slipping away. She is counting down in a lilting, hypnotic (literally!) voice. My breathing slows and steadies. I am at peace.

I am not, however, asleep. That would ruin the whole point, which is to extract material buried deep in my subconscious. I'm halfway between sleep and wakefulness, oddly alert. But today is strange. Because the session was interrupted at the beginning, because Krozgrow robbed me of A-time, because I'm feeling guilty about having rummaged Dr Diane's things, the trance doesn't take. Not completely. I float about aimlessly, and the more I try to focus the harder it gets.

She is wooing me to talk about a specific incident in childhood. I was thrown out of high school. It's more complicated than that. I had to leave, but . . .

Okay, sure, this is stuff Dr Diane really has to know about. But I've buried it deep. It's disturbing; whenever we circle around this territory my body twitches, my eyes roll, sometimes my hands jump right off the couch. We both know it's holy ground. We can't break through. I *want* to, and I don't want to.

I was thrown out of high school, and deep down I knew why, and I'm damned if . . .

'There was this boy you hated,' says Dr Diane, 'and you hated him . . . you played a trick on him . . . the trick went wrong. The trick misfired . . .'

'Fire.' My hands throw themselves around like they belong to an epileptic.

I don't know why I said 'fire'. Echoing her? Maybe it's too important, too close: I start to disengage from the trance. My eyelids open a tad. She doesn't notice, of course, on account of the way she's sitting. And the weirdness that has overshadowed this session from the beginning screws my head tighter; for opposite me hangs a mirror, so placed that Dr Diane's computer screen is reflected in it.

The screen shows capital white letters on a dark blue background: very high resolution. My vision's twenty-twenty. Some force begins to draw me away from the session, into the mirror, into the screen. I am aware of Dr Diane's voice asking questions, and of my own trying to answer them. Fire, fire, an important, vital fire . . .

One by one I take those white caps on dark blue and turn them around . . . only it isn't a conscious process like I've described it, there's something eerie about it, a magic transformation of secret writing without the interposition of a translator. Minutes pass, I don't know how many. What I end up with is this . . .

1. * RAY ARTHUR DOUGGAN. 20. ORCUTT HIGH. APRIL 25. FOLIO 19.

2. * CARL JENSEN. 19. NORTH ABBEY SCHOOL. JULY 4. FOLIO 25.

3. RANDY DELMAR. 19. PARADISE BAY WASHINGTON STREET HIGH. [N/A] FOLIO 26.

4. HAROLD ANDREW LAWSON. 18. P.B. NORTH STATE HIGH. [N/A] FOLIO 26B.

5. TOBES GASCOIGN. 20. ARCADE HS#3. [N/A] FOLIO 21.

CHIPP RECORDS ARE PASSWORD-PROTECTED – PASSWORD? . . .

I have been silent for a long time. I hear Dr Diane's pencil scratch on her pad. Then she says, 'When did you first come across Alice Mornay?'

She has questioned me about the clearing many times since I first let slip its existence. When under hypnosis you retain a degree of control, but that degree varies during the session.

'Late last year.'

'By accident?'

'Yes.'

'Does anybody else know about it?'

I am about to say, 'Johnny knows,' when I remember where I am and murmur, 'No.'

'You feel safe there, don't you?'

'Very.'

'There, you become a different person?'

'I . . . guess.'

'No one can reach you there.'

'No one.'

'Not even me.'

Those words are spoken so softly that I'm not sure if I'm supposed to hear. But I reply anyway: 'Not even you.'

'And how is Alice?'

'She's fine.'

'Still your friend?'

'Friend.'

A pause. Then – 'Have you talked with Johnny Anderson about Alice?'

'No.'

There's a longer pause, suggesting she doesn't believe me. I'm pretty sure Johnny's spilled the beans about me being Alice Mornay, but I lie anyway. Then she goes on, 'I don't think that would be a good idea, do you?'

'No.' But my heart seethes with rage. *How dare this woman interfere? Is she so jealous that she must have every morsel to herself?*

'Okay, Tobes, I want you now to start floating gently up to the surface of this beautiful placid lake, it's getting lighter now, the sun is warm up there, you are rising, rising, floating quietly upward through the tranquil water . . .'

I open my eyes fully. She's already over by the computer, tapping away. By the time I'm on my feet and around her side of the desk, she's cleared the screen I read earlier and is calling up my notes.

'Shoo,' she says with a smile. 'These are *my* secrets.'

I laugh and make for the door. 'So,' I say. 'Same time next week?'

'Same time. Tobes, wait a moment . . .'

She rises and approaches across the carpet, her face serious.

'We can't go on with this for ever,' she says. 'You have to break with therapy soon. Frankness coming down the pipe, okay? Your response has been poor. You won't give . . .'

Well, I can't remember her exact words, but the essence was thus: she accuses me of concealing my past, sometimes deliberately; without access to more of my memory-bank, she can't help. That will mean throwing me back where I came from, letting the lawyers have me. She wants to see my writings and drawings, disgusting though they may be. She wants to hear about my school-days in greater detail. She allocates me one more month, another four weekly sessions, to shape up. Unless she can see signs of real progress by then . . .

She punctuates her last sentence with a shrug and turns away.

That's when it happens.

I draw the gun, a Colt-Browning pistol. I point it at her back. The hammer rises slowly, oh so slowly. I don't mean to do any of this. *But I am angry.*

She is going to abandon me.

She means to take The One away from me.

She is too evil to live.

She reaches the desk. She stops, keeping her back to me, and drums the fingers of her left hand on the desktop.

The hammer falls on an empty chamber.

Distracted by the unusual noise, Dr Diane raises her head. She is looking directly into the mirror that caught my attention whilst in a trance.

But by that time my hand is back in the pocket of my windbreaker. By that time, I have regained my self-control.

I didn't mean to take Dr Diane's life. I would never do a thing like that.

Never.

*   *   *

Now this really is a new page. I am starting to do things with the Wicked Witch, and the first thing I am doing is to quit calling her that. I shall call her Nicole. She's not totally un-nice.

Today, we went on a trip with the neighbour. We have two neighbours, Diane, one on the right, the other you-guessed-it. The you-guessed-its are called Keeton.

Conversation as follows (in back yard) . . .

Nicole smiled. 'You know, Jeannette, I hope you won't mind me asking, but I was wondering if you were by any chance related to Diane Keeton?'

Johnny put in, 'Or Michael? Are you Batman's sister?'

'They're both Keaton with an "a", sweetie,' Jeannette said.

Mrs Keeton was the same age as Nicole, but she cared less about appearances: torn jeans, faded blue shirts that had come out of the wash all funny, hair like a string-knot puzzle, these were her trademarks. She let her kids do whatever they liked, but the funny thing was they both were A-grade students. Johnny thought Marcie okay, for a girl. Tom might become a friend, if Johnny let him.

It was Thursday, after school. Tobes hadn't shown up today. Maybe it wasn't one of his days. Anyway, Jeannette Keeton said, 'You guys want to come for a walk? I'm taking the kids down to the meeting.'

Nicole asked, 'What meeting?'

'The protest about the building plans, you know – the development in the cemetery.'

Now the idea of a walk with Nicole this time last week would have been death with extras, as far as Johnny was concerned, but that was before Tobes had scared the socks off him and Nicole had comforted him, and today he didn't mind. Besides, he really liked Jeannette Keeton, who used to invite him over for ice-cream, so when Nicole said, 'Um . . . I don't know,' he felt disappointed.

'Come on,' he said, tugging her.

'I'm not sure you ought to go in the cemetery,' she said, giving Johnny a funny look. But he was feeling brave, and anyway, what could happen in daylight with two women plus Marcie and Tom?

'Well,' Nicole said, kind of slow; then she smiled at Jeannette, but shyly, and went on, 'It's a little difficult for me, what with Mike . . . you know?'

'But maybe if Mike knew the strength of local feeling . . . ?'

'Mmmmm. Okay. We'll come.'

So they all set off down the path. Marcie had long brown hair that had recently been plaited. Johnny twisted the plaits together in his hand. 'Ow!' she cried. 'Don't do that!' She punched him. Johnny hit back, natch, but gently, because she was a girl and *he* was a little gentleman.

'How're you doing at school?' he asked her. She was a bit younger than him, a fourth-grader.

'Okay. I *hate* math. Tom likes it.'

Tom was following a few steps behind, his nose in a book. Tom's nose was always in a book. He didn't speak much.

Johnny's heart beat fast as they approached the side-path. He talked busily with Marcie to cover his fear. His head stayed turned to her until the side-path was safely behind, and when he finally stopped talking he found they were in a part of the cemetery he'd never visited before. The big track went on down, down, down, then it started to rise again until it became a sort of avenue: wide, with trees still on both sides, but no houses any more, and proper gravestones, in rows, with crosses and scrolls and brass plaques. Johnny could see a road ahead of them, and cars parked in rows. There were lots of people milling around, and a few guys with placards, and a bullhorn. Marcie took his hand. They ran.

There must have been hundreds and hundreds of people here, Johnny thought, though later Nicole told Mike Anderson there were only about sixty, but then that was her for you. A man stood in a pick-up with the bullhorn, speechifying. The people shouted and hollered and cheered.

'Look, Marcie,' Johnny said, 'hard hats!'

There were men working to one side of the roadway, in among the graves. They had this long, upright pole and a tape-measure and something on a tripod that looked like a camera.

Tom said, 'That's a theodolite.'

'A troglodyte,' Johnny yelled to Marcie. 'Tom thinks it's a dinosaur!'

'You're infantile,' Tom said, which was good from him, as he was only twelve. Johnny chased him, but Tom could run a whole heap faster.

Nicole and Jeannette finally caught up. They stood there, listening to the guy on the truck. Johnny got tired of chasing Tom, so he went back to Nicole and said, 'What's this all about?'

'There are plans to build houses here. Won't that be nice?'

'Houses? Oh, yeah: Dad's company, I know.' Johnny looked around. 'But . . . this is a graveyard. People can't *live* here. Funny, I never thought about that.'

'The ground can be what's called deconsecrated. You dig up the bodies, and bury them somewhere else. Then you can build houses.'

Johnny remembered how sad Tobes had been when he'd learned they were going to build on the cemetery. He tried to pay attention to what the man was saying, but the words went over his head in more ways than one. There was a lot of clapping.

'Doesn't the man want the houses?' Johnny blurted.

'No,' Nicole replied. 'This is a protest. None of these people want the houses. The cemetery's a sacred place, some of them have kin buried here.'

'It's a dump,' Tom volunteered. 'There are some terrible people in this cemetery, at night.'

259

'How would *you* know?' Johnny flared. But before Tom could answer, '*Look!*' Marcie cried. 'A TV camera. Let's go see!'

They ran over to where some men were setting up a camera, and a big, long microphone. Lots of other kids crowded around, but Johnny stood at the back. This was becoming creepy. A whole lot of stuff was going down, and he couldn't piece it together. Tobes had said he felt this was his place, his 'home' . . .

The sun was going down, the air grew cool. People started to drift away even before the speeches were done. At last Nicole said, 'Let's go home, I have to make dinner.'

They wandered back up the path that led to Court Ridge. Johnny still felt troubled. Nicole maybe saw that, for she took his hand and said, 'What's wrong?'

'I'm worried for all the dead people,' Johnny said, after a pause. No point in dragging Tobes into this.

Nicole thought a bit. Then she said, 'They're dead, Johnny. They don't care what happens to their bodies any more.'

'What about the ghosts, then?'

Whoops. Too late now. Whoooooooooppppps!!!

'Johnny, there are no ghosts; you know that.'

'I guess not. Only . . .'

'Only what?' There was a snap in her voice.

'If there were ghosts . . . there'd be a guardian, wouldn't there? And he'd have to take care of them . . . he'd have to stop the building, right?'

Nicole didn't say anything for a long time. At last she spoke. 'There are no such things as ghosts, Johnny. Therefore, there can't be a guardian ghost.'

'But I've . . .'

'Yes?'

'Nothing.'

Nicole stopped. Johnny stopped too. He sensed his stepmother's eyes upon him, but kept his eyes on the path. She lifted the boy's chin. 'What were you going to say?' she asked.

'I've . . . seen him,' Johnny replied, in a small voice. 'Maybe.'

Nicole said nothing for a while. Then she said, 'Look, Johnny, I don't know how to answer you, not really. But I do know this: Dr Cheung should hear what you've just told me.'

'Uh-huh. Right.'

'Will you promise me you'll tell her?'

'Promise.'

'That's good.'

They walked on together, hand in hand, the twilight lengthening their shadows to one side, like two more people, people without faces. Suddenly Nicole said, 'You know what I think? It's time we gave a party.'

*   *   *

This is getting tense.

It is three days after my last session with Dr Diane, late morning. I've just finished reading Julia's note to her, the one I lifted from the desk, for the nth time. There's the usual noise in the street, nothing special. A car pulls up, door slams, and so what? I go put the note in Dr Diane's box (memo to self – get a filing system), along with my reconstructed version of what was on her computer screen: I've copied it from memory, word for word, because it intrigues me and I don't know why but it just does, all right?

So I'm passing the window and I look out and there are these two *hombres* on the sidewalk looking up at my place. Cops. Instinctually, I am very, very good where cops are concerned. No question about it: cops.

They needn't be anything to do with me. But, they come inside. Footsteps on the stairs, clump-clump-clump. Bad feeling, *bad*.

First thing is, I throw a towel over the wire that connects me to the Paradise Bay power grid, reasoning that these visitors should not be alive (JOKE!!!) to my electronic wizardry. My coverlet goes over the boxes, but only half, because coverlets belong on beds, am I right? And if they see it lying over these suspicious shapes on the floor . . .

My plans are interrupted by a tat-a-tat, followed by illegal entry. They should wait for my consent, but they come in anyway, which I do not mind, because anything they now find is inadmissible in evidence; although to keep up appearances I say, 'It is customary, gentlemen, to wait for a "Come in" on the part of the occupant. Either of you got a no-knock warrant?'

You can see at once which is the bad cop and which is the good. The good one smiles as he produces his tin; the other one scowls. The good one has rich, chestnut hair, an honest face and squeaky-clean shoes. He could lose a little weight and profit. His *confrère* (that's French) could lose a ton and not miss it. He stinks of stale, sour tobacco. It's been snowing on his suit. No, dandruff, excuse *me*.

'I'm sorry,' says Mr Nice-Guy, 'but the door was ajar. I'm Detective Edwin Hersey, this is Detective Leo Sanders. Are you Tobias Gascoign?'

'Yes.'

'We'd like to ask you a few questions if it's convenient.'

And all this while I am watching Grunter the Pig (which is how I think of the *confrère*), as he roots around my pad in search of truffles. Greed is his thing. And imagine this guy on the toilet with a bad case of constipation, oh *God*.

'Do you think,' says Mr Edwin, 'we could turn that down a bit?'

The Dutchman, I have to admit, is occupying rather a lot of aural space.

> *'Up from forgotten depths of years long vanished*
> *Beams now this maiden's face on me:*
> *Dream-visions seen in days and nights unending*
> *Now turned to substance here I see.'*

Beautiful, beautiful . . . but lost on these two. I move towards the CD player. Piggy-wig growls, 'Yeah, turn that junk off, will ya?' I nearly change my mind and turn up the volume, decide to play things cool after all.

'Thank you.' Edwin Hersey has nice manners. 'We want to ask you about a couple of teenage boys who've been missing for some months now. Hal Lawson and Randy Delmar. Names mean anything to you?'

'No, sir.'

'How about Ray Douggan?' asks Piggy-wig.

'Who?'

'Guy got murdered a few months back, maybe you read about that?'

Click-click! Dr Diane's screen, Ray Arthur Douggan, April 25 . . .

'I may have heard something. In fact, I remember now: some of you guys came and asked me a whole heap of questions then.'

'Uh-huh. What about the name Jensen; mean anything?'

Click-clickety-click, Carl Jensen, July 4.

'He got killed too, right?'

'On the night of Saturday, July 4 last. Know anything about that?'

'Only what was in the papers.'

'Where were you' [this is Pig speaking] 'on the night of July 4?'

I pretend to cogitate. 'I think,' I say cautiously, 'I may have been at Harley Rivera's place, up by Point Sal. Partying. Traditionally a day for partying, *n'est-ce pas?*'

'Hey, would you look at this!'

I turn. Detective Sanders is fingering my officer's uniform with admiration. And I must say, it does look good: I found some stuff to clean the webbing shoulder-straps and belt, and I had the khaki jacket and pants dry-cleaned. The calf-length brown boots glisten.

'My dad used to wear something like that,' says Detective Pig-shit.

'So?'

He swings around. My voice just told him he's got to me and he wants to see why. I don't like talk of fathers. Why the hell should I care what his damn, fucking father wore?

'Bet you look good in that,' Pig grunts on. 'Along with lipstick, hey-hey-hey, look what I've found.'

He is holding up Dr Diane's plastic lipstick, the one she'll never miss; I'd carelessly left it by the bed,

'What the fuck do you think you're doing?' I scream. 'You got a warrant, or something? *Answer me.*'

They look at me appraisingly, as if I'm a steer and they're a couple of sophisticated buyers in no big hurry.

'Would you put that down?' I say. 'Please.'

264

Piggy puts it back, but only after making me wait. 'Touchy,' he says, 'ain't you?'

'Mr Gascoign . . . ' [this is Edwin Hersey, as if you needed telling] 'we don't have a warrant, and we don't plan on getting one, at the moment. We're here purely by your invitation, if you ask us to leave we must leave, but we would then come back later. If you know what I mean.'

I nod. I know.

'So if we could keep this nice and low key, that suits us just fine.'

'Yeah,' says Piggy. 'So first of all, tell us why you like dressing up in uniform, with lipstick.'

'Amateur dramatics.'

'Which play?'

'*Pearl Harbor.*'

The two cops speak simultaneously: 'That's a movie'; 'I never heard of that.'

It's their collision, I wait for them to sort things out. Edwin says, 'I didn't realize it was a play, as well as a movie.'

I say nothing. They look at me with raised eyebrows, but *still* I say nothing. I know my rights.

'Do the GIs wear lipstick, in Pearl?' asks Mr Pig-face Pig-shit.

'Actors wear make-up, Commissioner.'

Sanders opens his mouth to say he's not a commissioner before realizing I know that, and shuts it again.

'Anyway,' says my pal Edwin, after a pause. 'Let's get back to basics, shall we?' [I am starting to entertain tender feelings towards this man, and know it's time to be on my guard. Mine is precisely the reaction they want.] 'You were working for Harley Rivera at the time Lawson and Delmar went missing.'

'So?'

'There may be a connection between the boys' disappearances and Harley's place. We know you were working there, Harley told us. We honestly do not care about your relationship with him. We are not working for the Internal Revenue.'

'Speak for yourself,' Pig-shit puts in with a fake laugh. 'I work for 'em three hours out of every eight. Nice CD player, where'd you get it?'

'But those two used to frequent Harley's and it's likely you were among the last people to see them.'

'You got a receipt for this thing?'

I turn to find Detective Sanders holding up my CD player. He pulls too hard and the speaker-cord disconnects. I reach out to snatch it from him but he wrenches it away and says, 'Please . . . ?', spinning out the word.

The other cop says, 'Come on, Leo, we're wasting time.'

'Say please,' Pig repeats.

'Please. Now would you mind leaving?'

'Mr Gascoign,' (says Edwin), 'I've already explained: we can do this quietly, or the other way. Now which – '

'If this asshole friend of yours is going to toss my stuff around, we'll do it formal.'

They look at me. Their mouths are bad, bad, *bad*. I've boobed. But then Pig-face grins at me and meanders over to the door, where my towel conceals the electricity meter . . .

'Tell you what,' I say, 'I'd prefer to answer your questions at the station, with my lawyer present.' Which is absolutely untrue on all counts, not least because I don't have a lawyer, but I have to stop Leo Sanders, Detective, from lifting that towel. 'And although I have nothing to hide,' I ramble on, 'if you

266

touch another thing in this room I'll sue you to Mexico and back.'

Leo stops. He turns. Edwin is looking at me with a disappointed air. He has been writing in a book. Now he puts it away and caps his pen. He glances at Leo, who shrugs.

'It's your choice, Mr Gascoign,' Edwin says. 'We have a lot of other people to see.'

'Court-referrals,' I sneer. 'Dr Diane's puppies, yes?'

'Yes, and at least a dozen others.'

'What do you mean, "Dr Diane's puppies"?' Sanders is puzzled. 'What are they to you?'

'They're my friends. Co-patients.'

'Jesse Brown?' Sanders asks.

'And Ramon Porras and Billy-the-Kid Ryman and I know you're persecuting the four of us but I don't know why.' My heart's pounding, my face is hot with flush, I'm letting it get away from me. But I have to say something to keep that dumb fat cop's hand from off my towel, and anyway I'm mad now.

'Come on, Leo.' They start to leave, but at the door, Edwin pauses. 'We'll go see Billy Ryman, see what he knows about this guy.'

'Yeah.' Sanders's face lights up. 'Get what we want by the back door. Like this guy, here. Don't forget your lipstick, honey!'

For a second it doesn't register. No, honestly: I don't get his meaning. Go in by the back door. Lipstick . . . then it dawns: he thinks I'm a faggot, into anal sex.

'*Get out!*' I do not mean to scream at them, but I snap. Edwin lays a hand on Leo's shoulder; Piggy shrugs him off, his eyes ablaze with fury.

'Hey, kid,' he says suddenly. 'Did you kill Jensen? Kill Douggan, did you, eh?'

267

'No. I did not.'

'Know who did? Eh?'

'No, sir.'

'Yes, you do. Come on, come on.' Sanders stands so close to me I can smell his breath. It's rank. He grabs my shirt, pulls me close. 'Tell me, kid. Come on. Come on. Come on.'

'Diane Cheung.'

Leo Sanders drops me. There is a palpable change of atmosphere. Until this boo-boo of mine Ed has been an innocent bystander, looking on with some distress. Now pee-ow! He says, 'Are you in the habit of accusing your analyst of felony?'

I stare at him. Can't think what to say. Let me tell you what happened here, Ed, in case you one day read this (as I increasingly think you may). My mind had jumped ahead of yours in an effort to display its superiority. I badly needed to get the upper hand and I wanted your side-kick to let go my shirt. So I accused Diane because I knew you'd found one of her name-cards by the body and it seemed like a good, if cheap, shot. But it misfired. It misfired, because I remembered, too late, how I knew about that name-card. (It wasn't on the TV, it wasn't on the radio.) I'd been snooping around in the cemetery, eavesdropping your fellow detectives. That's how I'd learned about the card. But if I admitted that, you'd soon know that I'm in the habit of going there a lot. Which might be uncomfortable for me.

And I, too, have a stock of Diane's name-cards . . .

Oh dear.

So I say, 'No, I'm sorry, I don't know what came over me there. Not been sleeping well lately.'

But Ed persists, 'That's a very serious allegation you've made about a professional lady.'

'She's got an alibi for Jensen,' Sanders puts in. 'So.'

I close my eyes, striving after something, anything, that will get me out of this. But then I hear Ed say, 'She's got a *what*?'

I open my eyes. The two cops have forgotten me and are eyeballing each other.

'Yeah,' Pig-shit says, all innocent. 'She was in San Diego the weekend Jensen got killed. It checked out.'

'You . . . you *checked out* Diane Cheung for the night of the murder?'

'Gotta check out everybody.' Piggy's eyes slither onto mine and away again. 'You want to pursue this elsewhere, Ed?'

'Yeah. Yeah, you could say I do, Leo.'

They both turn and stare at me. I'm their lightning rod. For a bad, mad moment the situation can go either way. Then something untwists a quarter turn, and we're free of it. They go out, I fall down on the bed and stare at the ceiling.

From now on, I'm going to keep records more carefully. I've got to start grappling with the detail, and with history. I can't just go on leaving these holes.

I get up off the bed. I take out my notebook and a ballpoint. Suddenly I'm not sure how much time I have left to make all clear. I start to write, constantly forcing myself to slow down. My handwriting is clumsy, but one day other people are going to have to read this. One day, it's going to matter.

Who am I writing this for? Maybe it's for you, Edwin. Somebody's got to understand.

My mother was the most beautiful woman you ever saw. I have a photograph of her. She looks like a forties movie star, with permed black hair, and a row of pearls around her neck, and ear-rings. The pose is artificial,

269

like they did in those days: her head's tilted to one side, half turned towards the camera. She's smiling, in the photograph. I remember that smile in real life. I was four, I guess. We were in the park. I kept riding the slide. I'd climb up to the top and coast down, sometimes sitting, sometimes on my back, sometimes on my belly. She'd shade her eyes against the sun, and say, 'Take care, now!', and smile. I was doing the slide to impress her. I wanted her to see I was a real man, not like my father, the man she'd married.

I remember my mother as tired, always tired. Then one day, soon after the episode with the slide, she wasn't there any more. She dumped me. She left me alone with Dad.

It took me a long time to start this where I should have. I've got pages of notes, and yet this is the first time I've ever written about how it began. Because I'm so scared.

Edwin, that blotch is my tears. I'm crying so much, I can't write.

*   *   *

Diane was in a catatonic stupor. Far out over the sea the clouds had formed themselves into a mountain range, smoke-grey at bottom, overlit pink with the dying sun's rays on their peaks. The oil-rig was invisible this evening. The September evening retained heat like an oven not long switched off. She couldn't move. She stood in the kitchen, staring into infinite space.

She had come home early. There was so much to do and she needed space. She'd been invited to address a conference on Play Therapy in Washington next month and she'd made scarcely one note. She was late with an article for the *Journal of Child Psychology and Psychiatry*. Her accountant was pressing her to send some vouchers. One of the surgeons at St Joseph's was giving a barbecue tomorrow, Diane had promised to phone and say if she was coming, and she hadn't. Gracie Marlow, a ten-year-old victim of self-inflicted injuries, was getting worse: Diane had stuffed her notes in her briefcase to review this evening, along with notes on Peter Field, Sonny van Trong and three-year-old Susannah Levy, all problem children, all in need of her urgent attention. Her auto needed servicing. If she didn't start work on the garden soon she'd have lost it for the year, and next spring it would be twice as hard.

There was so much to be done, and she could not move. How right it once had seemed that a psychologist should own a house on a high bluff, from which she could look down on everyone and everything: mapping, analysing, but above the storms of human existence . . .

She had this obsessive fear: one day she'd be in full flow, chairing a committee perhaps, or analysing a patient, and the Angel of Death would come into the room and say, 'This meeting stands adjourned; all unfinished business is lost.' Just like that. No appeal.

Or worse, Death would say: You've got one minute. One minute to achieve all the things you've wanted and never done.

'What made you choose that one?'

'He presented himself, Mother.'

The silence continued unbroken for a long time. Then, slowly, slowly, realization seeped through to Diane that *Ma-ma* had spoken and she'd answered and she didn't even find it disturbing any more; that *Ma-ma* was here beside her, a physical if invisible presence, part of the furniture, and also inside her brain.

She looked down at her hands. They were playing with the chopstick Ed had given her that night at the Moks' restaurant. Funny, she couldn't remember picking it up. So anyway, she laid it down, and she said to herself, Diane, don't go mad, get busy.

A couple of days ago she'd made time for a mega shopping spree, buying the wherewithal to cook good, fresh, food: pans, tongs, wooden spoons, a pepper-grinder, a mound of household objects. Everything was still sitting on the floor, shrouded in plastic. She'd broken the hex on this house; from now on she'd shop until she dropped. Starting with a Manuel Ocampo canvas, next week. *For now, however, unpack. Bustle.*

Diane unwrapped, stacked and cleaned, almost without a break, for two hours. She did stop once, however. The last thing she unpacked was a bottle of pink champagne. She held it in both hands for a moment. Then she went to put it on the table, and sat with her chin cupped in her hands, regarding the elegant bottle in front of her, and she thought about Francis Baggeley.

When she and Francis were co-students at the University of Michigan they used to attend weekly seminars together at the house of a junior professor called Roger Sanction. Sanction was a bachelor who lived for his work and rarely cooked, but he'd make coffee for the students he liked. The first time she'd gone there, Diane had noticed a champagne-bottle in the rack of his refrigerator door. Apart from that and a carton of milk, the ice-box was empty. After a while she knew Sanction well enough to ask him about the bottle, and he'd told her, he was keeping it for the day he got tenure.

She remembered how he'd proudly brought it out and set it down on the table of his own kitchen. Laurent-Perrier, the first time she'd ever heard that name. He said it was a wine for celebration, and only for celebration: a sacred wine, he'd called it. With the kind of fervour most men keep for their women, he'd described its peerless bouquet, delicate savour, exquisite 'bite', lingering after-taste. Diane and Francis had looked at each other over the neck of the bottle and in that moment she'd felt, yes: she would go to bed with this man, and afterwards they'd sit propped up on pillows and drink Laurent-Perrier pink champagne until it came out of their ears . . .

She and Francis never had become lovers; Roger Sanction never got tenure. She wondered what had happened to his bottle of Laurent-Perrier, whether he'd drunk it anyway. She hoped so.

Diane, back in the present, picked up her own bottle. It was a marvellous shape: squat, solid, heavy, with broad shoulders like those of the man she was saving it for. She ran a finger over the round, gold label – Champagne Laurent-Perrier, Cuvée Rosé Brut – then up to the die stamped into the green glass. She wanted to drink this, but . . . not tonight. Soon, though. Soon.

She firmly thrust the bottle back in her ice-box, hauled out a mountain of food and rolled up her sleeves.

By six fifteen her place was not only starting to look like a real home, it smelled of something rich and wonderful. She lifted the phone and dialled Ed at third precinct. He was in, he answered, her heart lightened further.

'Why not stop by my place for a drink?' she said.

'Aw,' he said, 'aw, that's nice, Diane, but I've got a mound of work to do.'

'Me too, but I'm ignoring it. You should take a rest.'

'Mm. I know: why don't you come into town, I'll break for dinner. We can go to this little place in Fountainside . . .'

'Uh-uh.'

'Why not?'

'Because your little place doesn't have freshly made *fettucini alla Romana* just coming up to a state of utter perfection, whereas *my* little place does.'

There was a pause. She imagined Ed rubbing his unshaven chin, could almost see the longing in his eyes, and she gloated.

'You're a wicked woman; know that?'

'Mirror, mirror in the ditch, who d'you think's the biggest bitch?'

His laugh echoed down the line. 'See you in an hour,' he said.

Ed put down the phone and Diane did a happy march-time drum solo on the dresser with her solitary chopstick before busying herself with the food. She wished she'd bought an apron, it would have completed the new-found picture she had of herself as a domestic wonder.

Ed made it to her door in ninety minutes, not sixty, and looked every bit as unshaven as she'd imagined him.

'Sorry,' he said, pushing a bunch of tulips at her. 'Just as I was leaving we had a warehouse robbery come up. For a moment it was touch and go, then Sam Trevors stepped in early for his shift and I ran.'

'That's okay. Mm . . . tulips, wonderful.'

The sight of that drawn face, the drooping eyes, the tummy pushing against the shirt a size too small, was enough to bring out her innate sympathy. She forgot about how the food was now looking as tired as he was; she sat him down with a glass of chilled Raymond and told him not to get too comfortable, because she'd be serving within seconds.

As she tossed salad she heard him get up, and a moment later Barbra Streisand infiltrated the kitchen.

'Nice hi-fi,' Ed called.

'Thank you. Wow, you know how to work it! Took me a day and a half just to hook everything together.'

Barbra was in New York frame of mind tonight: perfect for two tired people who wanted to eat and drink and refuel and recharge without the burden of excessive conversation. The pasta was fabulous, better than Diane thought herself capable of producing. But as her eyes surveyed the latest purchases – Swedish crystal, English china, glass bowls for liquid candles, a wooden salad bowl from Indonesia – already she felt the seeds of doubt. Were these things right for her house? Were they what she really wanted?

Diane raised her glass, pushing these thoughts to the back of her mind, and she said, 'To the first male guest who's ever set foot here.' They drank. Wine filtered through her cracks and crevices, loosening a little bit of her here, a bit there. The memory of her mother's manifestation, mere hours ago, seemed nothing but a bad dream.

After dinner they went on the patio and stood by the rail, watching the ocean. A cool breeze swept off the sea, it was pleasant out there. They didn't speak for a long time. Then Diane laid a hand on Ed's and said, 'You saved my life by coming. Thank you.'

'Bad day?' he asked, turning towards her.

'Not good. A lot of pressures.'

'Me, too.' He paused, as if not sure how she might take what was coming next. 'I saw your patient a few days ago. Tobes Gascoign.'

Diane removed her hand. 'Really?'

'He was cool. Until Leo started tossing his stuff around, that is.'

'Leo should know better.'

'Mm. Gascoign's volunteered to come by the station for questioning, bringing his lawyer.'

'Does he have a lawyer?'

'We'll see.'

'But admit it, Ed: that's the action of an innocent man.'

'Possibly. Was it innocent of him to accuse you of murdering Jensen and Douggan?'

'He did *what*?'

'You heard me. In front of Leo. Said you'd killed the boys. It is my duty to inform you that you have the right to remain silent, but that if you choose to speak –

She punched his arm and he said, 'Ouch! That hurt.'

'Serve you right. It's not funny.'

'Leo and I agree. Gascoign's unstable. He may be innocent, like you say, but that didn't stop me having him profiled by Quantico.'

Diane looked into her glass. A while back, Daniel Krozgrow had stopped by her office to seek her assistance in this very thing. Funny, now she thought of it: Tobes had been there at the time.

'When will you have the profile?' she asked Ed.

'Sometime next week.'

'You're profiling all of my court-referrals?'

'The four current ones, yes. We also have a couple of other suspects, nothing to do with you.'

'What did you make of Tobes?'

'He's a jerk.'

'He's not a murderer, Ed. I've seen enough criminals to know.'

'Then you've seen enough to realize that the most unlikely people do kill.'

'But he's got an alibi!'

'For *one* of the murders. And what about Lawson and Delmar, the two kids that are still missing?'

'Oh, Ed . . . ' Diane heaved a great sigh, lacking confidence in her ability to get through to him. 'Why do you have to persecute my boys?'

'Funny . . . that's the word he used. Like, well . . . the Holocaust, you know?' Suddenly Ed rounded on her. 'Is that how you see me?'

'Of course not. It's just that all my experience as a clinician points the same way: my four are innocent.'

'Then how do you explain the name-card by the body?'

Diane made a face. Should she put him straight about how those four miserable creatures had stolen her cards during group therapy? While she was still deciding, Ed said, 'Let me turn the question on its head, Diane – what makes these guys so special, why do you so readily assume they're *not* capable of violent crime?'

'Because they're my patients! My duty to them – '

'To them? I thought your concern was for the truth.'

'Oh, I see, I see: it's back to this, I don't conform to police ideas about how their tame shrink ought to behave. Because I have patients who are suspects, I've got to throw them to the wolves, right?'

'Diane – '

'I've been working damned hard on those boys and it's time we straightened this thing out. Take Tobes:

he's got a new job, he's attending sessions conscientiously, you won't see him in court again.'

'What kind of a job? We had him down as unemployed.'

'Gardener. With the parents of another patient.'

'Another *patient*? You mean, one of your kids?'

'Yes.'

'Diane, am I hearing you right? You . . . have put Tobes Gascoign, a court-referral, with a criminal record, next to one of your child patients?'

'Why not, if I deem it suitable?'

Ed threw his hands in the air and turned away. In the silence, Diane became aware of how cold the evening had grown. The sun was going down now. Johnny's word, 'gruzzled', came into her mind.

'Did you see what's playing at the Ritz?' Ed asked suddenly. 'That French movie, the one you were talking about.' He looked at his watch. 'We could catch the nine-fifteen showing.'

'Sure,' Diane said. 'Why not? Take my car.'

Diane wanted to see that movie, but not tonight, but she was desperate not to fight with Ed any more and if two people are sitting side by side in a theatre it's harder for them to quarrel. She wanted to patch things up. She wanted them back where they'd been an hour ago, when Ed had settled down with his glass of chilled Sauvignon blanc and Streisand was still in a New York frame of mind. So Diane did what women always do, she said yes, yes, oh fuck, *yes*. Though not quite in those terms.

In the car, Ed put his hand over hers on the wheel and gave it a squeeze. 'Fighting with you's no fun,' he said.

'Why?'

'Doesn't feel right.'

Diane mellowed. She didn't want to, but she did. Somehow, somewhere along the line, Ed and she had begun the painful process of transmogrifying into a couple. Shades of Norman Rockwell clouded her mind, but without undue pain.

'Feel like doing me a favour, then?' she asked.

'Maybe. What?'

'Let me eavesdrop when you question Tobes Gascoign?'

For a moment Ed couldn't believe she'd actually said that. Then he snorted in derision. 'No way.' When she tried to speak again he held up a hand. 'Don't even think about it.'

Diane didn't want to antagonize Ed, because sitting in the car next to him felt good. Besides, she knew another way of getting what she wanted.

*   *   *

Dr Diane, there are things we need to address together, things I haven't been able to bring myself to say. Events I've kept secret since they happened, but which have shaped me. You sense what those things are. I need to talk about them with you. But when we're together, this mighty steel door comes crashing down, the drawbridge is hauled up, the portcullis lowered; the keep stands secure against any attack.

So what's going to happen is this: I will write it down. Then, next time we're alone together, I'll read out what I've written.

I will begin by showing you my mother's photograph, let you see how lovely she looked. Then I will tell you how she walked out on us, on him and me, and what happened thereafter.

I will no longer write only what it suits me to reveal. Thus it goes . . .

Until I was five I lived in Arcade, a small burg in Wyoming County, upstate New York. It was very cold in winter, with deep snow. There was a railroad station, but I don't recall any trains. The main drag was one hundred fifty yards long: a pizzeria, a tiny, dark restaurant and a modest hotel, some stores, and that was it. The school I went to was a square, brick block: my heart sank every time I clapped eyes on the place. In winter there were always lots of snow-days, when school was shut; I used to listen out for the announcements on the radio.

Mom left when I was four. Five, maybe. I went to school one morning, came back (I walked, the house we lived in was only a quarter of a mile away), she'd gone, leaving a note for my father on the kitchen table. I didn't realize she'd gone, of course. I thought she must be visiting a neighbour. Then it started to get dark. My father came home. He read the note. He screwed it up, tossed it in the trash; he turned to me and said, 'Good riddance.' Rest of the night, he was drunk. Sour mash whisky.

Let me summarize, Dr Diane: the years that followed were unhappy. That's all you need to know, isn't it?

No.

For a while I was sent to stay with my father's sister, who lived with her husband and two kids in a bad part of Buffalo. There wasn't much money, but I was used to that: my dad worked as a shoe-salesman, always travelling, never solvent, and if we'd had things at home it was mostly because of mother's salary as a kindergarten teacher. Now that had dried up, of course. I guess we were always poor but it didn't matter, because I'd never known the other way. I remember my aunt as a thin, sad woman who treated me like the lodger I was and never smiled. She wasn't cruel, don't get me wrong – just cold. I hated my cousins as much as they hated me. I was happy the day my dad phoned and said he'd take me back. I was seven then.

He'd moved outside of Arcade, was living in a trailer parked on land belonging to a farmer friend of his. Then I did know for the first time what it meant to go downhill. At least my aunt's place had been warm and dry, and there was food on the table three times a day, even if not much. Now none of these things was true.

My father was working as a hired hand; no more shoes, no car paid for by the company. Which meant he didn't get out. Which in turn meant he stayed in all evening, drinking and amusing himself with me. I was his entertainment. He had an imaginative turn of mind, did Dad.

I was still attending school, then. It never occurred to me to run away. Where would I run? Besides, as long as I was at school I didn't have to go home. In those days, I still had a few friends. Their mothers must have gotten tired of this pale waif who would turn up on their doorsteps of an evening, always synchronizing his arrival with the rattle of cutlery.

I could never take anybody home, you see, and so after a while it seemed less of a strain to see less of my friends. Then, quite soon, there were no friends.

I had one nice thing in my life. When I was about nine, I got myself a little kitty, called Spruce. He just wandered in one day when Dad was working in the fields – must have been a school holiday, I guess – and mewed at me. He was so tiny! Ginger and white . . . all fluffy and warm and he had a big long scratch on his nose that I bathed. I found him a box, and some straw. I opened a tin of tuna for lunch, and shared it with Spruce (I'd already chosen that name for him by then, on account of I'd been cutting spruce logs when I saw him).

Funny thing was, Dad didn't have anything to say against Spruce, not at the start. Gave him an odd look, that first evening, but didn't say much. Spruce was with me for three years, and all that time I fed him out of my own food allowance. My father was strict where rations were concerned. Spruce didn't grow much. The day he died, he was still only a kitten, in my eyes. I have heard adults say that children never grow up in the eyes of their own parents. I understand that, when I think of Spruce. My little Sprucey.

Dr Diane, did you know that the famous Soviet writer, Alexander Solzinitsin, put in the preface to volume two of his great work, *The Gulag Archipelago*, this: 'All one needs to taste the sea is one gulp.' I have read that book twice, but all I can remember of it is those words. I first began to read it when I was nine, in the library, where it was warm, and where my father was not (and where there were books about everything and anything, including Gainsborough hats, and *robes à la française*), and where the nice lady who looked after the books turned a blind eye when I smuggled Sprucey in under my parka. So now I am going to give you one taste of the sea.

In the library, I learned many things: among them, how to cook. I was never a great chef, but somebody had to cook if my father and I were not to starve. I think I may vaguely have realized that my life was not quite normal; that there were children who did not have to prepare each meal and wash up the plates and saucepans afterwards, but at that age (I am sure you know this) children adapt to the most extraordinary things and somehow make them tolerable. I learned to cook simple dishes.

One evening, very late, I was heating oil in a saucepan on our portable gas-stove. It was cold outside: December. I know it was December, because I'd made some effort at hanging paper decorations, to make Dad happy. Sprucey was lying by the door, playing with a paper ball. I'd turned the radio on low. Some people were singing carols, sweet and soft.

The oil began to bubble. My father came home. He was drunk. Being drunk, he stumbled over Sprucey and went flying. He picked himself up. He swore. Sprucey had scratched his hand in his confusion and fear. My father, staggering, looked at the blood as if he'd never seen it before. Then he turned and made a grab for Sprucey.

'Dad,' I said, 'don't. Sprucey didn't mean any harm.'

Sprucey scratched my father again and looked for a way of escape. But there was no escape from my father; we both knew that. He picked up Sprucey by the scruff of the neck. I knew from the look on Sprucey's face he realized he was gone. He went quiet. He went still. Then, when he saw what my father had in mind, he went mad.

My father plunged him into the saucepan of oil, and held down the lid. After a while, the oil started to burp out from beneath the lid and hiss onto the fire, but still my father held it down. He'd scalded himself badly. That was the first time I took pleasure in another's pain.

Afterwards, he made me clean the saucepan.

Dr Diane, I am going to take this up to your house now, and I am going to read it to you, and we are going to sit down and talk. I'm sorry if my arrival spoils your evening, but I haven't been able to reveal this to anyone for over ten years, and now that I've started I don't think I can stop.

All you need to taste the sea is one gulp.

*   *   *

When they came out of the movie Diane's eyes were wet with tears. Ed put an arm around her as they walked to the car. It helped. But her mind was still seething with the knowledge that she had to move forward with this man if they were to survive: that it wasn't enough to get on well, to laugh and joke and (occasionally) disagree about work matters. That was why she kept on crying, maybe. When Ed invited himself back for a night-cap she nodded dumbly, glad not to be left alone just yet.

Two miles short of her turning, there was a side-road that led nowhere except to a steel radio mast in a wire compound. Diane's friend at the sheriff's office had once told her it was used for air navigation by the big jets, an NDB he'd called it, but to her it was just an eyesore on a rolling green landscape that sloped gently down to the sea. No one ever seemed to visit, except her. She drove there sometimes late at night when she wanted to sit and think, and maybe even wonder what the mast was whispering to the planes that flew overhead.

Ed looked at her enquiringly when she took this turning, but Diane just drove on. There was still a vestige of light in the western sky when they pulled up beside the compound.

Diane got out; Ed followed. The cliff here was only a few feet high, but Ed had parked on a knoll and there was no beach, just rocks. Diane sat with her legs folded up and her arms around them, looking out to sea. When Ed moved to join her she said, 'No, you sit over there,' and pointed to a boulder.

'What's wrong?' he said, settling down.

'Nothing's wrong.'

A light breeze scarcely ruffled Diane's hair, but the taste of salt was strong on her lips. Something was brewing out there, beyond the edge of the world; something with furious winds and the smack of thunder in it, a storm content to take its time. She nodded at the mast. 'That's an NDB transmitter-mast,' she said confidently.

'I know.'

'Planes can steer towards it.'

'Or away.'

'Yes. A kind of beacon . . .'

They sat in silence for a while, but the tranquil evening was drawing to a close and Diane had to speak.

'Ed . . . Before, we both got it wrong. I don't want that to happen again. You got it wrong because you should have told me you were married. And I got it wrong . . . in bed.' She couldn't meet his eyes. 'I was useless in bed, as a lover, and it never got any better, and you must have wondered why.'

He hesitated. 'Yes.'

'I'm going to tell you why.'

*   *   *

I've already written about why I went to your house tonight. Why I broke in is more complicated. Is there a literature on the image of the sliding double-door as

285

vagina-substitute? All I know is that I wanted to penetrate your domain, to find out about the real *you*. The you we never get to see in therapy. The id of Dr Diane Cheung.

I couldn't make anyone hear. No lights on. Your patio doors are a joke: one heave with my Swiss army knife, and hey presto! *Entrada*.

What a place. What an *extraordinary* place.

It's almost dark. I drift through the grey dusk from room to room, marvelling at such dry-bone whiteness, the elaborate flower arrangements, the absence of any furniture except books and the barest essentials. You live in a palace, Dr Diane. An ice palace.

After a while, it grows dark. I don't need to switch on the lights. Moon-rays flood through the house, excavating caverns of shadow, hewing *yin* from *yang*. I go upstairs. Your bedroom is so *bare*! It's large, like all the rooms in this sepulchral house. There's a balcony overlooking the ocean. The simple bed, with its white coverlet, draws me towards it. I run my hands over that coverlet more times than I can count. I rest my head against the cool cotton and sniff in and in and in again, until I begin to feel dizzy.

I want to see what's in the drawer of your bedside table. Aha! – a beautiful bound book of blank pages, creamy coloured and silken-smooth to my palpitating fingers. No, not all the pages are blank; you have written on several.

I carry the book across to the french windows, where the moonlight is strongest, and go out on the balcony; as I have already mentioned, my vision is twenty-twenty, so I do not need to turn on the light. I read on, absorbed. I forget where I am, who I am, why I came here. The things you have written are terrifying. Your dreams . . . and not only your dreams.

The night I telephoned you, over and over again, afterwards you called your Ed. Who is this man? Do you love him? Yes, you must do, to write such things about him. Have you been to bed with him, have you?

Jealousy can drive a man insane. I get up and swirl around your room, taking deep breaths and trying to be calm. Sometimes, Dr Diane, I hate you more than you'll ever know: you steal my Johnny, you bed down with men, you are a whore and a thief, Doctor . . .

But in the end, my pain succumbs to curiosity. You have written a great deal recently, and I do not understand all of it, though I want to.

Why does Alice Mornay fascinate you so? Because of what I tell you under hypnosis, of course. And yet, how to explain this entry . . .

Alice Mornay again last night. Oh, why did Tobes have to tell me about her! I cannot now remember for sure whether I dreamed of Alice's history before T revealed it or after, but it seems the former, which troubles me.

It troubles *you*, Doctor? Well, gee-whiz, what do you think it does to *me*?!

What it does is cause me to concentrate so hard on what I'm reading that I don't hear the car-engine until it's almost too late. A beam of light sweeps across my eyes. I leap up. I'm trapped. What will Dr Diane think when she finds me in her bedroom? I will be accused of robbery, attempted rape, felonies without number.

I race to put the book back in the drawer. In my haste, my hand shoves in too far, encountering something solid. *What?* A gun, no, can't be . . . My fingers barely brush this metal object, they are shaking so much that when I push it back in place it makes a clunky noise that must be audible in San Francisco. I *think* it was a gun. *Think* so . . .

Voices in the hallway, the sound of the front door closing. It is a long drop from your balcony to the ground. Be patient, do not panic, I tell myself. The worst that can happen is that you will go to prison for a multitude of years. Dr Diane is not a lynch-mob *aficionada*. I close the french windows silently before scuttling off to hide.

Outside the good doctor's bedroom there is a landing: go right and, after passing other doors, you come to the stairs that curl down one wall to the big central room below: part hallway, part dining-room, part living-space. But exit from the bedroom and go left, and you come immediately to what I term 'the gallery'. It's square, with a huge, round, external window consisting of many panes, shaped into a gigantic eye. This square space overlooks the main room below, protected from the drop by a metal balustrade of intricate workmanship. If this house belonged to me, I'd use this area as a minstrels' gallery: hence my name for it. I go there and lie on my stomach and try to work out an escape route. While I watch, I listen.

Two voices. Dr Diane's is uncharacteristically shrill. She is laughing now, but the kind of laugh that betokens strain. My kind of laugh. As they pass through into the kitchen I get a look at the face of the guy she's brought home. Edwin Hersey, Detective of this parish. Edwin. Ed. Ed in bed.

Suddenly any notion of leaving vacates my mind, rendering it a lean, clean machine, firing on all cylinders. Tobias, uninvited though he be, intends to stay a while.

They return to the central room, still chattering. Diane cracks open a couple of beers. She sits on a cushion; he on a white sofa. I wonder why he doesn't smooch up to Dr Diane on her cushion.

'Anyway . . .' she says, in a dying fall, and there is silence for a while. 'Anyway,' she says again, 'it wasn't like it is now, not in those days. Counselling, video-cameras to spare kids the trauma of testifying in open court, play-dolls with penises.'

Ed nods, but says nothing, for which I am grateful because I need to concentrate without distraction. *Play-dolls with penises?*

'I suppose if it had happened now, I'd just be part of CHIPP. A name on a screen with a password attached.'

There is a pause. Then Ed says gently, 'Chip? I'm sorry, you've lost me.'

'Oh . . . Child Incest Protection Programme. It's a state database of abusers and abused. I have access to it, but not many other people do. You don't.'

'I don't?'

'It's a clinician-driven network, not something to be shared with the police. A bulletin-board and database. Forget I mentioned it. I'm not . . . not myself tonight.'

I know about this CHIPP thing. But how, why, where . . . ?

'Whenever I think about Mother, I still get all weepy. She loved me so much, I loved her so much . . . I . . .'

Dr Diane holds a hand to her face. Ed doesn't move. I want him to go across to her and put a protective arm around her shoulders and pull her to his breast, but Ed doesn't move.

'She had to put up with so much from Larry. Tantrums. Rows. Lack of attention, lack of consideration.

Her first marriage had been so wonderful, and her second was so . . .'

'Why didn't she leave him?'

'Chinese women don't.' Dr Diane's shoulders wriggle in a shrug. 'They just . . . don't.' A long silence. 'There's more.'

Ed slowly raises his head until he's looking straight at her. 'Tell me,' he says.

'It's about the things inside my head. The voices. Voice.'

'You're hearing voices? People who aren't there?'

'A person. One. She's dead.'

Another long silence. Then Ed says, 'Your mother?' And Dr Diane nods violently, once.

I can scarcely breathe. My throat squeezes up, my mouth is dry as sand.

'For months now,' Dr Diane says suddenly, 'I've been hearing her talk to me. Like . . . like she's there standing next to me, you know? And when I answer her, she . . . responds.'

'Can you *see* your mother?'

'No. But that doesn't stop me thinking I'm insane. And it's all to do with the sexual abuse, I'm convinced of that. Plus there's the dreams.'

'Dreams?'

'Flying. Dark, menacing figures that want to kill me. My own death. The violent deaths of others. Sometimes . . . sometimes it's my mother who wants to kill me . . . oh, Ed, do you think I'm mad, do you?'

She breaks down into sobs and now he does go to her: he takes her in his arms and rocks her against his chest while he strokes her hair. *I* think she is mad. She is totally cuckoo. And I am in therapy with this woman.

'You're the sanest woman I ever met,' Ed says, and I want to laugh. Maybe this is his way of keeping the situation under control until he can summon the men in white coats, in which case I go along with it, but not otherwise. 'Grief,' he continues, 'can destroy anyone.'

She nods her head in a series of quick, jerky movements that tell me she's still crying.

'Have you ever considered, well, you know . . . treatment?'

'I've thought about it.' Now she sits up straight, her hair a mess, her eyes turned away from me, so I can't see them, but I know they'll be red and horrible. 'The trouble is, I know all the things they could say.' She attempts a laugh. 'Why pay for what you already know?'

Ed goes on stroking her hair. *His* face I *can* see; it's unsmiling. 'I think maybe you should consult someone,' he says quietly.

More silence. She sits up and makes an attempt at straightening her hair. She wipes her eyes. After a bit she even reaches out for the can of beer sitting on the floor by her feet. She takes one sip, hiccups, holds a hand to her mouth. Then she leaps up and runs into the kitchen. I hear her gag. Ed goes to help her.

The room below yawns empty. I should run for it. I could pad down the stairs, be through the sliding glass doors and away, safe. Or maybe not. Ed looks like a fast runner. The slightest noise on my part . . .

I want to stay. I *have* to stay.

I can hear them talking in the kitchen, their voices just an unbroken murmur. Then they are coming out again. Dr Diane is saying something about how if they're to amount to anything he has to take this on board and decide.

' . . . And if tomorrow, or whenever, you call me and say, I really can't face this, then I'll understand.' She smiles, her heart not in it. 'I will. Truly.'

'I've told you,' he says, putting his arms around her, 'I love you.'

Flash, crash, slam, bam. *He loves her*.

And she . . . ?

'Maybe all the love inside me was killed. Not put to sleep, but killed.' Then Dr Diane sighs, and laughs. She's making a huge effort here. She says, 'I haven't shown you the place. Come, I'll give you the grand tour.'

It takes a second for this to register. Then my panic needle ups off the dial. *They are going to come and find me*.

I'm on my knees in a second. This makes noise. Ed looks up. I freeze. Ed says, 'Did you hear something?'

'No. The wind can make strange noises in the rafters. Look, I want your professional opinion, about this alarm system.'

Ed chuckles. 'This non-existent alarm system?'

'That's the one. We'll start on the deck, come . . . '

She's halfway back to being her usual self. But as Ed arrives at the deck-doors he glances up and back, still seeking the source of that irksome noise . . .

Over the next five minutes they move in and out of my view while I wait for an opportunity to flee that never comes. Just as I think it's safe to tiptoe down-stairs one or other of them speaks, the voice telling me they're coming back. My lips are sore where my teeth have ground into them. There's blood in my mouth.

I'm going to have to risk the drop from a first-floor window. But it's essential I choose a moment when they're on the other side of the house, or they'll hear me.

'. . . and the rape alarm there, by the front door, plus a back-up at back, and another in my bedroom.'

'Do you have sensors on all the windows?'

'Yes. Now, through here they wanted to run an infra-red beam, but I said . . . '

By now I have raised myself upright and am concealed in the square recess with the big round window, the gallery. 'Concealed' is a misleading word here; anyone coming upstairs need only advance along the landing to see me.

'. . . if you shouldn't ask them to resite the master-control away from those glass doors?'

'Mm-hm. What do you think?'

Mention of glass doors shakes me into risking a look downstairs. I snapped the lock with my knife. If they find that, I'm sunk.

'You see,' Ed is saying, 'if someone gets his hand in through the glass, and the box is within reach . . . '

'But he'd have to have a pretty long arm, no?'

I crouch by the balustrade, looking down. I can only see a tenth of Dr Diane's back, and nothing of Ed, as they stand to my left in the ante-room to the patio. Dr Diane says, 'These doors don't look very firm, do they?'

I shut my eyes, because I know the next thing I'm going to hear is her rattling the doors, that's what I'd do, that's what *anyone* would do.

'Do I get to see upstairs as well?'

My eyes fly open. The voices are approaching. Dr Diane did not try her doors, she is coming back into the living-room with Ed.

'Sure, why not?'

They are coming upstairs. Stealthily I retreat back from the balustrade. Dr Diane (I can just see her) is on the

293

lowest stair, looking down at Ed, invisible to me. I am in a blind alley here. Got to move.

'I don't want to pressure you,' I hear Ed say. 'Downstairs is fine with me.' Then comes Dr Diane's laugh, and this time she means it. She's almost back to normal. Only in my mind she can never be normal again.

'Come on up,' she says. 'Try anything and see what you get!'

'Well one thing I won't get is a bullet in my head.'

They are slowly climbing the stairs. I have no more time. I break. I retreat inside the nearest door, half open. Dr Diane's bedroom.

'Diane, seriously, I wish you'd replace the gun that was stolen.'

They are on the landing.

'I don't feel comfortable having a gun in the house. Whoever has it is welcome to it. This is the guest bathroom.'

The room is unsteady beneath and around me; the Big One has struck at last. We are having an earthquake. No, we are not. But equivalent to an earth tremor is the knowledge that Dr Diane's bedside drawer contains what may be a hand-gun, although she has just denied its existence. *Why didn't I make sure?*

Maybe she owned more than one gun and the cop is talking about a second one that was stolen.

They are back on the landing, nearer now. I step silently to the french windows.

' . . . and this is my room.'

I open the windows, glide through and close them behind me. As the light in her bedroom comes on, I flatten myself against the wall. For several moments all

I hear is the rise and fall of conversation. Then, suddenly, the french windows open and the two love-birds are standing on the threshold.

Nobody speaks.

I control my breathing. Six feet, no more, separates them from me.

I could kill them.

I could kill *him*.

What would she do if she saw her lover lying there with my Swiss army knife in his stomach and his eyes lying on the floor next to him like two toy marbles?

She's been letting this guy, this cop, screw her. This woman seems to recognize no limits, and now she is mad, too. The world does not need you, Dr Diane, the world has problems enough without you.

I finger the knife. I need both hands to extend the largest blade. I will have to take it out of my pocket. But if I do that, I risk making a noise.

I am not going to kill her. I am not going to kill anyone, ever.

'See how carefully they've done the contacts,' Dr Diane says in my right ear. 'Those guys cost, but they deliver.'

I open my eyes a slit. The balcony's empty. They're standing in the doorway, examining some-thing I can't see. If they take another step, just one, I'm dead meat.

I hear a long sigh. Then – 'What a beautiful night,' she says.

'Yes.'

'Ed . . .'

'Mm-hm?'

'Do you think I'm taking this electronic gadgetry too far?'

'No. Emphatically.'

'I mean, it's all so expensive and sometimes I feel like this crazy old spinster . . .'

'I only wish more women who lived alone had such good sense. And with your background . . . your history . . .'

'I suppose. It's just that . . .'

'Oh Diane, your stepfather raped you! And it isn't even as if he was content to rape you normally! I mean, these are sensible precautions for any woman living alone to take, but in your case they're doubly necessary if you're ever going to get over it.'

Then, Wham! Of course – CHIPP, the words on Dr Diane's computer screen in her office, Child Incest Protection Programme, 'your stepfather raped you'.

The windows close, not completely but enough to let me relax a fraction. I hear their voices murmuring inside the bedroom. Next second, I'm sliding down the wall to settle in a heap on the balcony.

Her stepfather raped her.

Her *step*father raped her.

Dr Diane had a stepfather. The stepfather. Raped. Her.

He raped her . . . not (as in NOT) . . . normally.

Wow.

Wow.

Wow.

Now I know she is not mad, she has merely suffered. She jumps into long-awaited focus, at last making perfect sense. But soft! What is this I hear . . . through the half-open doors, what sounds disturb Night's stillness?

The light in her bedroom has gone out. Yet they remain inside, talking.

I lift my head and survey the sky. There is no moon tonight, no danger of my shadow giving me away. I take a step forward, towards the windows. I wait a long time before proceeding further. Their talking dies away after a while, to be replaced by a succession of sounds, intermittent, of uneven volume. When Dr Diane cries out in a long, shivery moan of pleasure, the skin that covers my backbone arises to creep up and down before resettling into place, my guts liquefy and harden.

I press my ear against the tiny gap where window meets frame. I look through the glass, but darkness shrouds the figures writhing on the bed and I close my eyes, the better to concentrate on what my ears tell me. It is like a memory of home.

I was ten when my father sodomized me for the first time, and fifteen when he did it for the last. And in between, what sighs, what cries sang out upon how many nights; what tears were shed; what blood, what quantity of seed . . . ? To what suffering, and what pleasure and what shame, was Night sole witness as I grew from child to man?

What shit I write.

What . . . *soft* . . . shit.

Remind me one day to tell you, Dr Diane, what he said to me, my daddy, that first time. We can compare notes.

When the room has been quiet for half an hour or more, I pad to the opening and stand upon the threshold, looking in. I cannot see the bodies intertwined upon the bed, but I can sense them. Theirs is the deep, sated breathing of exhausted lovers. They will sleep for ever in each other's arms, let the last trump sound.

I stand looking down on them, as invisible to them as they to me, for a long time. At last I descend and let myself out through the glass doors. I walk away and don't look back.

*   *   *

Diane threw off the coverlet and sat up. Ed's regular breathing continued unabated. She quietly rose and pulled on a robe, shaking a little. The house lay steeped in velvety-smooth silence. At the head of the stairs she waited, listening. Her pulse beat fast; yet somehow Diane sensed there was nothing to be afraid of.

She knew who had stood at the foot of her bed, examining them. He had this certain smell, the sour, childhood scent of wet gabardine that clung to him like the mustiness of an ancestral tomb. Sensing his presence, Diane hadn't known what to do: wake Ed, put on the light? In the end she'd played dead and silently begged the intruder to go away.

Once downstairs she switched on the lights. A circuit of her house didn't take long. Every door was locked, except one: the sliding door to the deck. Somebody had broken the catch.

Ed was waking up as Diane re-entered the bedroom. He'd got as far as putting on the bedside light and was rubbing his eyes; then he sneezed and his hand groped until its fingers closed around the handle of her bedside drawer.

'What are you looking for?'

'Tissue . . . oh, Jesus . . .' He sneezed again.

'Not there. In the bathroom. I'll get them.'

When she came back with the box he was sitting up in bed. 'What time is it? What's the matter?'

'We've had an intruder.'

He came to life as if someone had doused him with the contents of an invisible bucket of water. Diane explained how she'd woken to the certainty that there was someone in the room, bending over the bed, but all she could see through her lashes was a figure that had moved and vanished.

Ed reached for the phone.

'What are you doing?'

'Calling the police, of course.'

'The police,' she reminded him, 'are already here.'

He gave her a look, but she didn't care. 'Ed,' she said, 'nothing was stolen, no one was harmed, the intruder has gone. I could not identify him – if indeed it was a male – to save my life.'

'Maybe the guy left traces?'

'Not nearly as many as *you've* left.' Diane nodded at the sheets, which weren't quite as they'd looked when she'd put them clean on the bed two days ago, and smiled.

His face told her he was thinking what story he should concoct to explain his presence here; the sad fact was, no story would do. Also, Ed was a cop and he'd lain there snoring his head off while his lady trembled under the very shadow of an intruder, too frightened to cry out.

'Ed,' Diane said gently, at just the right psychological juncture, 'go back to sleep.'

She stroked his cheek and bent forward to kiss him on the mouth. For a moment he did not react. Then he returned her kiss. Diane lay back, smoothing the bed beside her, and Ed followed, and when they made love it wasn't like before, it was perfect.

Later, when Ed had fallen asleep and Diane was drifting off, she heard her mother say, 'You never used to be this kind of girl.'

'Mother,' she whispered fiercely, 'I, a psychologist, cannot go on listening to voices inside my head. It's symptomatic of schizophrenia. It's unethical.'

'And it's stupid to live out here on the hem of the world.'

'Good*night*, Mother.'

'G'night,' Ed muttered.

*   *   *

A week later, at nine thirty in the evening, Johnny looked out of his window to see a man standing on the path underneath the light. He was wearing these funny clothes, though Johnny couldn't tell exactly what. Now the boy knew this was Tobes. Sort of knew it. The thought of going down to him was worrying, but he needed to test his courage. Also, he wanted to talk with his friend.

He hesitated for a long time. But, he went.

Nicole was out this evening. She'd gone to some party of other women; Johnny had heard them arguing about it earlier, with Mike saying You should go and Nicole saying But who will take care of Johnny and assorted crap. She'd gone, anyway. (It was to do with flowers, Johnny thought. Arranging them.) Mike was in the den, working on his laptop, desk piled high with papers. (Johnny peeked on his way out.) Mike wouldn't hear: when he was in that mode, nukes falling on LA wouldn't make much impression.

·Everything went fine till Johnny reached the gate. By the time he got there Tobes was already moving off, heading for the secret place. Johnny followed. Strange: all of a sudden he was giggling. Like there was this huge great bubble of gas inside him. He stuffed a hand across his mouth. Yet at the same time he shivered, which was weird, 'cause the night was warm.

Tobes had a flashlight. He held it so that Johnny could see the beam and follow the light. The boy looked back. They weren't alone. Some guys were lurking around up the path, but they didn't show much interest. Johnny wanted to run up to Tobes, tap him on the right shoulder and, when he turned, duck left to scare him. But he didn't. He didn't know why he didn't.

Tobes was wearing a uniform.

They jogged on down a steep side-path, bump-bump-bump, and the torch jiggled and every so often the boy caught sight of some new detail: what looked like a pouch, belt, cap. Weird.

Tobes vanished.

'Tobes,' Johnny whispered, 'where are you?'

No answer. Johnny looked around. And then he realized that here it was totally dark, like maybe he'd been struck blind. Bible stuff.

Something rustled in the undergrowth near his feet.

For a second Johnny wanted to cry, run, the usual garbage; but then the feeling changed and he felt proud of himself. This was going to be okay as long as he didn't panic.

Couldn't last, of course. A dog snarled, and Johnny's feet left the ground soonest. 'Tobes!' he shrieked. Something fell against a branch; leaves mushed together. He wheeled around and there was the flashlight, all by itself.

Johnny ran towards it. His legs got caught in a bramble. He tried to tear free, fell flat on his face. Another dog growled, or maybe it was the same one, and a fight broke loose: two dogs fighting over there, or was it over *there*?

'Tobes.' Johnny was sobbing now. 'Please . . . '

He heard. He was there. Johnny raised his head to see the flashlight standing on a raised grave. Tobes was coming up, up, up, *out of the grave.*

Maybe Johnny fainted. Stars jumped across his eyes. Then, it was like waking up in the morning, slowly rising to the surface, layer after layer of sleep falling away. And Tobes was there, sitting on the side of the grave, with the flashlight in his hands. He stood up. He went towards Johnny. He opened his mouth, but slowly lifted a white finger to his white lips and Johnny could not say one word.

The dogs had fallen silent. Not a sound disturbed the woods. Maybe God had forgotten to breathe.

Tobes shone the light on the gravestone, and Johnny read the words. Later he couldn't remember them all. Some guy's name, and dates: he'd died in 1941, and he was young. There was this text, too: 'Onward, Christian Soldier'.

'I was walking home that night . . . '

Johnny's heart felt horrible. It wasn't meant to beat that fast.

'Got in to LA little after six. Thought I'd hitch a ride up to see my ma. Not many cars. There was a war coming, and I was on my way to it.'

Tobes said nothing for a while after that; just kept staring into the space behind Johnny, who was shivering so bad he could hardly stand. He thought, *if I ever get back to my bedroom, I'll never, never leave it at night again, not even to go to the bathroom, even if I have to pee on the floor.*

'Had a forty-eight-hour pass. It had been raining for three days solid, was still raining. The man picked me up north of Oxnard. Brought me here. Did it here. They buried me not a mile away from where he did it.'

Seemed like Tobes didn't mean to speak again. Johnny wanted to say all kinds of things. Mainly: 'Stop kidding around, I hate this, take me home.' But even though he felt so scared, he realized something. He was in Tobes's power. What happened here depended on Tobes. Only him.

So Johnny asked, 'Did what?' And when Tobes still wouldn't answer . . . 'What did this guy do to you?'

'Pain.'

'What kind of pain?'

Tobes laughed. That's when Johnny knew for sure it really was Tobes, 'cause no one laughed like him and Johnny hated it. It skewered him, that laugh.

'You're not old enough to understand,' Tobes said. 'They found me. Next day.' And then there came a long pause. 'Both parts of me.'

Johnny couldn't figure that one out.

'He knew I was the guardian, knew I belonged here. He knew. He told me: Alice Mornay, I've brought you home. I was carrying one hundred seventy-six dollars that day. He didn't take a cent. They found the money next to my . . . my parts. And a name-card. He left his card. The name-card of the man who murdered me.'

Johnny stared at him, not afraid now, just absorbed.

'So they buried me here, not far from Alice's grave.' Tobes paused again. 'That was the second time they buried the guardian.'

For a while Johnny didn't get it. Then – 'Second?' he said. 'Wait a minute. . .'

'And there was a third time.'

Tobes advanced on Johnny, keeping the light on his face. The boy backed away. But as Tobes came on he kept talking in that relentless way he had, his black eyes boring into Johnny's skull, and Johnny couldn't stop looking, no matter how much he wanted to turn and run.

'My name was Carl,' Tobes said. (Which was wacko, because although the name on the stone might have begun with C, Johnny didn't think it could have been Carl; in fact, he was sure it wasn't.) 'There was a third funeral here. Next time, I'll show you the third grave.' He stopped, maybe a foot away from the boy, not more. Johnny could smell his breath. It stank. 'Next time . . . you'll be free.'

A dog growled, once, twice, closer.

'Don't move,' Tobes said softly. He let the flashlight beam droop. The dogs were six feet off, three of them, heads sunk low. Johnny could see teeth. Suddenly the front one lowered its body and he knew it was going to spring. Before he could move, Tobes jumped at the dog and swung the flashlight. The beam slithered all over the place. Johnny shut his eyes and waited, paralysed, for the teeth to bite into him.

The sounds coming in his ears grew louder, and muddled. He heard snarling and growling and thuds. A howl. Silence. Johnny opened his eyes. Tobes was standing to one side. The flashlight lay on the ground. The boy picked it up. He saw one of the dogs lying on its side. It didn't move.

Tobes had a knife. He looked up, saw Johnny staring at him, and deliberately shone the light in his eyes. Johnny closed them, blinded. When the bright red colour back of his lids faded away he opened them again, but couldn't see a knife anywhere.

Tobes pointed the light just in front of Johnny's feet. 'Walk.' They went home the way they'd come, Tobes behind, directing the light-beam. Johnny wanted to look back; something stopped him. Was Tobes still there? *Is he going to hit me?* Does *he have a knife?*

The boy walked faster. But then the light ran out, because behind him Tobes had kept to his own slow pace, and Johnny stopped. He *felt* Tobes easing up behind him. How close was he?

Johnny couldn't make himself turn.

The light was by his feet again. They went on.

There came this moment when they were walking up the main path, with the fences of the Court Ridge houses on their left, and they got close to the neighbours' lantern, so there was that light too, as well as the torch, and that was when Johnny knew he was going to make it. Knowing that helped so much, he could turn around again. He really was going to laugh in Tobes's face, say: *What do you think this was all about, you nerd? You scared the shit out of me. So what do you mean by it? Huh?*

But when Johnny did turn, the path was just a long, black void.

*   *   *

CASE-NOTES: *Johnny Anderson, September 9.*

Seventeenth session. Serious crisis.

Last night, the boy went into the cemetery again, despite my many warnings. This time (he told me) he saw a ghost, the ghost was Tobes dressed up, his name was Carl, and various other details, one of which was that *a name-card was found by Carl's body*. This 'Carl' was supposedly murdered in 1941, yet the coincidences are too pronounced to be coincidental. Tobes (if it was he) knows at least one detail about Carl Jensen's murder that the public do *not* know.

What does this mean?

I *must* discuss this with Ed/Symes. How?

Tobes is back in the frame as a suspect. By concealing what Johnny told me I'd make myself accessory to a crime.

I'm at liberty to disclose material if to do so will prevent harm to my patient. *Which* patient: Tobes or Johnny?

There may be a murderer in Johnny's household.

I have absolutely forbidden Johnny to enter the cemetery again. When I asked his permission to talk over his escapades with Mike and Nicole he got mad at me and clearly there was no point in pursuing it. 'I thought I could trust you,' he bawled. I advised him to tell his parents the story himself, in his own words. Also advised leaving Tobes well alone. Finally, I told him I wasn't prepared to keep my mouth shut for ever, and that next week we'd have to work out together what we were going to do.

It's my duty to neutralize any danger emanating from Tobes. For his own good, as well as Johnny's.

The Prophet Mahomet revealed that the insane are the beloved of God and specially chosen by him to declare the truth.

*　　　*　　　*

I'm very unhappy. So, I should make a list of whys.

One. Tobes is shitting me. I don't understand why he's doing all this ghost stuff. It bugs me. It scares me. He's creepy. He's a weirdo. He's nice, too. What am I

supposed to do? Diane said this morning that I was to
stay out of Tobes's hair. As if it was somehow my fault.

Two. I don't like Diane as much as before. She
doesn't understand how much I like Tobes, or how
maybe she should try helping him a little. Okay, I know
he's her patient too, like me, but she doesn't help him, I
can see that.

So: is she helping me?

Three. Last night, I really blew it with 'them', i.e.
the parent-type people in my life . . .

There was this party. Dad and Nicole decided they'd
give a stand-up dinner. They'd been talking about it all
last week, and yesterday morning at breakfast the
service finally broke down on account of the party, so
Johnny had to fix his own toast. Dad seemed pretty
happy. He told Johnny lots of the neighbours were
coming, and half a dozen guys from City Hall with their
wives, and one reporter, and Johnny didn't know who
else. Important people, Mike said, people with influence. He seemed *very* satisfied.

Nicole was less thrilled about this, because she was
the one who ended up doing the work. Didn't like
caterers. Anyway, she wanted Johnny out of the way.
And Lo! A new TV set was introduced unto the
Andersons. They put it in his room; Dad said it was his
for keeps. *But* – he was to stay up there all evening, and
put himself to bed at the usual time. A bribe-oh.

Nicole came up and settled Johnny on the bed with
his TV (turned down low) and the flinker (it even had
one of those) and a plate of cookies and a glass of milk
and she even brought the carton, one of those huge
Knudsden Full Creams, and Johnny kidded her, Maybe
I should have my own ice-box as well.

He was really pleased about the TV, though. So suddenly he had this idea, he'd tell Nicole a few things, like Diane had suggested.

'Nicole?'

'Mm-hm, honey?'

'Can we talk?'

'Well, not right now, I think.'

She was looking great, with this stunning black-and-white dress and her best jewellery and silvery ear-ring things shaped like miniature pestles. (Miss O'Shea had given Johnny a gold star last week for being the only one in class to know what a pestle was.) Nicole wanted to go down and greet her guests, she was worried, and all that stuff, but suddenly it was urgent, *he had to tell her*. So he said, 'Can Dad come up a moment? It's about the cemetery. *Please!*'

She looked uncertain, then smiled, and Johnny thought she'd do it, when suddenly Mike called, 'Nicole, sweetheart, where are you?'

'Tomorrow, pet,' Nicole said to Johnny. 'Okay?'

What could he do except nod and say, Okay? But after that, do you think he could get to sleep/watch TV/read? No. Because downstairs and outside, in the newly cleaned-up yard, grown-ups were enjoying themselves. They clinked glasses and clanked plates, and they made a lot of happy noise. It was a fun party, for them (*I'd hate it*, Johnny thought). But as the evening turned cooler they started to drift inside, until eventually the garden was empty. Johnny looked out the window, half expecting to see Tobes underneath the light, but he wasn't there. Of course, ghosts didn't like parties.

Johnny caught himself thinking that and it seemed weird. For a moment there he almost believed Tobes really was a ghost.

He flinked through the channels, but nothing grabbed him. He switched to a blank TV channel and watched the lines fizzle for a while, hoping they'd send him to sleep. They gave him a headache instead. Downstairs, the noise went on and on. *You'd think people would start to leave*, Johnny thought drowsily. *Grown-ups don't quit parties, they just get louder.*

He threw off the cover, jumped down from his bunk and padded along the corridor to look. People everywhere; some of them were sitting on the bottom of the stairway. Johnny kept to shadow, no one noticed him. Dad came to sit with a group of those other men on the lowest step. For a while Johnny couldn't hear what they were saying, but then the hallway thinned out and, 'Stanley, you're crazy if you think you can buy a bishop,' one of the men said.

'Cardinal Tom can fix anything,' another man replied. ''Cept his own conscience.'

They all laughed, Dad loudest of all. Johnny thought he shouldn't laugh so loud, then felt guilty about criticizing his own father.

'Mike . . . ' The man called Stanley put an arm around Dad's shoulders. 'I don't want you worrying about the deconsecration. At the end of the day, it simply isn't going to be an issue.'

'I don't know.' Mike slowly shook his head. 'We've not done a residential development in a graveyard before.'

Johnny was gliding down the stairs, like he, too, was a ghost, drawn to the seat of power by a magical incantation. His dad, Mike Anderson, was going to *build* on the cemetery?

Yes, of course. You've always known that.

Yes, but . . . Tobes's cemetery?

HIS CEMETERY!

'You can't,' said this voice. Johnny's.

The men all looked up, showing surprise that turned quickly to smiles. Why, wasn't it cute little Johnny, their host's son?

'Dad,' the boy said, coming down the last few steps, 'is it true you're planning to build houses on the cemetery? I mean, really?'

Mike smiled, but Johnny knew him from *way* back, and this smile was an oh-oh number. 'That's right, son. I thought you knew.'

'I knew about the houses.' He had to break and swallow here. 'It's just that . . . well, I hadn't really thought about it before.'

'What's your problem, son?' Stanley enquired.

'It's a nice quiet place. I like to go there. My friends like to go there.'

'Well, it's going to happen.' Dad's smile was giving Johnny the heebie-jeebies, but he was in too deep to care. Maybe he *had* been scared to death in that cemetery, but Tobes was a part of it, and he liked Tobes (kind of), and he'd felt *real* there. The thought of dozens of little houses, back to back, side to side, sprawling concrete and brick over the hills beyond the back gate suddenly made Johnny want to puke.

'Dad,' he said. 'Please don't do this.'

But all Mike said was, 'Time for you to get back to bed.'

'What about all the dead people? Who's going to take care of them?'

'They're dead,' said another guy. 'They won't mind.'

'They will, they will, they *will*. A friend of mine is buried there, three times, he's going to hate being built on.'

310

In the silence that followed, Johnny realized he'd blown it, mega. They were looking at him intently, like scientists poking around a specimen. Dad's face was horrible. He reached out to take his son's hand. Johnny ripped it away.

'None of your friends is buried in that cemetery,' Mike said.

Johnny mumbled something about Alice and Carl, but what was the point? This had gone beyond help. Hope, too. And when you're hopeless, really without hope, you do brave, stupid things. Johnny said, 'The guardian ghost isn't going to like you.' And because he was in control now, he could see that from their faces, he went on, 'Any one of you. So better watch out.'

And with that, he ran upstairs.

He wrote it all down in his diary, as the guests went out, slamming their car-doors, shouting, laughing, drunk maybe . . .

Jesus, tomorrow's going to be terrible. Did I dig myself into a hole . . .

I wish I'd never met you, Tobes.

*   *   *

For Diane, that Friday started so well.

She left home early, leaving The Safety Net ensconced in her living-room with their screwdrivers and junction-boxes and cute tan legs in sawn-off denim shorts, safe in the conviction that when she returned home that night her house would be a fortress. *Good* feeling; the last she was to enjoy for some time.

First person she saw as she ran up the steps of the police HQ was Ramon Porras, coming out. He was wearing black jeans, a grey T, and a sad, sad expression.

'Hello,' she greeted him. 'What brings you here?'

'Q and A.'

'About what?'

'Everything that ever happened in this town.' He became animated. 'Dr Cheung, I tell you, if someone stole a postage-stamp, they want me to confess to it. Murder, torture . . .'

But for all his anger, Diane could sense tears near the surface. 'Did you have a lawyer?' she asked him gently. He shook his head. Like so many misguided people, he thought innocence was a defence in law. Without another word he slouched away without saying goodbye or looking back: a troubled mind.

The muster sergeant told Diane where to find Ed: on the second floor, interview room 5. She met him coming out.

'Hi,' he said, surprised. 'What brings you here?'

'Have you been giving Porras a rough time?'

Ed thought about that for a second. 'Yeah,' he admitted. 'Maybe I have at that.'

'And?'

'He's got an alibi for Douggan, none for Jensen. Anyway, what can I do for you?'

'I'm here to monitor your interrogation of Tobes Gascoign.'

'Oh, Diane, we went into that, and – '

'I cleared it with Peter,' she said, pushing past him into the room. 'Check it out with him if you don't believe me.'

Rather than have a big argument then and there he went out and checked with Peter's office, who okayed

Diane, and he came back in a temper so bad you could see smoke coming out of both ears. 'You going to make a habit of this?' he asked.

'Of what?'

'Cutting off my balls.'

'How many balls do you have? I mean, a habit implies – '

'Oh, for Christ's sake!'

Diane dropped a pause into their conversation and then she said, 'I'm not going to apologize, any more than some of your men are for trying to block my Juvenile Crime Unit's effectiveness with red tape, and regulations, and goodness knows what else. I told Peter this was an experiment and he agreed to it.'

'Diane, we are lovers. This is a major, *major* betrayal.'

'It has nothing to do with our being lovers.'

'You can't dissociate the two.'

'That's precisely what we must learn to do.'

The phone rang. Ed answered. 'Yes? Put him next door. Thanks.' He looked at Diane. 'Gascoign's arrived.'

She switched out the light. This room had no window, it was dark, but she knew her way around it from past assignments. She went over to the far wall where a curtain hung, and drew it aside to reveal a sheet of glass giving a view of the room next door: a two-way mirror, like the one connecting her office to the playroom at St Joseph's.

The door of the other room opened to admit Tobes, in custody of a uniformed cop, who left him alone there. Tobes spent a few moments wandering around. He examined the tape-recorder, the desk, the four chairs, before finally going over to the window and staring out.

'We'd better continue this later,' Ed said in a cold voice. He phoned down for a stenographer and video-equipment. Diane glanced next door, through the mirror. Tobes had put on his headphones and was listening to that portable CD player he always carried around with him, a dreamy expression on his face.

'Ed,' she said, 'let's talk this out.'

'So what's to talk?'

'I know I'm not doing this as tactfully as I might. But I *am* doing my duty. And I swear to you, if today doesn't work out it's the last time.'

'Oh, yes?'

'Yes. And please don't get sarcastic.' She pointed through the mirror. 'He's starting to worry me terribly.'

'And why?'

'You remember the other night, at my house?' Ed eyed her, not sure which bit she meant him to remember. 'We had an intruder. You've got to promise me not to use this, because it's not evidence, it's things I feel inside me, but . . . I believe the intruder was Tobes Gascoign.'

Ed said nothing for a while. They both stared through the glass at their suspect, two voyeurs in an aquarium, trying to figure out if what they were looking at was barracuda or cod.

'He has a smell,' she went on. 'Dank, musty.'

Tobes seemed to have registered the mirror. He was gazing straight at them, unblinkingly. Sometimes a hand went up to the earpieces of his CD player; apart from that, he didn't move. Except that his smile deepened, and Diane noticed that his eyes were wide open, alert.

'Is that it?' Ed asked.

314

'Not quite. It seems logical to suspect one of my court-referrals, especially in the light of that name-card I found in my garage.'

'And blamed me for.'

'Patients sometimes get these fixations with their therapists.' *Often*, a voice recited inside her head, often they do . . .

'File a complaint. I'll back you, and to hell with the gossip.'

'Ed, I am talking about a smell and a hunch!' Diane's exasperation came back at her, reflected in his eyes. 'I'm muddled, I'm sleeping badly, I'm, I'm . . . tortured by these bad dreams, I . . . '

'I'm worried about you.'

Damn, why do women always cry at the worst times? Diane groped for a tissue. Ed tried to clean her up with a handkerchief, but she pushed him away, and this action brought her around to face the big sheet of glass again.

Tobes, still facing the mirror, still had this dreamy look on his face. He had unzipped his fly and taken out his penis. Fully erect, uncircumcised, it stood out at an angle of twenty degrees from his body, absurdly reminding Diane of an Oscar statuette. Tobes was masturbating, slowly.

For a moment Ed and Diane stood there, stricken into silence. Then Ed made a dive for the door, but she was quicker. She grabbed his arm and she shouted, 'No!'

'You can't just . . . let . . . '

'Wait!'

They glued themselves to the mirror. Ed's horror shivered and shimmied all around her, like an alien force, but she made herself ignore it. Tobes's hand was

315

moving faster now. His eyes were shut, his teeth ground, he started to lean backwards. And then sperm flew out, he came so hard that a few drops landed on the mirror, grey blobs with a luminous white surround, and it was funny, but both Ed and Diane recoiled at that, as if they were under attack, and vulnerable.

Tobes knew they were there.

On the other side of the mirror, their assailant was cleaning up. Tobes rubbed his side of the glass with lazy strokes of a soiled handkerchief, smiling the while. Because he didn't know where they were standing his eyes didn't quite meet theirs, but that was chance, and part of Diane saluted his courage.

'Okay,' she said briskly. 'Take the interview as if nothing has happened. Heat up your grill, Detective. Stay *well* away from the break-in to my house. Go over early history, childhood, school.'

'What?'

'I need to have you, Authority, Power, ask him the questions he ducks when they come from me. They're the key to this. Ask him if he was sexually abused as a child – that's very important.'

Ed was starting to make notes. Diane paced up and down, numbering points off on her fingers.

'Take it fast, then slow, then fast again: I need to watch for word salad. Know anything about kinesics . . . ?'

'Huh?'

'Body language. Never mind. Find out what you can about his mother. Quiz him on the difference between right and wrong, and don't let him get away from you on that one. Press him on his history of school-refusal.'

'Slow down.'

'Oh yes, another vital one: ask if he suffered any kind of head injury as a child. Keep him on the hop: be nice, horrid, fast, slow, logical, instinctive. Don't let him rest.'

'Am I allowed to ask him about these crimes he may have committed?'

'Sarcasm again.'

The door of the far room opened to admit a stenographer; Tobes was over by the window, innocent and unconcerned. Diane continued to watch him while Ed went out and a few seconds later materialized in the far room. She adjusted the sound-speaker volume. Ed took a few moments to get a grip on himself. He made Tobes sit down opposite him. Diane studied their body language: very hostile.

She wanted to believe the incident they'd just witnessed wasn't serious. But she kept remembering Bruce Lyons, who used to hold up underwear shops in Los Angeles, order some woman to remove her panties, and then masturbate with the garment draped over his face before robbing the till. He didn't care if people watched: the more the better. He became California's public enemy number one, and they sent him down the river for fifteen years.

Ed started in.

Diane had fought against giving vent to her deepest suspicions about Tobes. But as the interrogation progressed, she found herself putting away doubt. The more she heard, the more convinced she became that her first, instinctual hunch was correct.

It turned out that Tobes had been dropped on his head as a baby.

He had a record of petty theft.

His kinesics signalled he was petrified of talking about his mother, which she already knew; but now for

317

the first time she was seeing him under pressure from a third party, and the reinforcement was remarkable. This boy didn't want to acknowledge he had parents, period.

Then came this exchange . . .

Ed: Date, I must have the exact date.

Tobes: I don't remember, I'm telling you.

Ed: Well, do you have a friend, a –

Tobes: I'll look it up in my journal, okay? I'll tell you then.

Journal, what journal? Diane knew nothing of that. Keeping a diary was one of the hallmarks of the self-esteem killer. What would Daniel Krozgrow make of it?

Ed was good today: wide-ranging, imaginative. A new picture of Tobes started to build as Diane listened. In some ways this was the young man she already knew, in others not; two images came together, faded apart. The words 'malignant narcissism' swam into her mind. Symptoms: paranoia, total self-absorption, inability to empathize with others, absence of conscience . . .

Vesti la giubba, Tobes said suddenly. When Ed looked blank: *Pagliacci. On with the motley, in case you don't happen to have Italian.*

. . . The need to reassure yourself that you're more intelligent, more valuable than those around you. Saddam Hussein is thought to suffer from malignant narcissism.

At last the interview was winding down. Diane checked the time: nearly two hours had passed. She watched Ed and Tobes go out, followed by the stenographer, and mentally began to compose her analysis.

The door of her room banged open. 'Hi!' said Tobes. 'And what brings you here today, Dr Diane?'

'What the hell do you think – ' Ed grabbed him by the arm. 'I said, *down* the corridor, you – '

All wrong, and too late anyway.

'Hello, Tobes,' Diane said. 'How are things?'

He was looking at the glass panel. 'So,' he said cuttingly, 'a spy, huh? Habit of yours, yes?'

He threw off Ed's arm. His eyes blazed with malice towards her, towards the world. 'Well, fuck you!' he hissed. 'Fuck you all.'

Then he was out like a whirlwind, Ed in hot pursuit. The door closed. Diane sank into a chair, trembling. She was still there moments later, when Ed came back. 'Sorry,' he said, sitting down opposite her.

'It's okay.'

'I told him the way out but he made a dive . . .'

'He guessed I was here, or somebody was. Never mind. You were brilliant.'

'So, what's the verdict?'

He looked at her like a dog expecting a long-merited walk. Diane was trembling on the abyss now. Whatever she said next was going to affect Tobes Gascoign for the rest of his life.

'You're having him profiled by Quantico, right?'

Ed nodded.

'Tell them it's urgent.'

He was surprised; which of itself was hardly surprising, in view of her earlier attitude. 'You think – '

'I think he has psychopathic tendencies.'

Ed leaned forward. 'Give.'

'That's it.'

'It can't be! There has to be more. You're changing your whole approach to this guy, you're turning against him, and you have to have a reason.'

'Professional instinct, based on what I've just seen and heard.'

'You mean, he jerks off.'

'Not just that.'

'Well, *what*?'

'There's little to be gained from shouting.'

Ed thumped the table with his fist. He stood up. 'Come on, I want you to see something.'

When she was slow he grabbed her hand and pulled her out of the chair, into the corridor, along to a big room at the far end, where half a dozen detectives were hard at work. He hauled her up to a filing-cabinet and wrenched open one of the drawers to show her its contents.

'A month's work, Doctor. Two hundred separate files and over, and these are just the interviews, the suspects, that we deemed worthy of taking out of the computer and translating into hard copy. There's the same number again on disk.'

He took out half a dozen folders and slammed them on the top of the cabinet. Diane was aware of eyes scalpelling her back. Her skin froze. Ed tossed papers around like there was a storm blowing through the office.

'Two, three, four thousand man-hours, stenography, photography, forensic, tech reps.' He thrust an enormous orange folder into her chest. 'The Quantico file. Have a guess, go on, guess, how many pages?' He raised his voice, addressing the room at large. 'Hey, guys, a sweep! Come on, how many pages in the Quantico file, buck apiece, nearest wins all.'

There is only one thing to do with a patient who loses control and now Diane did it: she withdrew. She turned, she walked through their laughter – not all of it hostile – and made for the exit. Ed ran after her. He tugged her arm. Because he was stronger than Diane she made no effort to shake him off; she went limp, refusing to look at him.

'Why won't you do one damn thing to help?' he snapped. 'Those files add up to zero. Now. You heard, and saw – but my God, you saw – Gascoign this morning. You tell me he's psychopathic. You tell me he broke into your house. You have the power to put him away, to make the streets that little bit safer, and you will not do it and I demand to know *why*?'

On the last word he hit the wall with his hand, making her jump.

'Diane,' he said. 'Make a report, a complaint, about the break-in that night. That gives us probable cause to hold him. It buys time.'

She wanted to so much! *Oh Ed, how can you not see that?* But instead she did a desperate, dangerous thing: she let herself go, which she had never done before, no, not even when *Ma-ma* died. She turned her back on Ed and walked out of the headquarters. She got in her car and she drove, not to St Joseph's, where she had a frantic schedule this Friday afternoon, but home. She stormed past The Safety Net, who were packing up, threw herself on the bed, and howled for a long, long time.

The storm blew itself out, eventually. '*Ma-ma*,' she cried quietly into her pillow. 'When will I ever learn to grow up?'

Ma-ma was there for her, as always. 'When you grant yourself permission.'

'But Larry, my stepfather . . . '

It was like when there's nothing being broadcast on a particular wavelength, though you sense there's someone out there. *Ma-ma* hadn't gone away, but nor had she anything to say about her second husband.

'I don't have any friends,' Diane sniffed.

'Which makes you doubly strong. And there's Ed.'

'There *was*.'

Diane started to sob again. The ether hissed. She knew *Ma-ma* was still there. The knowledge eventually gave her the courage to sit up, clean her face, manage a smile. She did some meditation. That helped. *Phone the hospital, struggle to put your career back together again.*

Diane made an infusion of raw tree peony bark, with cinnamon and walnuts: the most soothing concoction she knew. As she sat sipping it, she reviewed the situation and tried to work out what should happen next.

She must confront Tobes and have things out with him. But . . . 'He's dangerous, *Ma-ma*,' she heard herself say.

The ether was silent. *Ma-ma* had gone. As the certainty solidified inside Diane's brain she felt her sense of humour return. 'I bet Tobes talks to people who aren't there, *Ma-ma*.'

When there was no response, Diane laughed.

*   *   *

It's school vacation. Dad was talking about a week in Orlando so as I could take in Disney World, but now it seems like business is shaky and he wants to stay around for the summer. Nicole bought me a Lynx hand-held for my birthday last week. Dad was so busy in meetings then that he had to bring my present home on my actual birthday, along with a card. (He'd gone to work before I woke up that morning.) Nicole's brother and his wife sent a card plus dough. My mom's sisters both sent presents: a book on vampires from Auntie Elaine, and a skateboard from Auntie Pat. I had to write thank-you letters. Yech! (I'll never get the hang of that board.)

They're starting to do bad things to the cemetery now. There's wires up, and holes being dug. Not near our place, thank goodness. But every day it sounds a bit noisier back there. I like watching the earth-movers but I'm only allowed to go with Nicole or Dad, and they're often busy.

Went to the ocean a couple of times with guys from school, but that Arnie Krantz was there, too. He didn't fight with me, but he kept talking about me behind my back, and the other kids would laugh. I just pretended I wasn't interested, but I don't think I'll go again.

It's so boring around here.

Every night I look out of my window at nine thirty. He's never there. I give him until ten, then go to sleep. He's still my friend, though, my one and only. Wei yi, in Chinese. Dr Diane showed me how to draw it, the Chinese for 'one and only', and how to spell it in real letters, too. We're getting on well. She said I should write my diary more, but why, when nothing ever happens?

Maybe I should run away from home. I'm frightened to do that. But I can't see any other way. I won't think about running away yet. Only if things become unbearable, then will I run away. I know where I'll go. He won't reject me. He promised.

Diane said: Try to sort it all out on paper. Write it down, then you control it. As if things were so easy! Dad hasn't said anything about the party the other night, not yet. He will, though.

Funny: Johnny had just finished writing that when the sky fell in.

It was Saturday: three o'clock in the afternoon. Mike came back from his golf game. He walked in the kitchen, where Johnny was still writing, and this was how it went.

'Johnny, I want to talk to you.' Mike raised his voice. 'Nicole, can you come in here a moment?'

She came in from the garden, and ran a hand through Johnny's hair, and he was grateful. At that very precise moment, he actually liked her more than he loved Dad.

'Johnny,' said Mike, sitting down, 'we need to have a serious talk about what happened the other night.'

The boy nodded. He wanted to say something, but his chest felt all tight, his throat ached, he was gruzzled.

'You said one of your friends is buried in Court Ridge Cemetery. You said it in front of my business partners. You said your friend wouldn't like being built on. And the guardian ghost wouldn't like it.'

There was a long silence. The boy looked at his father, contrite and wanting to make amends, but silent. Mike Anderson sighed. Nicole's hand strayed across to Johnny's: their fingers touched.

'Johnny.' Mike paused, as if he wanted to be *real* choosy with his words. 'There are no such things as ghosts.'

'You don't know that,' Johnny said.

'Has Dr Cheung been talking to you about ghosts?'

'Yes.'

'Uh-huh. I thought so.' Mike tapped the table-top with the flat of his hand and looked at Nicole. His eyes said, Case proved.

'Don't blame her,' Johnny flared. 'You should be grateful to her.'

'I should?'

'She's making me see you didn't kill Mom,' the boy shouted. 'Isn't that a plus? Huh? Mr Big-Shot Reckless Driver.'

There was this awful silence – you hear your heart beating and the tape's run out: Life Stops Here. Mike slowly regained control. His face was a picture. A horror picture.

'I'm not taking any more of this crap,' he said, standing up. 'Ghosts . . . guardians . . . what Johnny needs is a proper psychologist. Not a woman, not a foreigner: somebody competent.'

'Honey, hold on a moment . . .'

It was Nicole, riding to his rescue. Wow! 'Johnny needs help, Darling, and he likes Diane. They get on together. And you know how much sweeter things have been in this house since he started seeing her.'

Nicole was nervous, Johnny could tell. She hadn't had a lot of practice at contradicting Mike. But once she started, she pitched with the best.

'We shouldn't change just like that,' Nicole said. 'I think it's the graveyard. We should move house.'

'Oh, we've been through all that.'

'*You've* been through it. Your side of it. Now, if we're going to stay, I want some ground rules. Mike, you say the cemetery's okay, that there are no ghosts. Johnny doesn't agree. Why don't we all take a walk there now, as a family, and discuss it as we go. Because what we three need to do is *talk*.'

Mike and Johnny stared at her. They were neither of them accustomed to hearing propositions advanced from this quarter with feeling and rationality. Now Nicole stood up and headed for the back door.

'Come along,' she said. 'You're not going to change Johnny's psychologist without listening to him first, and doing something to help him, and treating him as a father should.'

Johnny couldn't believe Nicole had said that, even later. Mike looked like he was going to explode, but a few minutes later the three of them were walking through the back garden, which had become spectacularly neat and tidy since Tobes got his machete into it, and out onto the path.

'Okay, Johnny,' Nicole said. 'I want you to give us a tour. Show us your turf. And whenever we get near a place where you've met a ghost, tell us all about it.'

'Yeah,' Mike put in, 'you can introduce us to your new friend, this guardian . . . whatever.'

Now this was rapidly turning into a problem. The only ghost around here was Tobes, and Johnny might not be a grown-up, he didn't have the brain of an Einstein, but even he dimly appreciated that getting this across would not be straightforward. *He* didn't understand it, so how to convince other people?

While Johnny was mulling that one over, they came to the fork in the path. If they turned left, they'd be entering Tobes's territory: the world of dogs, and their shit, and old graves. Johnny didn't want to risk that. And yet, Nicole had definitely got something. He wanted to go back to those places with a couple of adults holding his hands, in daylight, without Tobes.

So he made a left.

It was amazing how quickly they passed from one terrain to the next. Within yards of leaving the main track, the going got harder. They pushed through some brambles. Mike swore, but softly, so Johnny couldn't hear the bad word. After they'd been battering their way through the jungle for a bit, Nicole asked, 'Are you sure this is the right way?'

'Yes.'

'I never realized it was so big,' Nicole said. Her voice was quiet, awed.

'Big place,' Mike agreed. His breathing was funny now, as if he'd been running. They pushed on.

'Okay,' Mike said after another five minutes or so. 'Enough. No ghosts. Home, now.'

'It's this way,' Johnny said. 'The place where the ghosts are.'

He wasn't bullshitting. He remembered this place. He knew where Tobes's secret hideaway was, and suddenly he wanted Dad to see the grave of Alice Mornay. Maybe that'd satisfy him.

'Johnny,' Nicole said. 'Did you come here *alone*?'

The boy saw her point. They were a long way from the reassuring safety of home. Too late, he realized he should never have let himself be sucked into this. It was a trap. Nicole had laid it.

Should have known.

'Sometimes,' he said.

'Well, who went with you at other times?' Mike was angry. 'Have you been making friends and not letting us meet them?'

'I came here when I got lost that Saturday, remember?' Johnny didn't mean to shout, but things were getting desperate.

'Don't you take that tone with me.' Mike grabbed his arm. 'We're going home and I'm going to phone that Chink shrink . . .'

'No!'

Johnny wrenched his arm free and broke into a run. Mike chased after him. Johnny dodged this way and that, but they were out of open space now, heading deeper into thorns and thickets. Suddenly he saw a tree he recognized. Tobes's clearing! It was nearby. Yes! He dropped on hands and knees and crawled through the hardly visible opening. He'd found it!

But he wasn't quick enough to prevent Mike from seeing him. Mike crawled through the tunnel. Johnny backed up against a tree. There was no way out of here except through the tunnel, and Mike was blocking that, swearing like a marine. He burst through, face all scratched. Outside, Nicole was calling – sounded like she might be crying, too.

Mike stood up and dusted himself down. He glared at Johnny. He took a stride forward. He fell flat on his face. Johnny didn't laugh, he was too scared. Dad got up. He looked back to see what had tripped him. Johnny looked too.

There was a hand sticking out of the big mound of soil, next to Alice Mornay's grave. It was black. Not all its fingers were present and accounted for. Johnny guessed this must be the equivalent of a cheese-flavoured nacho, if you were a dog.

He started to laugh. Then he couldn't stop.

*   *   *

The day after Tobes's extraordinary interrogation was a Saturday. Diane slept late and went down to St Joe's after lunch, meaning to cut a swathe through all her paperwork. Things went well, at first; but then Ed zapped her by stopping by the hospital about three o'clock. She'd thought she wouldn't be seeing him again, at least not socially. He put his head around the door, cutting off the breath in her throat, and asked if she could spare a moment.

'Come in.'

The rest of Ed came around the door, lugging this big bunch of flowers.

'Oh, Ed . . .'

They were beautiful: wild roses, larkspur, California poppies, and they came wrapped in newspaper . . . 'You *picked* these,' she burst out. 'You actually went and picked them yourself.'

'I'm too cheap to buy a girl flowers.'

Diane's heart just melted and melted and went on melting. Women were so stupid; it was their greatest charm. 'Does this mean we're friends again?' she asked.

'Yes and no,' Ed replied. 'Mind if I sit down?'

Looking into his eyes, she saw this was heavy stuff.

'I was talking with some of the guys,' Ed said. 'That unit of yours is starting to get popular, you know?'

Diane shook her head.

'Plus you're starting to change the atmosphere, down at the station. And that can only be good.'

Diane opened a desk drawer and pulled out a sheaf of notes. 'My first quarterly report to Peter,' she said. 'Draft only. But there *is* movement. Counselling of officers is going well, especially after that hostage take last month. Fewer juvenile arrests.'

'So why do I feel afraid?'

Diane stared glumly at her mate, having no answer. He sat with one leg resting on the other knee, hand to ankle; she could see his white socks, a little frayed around the tops. She was not one of nature's sock-menders, but the sight tugged something deep inside her.

'Diane,' he said, 'we have to separate out your roles. We have to make the best deal for all concerned.'

'Are you sure?'

'Meaning?'

'Is this really about deals and demarcations, or don't you like seeing an amateur do your job better than you can?'

Ed's face hardened, his movements became twitchy. 'I don't think that enters into it,' he said. 'What I want from you is a commitment not to go to Symes behind my back again.'

She considered the wall while he regarded the state of her carpet. Outside the sun continued to shine, but it sure was raining in Diane's office.

'Do you think we can work together and still be lovers?' he asked, surprising her by actually coming to the point. 'Or should I apply for a transfer?'

'I'd *hate* that.'

'Not as much as I hate my lover going behind my back to get me overturned.'

'You'd leave the unit?'

'I'd leave the precinct. Maybe even the state.'

He'd obviously been thinking about this, it wasn't a temper-inspired whim. He might up and go. Leaving her where? Ah! – Diane shouldn't care about herself, she should think only of the good of the force, of the patients, of the criminals she was helping stay out of jail. Whereas all she really cared about at this moment was her, her, again her.

Ed's bleeper jolted them out of their respective day-mares. He gestured at her phone, and she nodded.

'Ed Hersey . . . yuh. Yuh. *What?*' Ed swung around in his chair, groping for notebook and pen. 'When did this happen? . . . Where?'

He wrote busily before hanging up, then wrote some more. Diane was half curious, half bound up in her despair of ever making a viable future for them both. Then Ed said, 'They've found the Delmar kid.'

'Alive?'

'Uh-uh. Buried in Court Ridge Cemetery. A family was out walking, they stumbled over it.'

Diane didn't know why she asked her next question; there had to be hundreds of families who walked in that place, it was just that she happened to know one such family. 'What's the name of the people who found him?'

'Anderson.'

Diane rested her head in her hands. Ed said, 'I have to go, what's up?'

'Coming with you,' she said, rising. 'Johnny Anderson's my patient. The patient I found Tobes a job with.'

'Oh, Jesus . . .'

They drove up to Court Ridge at speed. The Anderson house was under siege from the usual assortment of animal life that slithered out of the thickets on these occasions: reporters, interviewing themselves for want of a better victim; cameramen; ghouls; neighbours with an angle. Yellow-and-black incident tapes ruled off a sanitized area in front of the main entrance, with two blues standing behind it. Ed and Diane drove through in a hail of flash-guns and shouted questions.

Inside the house were a lot of officers, two guys from homicide Diane vaguely recognized, an assistant medical examiner she saw down at the tennis-club sometimes. The Andersons' house had been transformed into a temporary HQ, with comings and goings and handheld transceivers and portable fax machines. Ed conferred with a deputy inspector; the two of them went out back. Nicole plucked Diane's arm. 'Thank God you're here,' she said.

'Luck. Where's Johnny?'

'In his room.'

The two women climbed the stairs together. Diane used the opportunity to quiz Nicole about events, and Johnny's state of mind.

'He was hysterical at first. I didn't see it, but there was this hand sticking up out of the soil . . .'

Johnny looked up quickly as Diane knocked and pushed open his door. 'Hi!'

Her first impression was that the incident had interested rather than scared him. There were few signs of negative affect. He seemed eager to talk.

'Gee, Diane, you should have seen it. It was awful. This hand, four fingers sticking out, like in some movie, y'know?'

'I can imagine.'

'He'd been eaten, it was a he, a guy, I heard. They say I've got to stay up here until they're ready to ask me some questions.'

Diane had a question of her own. 'Johnny, can you describe the place where you found this . . . this?'

'It was a clearing.'

'Near here?'

'Half a mile, maybe.'

Diane knew kids of his age varied tremendously in their ability to interpret distance. 'Anything strange about this clearing?' she asked.

'No.' He didn't quite meet her eye.

'No gravestone?'

He looked at her in astonishment. 'You've been there?'

'Something's written on the stone, yes?' When he didn't reply, she prompted him. 'Alice . . . ?'

'Mornay.' Johnny mooched over to the window. Diane expected him to come back after a while, and when he didn't she went after him. He was staring down into the garden where Tobes was busy with some rose bushes, near the wall of the house. If he was aware of the pandemonium around him he gave no sign.

Diane said, 'Johnny, you mustn't be surprised if Tobes doesn't come here again.'

He wheeled around. 'Why?'

'Until we get this mess sorted out, he needs to stay away from you. For his sake, and for yours, and, yes, for mine, too.'

Diane feared she'd have to explain more, but the boy merely nodded. 'Let me say goodbye,' he murmured. 'Please.'

'That's up to your parents.'

Diane left him in his bedroom and went to find his stepmother.

'Nicole,' she said, taking her by the arm as they descended the stairs. 'Maybe I was wrong about Tobes. You'd better let him go.'

'But . . . why? He seemed such a nice young man.'

'Trust me on this one, okay?'

'But he's so cheap, and he's done marvels in the back yard. I don't know what Mike's going to say.'

'What Mike's going to say about what?'

They turned to see the master of the house emerge from his den with a couple of officers. Mike's face was flushed. He'd been making a statement, and obviously he didn't like the way his house was being upturned by a murder investigation. 'What am I to say?' he repeated.

'Tobes Gascoign,' Diane said crisply. 'I think you should let him go.'

'Why?'

'I'm not at liberty to say more than that he's my patient and I have professional reasons for thinking he could be a malign influence on your son.'

'How come you didn't think to mention that before, when you were selling him to me?'

'It didn't seem relevant at the time. And . . . and I didn't know then what I know now.'

They locked eyeballs. Diane couldn't think what to do if Mike pushed this, because she owed Tobes a duty of confidence just as much as she owed one to Johnny.

'You're saying he's connected with that thing we found in the cemetery?'

'Not as yet.'

'But you think he might be?'

'Not as yet.'

Mike Anderson looked into Diane's eyes like he wanted to pluck out her soul. She was mentally preparing herself for a fight; but then he said, 'Okay. If that's what you think.' He marched across the hall and into the big living-room. Through the french window Tobes could be seen, working away on his rose bushes. Mike opened the window. 'Tobes, come in here a minute, will you?'

Tobes entered. Diane, hearing a noise behind her, half turned to see Johnny at the foot of the stairs. As he caught her glance he stopped, putting his hands into his hip-pockets, and stared at the floor.

'Tobes,' Mike said, 'this lady is your shrink, isn't she?'

Tobes looked at her. 'Hello, Dr Diane.' And then to Mike, 'Yes.'

'And she's good, isn't she; you do what she tells you?'

Tobes said nothing.

'Well, son, I'm sorry about this, but she says I have to let you go and I'm not about to take chances. What do I owe you?'

Tobes gazed at Diane, but she couldn't read the message.

'Son? You hear me?'

Tobes seemed to gather his senses. 'Oh, uh . . . yesterday and today . . . five hours, say thirty-five dollars.'

'Say fifty.' Mike took out his bill-fold and gave him a fifty.

'Thank you,' Tobes said.

Diane watched him narrowly all the while. 'Tobes,' she said, 'I'm so sorry about this. Come to my office nine o'clock Monday; before you leave I'll have gotten you a job. That's a promise. I'll call in favours, I'll do anything, but you'll have another job by Monday lunchtime.'

His smile was thin, but he remembered to say, 'Thank you.' And then – 'I'd like to say goodbye to Johnny; may I?'

Nobody said anything. Mike looked at Nicole, who looked at Diane, who was too busy staring at Tobes to register. So Tobes took things into his own hands. He walked into the hallway, where Johnny was waiting. The two of them went to stand over by the front door, and they had their heads close together, but they didn't quite touch. The grown-ups felt, Diane knew they all felt, that this was going to break up any second now, so where was the harm, what was the problem, with so many policemen around . . .?

*　　　*　　　*

Johnny watched.

Tobes was in the living-room with Mike and Nicole and Dr Diane. He stood there with his head up, looking

335

everybody in the eye, and Johnny felt so proud of him. Any minute now, Tobes would leave this house for ever. All the boy cared about was saying a real goodbye.

The adults finished their business. Tobes walked right through them, coming straight towards Johnny, and from the way he carried himself the boy knew Tobes felt the same way about this as he did. He was Johnny's big brother, his John-Boy Walton who took care of him and put up with him, and now he was leaving and Johnny wouldn't be seeing him again.

'I love you,' Johnny said as Tobes came up.

Tobes smiled. First his smile said, 'I love you too,' and then his mouth said it. 'But they won't let me stay here.'

'Why?' Johnny whimpered.

''Cause they think I had something to do with what you and your old man found today.'

'Stupid! It's all my fault.'

'Don't say that.' Tobes had moved close, they could have kissed if they'd wanted.

'But I told Diane some of the things you said to me!'

'Oh.' Tobes bit his lip. 'Be a bit careful what you tell Diane, okay?'

'Why?'

'Doesn't matter.'

'Nobody loves me, except you.'

'Your old man loves you. Even the Wicked Witch does. You're lucky, Johnny. Don't throw it all away.'

'I just wish I could live with you.'

'Maybe one day I'll have a great place of my own. Then I'll visit you.'

'No, you'll come and rescue me. You will, you will.'

With a frown Tobes warned Johnny to keep his cool, or the adults would come and break them up. The boy chewed his lips until they bled.

'I'll come and rescue you,' Tobes agreed. 'On a big white horse.'

'Oh, stop shitting me.'

'You see – I'll be back. Once this has died down. The fuss about the stiff.'

'You didn't know anything about that, did you? Tell me you didn't.'

But Tobes only smiled, and said nothing.

'Tobes . . . ?'

Still nothing. And all of a sudden Johnny couldn't take any more. He turned and started up the stairs to his room, unable to see a thing. Funny, he didn't sob and cry out, but tears rolled down his cheeks, it was like the worst headache in the world; he heard the front door open and shut, he knew Tobes had gone, when he'd been hoping he would run up after him, but no, of course, the grown-ups would jump on him if he did that . . .

Johnny fell asleep on his bed. He woke up an hour later, still feeling terrible, gruzzled as hell, desperate to know where Tobes was, and if he was happy. Him, he'd never be happy again.

After a while, he pulled out his diary. *Tobes won't come back*, he wrote. *Ever.*

*   *   *

This is heavy, serious stuff and I'm going to take my time. No rush. What's important is setting down the *order* in which events transpired. I need to be able to fix the moment, the precise moment, when I realized Diane Cheung could be the killer. Because if I get the timing right, that'll be a first step towards clarifying my reasoning.

This Friday, I went downtown to be grilled at Police HQ. Which was kind of fun, y'know? Ed was clever, but I was cleverer: and I liked the danger, the walking out on the high-wire, running every word I spoke through the computer before I spoke it, analysing the next fifty billion moves. But all the while I had this creepy feeling there were people watching us through the mirror. (After months of therapy with Dr Diane, I am well aware of the possibilities two-way mirrors afford.) And sure enough . . . DR DIANE CHEUNG WAS NEXT DOOR!

I was kind of rude. I'm sorry, Dr Diane. But I'm really glad I jerked off over you. Did you like that? Is mine bigger than Ed's, by the way? I think so.

So I bike home feeling pretty good.

Next day, I am fired from *chez* Anderson.

This I have been expecting for some time, on account of I can be close to Johnny every day and some things are too good to last. So I am fired. Diane did that, which makes me angry. Sad also. I really love that little guy. (Probably his folks saw that and guessed I was queer for him. Sicko.) As I walk down the drive, scattering the riff-raff of the world's press, I half expect the sad feeling to lift, but it doesn't. It stays with me all the way into town, along with the memory of that tearstained, upturned little face, his wet, pony-eyes gazing into mine.

Whenever I was down, Mom used to make chicken soup. We didn't have much moolah, but she was always good for chicken soup. Took her time over it. Rich-coloured it was, almost yellow, with corn in it, and bits of breast, and smooth as cream. So if some kid had beaten me up at school, or Dad was drunk, or whatever, out would come the chicken soup. It tasted wonderful, it felt good going down, and the goodness remained long after the soup had gone.

Then one day I saw Mother add a shot of Dad's vodka to that wonderful soup and I realized that not everything is as it seems. A staging-post on the road to manhood. (Dr Diane, I am troubled by this memory. Mom left when I was five, I think. Yet I can remember all these chicken soups, and lots of them seem to belong to when I was older. Why?)

Now I want that taste, that goodness again. So I buy a tin of Campbell's and bring it home to heat up. Also, a Crunch bar that I eat on the way home – comfort foods. The soup's okay, but it's not magic. As I sit there sipping it, I start to cry. I put down my bowl and give way to it. Don't know what I'm crying for. I'm just so unhappy.

I dry my eyes and fall to thinking about Dr Diane. She's fixed me good, this time. And I'm facing up to a discovery: I don't actually like her any more. At this point, you understand, it never occurs to me that she's homicidal, just that she worries me. And from there it's a short, instinctive jump to: she's dangerous.

Why am I thinking that?

By now it's dusk. I put away the soup things and lie on my bed, with the beloved Dutchman for company. I turn the music up loud and seek inspiration in my ceiling. Why do I find Dr Diane Cheung a threat all of a sudden?

Well, there are several reasons, and listing them helps keep the sad feeling at bay.

One. She got me fired. (Small thing, but she was supposed to be on my side.)

Two. She had a gun, and it was stolen. Only, it wasn't stolen. Or *maybe* it wasn't. In her house that night, I touched what I think may have been a gun, only to hear her say to her tame cop that she hadn't bought a replacement yet. (So, if I'm right about the gun, she's two-timing the cop on a firearms rap, and I can relate to that.)

Three. She's all tied in with Alice Mornay and my clearing in the cemetery. See her Dream Book, or whatever she calls it. She knows about that place. I told her about Alice. But I can't remember saying how to find her, or at least, not too clearly. Sometimes those hypnosis sessions can be eerie. Maybe I did it when under the influence.

Four. I keep coming back to that CHIPP business. Now, I know what I saw on her computer screen that day: the names of boys who were either dead or missing. Why? What's it to her? (Okay, so there's nothing in that. She's a psychologist, she could have any number of reasons.) (And that stuff she told the cop about child incest, and her having been raped by her stepfather.)

There is no Five. And yet, in a strange way, there is.

I get up off the bed and hightail it over to Dr Diane's box, where I rummage. My drawings. She encourages me to draw and show her the results. Freestyle, she calls it. So one day, feeling horny and brave, I said to her, 'What about some steamy stuff?' And the odd thing was, instead of turning cold on me, her eyes kind of lit up, and she said, 'Yes! (With an exclamation mark, as in YES!) Why not do that, lots of that?'

And so here it is. My hard porn.

There are maybe fifty sheets of paper by now. I favour pastel crayons: they flatter human skin-tints. My imagination is the biggest thing about me, I conclude as I flick through my handiwork. Men with women – well, I soon grew out of *that*. Men with men, animals, children; women with ditto, children with children, hordes, singles, shit, piss.

I have never been in therapy before. I only took it this time because the alternative was the pen. But surely it cannot be altogether typical for your female therapist to insist on the mass-production of pornography? (One thing I do know is this: it's not normal for a psychologist to hear her dead mother's voice speaking to her all the time. I mean, with this we enter the realm of Ripley's *Believe It Or Not*, am I right?)

Diane did not ask Jesse, or Ramon, or Billy-the-Kid to do any of this porn-stuff, that I did ascertain.

I haven't shown Dr Diane any of it yet. She keeps asking to see my artwork, though. I'm too ashamed.

The sight of my craft-products begins to excite me. I stuff the drawings under the sheet, ready for later. The World War II uniform Maxine lent me (nice girl, Maxine; too bad she got afflicted with serious hots for Harley Rivera) hangs on the wall opposite. I get up, the front of my pants expanding like a gas-balloon, and go over to it. As I reach up for the holster, there's this soft tapping at the door and I turn. Fortunately, my cock has deflated. Fortunately, my drawings are hidden beneath the sheet. Fortunately, for who should my visitor be but . . . Dr Diane Cheung.

She looks at me without speaking; I guess my face isn't exactly shouting, 'Welcome!' But I remember my manners. *'Huan-ying guang-lin,'* I say. So glad you could come, so honoured.

'You speak Chinese?'

'You know I don't.' (She comes in, eyeing me up in that ironic way she has.) 'I've studied a lot about China lately.'

341

'Could we turn the music off, do you think, or at least, down?' (I make no move.) 'What *is* that music? Very serious . . .'

I turn off the CD player, my bones not telling me that music is likely to be today's special.

'Can I help you?' I say in a cold voice. I wish she would leave. For a while she doesn't answer, just saunters around my place like she's thinking of renting it. She sees my green jeans hanging up by the window to dry. Seems fascinated by them. Will she ask me about them? She doesn't.

'I felt we should talk, outside of the structured atmosphere in St Joseph's,' she says at last. 'More as friends than as doctor–patient.'

'Oh, yes, we're friends, fine, that's why you had me fired, right?'

'I had a duty to Johnny.'

'Why did you have me fired?'

'I'll find you another job, I've already – '

'Why, why, why?'

'Why did you never tell me about your job at Harley's Diner, why must you suddenly smoke all the time, what do you mean by scaring that poor little boy halfway to death in the cemetery at night, why is there a body buried next to Alice Mornay's grave?'

It all comes out just like I'm writing it, whoosh! Rocket-stuff. She is on the verge of breaking down. I see tears. I am glad.

'Tobes,' she says, 'answer me truly: did you kill Douggan, did you kill Randy Delmar?'

'No.'

'Then isn't it time you came clean about what attraction Court Ridge Cemetery has for you?'

'Don't mess with my cemetery, lady,' I burst out. I'm angry now: how dare this bitch . . . 'Don't ever go there. You've been there, haven't you? Don't go again.'

She seems perplexed.

'It's dangerous for people like you. There's queers there, men with knives and guns, I've seen them, fought with them even. You're a nice lady, Diane, you don't mind if I call you Diane, do you, we've been intimate for a while, time for first names. You're too beautiful for the Court Ridge crowd. That dress you're wearing, it suits you so well, white, white is your colour, and that black belt with it, magical. Did you care for some coffee?'

'I used to wonder why I was the only person interested in fighting your corner,' she says quietly. 'Now I'm beginning to see.' She stamps her lips together, like she's biting back words; then . . . 'Tobes, let's work through this. Johnny Anderson: you like him, he likes you too. It's only natural that his parents be concerned. There are a lot of men who feel a need to get close to young boys. People are wary these days.'

I want to shout at her, but what's the point?

'And your relationship with Johnny has been a little . . . well, odd. Wouldn't you agree?'

'No.'

'No? What with taking the boy into a graveyard at night, that self-same graveyard you've just told me is so dangerous, and pretending to be a ghost? And while we're on *that* subject, why on earth did you tell him about a name-card being found beside the body?'

Shit!

I want to bluff, but she's hit the nerve dead centre: this has been bugging me for days. *Why did I have to be so dumb as to mention those fucking cards to Johnny?*

Because they were on my mind, that's why. The cops were talking about them. Dr Diane was talking about them, on account of she wanted us to bring them back to her. And I knew something nobody else knew and because I was so damn proud of it I had to go blurt it out to Johnny that night I pretended to be Carl. Ever since which I've been waiting for somebody to come calling, since I know Johnny tells Dr Diane everything.

I expected the cops, though. Not her.

Only one way to deal with this question-that-I-cannot-answer: ignore it totally. 'And why not?' I say.

'Why not?'

'Sure. Johnny's heading straight for the trashcan. I mean, just like my parents wrecked me, y'know? Johnny's got no friends, he has no fun, he's over-protected, he's a wimp. I'm showing him a beautiful new world, scaring him a little, stretching him lots. All the things you should be doing, lady.'

While she's still swallowing that one, doing a real python-goat act, let me tell you, I heat water for coffee. As I hand her a cup I say, 'Sure, I killed Douggan. Delmar, too. How else could his body have got into my clearing? And if you don't lay off me . . . I'll kill you, too, Diane.' I sip, gazing steadily at her. 'There's no sugar in that, did you care for some?'

She's cool, you've got to hand it to her. She places the cup of coffee on the floor and comes upright again. Many a woman would have flung it in my face; not my Diane, my sweet Dr Diane. She smiles, says, 'Well . . .' and heads for the door. I wait until she's opened it, on the threshold. I say, 'Just because Stepfather Larry had you in the ass, doesn't mean you can bust my chops, lady.'

She does not look back. Only thing tells me she's less than cool is, she leaves my door wide open.

I don't know who I should send this too. It's not a memoir any more. It's a deposition.

*   *   *

'I have your killer,' Diane said as she entered. 'Sooner you arrest him the better.'

Peter Symes was standing hunched over his desk, a plan of Paradise Bay in front of him. He looked summery-good: long, navy blue shorts, a yellow T-shirt, blue baseball-style yachting cap with 'Captain' emblazoned on the front, his glasses dangling from a chain of little yellow balls around his neck. Today, a Saturday, was evidently his day off; he must have been on the water when the radio message got to him: we have another corpse for you to look at. His chin jerked up, he glared at Diane. The court likewise.

The court consisted of the usual crowd: homicide dicks, Chief of Patrol, assistants from the DA's department, and Daniel Krozgrow. Daniel, also hunched over the plan, now rose and saluted Diane with a smile.

'What are you talking about?' Peter's innate charm was low-level today.

'Peter,' she said, 'five minutes alone with you, Daniel, and Ed Hersey. Please. Trust me.'

He didn't like it, but he said, 'We were just breaking up anyway.' The room emptied, all except for Peter, Ed, Daniel and Diane. Peter sat and indicated the others should do likewise, but Diane couldn't. She paced.

'I just came from Gascoign's place,' she said. 'He confessed to Douggan and Delmar both.'

Peter leaned back in his chair and rested one ankle across the other knee, holding a pencil before his face. He rocked to and fro, sapping her confidence with each sequence. Nobody spoke for a while. Then Peter said, 'You got him to confess to two murders?'

'Yes.'

'Was there anyone else present?'

'No.'

'Did you record what he said? Did you read him his rights? Offer him one phone call?'

'No. It wasn't like that.'

'Then it wasn't like a confession either.'

'There's more,' Diane hurried on. 'Listen . . . ' And she told them about the break-in to her house, leaving Ed out of it; how Johnny had admitted to being lured into the cemetery by Tobes at night, the bit with the soldier, the name-card and everything. She told them Tobes had revealed the Alice Mornay gravestone under hypnosis, showing his familiarity with same. And the more she ranted on, the less interested they seemed.

At last she fell silent. Peter started to speak, then irritation got the better of him; he looked at Daniel and said, 'You tell her.'

Daniel smiled, shrugged and sighed all at the same time: a brilliant display of sympathy mixed with condemnation.

'Well, Diane,' he said, 'it's like this. We've profiled our killer, and we've profiled Tobes Gascoign, too, along with lots of other people. And what we've got is this. Whoever killed Delmar and Douggan is an organized nonsocial type. You know what that means, don't you?'

'A methodical person who usually lives some distance from the scene of the crime. Hostile to society generally, wanting to get even all the time. Needing a regular fix of publicity.'

'Right. And Tobes is your typical asocial disorganized personality. You could say: the opposite of our posited killer in this case.'

'But he *confessed*!'

'Oh, Diane, come on.' Daniel's smile was kind, but his eyes had become judgemental. 'A cry for help? For attention? Addressed to the one person who might be expected to respond?'

Diane stared from face to face, seeking understanding, sympathy, agreement. In vain.

'Just a minute.'

Peter Symes had spoken. Diane's heart gave a great big thump of hope. He had spotted Daniel's flaw! He was going to tell them what it was. Her rescuer, her hero.

'Are you seriously telling us, Diane, that you let a court-referred patient work in a household where there was a vulnerable ten-year-old boy?' He was leaning across the desk towards her, like a judge. 'You knew this guy was capable of breaking into a house – yours. You didn't bother to report that to the police. And that he masturbated all over one of my interview rooms. And you still let him go on working for the Andersons, in close proximity to an impressionable minor?'

'Yes, but . . .'

Diane could not think how to finish that sentence. Fortunately, there was somebody in the room who could.

'Yes, but . . . wait a minute,' said Daniel Krozgrow. Now he too was pacing the room. His voice had lost all its earlier confidence. 'This stuff with the ghost . . . '

He stopped and wheeled around to face her. 'Mixed characteristics are not unknown. Disorganized asocial and organized nonsocial sometimes mix 'n' match. This stuff about pretending to be a ghost is new, I haven't had that before. It's extraordinary.'

Unitl now Ed had been engrossed in the carpet. Suddenly he looked up at Diane. He said, 'Why not let me go question Johnny? Just me. Alone. No squad car, no partner, no parents listening in.'

Daniel Krozgrow frowned. 'I'm not sure he'd relate to you sufficiently to make it worthwhile. Does he know you?'

'Not from Adam,' Ed replied.

'I could vouch for you,' Diane said. 'What if I speak to Johnny on the phone, here, now, so you can monitor what I say? I'll tell him to expect Ed and just say he's to answer truthfully.'

'One thing, Hersey,' Peter put in. 'You go with your partner.'

Ed glanced at Diane, then nodded. 'Leo will be okay,' he said. 'I'll see to it.'

What could she lose? The score had sunk to forty-love and she'd fought back to deuce. 'Peter, let me use your phone.'

Johnny was in; it was Saturday evening, where else would he be? (With Tobes, her dark muse murmured.) He listened to what she had to say and agreed at once. Diane then spoke to Nicole, who acquiesced. Ed, meanwhile, had rounded up Leo and the two of them set off.

By now it was about eight o'clock. By common consent, nobody was going anyplace. Peter hauled a bottle of rye out of his bottom drawer and fixed a drink for himself and Diane. Daniel stood by the window, nursing a ginger ale. Time passed, but slowly.

Diane's mind hovered over this and that, like a butterfly. What music had Tobes been listening to in his room? Something heavy, dreary. Melancholy music. Perhaps she should have paid more heed to his musical taste: he so often wore his Walkman. He was never without it.

Maybe if she knew what music fascinated him she'd have a lead on what he really wanted.

What would Daniel Krozgrow normally be doing on a Saturday night? Why didn't he go someplace else, instead of hanging around here?

Peter Symes pulled the top half-dozen files off his in-tray and started to read. After a while he took out a pen and began to make notes. He fielded a couple of phone calls. At odd intervals, people came in with info or updates. There were many priorities in a murder inquiry; right now what weighed heaviest was the length of time the medical examiner was taking over Delmar's remains.

Would Ed still love her after this? Diane wondered.

Was she capable of receiving, let alone offering, love? Could the two be separated?

Ed had been gone an hour.

Diane walked around a bit, to stretch her legs. Peter didn't look up from his reading. Her bladder was aching. When she went to the door and mumbled, 'Back in a minute,' the other two ignored her.

Dabbing her face dry, considering it in the mirror, Diane wished she'd done more background work on serial killers so as to impress Daniel. Was he married, by the way? He could look cute in boxer shorts . . .

Back in Peter's office, nothing had changed. Daniel was in the act of pouring another ginger ale, only his second in – Diane glanced at the clock on the wall – one hour and forty minutes.

The flow of personnel abated somewhat. She counted only three more phone calls before Ed and Leo came back.

They returned two hours and twelve minutes after they'd left.

'So what did the kid say?' Peter asked, capping his pen.

Ed was spokesperson. 'He said, he's never been inside the cemetery except three times: once with Diane, once with his stepmother, and once with his dad one Saturday morning when he got lost and Gascoign rescued him. No, he never went into the cemetery at night; no, he never saw ghosts there. Seemed kind of indignant we might think he had.'

No one looked at Diane, not even when she protested, 'But he told me about going, I've got case-notes to prove it!'

Ed held up a placatory hand. 'The stepmother does agree that Johnny claimed to have seen a ghost, and that he was fixated with them. She also thinks he may have gone into the cemetery one night, alone.'

'But that's not all,' Diane exclaimed. 'Johnny told me Tobes mentioned finding my name-card by one of the corpses. You never made that public, so how can Tobes have known unless he was implicated?'

'"He told me Tobes mentioned . . . " Diane, don't you know any law at all?' Peter made no secret of his exasperation. 'This is double hearsay! Either the kid's going to back you or he isn't. And guess what? He isn't.'

'Something else I want to clear up,' Ed said, unexpectedly. 'Diane, here . . . she did kind of report the break-in to her house. To me.'

Peter shook his head. 'I don't get this.'

'I stayed over, that night. I was asleep when the intruder called, but was with Diane when we found evidence of entry.'

Ed had an audience any actor would die for.

'Why didn't you make a report then?' Peter enquired.

Ed didn't answer. He continued to gaze straight ahead, a good soldier on trial for doing his duty.

'There's a rumour,' Peter cautiously began, 'that you and Diane have been seeing a lot of each other. I now gather this is true?'

'Yes.'

'No!' she shouted. And then Ed did look at her: he stared into her eyes and he said, 'But I can't go on with this. I don't believe Diane's in the real world at all.'

A long silence followed. All Diane wanted was for this to end. She could go, just walk out; but that would leave them in command of the field.

Peter said, 'I don't understand you, Diane. Couple of hours ago you stormed in here, cleared the room, said you'd found us our murderer, and now look. But those hours haven't been wasted, I've been thinking a lot. Just tell me one thing: where do your loyalties lie? Who are you rooting for: Johnny Anderson, Tobes Gascoign, us? Yourself?'

Diane realized she must say something. 'It won't happen again, that I promise you.'

'That I promise you,' he echoed. 'The Juvenile Crimes Unit will be disbanded formally on Monday. There'll be a statement. Kindly prepare an invoice showing what this department owes you down to and including' – he looked at his Rolex Submariner – 'twenty-two thirty-eight, Saturday.'

He stood up, a judge going into recess. At the door he said, to no one in particular, 'I'll be in Incident.'

He went out, followed by Daniel, who looked upset. Diane walked towards the door. Leo made way for her. She had to manoeuvre around Ed. She got the feeling he might fall down any second.

'Goodbye,' said a voice behind her. Diane guessed it belonged to Ed; it didn't sound human at all. She wanted to say goodbye and she thought she'd managed it, but no sound came out. Then it was the stairs.

*   *   *

So Mike Anderson and I stumble across a burned, half-eaten corpse, and Tobes gets fired and for a long while after that I just cry. Nicole brings me food on a tray. I eat some. She sits with me, holding my hand, and I don't mind. After a while I tell her I want to read, and she takes the tray downstairs. By this time the house is pretty quiet . . .

Johnny was thinking of going to sleep when the cops called again. There were only two of them this time, but one stayed outside on the landing, half in and half out of the conversation. Nicole introduced them: Ed was one, and Lennie the other (Johnny thought it was Lennie), Lennie being the one who stayed outside.

Ed acted cool. He treated Johnny as a grown-up. The boy asked to see his badge, and he flashed it right away, like Johnny was a citizen. He asked to see his gun, but Ed said he hadn't got it with him. Then he started in with these questions. About Tobes. Whether Johnny'd gone into the cemetery with him, if Tobes had pretended to be a ghost, all stuff like that.

Johnny lied.

He wasn't sure why he lied. All he knew was, this stuff couldn't exactly help his one and only, his *wei yi* friend. He'd had time to think about the things they'd done together. They'd made a lot of sense to Johnny then, but they wouldn't have made sense to anyone else, and frankly now they didn't wholly add up for him, either. Some of them had been downright scary.

Also, it occurred to Johnny that he, too, might be in trouble if he owned up to all this crap. He didn't want to be sent to the funny farm. So taken all round, it seemed easier to duck.

He told Ed that he'd only ever been in the cemetery three times: with Nicole, Diane and Dad (and Arnie). Also, he didn't believe in ghosts and had never seen one. Ed seemed kind of upset, but he didn't say anything; just patted Johnny on the cheek (why *did* grown-up type persons do that?) and went out.

Johnny heard him talking with Nicole downstairs. Later, she didn't say anything, so he guessed it was all right. The one thing that worried him was if they asked Diane some questions and she told them he'd said different to her. But he could always put it right by pretending he'd been joking with her, or something.

Johnny felt nervous the next couple of hours. As if something was stirring out there, coming his way, and he didn't know what. Stomach queasy, couldn't eat much. His heart beat fast at unexpected times, for no reason. Premonition, wasn't that what they called it? A grey, blankety feeling.

That night, the Big T showed!

He left it kind of late; perhaps Tobes knew Johnny would wait for him, that the boy was a sucker. It was nine fifty-four by Johnny's Casio Alarm Chrono when he stood under the light and waved. Of course, Johnny didn't hesitate, he went down.

'Hi,' Tobes said. He held out a hand. Johnny ignored it, giving him a hug instead. Tobes held the boy like he was an egg with a crack in it.

'How've you been?' he asked.

'Okay. You?'

'Okay. Hey!' He punched Johnny gently. 'Miss you.'

'Me too.' By now they were standing kind of close, not touching though. And Johnny remembered. 'Tobes, there was these two cops, and they came asking questions about the cemetery and ghosts and you.' Johnny filled him in. Tobes seemed pleased that Johnny had lied.

'I didn't say anything, Tobes, honest! I wouldn't do that to you.'

'Thanks, Johnny. Copacetic.'

'Are we going ghost-hunting again?'

'No, Johnny. We're going to take proper care of ourselves.'

'But . . . you'll come back?'

'Next week, maybe.'

'Not before then? Please?'

'Listen. You have to listen, okay? Your folks are great. You don't realize how great they are. You think they're terrible, but they love you and they don't . . . don't mess around with you. So you've got to start making the most of what you have. Understand?'

Johnny miserably shook his head.

'They love you, you dumb kid.'

'But so do you!'

'I don't want to come between you and your folks. I won't.'

'All I want is to *see* you now and then. Is that so terrible?'

'Johnny, why won't you understand? People want to protect you from me . . .' He was looking over Johnny's shoulder. 'Like now, oh shit.' Johnny couldn't believe it: one moment Tobes was there, the next he'd turned and bounded away without even saying goodbye.

'Johnny,' cried this voice. 'What are you doing down there?'

Nicole was almost her old WW self. 'I saw you,' she snapped, once Johnny had dragged himself back to the house. 'You were with Tobes, weren't you?'

'No.'

'Don't lie, I saw his face under the light.' There was this long, awkward pause. 'Did he, you know . . . do anything?' She must have thought Johnny didn't understand, because she rushed on, 'Did he touch you, dammit?'

Johnny shook his head. Nicole stared at him, and maybe she was going to cry, but in the end she just said, 'Do you know what time it is?' She looked at her watch. 'A quarter after ten at night, and you were talking with that . . . that person, at the gate. After you'd promised not to go in the cemetery again.'

'I was at the gate, not in the cemetery.'

Nicole stamped her foot. 'You're asking for a hiding; know that? Now get inside, and pray God I decide not to tell Mike. And if you ever do such a stupid thing again, I'll haul you up in front of Dr Cheung. Now get upstairs.'

She was frightened for him, Johnny knew that. Didn't stop him hating her, though.

*　　　*　　　*

The beach was firm where Ed and Leo parked, although further out, nearer the sea, it took on the consistency of

355

sludge. There was just enough dawn light to illuminate the retreating skin of water that shadowed each dead wave. They left the car and made their way towards the rocks. Ahead of them they could see spotlights, the medics, a man sitting down with his head between his hands while a black lab nuzzled him gently.

Ed made for the lab-man first.

'I'm Detective Ed Hersey,' he said, showing his badge. 'This is my colleague, Detective Leo Sanders.'

The man looked up. He was in his thirties, Ed guessed, with a day's growth of beard and a white face and black holes for eyes. He made a clumsy effort to stand, but Ed laid a hand on his shoulder.

'No need for that,' he said, squatting down beside the man. 'Nice dog . . . hey, how are you, boy, hey . . . ?'

'It's a she,' the man muttered. 'Patsy.'

'Hi, there, Patsy, good dog, good girl.' It was getting lighter now, Ed could see the guy was thin, shivering with cold inside his tracksuit, although the September morning was already warm. 'You're Gary Maudesley, right?'

'Yes.'

'And you found . . .'

Maudesley turned to one side and began to retch. Patsy wagged her tail disconsolately, looking between Ed and her master as if begging to be allowed to finish her morning's walk. Leo, who had been inspecting what lay by the water's edge, now came up and said, 'Young, white female, about twenty-four, -five, strangled, no sexual contact, been dead several hours. ID in the name of Maxine Walterton.'

Ed stood up, his joints protesting. He'd gone home last night and gotten drunk, only to be roused by Leo at four in the morning with news of the latest homicide. 'Why me?' he'd croaked. 'This is my day off.' Then Leo had told him what they'd discovered near the body . . .

'Gary,' Ed said gently to the guy in the tracksuit, 'I'm sorry to have to put you through this, but I need you to tell me about the things you found.'

'The name-cards?' Maudesley had recovered somewhat. He coughed a couple of times and succeeded in coming upright.

'Yeah.'

'I found them right by the . . . her.'

With a little encouragement from Ed, Maudesley accompanied them down to where assorted angels and ministers of death were methodically going about their business. Scattered around were a number of small, white, rectangular cards, protected from the elements now by a sheet of plastic. Ed went over to the medical examiner's man and got himself a pair of tweezers. He slid these under the plastic sheeting and fished out a card. 'Diane Cheung,' he read aloud.

'Hey,' said Leo. 'Maybe she's going in for that wave therapy stuff now.'

*   *   *

Diane awoke from a dark, suffocating dream. It was late, the sun already bright; surf was up, but she wasn't. She lay in bed, staring at the white-lit sky until her eyes burned. *I should dress, make coffee, eat something, or I'll get weak. I do not care. What reason do I have for getting up?*

She turned on the radio, eventually. After five minutes of light 'n' easy came a news bulletin. Another murder, a young woman this time. She'd been found strangled on a beach, not far from Point Sal. Harley's territory. The item dragged on and on. This used to be a peaceful stretch of coast; now young people were dying in droves, and the police are powerless; blah, blah, blah. Diane turned off the radio, and dozed. Her stomach hurt.

*   *   *

Johnny was doing math homework when the two cops came *again*. Only this time it was really heavy, and they interviewed Nicole first, for ages. And afterwards they all trooped into his bedroom together, Nicole, and Ed, the nice one who'd come before, and Lennie – who turned out to be Leo.

'Johnny,' Ed said, 'did you know that a young woman was murdered last night?'

Johnny said he'd heard something on the radio, not much.

'She was found on a beach, strangled. So this is very serious, right?'

Johnny nodded. That awful premonition feeling had come back three times three.

'Johnny, I want to ask you something. It matters a lot that you listen hard and get it right. Now. Did you see Tobes Gascoign at all last night?'

Johnny looked from face to face. He couldn't think what to say. While he was thinking, he could hear Nicole doing something behind him. She came around to face him again, only this time she had his diary in her hands.

'*Shit!*' he cried. Tears spurted down his face. How did she know where he'd hidden it? *How long had she been reading his thoughts?* He pounced, but Nicole was too quick for him, lifting the diary out of reach, while Leo grabbed Johnny. He kicked and struggled, but what was the use?

Leo continued to hold him as Nicole and Ed read his diary. 'Is this true?' Ed said, looking up. 'Did you see Tobes between five of ten and a quarter after?'

'Yes,' Johnny said sulkily. 'Ask her, she saw.'

'I know she did.' Ed handed Johnny the book with a smile. 'Thank you, Johnny. That's all we wanted to know.'

When they were at the door Johnny thought to ask, 'Who got killed, then?'

'Lady by the name of Maxine Walterton. Mean anything to you?'

'No.'

'She used to own a theatrical costumier's. Ring a bell?'

'No.'

After they'd left Johnny opened his diary and wrote a single sentence. *Got to find a better hiding place for this.*

*   *   *

In the kitchen Diane made a pot of chrysanthemum tea and sipped it scalding hot. It revived her to the point where she could essay a little *hatha* yoga exercise. That was going really well, until someone knocked at the door, ruining her concentration.

'Yes?'

As Diane admitted Ed and Leo she thought she'd never seen two such exhausted men in her life.

'Hi,' Ed said shortly. 'Mind if we sit?'

She gestured at the nearest chairs. Their relief at sitting down was almost tangible. Ed sat forward, holding out a white card. 'Recognize this?'

Diane took it. 'It's one of my name-cards,' she said wonderingly. 'Why, where did you . . . ?'

'Point Sal.'

According to the radio the latest victim, Maxine Walterton, had been found near there. Diane's legs gave way, she lowered herself into the nearest chair, nearly missing the edge; she said, 'Not the girl, tell me this is nothing to do with the dead girl.'

'Found it on the beach, next to the body,' Leo said. 'Along with a dozen like it.'

Diane sought to fight her way through to some light, but her mind was stuck in the mud.

Then her mind kicked in, and she remembered what Jesse Brown had told her. He'd taken her name-cards, just as the other boys had done, and thrown them away 'up Point Sal way'. Of course, he'd been to . . .

'Were they found near Harley's?' she asked weakly; and Ed nodded.

Diane got up. She made a move towards the kitchen, then stopped. She raised a hand to her cheek and stood there, swaying, like a drunk.

'Diane . . .'

'Give me a minute.'

The two men exchanged glances. Leo slumped further down in his chair and closed his eyes. Ed watched as Diane slowly drifted about the room, keeping her palm to her cheek.

'Ed,' she said at last, 'can I speak to you alone? Sorry, Leo . . .'

Ed said, 'I'd rather not,' just as Leo said, 'Best not, Diane.'

'Please.'

The two cops looked at each other again. Leo broke the silence by standing up and saying, 'Be in the car.'

'Five minutes,' Ed said.

'Yeah.'

When the door had closed behind Leo Diane said, 'Don't take me to court again, Ed.'

'What?'

'Don't do it. You can subpoena me, you can get a warrant, but don't do it, please don't do it.'

'I don't know what you're talking about.'

Diane stopped drifting. She took her hand away from her face and she said, 'I know how those cards got there. I think. And I'm going to have to betray a patient in order to tell you.'

She staggered. Ed ran forward to catch her. He gathered her up and laid her down on the sofa. Her head throbbed. She'd promised Jesse she would only tell the police about those cards if there was no other way of taking the heat off *him*. But she was going to tell in order to take the heat off *her*.

No, she was going to do it because she wanted Ed more than she wanted anything in the world, even self-respect, and this was the price.

'I have a court-referral,' Diane said. 'His name is Jesse Brown.'

Ed's frown deepened. 'Sure, Leo and I interviewed him.'

'He had a set of my cards. Stole them. Then he got scared and he threw them away on the beach, near Harley's.'

Ed was silent for a while. 'Well,' he said at last, 'according to forensic, those cards had been there a long time. Most of them were in the back of a cave, along with condoms, and Christ knows what else. But there were a few by the water's edge. As if someone had scattered them there.'

Someone who'd thrown them down in rage, she was thinking. *Someone who hates me . . .*

'You think it was Tobes,' she whispered. 'Don't you?'

'No,' Ed replied. 'We don't.'

Diane gazed at him. 'You . . . don't?'

'He's got an alibi Perry Mason couldn't crack. We have an eye-witness who saw Maxine leave Harley's and walk along the beach with a guy, and later this witness heard sounds of a struggle, screaming. This all happened at five after ten. Tobes was with Johnny Anderson just before, Nicole Anderson saw them together and anyway the kid confirms it. Whoever killed Walterton, it wasn't your prize boy.'

Ed had been kneeling beside the sofa. Now he stood up. Diane saw he was heading for the door and leapt to her feet. She ran to him. She clutched his sleeve and moaned, 'Please don't go. I don't want you to go.'

For a long moment he stared at her and then he turned his head, only his head, but she thought that was a prelude to him going, so she raised her hands to his shoulders. Ed hesitated a moment longer. Then he pulled Diane to him and their lips met.

The kiss was a long one. When they separated, Diane's whole mouth felt raw. As if he'd chewed it halfway to the bone. She wanted to speak, but Ed put a finger across her mouth and backed away, holding it there until he ran out of arm.

Leo was halfway up the path towards the porch. Seeing them emerge he tapped his watch and turned away.

'Is it the same guy?' Diane asked in a low voice. 'The killer?'

'Krozgrow says not.' Ed stared at the ground between his feet as if it held the key to the universe. 'Krozgrow says, if it ain't in the cemetery, it ain't our friend. Maxine was strangled beside the ocean. Plus, she's a woman, no mutilations, no burns.'

They stood there a moment longer, side by side but apart. There was nothing either of them could say to mend things. But as Ed took off down the path Diane called after him, 'No court order. No contest. You owe me.' And when he didn't reply, *'You owe me!'*

*   *   *

Come Monday Diane rose all bright and breezy and was in her office by seven a.m. She used the next couple of hours to start putting her baby, her Juvenile Crimes Unit, to rest. There were reports to be drafted, loose ends to be tied.

Shuffling through the files, Diane sighed. How hard it had been to put together; how amazingly easy to dismantle. So much effort, to such pathetic effect. First, getting Peter Symes to buy the idea, lobbying down at city hall, in the press, on daytime TV; overcoming the cops' resistance to being lectured by a woman; then putting together the programmes, the workshops, the reading-lists; fitting things into other people's schedules, always according with theirs, never imposing her own; being endlessly patient, sympathetic . . . what a price she'd paid. For nothing.

Tobes Gascoign was due at nine. By nine fifteen he hadn't shown. Julia Page came in bearing an envelope. It contained one of Diane's personal name-cards, showing her home address and number. On the back was written: 'STARTING TO HATE YOU NOW'.

'Who delivered this?' Diane croaked.

One look at her face showed Julia how distressed she was. 'Why . . . I can find out, I mean . . . Diane, what ever's wrong?'

Diane handed her the card.

'Do you recognize the writing?' she asked.

'It could be anyone's. Capital letters.'

Diane stuffed the card back in its envelope and slipped the envelope in a drawer. She felt certain Tobes had done this, but how to convince others? And why hadn't he shown?

Suppose it wasn't Tobes who'd delivered the card, after all? Who *else* was out there?

Diane tried to put the incident from her mind, but it was hard. Julia made her tea, unbidden, and poured a cup for herself. 'You've not been yourself lately,' she said. 'Want to talk about it?'

Diane thought to side-step her by explaining what had happened to the Juvenile Crimes Unit. At some point this blended into telling Julia everything that had ever happened between her and Ed Hersey.

'Why don't you see a therapist?' Julia asked.

'I've been thinking about that. The problem is: who to see?'

'Don't you have any friends who are in the biz?'

'I know a good few, but that's the problem. Francis Baggeley, perhaps . . . ? No, he's miles away, and besides, I need a stranger.'

'Maybe you should take a quick break now? Why not fly down to San Diego? Remember that time you couldn't make it, and gave me your ticket? Well, I had such a good time I can't tell you. I'd just broken off with somebody, and – '

'Julia. Julia, do me a favour. Don't tell anybody about that trip. About how I gave you the ticket I mean, okay?'

'Sure. Okay.' She spoke slowly, obviously puzzled.

'Only those perks are non-transferable and I don't want the airline to revoke my frequent-flier status. It

364

was saving me more than two thousand a year, last time I costed it out.'

Julia grinned. 'And I bet you don't want the Internal Revenue to know, either. Don't worry, I've no intention of going to jail for your tax frauds.'

'You're a first offender. They'd sent you to a shrink. Me.'

Their laughter didn't quite cover Diane's embarrassment; she was glad when the phone rang.

'Hi,' said a man's voice, and for a long time after that there was silence, because Diane's vocal cords had seized up.

'Is that you, Ed?' she asked, feeling stupid because she knew damn well who it was.

'Uh-huh. Listen: that information you asked me to get . . .'

'What information?'

'About Gascoign's school records, remember?'

She did remember, then. A long time ago, when life had seemed rich, she'd asked Ed if he could help track down Tobes's papers.

'Diane . . . are you there?'

'Yes. Sorry. Only I . . . I really wasn't sure if I'd hear from you again.'

'Oh. Well . . . anyway, this morning something came in. Took 'em a long time to piece this together. But I got a name for you. Samuel D. Baker. Lives in Queens, New York City. Gascoign's old school principal.'

He dictated an address; no phone number.

'Thank you, Ed. I owe you.'

'Thought it was me owed you.'

Diane could say nothing. Her lips still burned where he had chewed them yesterday; she wondered if his did, too?

Ed cleared his throat. 'Problem turned out to be that the school had closed down. Not enough pupils. And there's one more thing: Gascoign's records are definitely missing, believed destroyed.'

'Ed . . . thank you. In the circumstances, I . . . well.'

'Yeah. Well,' he said. 'See you soon.' Then he laughed, quietly, and put down the phone.

Diane got a number for Samuel D. Baker of Queens from information. When she called, a female answered; she sounded too young to be Baker's wife. Diane told her who she was and what she wanted. The woman said to wait. After a long pause, Baker came to the phone. Diane went through her spiel again.

'I remember him.' There was no warmth in Baker's voice. 'Who did you say you were?'

Diane explained about Tobes's previous record, Judge Cyril DeMesne, the Californian court-referral system. 'Do you know where his school records might be?' she concluded.

'They were destroyed.'

'When the school was closed, you mean?'

'I mean they were destroyed.'

'Mr Baker, I'm sorry, but I don't understand what you're telling me.'

Another long pause. She heard the woman's voice in the background; Baker muttered, 'Yes, today, six.' A door slammed. The woman had gone out, but Baker still didn't speak. The hairs on the back of Diane's neck prickled.

'Mr Baker, Tobes is under suspicion for murder. Several murders, in fact. I don't believe he committed them. Can you help? Please.'

'Look,' he said. And then again, 'Look . . . ' as if he was making up his mind, and Diane knew, she just

366

knew he held Tobes in the palm of his hand. 'What kind of murder?' he said at last.

'What *kind*?'

'Yes, what *kind*, is that so difficult a question?'

She heard deep breathing down the line. Eventually Baker mastered himself. He said, 'Was there any burning involved? Or sex?'

Diane forgot to take notes. She stared into space, terrified of moving, of saying the wrong thing and causing Baker to cut off.

'There was both,' she breathed.

Baker made her wait a long time. 'Do you ever come out this way?' he said eventually. 'It's not that I don't trust you, but walls have ears.'

'If it would help, I'd come specially.'

'I don't know if it would help or not.' Another of those long, ominous pauses. 'Guess it might.' His voice was quieter now, in sharp contrast to the rage of before. Then he said something weird, something that stayed in Diane's mind ever afterwards. 'I've been living with this thing, and dying of it, for years.'

'When could you see me?' she enquired.

'When could you come?'

Diane started to leaf through her diary, registering horror. Impossible, impossible; maybe the weekend after next . . . but her court report about Tobes must be on Judge DeMesne's desk the day after that; no time . . .

She heard herself say, 'How about tomorrow morning?'

*

By a quarter of eleven next morning, she was pacing the pavement a block away from Baker's house.

It was a hot, sultry day. Every minute or so a big jet howled in to land downwind at Kennedy, so low she could see inside its wheel-bays. She wondered how the residents of this neighbourhood could stand it. At five to eleven she broke, and rang the doorbell.

No one came for a while. Diane examined the exterior: a wooden-shingle house painted canary yellow, with dark red windows and front door, and a tidy but bleached-dry garden. In the sloping drive was parked a small black Ford, of a type they didn't make any more. A child's bicycle leaned against the garage door: unlike the car, that was new. Grandchildren . . . ?

Diane heard steps inside. A women opened the door: tall but stooped, with an expression that spoke of low expectations, she reminded Diane of some bit-player in *Roseanne*. She wore glasses that made her look fifty, though as they talked Diane revised her age downwards.

She introduced herself and the woman said to come in, sounding like one of those ickle-bickle actresses acting child roles. She ushered Diane into a back room. 'Would you like coffee?'

This was addressed, not to Diane, but to the room's other occupant: a man. He looked up, first at the woman, then at his guest.

'Oh,' he said, struggling up. 'You must be Diane Cheung.'

They shook.

'Yes, coffee . . . you want coffee?'

Diane nodded.

'Two. Thanks, honey.'

The woman went out, closing the door behind her. 'My daughter,' Baker explained. 'She takes care of me.'

'That's nice.'

'Sometimes. It can be tough on her husband and kid. I keep myself tucked away here, most of the time. Eat

368

here, mostly. 'Cept Thanksgiving and Christmas. Sit down.'

Baker had a rocking-chair in the window bay, looking out over another bleached and drought-ridden patch of garden. The room was icy cold and smelled of last week's meals. The windows looked like they were triple-glazed – no doubt to keep out the noise, although they didn't do that too well – and an air-conditioner was set high up on one wall. It was an old, noisy model: Diane could see a threadbare patch in the blue carpet where water had dripped over the years. She wished she'd brought something to cover her arms. Baker was wearing a short-sleeved white shirt, crumpled, not fresh from the wash, and corduroy pants. One of his slippers was holed where the big toe had pushed out of it. His spectacles had pebble lenses that made his eyes look unnaturally large. While he rocked gently to and fro, staring at her, she moulded her face into a polite smile and covertly examined the room.

Along one wall stood what she guessed must be his bed, now folded back into a sofa for daytime use, with a wad of paper under one castor. Above it hung two reproduction New England scenes, part of a cheap set. At the foot of the sofa rested a tank of tropical fish, air-bubbles rising to the surface in a continuous, soothing stream. Bookcases took up most of the remaining space. Diane read a few spines. 'Eng. Lit., huh?' she ventured brightly.

'Forty years of it.' Baker's hands gripped the arms of his rocker. 'Went into teaching to earn a little money after college before starting real life.' He laughed: an ugly grunt. 'Well, that *was* my life, and nothing much real about it.'

An uncomfortable silence was interrupted by the daughter bringing two mugs on a brass tray, the kind you can pick up at any budget store for less than ten dollars. Diane's coffee was made with full-cream milk; no one had asked her if she took it. Sugar came in a polystyrene cup, so at least sweetness was optional. The woman set down the tray on a table and left without saying a word.

Baker sat thrust well back in his chair, looking down his nose for a while. Then he picked up his cup and started to sip, continuing his observation of her over its edge.

'You know,' he said eventually, 'I've been having second thoughts about this.'

Diane's heart sank. He was not a prepossessing man: aged about seventy, fat around the midriff, with skinny arms, sparse, neglected hair and a challenging tilt to his chin. She tried to imagine him enforcing law and order on a class of twenty sixteen-year-olds and could summon up the image, just, but only in the same way he must have done his job: by dint of sheer hard work.

'Some things,' he said, in his gruff voice, 'best stay hidden.'

'A long journey, just for a cup of coffee.'

He grunted, and looked away. A lump of resentment began to form in Diane's stomach. She should fight this man, but the bitterness emanating from him like poison gas deterred her.

'Forty-one years,' he said abruptly. 'I had a bellyful of the American public school system, Doctor.' He tossed his head, making a noise like 't'chah!' – Baker's substitute for spitting.

'You taught at Arcade,' she prompted him, 'all that time?'

'Jesus, no; what? You kidding, or what?' His voice slipped momentarily into 'New Joisey' ways. 'Ever been to Arcade? Had more snow-days than school-days, most winters. Mile after mile after mile of white fields and woods, then half a dozen houses, village store, church, and a sign saying, "Thank you for driving carefully through Nowheresville." Blink and you miss it. Blink twice and you miss the twin town.'

Again the toss of the head, again the 't'chah!'.

'Arcade was the pinnacle of my career.' he said. 'Assistant principal came up. I went for interview. Only five others had bothered to apply; two of us showed up for the Board of Supervisors' meeting; I got the job. Remember going home to Gwen – my wife, her name was Gwen – feeling proud I'd got the job. Didn't know it'd kill her. The cold, I mean.'

His voice had sunk lower and lower, like his chin. Slowly, hoping her actions were unobtrusive, Diane took out her portable dictating-machine and set it going. Later she transcribed the entire interview herself. Although it occupied only a few pages, their talk was interspersed with long pauses; Diane edited out most of those, along with some of Baker's expletives and repetitions. But whenever she scanned the transcript later she could hear his 't'chahs!', see his fat stomach wobbling when he grew animated . . . recall in perfect detail his face, his troubled face, and the sorrow that lined it . . .

BAKER: *So. Want to have it all down on tape, huh?*
CHEUNG: *Do you mind?*
BAKER: *Don't much mind, I guess. Who's going to listen?*
CHEUNG: *Me. I do my own typing. I'll make one copy, then blank the tape.*

BAKER: *Yeah, yeah, and there it'll be on your computer for all time. What does it matter? Can't do much to me now. Your thing picking me up all right?*

CHEUNG: *Fine.*

BAKER: *That's good. You want to know about Tobes Gascoign. Well. When I joined Arcade –*

CHEUNG: *Excuse me, when was that?*

BAKER: *Fall of eighty-six.*

CHEUNG: *Sorry. Go on.*

BAKER: *When I joined the school, he was the worst-behaved kid they had. Long record of school-refusal. Disobedient. Flunked every test, except music, he was good at that. Showed no interest. The other kids hated him. No friends. No future. No hope. So I said to myself, right. You've landed this job as assistant principal, for your sins, and you're going to sort this boy out. So I started to dig around. At first, just that: made enquiries, reading his records. And there was the familiar pattern. Mother gone off, she couldn't take the father, I guess. The father, Terry Gascoign, was a pain in the butt. Drink. Idleness. Out of work, mostly, living on welfare. You could see it just coming down the pipe: like father like son.*

CHEUNG: *Did you meet with the father?*

BAKER: *Oh, yes, couple of times. Terry didn't want to know. He used to beat the crap out of the boy, was quite open about that. Wanted to know why I didn't take my belt to him if he was a problem.*

CHEUNG: *Were any outside agencies involved?*

BAKER: *(Laughs.) Doctor, in rural upstate New York, an outside agency is a realtor with an office five miles from the centre of town.*

CHEUNG: *So you're saying . . .*

BAKER: *No. I'm saying no.*

CHEUNG: *Go on.*

BAKER: *Well. We got to the summer of eighty-eight. Tobes was, oh, let me see . . .*

CHEUNG: *Fifteen?*

BAKER: *That would be about it. He was in tenth grade, anyway. No, he wasn't, he'd been held over, ninth grade. He had some kind of a rapport with the ninth-grade form teacher. Dick Tunbridge. Dick was a beer 'n' bowling type. They weren't confidants, or anything like that. (Long pause.) So there we all were, heading for hell in a snowstorm. And that summer, by that time, Tobes had become a real full-time freak. He was obsessed with executions.*

CHEUNG: *Executions?*

BAKER: *Yes, burning at the stake, guillotines – he built himself one of those, a toy, but it could slice a banana in half, remember seeing it. But mostly burning. And I remember thinking, that boy is a fire-setter in the making.*

CHEUNG: *Excuse me. Did you write any of this in his reports? Would it have been in the records that are missing?*

BAKER: *Might have been a hint or two. It's irrelevant, anyway. Those records don't exist any more.*

CHEUNG: *Please go on.*

BAKER: *So then we got to it. The thing with Joel Hagen.*

CHEUNG: *Yes?*

BAKER: *He ever tell you about Joel? In therapy?*

CHEUNG: *Well, I shouldn't really discuss . . . No, he didn't.*

BAKER: *I'm not surprised. Everything got hushed up. And then the school closed, so . . . (Long pause.) Joel was same age as Tobes, but a whole lot brighter. His father was an attorney for one of those advertising set-ups, with fancy offices in Manhattan, and he lived there most of the week, but the mother was running her parents' farm. Big spread, profitable in those days. Her folks were getting on, she loved the work, the life. (Laughs.) Hated Manhattan, all those whores in heels, that's what she used to say, nothing but whores in heels, Mr Baker. And she kept Joel by her, which is why he was at the school, and he did just fine.*

CHEUNG: *You sound as though you were fond of Joel.*

BAKER: *I was fond of all the smart kids who worked at it. Don't go putting things into my mouth I didn't say, please.*

CHEUNG: *Sorry.*

BAKER: *Yes, well . . . One day, I got to hear a rumour. Joel was accusing Tobes of having made a pass at him.*

CHEUNG: *A pass? Sexual advances?*

BAKER: *Yes. The kids were going spare about it. Every time I picked up on it, it had gotten worse. At first, you know, it was kids' stuff, gangs in corners at recess: 'He put his hand on my knee'. Then it was serious. 'He made Joel strip, and then he did this, and then he did that', you know? And – 'He forced him to . . . ' Well, I guess you see more of this than I ever did. So the next thing we know is . . . Joel nearly dies in a fire. And I reckon, we all reckoned, Tobes set that fire. He as good as admitted it. Dick Tunbridge and I grilled him good, we –*

CHEUNG: *Just a moment, please. What were the circumstances of this fire?*

BAKER: *Very strange. There was an old, semi-derelict house, on the outskirts of Arcade, heading north out of town. Late one summer night, it caught fire. The fire-fighters turned up, and heard someone screaming. Joel was in the basement. They got him out. Seemed he'd been hit over the head and just left there, by whoever started the fire.*

CHEUNG: *You mean it was attempted murder?*

BAKER: *Kind of looked that way. So Joel came out of hospital – shock, burns, concussion, a pretty rough deal – and the police wanted to interview him, and so did we. And this is what we got. That evening, late, Joel had been out with friends, and he was walking back to the farm. Had to go* right past this old house. And there was this really pretty girl, wearing shorts, and with long blonde hair, and she whispered to him, all cute and sexy, 'Hi, Joel, want to make out? I know a place we can go.' And she smelled gorgeous, according to Joel, but because it was nearly dark he couldn't see her face properly, though he realized she was a stranger to him. So he went with the girl, to the old house. And the next thing he knew, he was coughing up his cookies in some fireman's arms with a bump on the back of his head the size of a Fabergé egg. Now Joel hadn't seen anything, apart from this girl, and right from the start people were saying that he was making up a story to cover some funny business of his own. You see, Arcade's a tiny community. People there knew each other. There just wasn't a girl who fit the description of Joel's siren temptress.

CHEUNG: *How did Tobes come to be involved?*

BAKER: *Well, of course, his was the first name everybody thought of. Joel had no enemies, apart from Tobes, and Tobes was there in the frame on account of all these rumours.*

CHEUNG: *Excuse me, but did you think Tobes was or might be gay?*

BAKER: *Not then.*

CHEUNG: *But later?*

BAKER: *Best if I tell it how it happened. Dick Tunbridge and I were appointed as a kind of inquisition.*

CHEUNG: *By who?*

BAKER: *The principal. Man called Otis Lake. Not my favourite fellow, but that's irrelevant. Lake wanted everything kept as quiet as possible. He was due for retirement in twelve months' time, didn't plan to go out on a scandal. Lake said to me, Look, you and Dick talk with these kids, I'll try and keep the police out of it until you've done that.*

So we did. Joel was just confused about everything. And Tobes, well, he just sat there and said, Prove it, over and over again. With this great big smirk on his face, that said, Sure, I did it, and so what? But he hadn't reckoned on Joel's father, Dale Hagen. Suddenly he got into the act. And everything changed.

CHEUNG: *How?*

BAKER: *Dale Hagen threatened to hit everyone with a lawsuit. Failure to supervise, in essence. Which looked crazy, because the kid was out of school at the time, but Lake took it to the Board of Supervisors, and they brought in a lawyer of their own, and things weren't as clear cut as we'd thought. Personally, I never liked our lawyer. I thought he was overawed by Hagen senior. Anyway. Hagen was going to name Tobes as party to the suit. One evening, there was a meeting with Hagen, to see if we couldn't come to some agreement with him. Lake, me, Hagen, our lawyer. And Tobes Gascoign.*

CHEUNG: *What?*

BAKER: *He hadn't been invited, of course. Just turned up. He was ice-cool, very polite. Said he had some evidence to throw light on what we were discussing. At first we wanted to kick him out. But I guess everyone in that room was curious to hear what he had to say – we had half the picture and he had the other half. So he sat at one side of the table, see, opposite us, and he produced these photographs. Spread them out in front of us. In colour, high quality. None of us could figure out what we were looking at. So we asked him. And he said, 'Those are photographs of my asshole. I took them myself. As you can see, I've been anally raped. If you doubt me, look.' And he dropped his pants. He turned around. And he bent over. (Long pause.) Well. Let's just say, we saw what he meant. And after that, we had a handle on those photos all right, boy! . . . Anyway.*

He said, Joel Hagen had raped him, and all the rumours
we'd been hearing were spread by him to cover up his own
evil proclivities, that's what he called them, evil proclivities,
and if Hagen went ahead with the lawsuit he'd cross-claim
for damages of one million dollars. Hagen sat there, quiv-
ering. Looked like a man who might explode. And he did,
in a sense. He led off with all the usual stuff you might
expect. Tobes waited until he ran out of steam. Then he
said, Hold on a minute. There's a way out of this. I want to
quit school, and I'm going to. I'll go quietly, if you drop
this stupid case, and if you lose my school-records. I don't
want any dumb teacher's fantasies clogging up my life,
see? I want a fresh start. And I want an answer now.

CHEUNG: *Did he get one?*

BAKER: *Yes. We all expected Hagen to loose off again. But*
he didn't. He sat there for a long while, thinking things
over. Then he turned to Lake and he said, 'Can you lose the
little fucker's files?' And straight away Lake said, 'Yes.'

CHEUNG: *How did you feel about that?*

BAKER: *Relieved.*

CHEUNG: *I'm sorry?*

BAKER: *By then, we all knew the school was headed for*
closure under a streamlining programme. None of us older
teachers was ever going to work again. None of us fancied
spending the rest of our lives tied up in court hearings. I
think we'd have done a whole lot more for Tobes, if he'd
asked us. As it was, losing a few records seemed like a cheap
way out. Cheap snow job. Lake and I burned them later that
same night, in a field. (Long pause.) Been troubling me ever
since. Somebody raped that boy. Somebody did it.

CHEUNG: *Mr Baker . . . do you think Tobes was capable of*
murder, then?

BAKER: *(Long pause.) Yes.*
(End of tape.)

Diane didn't know what prompted the question, really. But as Baker was showing her out, somehow conveying the impression that this was the first time he'd left his back room in years, she asked, 'Was there anything you liked about Tobes? Anything good at all?'

Baker thought. 'The music. Pity he didn't pursue that, he might have amounted to something.'

'Did he play?'

'No, he just listened, every opportunity he got. Had those headphones, you know? Never saw him without 'em. Used to be a tussle in class sometimes, to make him take 'em off.'

'What did he like best?'

'Wagner, mostly. Always the same tune.'

And suddenly Diane became very alert. 'What tune?'

Baker shrugged. 'I'm no Wagner fan. Somebody did tell me once, but I've forgotten.'

'Did it sound anything like this?'

Diane hummed what she could remember of the music she'd heard in Tobes's room. She sounded terrible. Baker listened with a frown. At last he said, 'That could be it. All those heavy notes, da-dum, da-da . . . da . . . da . . . da . . . da . . . DAH.' (He hummed much better than Diane.) 'Familiar, I will say that.'

Diane wished she knew more about opera. She took the dictating-machine out of her purse and added a note to herself: bone up on Wagner.

She was on the point of saying her final farewell when she fired one last, forlorn, hopeless shot, and scored a bull's-eye. 'Tobes's father . . . what happened to him?'

'What, Terry?'

'Yes. He was a drunk, wasn't he?'

'And a chain-smoker, and a thief, if the rumours were true.' Baker threw back his head and laughed, as if now, right at the end, Diane had said something really worth hearing. 'Well,' he said when he'd finally mastered his guffaws, 'you could kind of say they locked up Terry and threw away the key.'

*   *   *

September 28

> *Dear Mr Hersey,*
>
> *I don't really know why I am writing to you. It's likely you'll read one or two pages, then just throw this in the garbage. Maybe it's better that you should.*
>
> *I hope you remember me (Tobes Gascoign). You behaved pretty well towards me, all things considered. I wish I could write to somebody else in the force. I would if I could. But I don't know any other cops, except your sidekick, and I don't like him.*
>
> *You'll see why I don't want this letter to go to you in a moment.*
>
> *First thing is, I'm very, very frightened. Not only for myself, but also for Johnny Anderson, who lives at #15, Court Ridge, above the old cemetery. Johnny is my friend. I believe he understands me better than any other person alive. I know that he is unhappy at home and it worries me. We are similar types. We care about each other. And we're both in the hands of Dr Diane Cheung, who is your lover, and I believe she has killed more than one person. Ray Douggan, Carl Jensen, and Randy Delmar. Maxine Walterton, I'm not sure. Dr Diane has it in for young males, on*

account of being raped by her stepfather. But you know all about that, too.

You see now why I'd rather write this to anyone except you.

I realize this is a serious allegation. The most serious allegation one human being can make against another. And yes, I know I accused her before, and you laughed at me. Then, I had no evidence. Now I do.

Okay, so you will want to see my evidence. It's not complete yet. I need your help in completing it.

One. Diane reported her gun as having been stolen. Well, I'm pretty sure it wasn't. There is a gun (I think) in the top drawer of her bedside table, which I am sure you remember and know well. I can't swear it's the gun she reported lost. But you can check it out. If there really is a gun in her drawer you can test it with ballistics, can't you? Find out what bullets killed the boys, see if it fits?

Two. Her name-card was dropped by one of the bodies, Carl's, I think. I heard you guys talking about it in the cemetery (where I spend a lot of time) which is how I know, because you didn't put that in the papers. I mean, didn't any of you think, even once, that the obvious answer was the right one: that the killer had left her calling-card for you to find?

Three. You found Jensen next to the grave of Alice Mornay. Well, Diane knows about Alice. Alice is in her Dream Book, the one she keeps in the bedside table alongside the gun (see #1). Now Alice is pretty hard to find, I think you'll agree. Maybe I told Diane about Alice, it's possible. But does it matter who told her? Fact is: she knows about Alice. In other words, she was familiar with the place you found the corpse long before you found it. Suspicious? I think so.

*Four. She has a computer programme called CHIPP.
It's Child Incest Protection Programme. I saw a screen-
ful of it in her office one time. On that day, only two
bodies had been found, and their names were on the
screen, starred. Randy's name was there, too, but it
wasn't starred,* because it hadn't been found!!! *Get
it? Exciting, isn't it? Once you start to piece it together,
that is. And I'm pretty sure the dates when the first two
bodies were discovered were on that screen, too, but the
other names (Randy and Hal's) didn't have dates. Bet
they do now, though. Or at least, bet Randy's does. Go
check it out. (Go soon: my name's on that screen too.
I'm next, you see, unless she can hang the murders on
me, which I feel she will try to do.)*

*Five. This is the freaky one. Do you remember Diane
going to San Diego, on a weekend trip? Well, she didn't
go! She sent Julia Page, her gofer, instead, and Julia
pretended to be Diane, so as to give her an alibi, and it's
all a cover-up, because that was the weekend she corpsed
Jensen. Now me, I can't check that. You did, though:
your co-cop said so, here in my room, when you called
that day. BUT YOU ASKED THE WRONG QUES-
TIONS. You asked if a white female of a certain age had
checked into the hotel, name of Cheung, and they said yes
and that was it, because you knew her and deep down
you trusted her and you had lots of other things to do.
But if you send someone to the San Diego hotel, and
check the clerk's memory-banks against photographs of
Diane AND JULIA, bet he'll say: JULIA. And here's
something to help you: a note from said JULIA, saying,
'Thanks!' So you see, it all adds up and it all makes
sense. (NOTE: I'd like the note back, please.)*

*And Six. You know about six already, don't you?
She's hearing voices, her mother's in particular. (Don't*

*ask how I know, I just do, okay?) This is not normal
behaviour for a psychologist, am I right? This is mad-
person type behaviour. Mad people sometimes kill,
don't they?*

*I'm sorry to do this to you, really. You're an okay
guy, Mr Hersey, for a policeman. But I can't take the
risk that she's out to corpse me, too. Me and Johnny.
She should be locked up, or given one of those lethal
injections.*

*I'm not going to mail this right away. I'm not sure
yet. I'm pursuing my enquiries. When I have something more concrete, you'll be the first to know.*

Sincerely, your friend,
Tobes

*   *   *

The room was white, all white, and Diane was alone in
it. She sat at a square, rough-hewn wooden table on
which stood a glass of water, sparkling cold. Opposite
was an empty chair, hard and right-angled, like her
own. Above her hung a light-bulb, shaded by a globe of
textured paper. The floor was tiled. One wall held a
window, protected on the outside by a grille.

This room smelled faintly of disinfectant. Its atmosphere was hygienic, unemotional.

Behind her, the door opened. Diane was about to
turn when a hand descended on her shoulder, making
her jump: somebody had managed to creep up on her
in total silence. Seeing his face, however, she smiled.
This was Father Benedict.

Diane had come to New York City, the upper west
side. The upper *upper* west side. Her cab-driver, a
young Puerto Rican, hadn't wanted to take her here.

She'd bribed her way past his sensibilities. Here, in the House of Christ the Risen King, a small community of brothers brought soup, faith and hope to the derelict bodies and souls around them. There were bullet holes in the walls of their house, and several windows had been smashed, but the brothers (there were eleven of them, one for each *good* disciple) had no money to waste on repairs. Their resources went on rescuing young men and women from street gangs, and from the evils of Charlie-crack. Father Benedict did not altogether trust Diane – in his place, she wouldn't – so she'd had to piece together much of this for herself.

On her way up to this austere room she'd passed a doorway. A glance inside had showed her a man wearing a monk's robe, in earnest, quiet conversation with three black women. There were airline tickets on the table between them. She'd guessed, then, that this must be a staging-post in one of America's most secret underground railroads: Project Freedom, an organization that transplanted gang members and their families out of state as the only way they could renounce their membership and live to brag about it.

The monk looked up, saw her staring, and covered the tickets with his hand. After which she no longer had to guess; she knew.

Father Benedict had listened kindly to her story. His was a pale, thin face with a beard resembling a series of cuttings from another man's that had never quite taken. His eyes were between grey and blue, framed by worrylines, intent, careful. He was perhaps twice Diane's age.

'Diane,' he said, sitting down in the hard chair opposite hers, 'you realize, I'm sure, that no brother is obliged to speak of his past.'

'Yes.'

'All I could do was ask Brother Michael if he would see you. I have asked him, and explained the circumstances as you've explained them to me.'

He had a cultured, soothing east coast voice. Diane found herself nodding agreement. There was a long silence.

'And Terry . . . Brother Michael . . . says what?'

Father Benedict didn't answer directly. He raised his eyes to the door behind her. This time Diane was not taken entirely by surprise: she heard the swish of a broadcloth robe. She rose, clumsily, upsetting her chair. Brother Michael set it upright with deft, businesslike movements: she could envisage him wading into a brawl to great effect.

The two men stood side by side, looking at her. Father Benedict eyed Terry (Diane could not think of Tobes's father as anyone other than Terry), received some covert signal and took his leave. Terry continued to stare at her through expressionless eyes.

He was perhaps forty-five, clean-shaven, alert and strong. Not enough flesh on him to stuff a *guo-tieh* dumpling, as *Ma-ma* would doubtless have said, but wiry. He was tall, or rather, he *used* to be tall: now his shoulders hunched.

'How can I help you?' he asked, sitting down opposite her.

There was nothing soft about this man's voice. His tone was sharp: a chairman calling the board to order.

'I'm Dr Diane Cheung . . .' She explained, for the second time this afternoon, about Tobes's predicament. When she had finished, he said nothing, just stared at her, until in the end she was forced to ask, 'You are Tobes's father?'

'In my past life, I was lots of things.'

384

There was something final about that pronouncement, as if he meant to terminate their meeting, but he did not rise, and they continued to look at each other for the space of half a minute.

'You can help him,' she said.

'How?'

'By filling in the gaps in my knowledge.'

'About his childhood?'

'Yes.'

'Ask him. If he wants to tell you, he will. If not, not.'

But still he did not rise. They might have been discussing any recalcitrant youth who had given the Brothers grief; Diane reminded herself that they were discussing this brother's son, and continued, 'He's blanked off his childhood.'

'As have I. Yes, I am the father. That was all long ago. Unless you can convince me there's some purpose in talking over the past, I can't help.'

And *still* he did not rise, this man they'd locked up before throwing away the key, this penitent. He longed to be convinced, or so her professional instincts shrieked. *How?*

'Do you think him capable of murder?' she asked.

With a quick movement of his upper body and hands he brushed back his long hair to reveal a white scar, the needle-marks still visible, extending off his forehead towards the back of his skull.

'The day we parted,' he said, 'he came at me with an axe. Luckily, we were *both* drunk.'

He allowed his hair to fall back over the grisly scar. Since entering he had never once smiled, but now he did. His teeth were pure white, innocent of coffee-stains, or tobacco, but there was an ugly gap in the lower set.

'My son's other legacy to me,' he said, pointing at the gap.

'And yours to him? Let's talk about that.'

His smile vanished instantly. Diane realized she'd been pitching for a saint when she should have been keeping her eye on the man. 'He's disturbed right off the scale,' she rushed on, 'he may be mad, may be a serial killer. I have to find out the truth, soon, now. He won't let me in. Won't save himself. You know all about him. I've just come from Sam Baker, remember him? He told me how . . . about the scandal at the school.'

No response. The face opposite hers did not so much as flicker.

'Tell me about Sprucey,' Diane said. 'The kitten your son loved.'

Terry stood up.

'The cat you fried. Tobes made a joke about it: "Cat in a hot tin pan, hold the chili", that's what he said to me in therapy one day.'

Terry was halfway to the door.

'Tell me about the soft shit,' she said. 'I still don't understand about that.'

Diane heard the door open. A strange, moral certainty rose within her breast; that, and rage. 'You were the one who raped him, weren't you?' she said. 'Why don't you make your confession, Brother, and find peace?'

*   *   *

Soon as I see her I say, 'You're brave.' I mean, coming here again, after what happened last time . . .

Diane Cheung enters with just a little knock to say she's there. *Fuck!* I could be jerking off, or whatever.

386

But then she's a vampire: once you've issued the original invite, that's it, you're stuck with them.

She's watchful, afraid. I mean, she *is* brave, no doubt about it. That or stupid. Or pursuing her plan of destroying me, which today necessitates a visit. So I leave my shirt where it is, I get a grip on my head and I say, 'Come on in, sit down. The floor's pretty clean.'

Her eyes rest on the flowers first. Does she recognize the patterns in the arranging? How they mirror the arrangements in her own, all-white house, the sepulchre-on-the-hill? Then her eyes go to the electricity apparatus, and widen. She turns her best ironic look on me, eyebrows riding high.

'Sure,' I say, 'I'm good with things like that. When it comes to the old juice, ain't a system Tobes can't beat.'

'No music today?' she asks, in a light, little-girl voice – not like her, that; she must be nervous as hell.

'I'm tired of the same old thing. Want some peace.'

'Wagner, isn't it? Your favourite?'

'Right, yeah.'

'The Ring, maybe?'

'Oh, so you know Wagner?'

'I'm interested, yes.'

'Then you'll know the motif without any help from me. I'm busy, Doctor. Another day. Please.'

I light a cigarette. Dr Diane examines the Marlboro pack with intentness. I offer it to her, gentleman that I ever am. She declines. She doesn't say anything for a bit. Then – 'Tobes, have the police been here yet? About Maxine Walterton?'

'Not about Maxine. Why should they want to see me about Maxine.' She doesn't reply. She's letting me twist in the wind, all right. 'Tough about Maxine,' I croak.

'You knew her?'

'Somewhat. Why – do they think I killed *her*, now?'

'Maybe. She was killed Saturday night; where were you that night?'

'Why should I tell you? I mean, who the hell – '

'Where *were* you?'

I stare at her, trying to figure out what's behind this shit. One thing's obvious, though: she has the initiative. She came here with a game-plan and at her elbow stand forces of darkness, ready to do her bidding.

'I was visiting the cemetery,' I say boldly.

'Alone?'

'Yes, alone. But you should be able to find someone who saw me there: I wasn't the only ghoul by a long way.'

'Ghoul?'

'Since they started turning up – how shall I put it? – bodies without *reservations*, you get quite an audience of an evening.'

'I want to be sure, Tobes. Were you alone?'

'Yes.' No way am I letting my Johnny down. *'Yes!'*

'Thank you.'

She hadn't moved from near the door. Guess she wants an escape route if things get tough. Now she smiles a bit, though her lips tremble. She looks around, nervous-like.

'You make this place nice.'

'Thanks.'

'Do I detect Chinese influence?'

'You know you do, Doctor.' I gesture at the pile of books on the floor: everything from Sichuan lean cuisine to *A Dream of Red Mansions*. (That's the English-language edition, actually. I don't bother to tell her I can't make head nor tail of it.)

'Confucius, is that I see?'

'Mencius.' Can't make head nor tail of him, either, but – 'The Analects. Very charming. He's excellent on dealing with the unwelcome visitor. Was there anything else?'

And now her eyes lock on to mine. 'Tobes,' she says, honey-tongued, 'have you ever been inside a real Chinese home?'

'I've never visited the far east.'

'I mean here, in America.'

She means: was it you, onlooking, that night I fucked with my cop?

'No.' A devil enters into me. 'I did, however, once go to a temple of the soul, where all was peace and harmony and natural beauty, a place I knew I could be happy, all white . . . '

'Temple? Where?'

'Oh, not so far away.'

'Are you religious, all of a sudden?'

'I'm toying with the idea of becoming a Buddhist.'

'Superstitious?'

'Maybe.'

'Me, too.'

'Really? Or is this just another of your cutesie-cutesie ways into difficult boys, Dr Cheung?'

She smiles ruefully and takes a step backwards. Suddenly I don't want her to go. I have items of my own on this agenda.

'Do you still think I killed those guys?'

'You told me you did.'

'That was just to get you off my back. To scare you a little. To be frank . . . I hoped it would scare you

389

from coming back.' I glance around my hovel. 'It's kind of embarrassing, entertaining a lady here.' My gaze again settles on her face. 'But I didn't kill anyone. Honest.'

'That's what I thought,' she says, after a pause. 'But it's good to have you confirm it.'

'Thanks. So . . . we can be friends?'

'I think so. But why didn't you show up for therapy the other day? I was going to help find you a job, remember?'

'Oh . . . ' I just shrug. How to tell her that I'm afraid of her, I lust after her, I'm jealous of her cop lover-boy, she's my mom and my . . .

'Tobes, do you remember Mr Baker, who used to teach Eng. Lit. at your high school? Only I met him the other day.'

'You did?' An interesting phenomenon: I'm stuttering. The earthquake's about to happen. My room sways with foreknowledge of its imminent destruction.

'He told me about Joel Hagen, and what happened to you. And afterwards, I went to visit your father. He's a minister now, kind of. A monk, in New York City.'

A belt of steel tightens around my chest. I can't breathe. I'm at the wall, knocking my head against it, what a stupid thing to do, I can't stop, I can't stop. *She* stops me. She puts an arm around me and holds me tight, tighter even than the band of steel that's suffocating me to death. 'Tobes, Tobes, what's the matter? Calm down.'

'You bitch,' I grind at her. I'm talking through a wall of teeth. 'You bitch, you had no right.' My nose is running. I wipe it. My hand is crimson-hot. Blood. A nose-bleed. She gives me her handkerchief, with that wonderful blossomy scent of spring. Within seconds, it's drenched, stained beyond cleansing.

'Tobes,' she cries, giving me a hearty shake. 'Snap out of it!'

I stand in the corner, shivering, avoiding her eyes. Now I know the dark forces riding on her shoulder, know her evil plan. This is the kill.

When she takes a step towards me, I shrink back into my corner, arms making an X before my face. Dumb! Do I imagine that by making the sign of the cross I can vaporize her?! But she stops. She says, 'Tell me about the thing you've always shut out under hypnosis. Tell me about the beast behind the wall.'

I stare at her uncomprehendingly. Suddenly this amazingly versatile lady has broken into Swahili.

'Tell me about the soft shit, Tobes. You've come close to it so often. Now's the time.'

The speech is there in my mind, clear, concise and long prepared: 'What are you talking about? I do not understand you. Kindly leave me alone.' It stays in my mind. My teeth, clenched so tightly a moment ago, are chattering. There is a bump, accompanied by pain: I have slid down the wall and am squatting in my corner, my hands, useless as a cross, stretched back to hug the back of my skull, the arms protecting my face.

I knew we would get here. I've let slip the vital phrase in therapy sessions, more than once, so I knew we would get to this point one day. But not yet. Not yet.

A long time passes. I guess. I don't know. I lower my arms, slowly. I look up at her. Diane's face is warm and kind. She crinkles up her wonderful slanted eyes, in sympathy and love. I turn to face the wall. And slowly, unemotionally, without knowing why I'm telling her, or indeed why it happened to me – most of all failing to understand why it happened to me – I explain everything.

I was thirteen.

My father and I were living in a trailer, outside of Arcade.

I was doing all the work, he was drinking all the money.

One night he came home drunk. I'd left food for him, on the stove. He actually ate it. For a wonder. The night was ultra-cold. December. Christmas season.

He climbed into bed. We shared a room, a section of the trailer, curtained off from the rest. Two beds, one against each wall. I murmured, 'Goodnight, Dad,' hoping he wouldn't beat me. He didn't. He got out of bed. In the dark, I couldn't work out what he was doing. I heard noises, like he was dressing. Or undressing. He came to my bed. He got in. He hugged me close. At first I thought he was cold, I was cold, it wasn't unpleasant to have a warm body next to mine, even if it stank of booze and tobacco and old, old sweat. Not so bad. He held me. He began to stroke me. His hand went down to my cock, and then to my ass. I struggled. He was stronger. He lay on top of me, pinning me to the bed, so I couldn't breathe. I kicked. No good. It took him time, but he managed it. He got it in me. And then he said.

And then he said.

(And this is what I tell Dr Diane Cheung.)

'Son, you have such soft shit up your ass.'

That's what my father said while he was raping me that first time, yes. Now you try it. Imagine it's your own father, doing it to you. Like one of those cut-out figures they have down at Laguna Beach, with a hole for your face, so you stick it through the hole and

392

become Ronnie Reagan, or Barbara Bush, and Click! They take your pic. Put your father's face in the sodomizer's cut-out, then lie on your stomach and shut your eyes. Then sleep, if you can.

*　　*　　*

It was late that night, in the library, when Ed found her.

He came loping down the stacks, his sneakers making mild squeaky noises on the linoleum, but Diane was so tired she didn't register until he'd almost reached her side.

'Hi,' he said, sliding into a chair opposite hers. She raised her weary eyes above the book-rest. 'Hi.'

'What are you doing?'

Diane gestured at the pile of books in front of her. 'Wagner.'

'Oh?'

'It's a key, of some kind. I don't know what. Look, there's something I want you to see . . .' Ed got up and came around the table so that he could read over her shoulder. 'Do you remember going to Harley's with me, to find out about a character called Besto?'

'Who turned out to be Tobes.'

'Right. Well . . . Wagner wrote an opera called *Tristan und Isolde*. It's derived from countless old legends. In one of the sources, the hero, Tristan, has to go in disguise. So he changes his name to Tantrist. Get it?'

'Tantrist . . . he reverses the syllables of his name?'

'Right. And if you do that to Besto . . .'

'You get Tobes, yes, of course. Didn't you realize that?'

393

Diane gazed at him. 'I know it sounds crazy, but I didn't.'

'It sounds crazy,' Ed confirmed. 'Is this leading anywhere?'

Diane sighed. 'I don't know. It's a bitch that I can't identify his favourite opera, and he won't tell me. If it was *Tannhäuser*, there's a source that talks of the hero meeting his rival in love and kissing him on the lips, thus burning him with a mark that will never fade until the giver of the kiss has been found again. Or there's *Parsifal*. Listen to this, it's from Wagner's prose sketch: "Elsa, deeply moved, describes in ecstatic terms the happiness that has come to her through him, how she could die of gratitude, of the sense of boundless love". Which is how I sometimes feel when I consider Tobes's relationship with Johnny, it's so hot, so . . . I don't know. And there's a character called Telramund. He sings, "Thus enters evil into yonder house!" Could that relate to Tobes's getting a job with the Andersons?

'And then there's *Tristan*. Oh, God, but that's the one I dread! All about following your beloved into death, and being united hereafter, and it goes on and on. Then there's the Ring, with fire motifs. Tobes loves fires. And then Wagner started to write music that contradicted the words, so it's not enough to read the libretto, you have to find out what was in his mind.'

Diane fell silent, driven to distraction, exhausted. 'God knows what I should be looking for.' She rummaged through her notes. 'Look at this . . . after Wagner finished *The Flying Dutchman* he wrote on the score, "*In Nacht und Elend.*" "In night and wretchedness." Jesus, I know how he felt.' She rested her head in her hands. 'I should have picked up on this way back. Oh, Ed, Tobes is dangerous, so dangerous.'

'I know. I came to tell you. Quantico have done a big turnaround. They're saying Tobes could kill, very easily, they think. It was that ghost stuff that did it.'

'But Johnny denied Tobes had pretended to be a ghost!'

'They think the boy's protecting him, which redoubles the peril-factor. Daniel Krozgrow made waves. Symes has sent me around to sue for peace.'

'Oh, Jesus.' Diane let her head flop forward onto the table. She was crying and could not stop. *Pray God Ed does not take this for gratitude.* 'Listen,' she said, pulling herself together. 'I know a whole lot more than I did.'

'Tell me about it. Not here, though. Over a glass of wine.'

Diane felt loath to leave, but she was getting nowhere. 'Sure, why not?'

The library staff were closing up now anyway. Then, surprise, surprise, in the basement parking-lot they'd already *closed* up. Her car was impounded. Diane just wanted to fall over and die, but Ed wouldn't let her. There was something gritty about this man, a person who refused to let go. What name did people have for such? Hero, maybe?

They went in his car. He knew a little Thai restaurant near police headquarters. Ed ordered. The Singha beers came first. Knowing its potency, Diane sipped. Then she swallowed. Then her glass was empty and another on its way.

'So,' Ed said, after she'd eaten six spring rolls, a Thai salad and half a bowl of scalding *kow thom* soup, 'tell me.'

It took a long time, she had much ground to cover. The basic message she had for Ed was that whenever she tried to diagnose Gascoign, it got worse. She told him how the day after Tobes was referred to her, basing herself on one read-through of the file and a preliminary meeting, she'd done a first take: here was a kid suffering from obsessive-compulsive behaviour with maybe some borderline neurosis to work on and impaired cognition. Now he'd developed into a hebephrenic malignant narcissist, and everything pointed to the next station down the line: psychopathic tendency to murder.

'It all hangs together,' Diane said. 'His father raped him and abused him in countless other ways. He was lonely at school, shunned by the other kids, shy, introverted. He hates his father, hates homosexuals, loathes being touched; he's utterly self-absorbed; you add in Baker's story, his jerking off in the interview room, the compulsive thieving . . . even that, the compulsive thieving, is a factor they find more often than not in classic serial killers. As is keeping a diary. Remember he told you in that interview how he kept a diary? Boy, I'd love to read it. He likes dressing up and acting out roles. *Cross*-dressing, if Baker's story was true, and if Johnny was right the first time about him pretending to be Alice Mornay. Tobes as good as admitted the boy was telling the truth about that. Did I mention the jeans?'

'No.'

'It's a small thing. The day Douggan was found . . . that morning, as I drove to work, there was a guy hidden in the bushes near my house, smoking. I think he stole my paper. Anyway, he was wearing green jeans. And I saw a pair just like them hanging in Tobes's room.'

'You think Tobes must have been there, outside your house, planning the break-in?'

'That's what I feel.'

'And the boy, what about him?'

'Johnny? He's protecting Tobes, I'm sure of it. That alibi for the Walterton girl's murder won't stand up.'

'Hm. His stepmother supports it. I'm just wondering if it isn't the other way around. Maybe Tobes is protecting Johnny, trying to keep him out of it: didn't you just tell me that when you saw him he denied being with anyone in the cemetery last Saturday night?'

'Ed, if Tobes really thought he had a shot at an alibi, he'd take it. No matter who got hurt. He's out for number one, period, and he'll exploit Johnny as far as he has to.'

'Well . . . you're the expert.'

'So what's next? You'll arrest him?'

'There's a conference set for tomorrow.' Ed glanced at his watch. 'Correction: today. Daniel, you, the *jefes*. Peter's going to pull a decision out of the hat at the end of it.'

'What's your guess?'

'I have to be frank: as of now, we don't have probable cause to arrest Gascoign for street-loitering. We need to find a murder weapon, we need latents on the gun, we need to destroy the alibi Harley's set up for him. The wish-list is long.'

They had run out of food, and beer, and words. They sat slumped in their chairs, staring through the candlelight at each other, not wanting to split, desperate to get some rest. Ed called for the check. He would have to drive her home: they both realized that simultaneously. As they left the restaurant he took her arm, perhaps sensing how much Diane longed to be comforted.

It was raining.

'Take you home,' he said, turning up his collar.

'I suppose.'

'You don't sound happy.'

'Oh, it's just that . . . I don't know. Maybe buying that house of mine was a mistake. At the end of the day, so far away.'

'And so lonely. Did you buy a replacement for the gun that was stolen?'

'Yes. Same model, so I won't need to re-train.'

'Good.' He squeezed her arm tighter. 'Not that you have to go home tonight if you don't want to. Come back to my place.'

Shit on him! They'd bust up, he'd betrayed her, and now, one cheap oriental meal later, all that was history. Detective/First Hersey had seen an opportunity to get laid. She shook off his arm.

'I'll get a cab.'

'Diane, don't!'

But she was already walking down the street. Swaying would be a better word. (How many of those Singha beers had she drunk?) Her hands were wet, her feet soaked, hair straggled down her face. She'd not felt so ridiculous since that time in sophomore college year when her sorority put on a play and she was cast as the Incarnation of Feminine Soul, rising out of what looked like a wedding-cake – the cake had slid off the stage, taking her with it, right into the arms of her behavioural science tutor.

'Diane, come back here!'

What am I, his dog or something? She walked faster.

'Diane!'

People, fortunately there were not many of them about, stopped to look.

'You never learn, do you?' Diane tossed over her shoulder. 'Always the personal, never the professional.' It was more effective if she turned around and hollered, so she did. 'Some things are more important than getting laid!'

'List three in order of importance,' a bystander helpfully enjoined, but Diane was blind to all but Edwin Hersey, standing with his legs apart, like a security guard, some twenty yards down the street. 'You know your trouble?' she yelled. 'You're anally retentive, you can't let go, ever!'

'At least I don't talk to my own dead mother!'

How could he! Diane puffed up like a toad, crammed full of dignity and self-esteem. 'You bastard!' she bellowed. 'You creep! You were repressed as a child, it all stems from that!'

'I was *not*. If you must know, I had an orgasm when I was ten!'

Their audience, which had expanded beyond all expectation, gave a ragged cheer.

'You did?'

'I did! With a stuffed bear called Egbert.'

The contest was all over bar the shouting, and it was Ed the bystanders loved. They crowded around to pump his hand. Diane stood in the rain with hair blotting out half the woeful sight of her vanquisher being congratulated, she wished it would blot out the whole. Ed was coming towards her, shedding well-wishers. He was laughing. What was worse, *much* worse, so was she.

'Oh, Ed,' Diane said, falling into his arms, 'take me home. Yours . . . mine . . . anybody's.'

They got in his car. Ed drove off. Diane lay against him, one hand casually draped across his upper thigh and moving north. He flicked through the airwaves, as was his habit, and tonight she didn't care: he could juggle dildos while standing on one leg atop an anthill and it wouldn't matter.

Ed lived in a newish apartment building behind Apollo Park, on the edge of the shopping district. As he opened the door he apologized for its state and size – divorced cops didn't have much spare cash – but Diane couldn't have cared less. She homed in on the bed as if following a nav-aid. They got undressed quickly and rubbed their bodies up against each other like sensuous cats who'd found their own patch of sunlight, and she could have gone on like that for a long time, only Ed was bending her back, and Diane knew how much he wanted her *now*. And that knowledge became a key to the passion she'd sensed inside herself but never unleashed.

She fell backwards onto the bed, pulling him down on top of her. 'Do it,' she cried. *'Do it . . . !'*

Afterwards she lay exhausted, wondering how long it would take her body to come down, hoping never. There was steam rising off the bed, must be; when she raised her head a tad and saw only the tranquil bedroom it seemed kind of hard to believe. A disappointment. A little death . . .

Ed had fallen asleep as if flattened by someone wielding a baseball bat. Diane realized the drapes had been open throughout their love-making; if she propped herself on one elbow she could just see the edge of Brunsekka and O's terrace restaurant, a block away. How extraordinary, she'd been the show for anyone who'd cared to take a look, and so what?

400

She had Ed and a future. Hope. Luxury beyond expression.

Diane felt something rustle beside her. She squinted down at Ed, whose eyes were opening. 'Hi,' he murmured drowsily.

'Hi.'

'Want anything?'

'Yes.'

'Me, too.'

'Let me guess.' Diane stretched, and felt lascivious. Every muscle in her body sang. 'A burger with ketchup.'

'No. I want to get married.'

Diane had been in the middle of another long, utterly enjoyable stretch. She froze. 'What did you say?'

'I said – '

'It's all right, I heard you, how about next Tuesday?'

He raised his head. 'Hey! I never said I wanted to get married to *you*.'

She hit him with the pillow; would have gone on hitting him for quite a while if he hadn't wrapped her up in the sheet and threatened to suffocate her. She asked for a truce; he agreed on terms that they make love again immediately; Diane was in no mood to haggle.

Hours later she awoke, feeling cold and worse than cold – apprehensive. She knew at once what had disturbed her: the clicking noise some phones make when they're about to ring. Sure enough, the bedside phone did ring. Ed awoke upon the instant. 'Yeah?' he said, already swinging his legs off the bed as he picked up.

Diane shivered. The air-conditioning had been set way too high. Her tongue was furred an inch deep with

gunge; why hadn't she drunk water last night? Oh yes, of course . . .

Ed was saying, 'What? . . . Yeah, I can hear you, Leo. Go ahead.'

Memories surged up in a great burst of happiness. Diane snuggled close to Ed, who leaned back into her embrace, letting her in on the conversation. Leo was saying, 'You want to hold your front page?'

'What gives?'

'Tonight we got a second eye-witness on the Walterton girl. He fingered Harley Rivera. Sent a couple of our own up there . . . and Rivera confessed in the car. They're bringing him in now.'

Ed's jaw dropped, but not as far as Diane's. 'Be with you in twenty.'

'Well, be prepared to stand in line around the block, 'cause the ladies and gennelmen of the press have beat you to it.'

Ed dropped the phone back on the hook and made a grab for his shirt.

'I'm coming with you,' Diane said, scrambling into her clothes.

'No, I'll get you a cab.'

'Stick that, buster. Here, pass me your comb . . .'

Ed didn't protest again. He wanted her, she realized as she settled in the passenger seat of his car; he wanted her near him. Briefly she laid her head on his shoulder. Ed started the engine, and they were away with a screech of tyres.

Because he was tense now he set the car-radio to 'scan', giving them five-second bursts of one station before moving on to another. A habit that normally irritated the hell out of Diane today seemed only endearing. She hummed a little tune of her own and gazed out of the window. She would need a trousseau. She wanted a proper wedding, not some hole-and-corner affair at city hall. On the beach, perhaps. In Hawaii, perhaps. Oh. How would Ed cope with her earning so much more than he did . . . ?

Then it happened.

Diane stabbed down on the radio's console, shouting, '*Stop!*'

Ed swerved, making the car lurch dangerously.

'That's it, that's *it*!'

'That's what, for Christ's – '

'The music Tobes was playing, the music he's been playing ever since he was fifteen, maybe longer.'

Her fingers found the right button. For five glorious seconds the car filled with sound to lift up the heart. She noted the station. 'Come on,' she said, 'come on, come on,' because any moment the DJ was going to say what the music was, and then Tobes's secrets would be hers.

The music changed. From one beat to another, it changed. Diane stared at the dial, aghast. What was happening? And then the music changed again, they were back in the realm of Burt Bacharach; had it all been a dream?

'I don't understand,' Diane said.

'Compilation tape. They keep 'em handy, to cover a gap in scheduling.'

'You mean, I could call the studio and find out what it was?'

'I guess.'

'Why don't you have a *phone* in these damn cars?'

Leo hadn't exaggerated; it was a case of having to fight their way through the crush. The Fourth Estate could have taught Achilles a thing or two about laying siege. As they were swept forward, past the muster desk and up the stairs, Diane caught a glimpse of her Versace-clad Nemesis speaking head-on to camera down a side-corridor. Tonight, however, was worse than last time. Then, Peter Symes had made sure the thing was sewn up for his own benefit. Now, events were ahead of him. Ed and Diane swept into Symes's office a short head in front of the human wave propelling them onwards.

'Got that one wrong,' Daniel Krozgrow laconically said as they entered. 'The boys at home said Harley wasn't in the frame at all. Hello, Diane.'

He shook hands, his friendly eyes crinkling at the edges. Diane smiled back, feeling good inside, but this was the last pleasure she'd know in a while, for there was a problem. The men who mattered around these parts, the *jefes*, as Ed styled them, were poring over a loose-leaf folder on Peter's desk. The state's media were clamouring at the door, and somewhere a fuse had tripped, a battery expired.

'You can stay, Detective,' Peter said, when Ed made as if to leave. 'You'll enjoy this.'

Alf Terrigo, Chief of Detectives, glanced up from the file and shot Diane the briefest of smiles. 'They fouled up the Miranda spiel,' he said. 'Don't know if we can retrieve it. The DA's on his way over now.'

'I thought you had a second eye-witness,' Ed said.

'We do, but hell, it was a dark night, you know what a good operator will do with that. We need the man's own words.'

'Is his lawyer here?'

'He hasn't asked for one.'

'But you gave him his phone call?'

'He didn't take.'

Ed whistled. 'Why not try him again?' he asked slowly.

Terrigo nodded. 'We were thinking along those lines. We haven't charged him formally, yet. Problem's this: if his first confession turns out good, will we be treated as waiving it by going through the whole to-do again? And what if he doesn't spill second time around? See?'

'What about the other deaths?' Diane put in. 'The young men. He's confessed informally to Walterton, right?'

'That's exactly where our two guys came unstuck an hour ago. They started talking to him about Douggan and the rest, and he went berserk. Said no way did he have anything to do with that; he killed Walterton because he was drunk, and stoned, and she wouldn't go down on him 'cause she said his cock stank. Crime of passion, *he* said. So unless we can find the gun that killed the boys, and show Rivera's traces on it, we're sunk.'

'But you think he did it?'

'Sure he did it.' Peter Symes now asserted his authority. 'How many murderers does a town this size need?'

'Pete,' said Alf Terrigo, 'if you'll forgive me, that is not terrifically scientific.'

'Well, tell *them* that,' blasted Symes, shaking an angry finger at the door behind which the press even now paced up and down as a composite raging lion. 'Have you heard of genetic fingerprinting? We test Rivera, match with traces on the boys' cadavers, that's it.'

'There were no usable traces on any of the corpses.'

Peter threw up his hands and turned to face the wall. 'I don't believe this,' he told his large-scale plan of Paradise Bay and Environs. 'Say it's untrue.' He swung around. 'Where the fuck is the DA?'

Diane knew she was not going to make any significant contribution to this assembly; fatigue and Singha beer argued cogently for a recess. Slowly she retreated until she could slip out the door without anyone noticing. At the far end of the corridor a sergeant kept the hounds temporarily at bay. She turned in the other direction, seeking the back stairs.

On the first floor she sweet-talked one of the younger Photo Unit boys into letting her camp at his desk long enough to use the phone. She called the radio-station that had played Tobes's theme. After being bandied from pillar to post for about twenty minutes, she finally got connected to a Voice. She had no idea whether it was male or female; it sounded androidal. This Voice confirmed the correctness of Ed's diagnosis: what Diane had heard was a compilation tape used, along with fifty or so others, to fill awkward gaps between scheduled items. No, there was now no way of discovering who'd compiled it or from what. She tried, without success, to interest the Voice in her problem. When she started to hum Tobes's tune, the Voice hung up.

Diane made one more call from the Photo Unit man's desk, this time to a cab-company. A nice black lady drove her home. She had Ketty Lester tapes, the best thing to have happened all day. It took them over forty minutes to get to the house, and all but cleaned out Diane's purse. As she was dredging around for that last darn dollar, her black lady popped out the tape, automatically substituting news for 'Love Letters'.

'. . . as yet unidentified male for further questioning. Police Chief Peter Symes made it clear, however, that his men have no plans to focus their enquiries elsewhere at the present time; although when pressed by reporters he did emphasize that, despite tonight's arrest, it's still too early to close the files on Ray Douggan, Carl Jensen, Randy Delmar, and the still missing Hal Lawson.'

'Do you think they'll ever find him?' asked her black lady. 'The one that's still missing? Oh, thank *you*, m'am.'

'I don't think so,' Diane said. 'Something tells me.'

As she went through the house, lighting up, she questioned her inner sense of dissatisfaction. Harley Rivera's arrest and confession, even if the latter was suspect, ought to be grounds for rejoicing. Most people would be quick to point the finger at Harley in connection with all the dead teenagers, because they needed reassuring that the streets were once again safe to walk. Simple answers were wrong answers: Confucius-he-say.

Diane approached her patio windows, meaning to draw the drapes. These were new: she'd gotten tired of waiting for inspiration to hit her and bought some soft-furnishings. There was even a second sofa now, and many more scatter cushions. She'd moved the hi-fi upstairs. The preponderant colour was no longer white. She was developing a feel for cool blue, and her patio window drapes were navy. She reached up to take hold of the edges. Something made her look down. A pallid face was pressed against the glass.

Diane froze. The face sucked itself, literally, to her window; its lips were red worms, with something flickering between them. One eye, magnified, glared at her balefully over a rounded blotch of white where a cheek was leeched to the pane.

Diane screamed.

'*You bitch!*' a muffled voice yelled. Tobes's voice.

He reached for the door-latch and rattled it. The whole frame shook, streaks of light danced before Diane's eyes as the glass vibrated. For a moment longer she hung in suspended animation, gazing, horror-struck, at the grisly white vision outside; then she was running. She hurtled to the box beside the front door and threw the master switch. A red light came on. Her alarm system was live. She was protected against all evil.

'Go away,' Diane screamed. 'I'm calling the police.'

'*Fuck you!* You steal Johnny away from me, you break my brain, you go see my father, accuse me of killing everyone, *fuck you!*'

'Go away! Now!'

'You get me fired, you set the police on me.' Tobes's voice, distorted by distance and storm-glass, was never-theless distinct. Frighteningly so. He must have been screaming as loud as a man can scream. She covered her ears. Still the voice penetrated. It was like being under attack from the air, like sheltering from the worst hurricane ever.

'You bitch, you bitch, *you bitch!* After you left the cops came around, trying to get me to say I killed Maxine!'

'They don't, they don't think that any more.' Diane was shivering uncontrollably.

'I really cared for that girl, she was kind, she was neat.'

'They know now, Harley killed her, get out, *get out!*'

'I would have done anything for Maxie, my Maxie, she was so cute, so cute . . .'

'*Harley Rivera killed her!*'

Diane's eyes lit on the phone. She ran towards it.

Tobes, as if sensing her intention, rattled the latch again. The alarm detonated into a hundred-megaton explosion of sound. The receiver dropped from her hand. She was kneeling on the floor, trying to pick up her phone. Drops of sweat fell onto the white plastic. The noise inside and out of her head was traumatizing, she had seconds left before unconsciousness superseded. She looked up to see the white face dissolving away from the glass.

'Hello . . . police, urgent, police.'

The alarm noise cut off in mid decibel, leaving her shaking like a jack-hammer.

'Caller . . . hello, caller, can you hear me?'

'Police. I want the police.' They had a minute's respite, the operator and Diane, before the alarm started up again. She could override it, but Tobes might still be outside. Suppose he was circling the house; what could she do?

Hurry, operator, hurry; forty-five seconds from now the banshee would open up again . . . Then she was speaking with the emergency services, giving her name, address, number and security subscriber code. Of course! How stupid! The alarm system had been wired directly to the sheriff's office, Sheriff Watters was probably on his way right now.

The alarm started up again.

Diane dropped the phone, shocked into imbecility. Was Tobes outside still? Jesus, what to do? She ran to the control-box, opened its perspex fascia and tried to remember which switch did what. She jabbed at two before the noise died. She ran back to the phone. The line was disconnected, though not dead: a comforting burr echoed down it. Diane dropped the receiver back on its rest, but *she* did not rest. She sprinted around the house, checking windows, doors, locks, keys.

She listened. The only sound she could hear was her own desperate panting. Then lights swept across her bedroom window and a siren sounded, but this one was a comfort, for it meant the sheriff had ridden to the rescue.

Sheriff Watters himself was doubtless at home with Mrs Watters, enjoying his well-earned rest. Jim Hall, a young, fresh-faced officer Diane knew slightly, stood at her door with a colleague. 'What's all the fuss?' Jim demanded.

Diane, still overwhelmed with relief and gratitude, let them in and slumped to the floor, a helpless woman, saved. Jim stared at her. 'Yes?' he said.

And suddenly Diane Cheung became the perp. The enemy.

It was like the end of some breathtaking, Olympic performance. Her adrenalin-flow was returning to normal. Things assumed their normal size and shape. Voices sounded reasonable. And internally there were big changes, too: she began to feel stupid, and then angry with herself for feeling that way when she was the one who had been wronged.

Diane explained, shakily, what had happened. Jim wrote it down while his colleague ambled through the house, his expression varying from bored to incredulous that anyone should have bought that chair, that painting.

'Was anything taken?' Jim asked when Diane was through.

She shook her head.

'Any criminal damage?'

'No.'

410

'Broken glass, stuff like that?'

Another shake of her bewildered head.

'Muddy footprints on the deck?' Jim said, buttoning his notebook into his pocket.

'He was going to kill me,' Diane said, with a lucidity she found amazing.

'Yeah,' Jim responded. 'Dr Cheung, did you ever think to move down the coast, to one of those smart new condos? They have security, and everything. Anti-rape alarms.'

'I'll think about it.'

'Yeah. Well. Goodnight, then.'

After their car had disappeared down her driveway Diane leaned against the wall and listened. She took the pulse of her home. Nothing. No one. Tobes had gone; she felt it. For the moment, she was safe.

He would come back. But not tonight.

Normally when under stress she concocted a herbal tea. Now, however, she went out to the integral garage and rummaged among her old suitcases and boxes until she found the one containing her mother's things. She'd still not been able to bring herself to sort them all. She knew there was a medicine box. *Ma-ma*, in some ways less oriental than her twentieth-century offspring, had gone in for Diazepam. Diane found, and swallowed, two pills.

That night, she did not dream.

*　　　*　　　*

Next day, Diane managed to organize a lift into town with Margie Adams, who was a radiologist at St Joseph's and lived two miles up the coast from her. She dropped Diane two blocks from the library. Diane retrieved her car. At work, Julia greeted her with the news that Peter Symes's office had already telephoned twice and would she call soonest?

Diane had appointments, two of them replacement hours for patients who'd been forced to do without her while she was in New York. These she must, and did, attend to first. But it was not without a sense of pleasurable anticipation that she called Peter at around midday.

'Diane,' he said, 'how are you?'

'Good. You?'

'So-so. Do you have time to talk? Only I was going to apologize to you, and I don't feel it should be rushed.'

'I always make time for apologies.'

'Okay. I was hasty, over-hasty, in ordering your unit disbanded. One of the more unpopular moves I made around here last week, let me say. You have many friends here.'

'Thank you.'

'Will you kindly agree to let bygones be just that, and come back?'

'I'll think about it.'

She would have to think about it a whole heap, she realized, if she wasn't to undermine her wedding before it happened. What would Ed say at the prospect of more rows, endless bickerings, over where stood the frontier between their personal and professional affairs? 'I'll think about it,' she repeated, with unnecessary firmness.

'That's all I can ask for now,' Peter said. 'It's more than enough. Diane, Sheriff Watters called me first thing. He'd just read a report about a visit to your place by two of his officers last night, and he was very concerned. Are you fully recovered?'

'I guess.'

'I took the liberty of filling Sheriff Watters in on some of the background: your assailant, his record, and so forth. The sheriff will be calling you himself to express concern that this incident may not have been dealt with as efficiently as it should have been.'

'There's no need. Why did Watters call you?'

'He knows you and I are personal friends, knows of our professional association; he felt I should have the information.'

A much more likely reason occurred to Diane: after last Saturday, word had gone out that she and her unit were dead meat and might start to stink a little, so any useful dirt peace officers could get on her was to be passed up the line to Symes.

'Diane, I hate to pile things on you, but . . . can we have you here, later today? As soon as convenient, in fact?'

'Why?'

'Things have reached a delicate stage with Rivera. He's offering a deal. Or rather, not offering it, but skirting around it, hinting, teasing . . . we need your assessment.'

'Has Daniel gone home, or something?'

'Daniel's as keen as I am that you should be present when Rivera gets around to pitching.'

Diane was enjoying this phone call. The creak of old rope as Peter dangled and twisted in the wind made for easy listening – and that had always been her favourite. 'I'll be there as soon as I can,' she said. 'Peter, I have another call on two, goodbye.'

Julia, standing in her doorway, watched her hang up. 'You don't have a line two,' she said, redundantly.

'Maybe I should get one, at that.'

It was eight thirty before Diane made it to headquarters. She took up position next to the mirror through which she could watch all that happened in the room where Tobes had jerked off that famous time.

Rivera sat with his elbows resting on the table and his head in his hands. Cigarette-smoke curled up from between the fingers of his right hand. Diane couldn't see his face, since he was sitting sideways-on to the mirror. He'd got a bad attack of the shakes. His lawyer, a middle-aged man with red bow-tie, anxious, square face and thick bush of white hair, watched him carefully. She knew that Rivera had asked to speak with Detective Ed Hersey 'and his girlfriend'. He'd been told that the girlfriend was not available and wouldn't be. For half a day, that had served as the official deal-breaker. Now Harley Rivera had cracked: Detective Hersey, flying solo, would do. No stenog, no Diane Cheung, no DA: just Ed.

Daniel slid into the chair next to Diane's. She nodded at the mirror. 'What's he on?'

'He's been a cocaine addict for over ten years, main-lining heroin for two. Nothing in reserve, now.'

'So he'll say anything. Can we use it?'

'Depends on the anything.'

The door to the far room opened; Ed came through it and took a chair opposite Harley. 'What's Ed been told?' Diane asked, while he was still running through the preliminaries.

'To listen to everything and agree to nothing, but to be sympathetic and supportive.'

'Isn't the latter part somewhat unusual?'

'We need a break.'

'You mean, Peter needs a break.'

'He's a little old to find himself unemployed. Ah . . .'

414

Harley had started to speak. At first the words came out real slow, and in no particular order. Ed didn't say anything, just slumped in his chair and rested one arm over the back, looking bored. When the lawyer tried to put in a word, Harley silenced him with his hand.

'Listen,' Harley said, and it wasn't much more than a whisper. 'I want to cooperate. I am a nice guy. I am. I didn't want to kill Maxine. Loved her. My girl. She was. It was accidental. It was.'

Harley had stayed silent almost a minute before Ed leaned forward. He'd been examining the fingernails of his right hand. Now he stuffed that hand into his pocket and he said, 'What do you want?'

'Manslaughter.' It was the lawyer who spoke, this time without objection from the piece of flotsam masquerading as his client. 'Mr Rivera will plead to homicide sub-division two, on the understanding that no evidence will be led of aggravating circumstances leading to detention beyond a normal expectancy of ten to fifteen years.'

'And in return?'

Ed and the lawyer both looked at Harley. For a long moment he didn't respond. Then his mouth worked, he chomped his tongue, he spoke.

'I can finger the man who killed Carl Jensen. I can do that. Can.'

Daniel was suddenly sitting ramrod-straight, hands on the tops of his thighs. Diane, too, felt her body adjust itself in unexpected ways. The lawyer shifted his torso back slightly, indicating that this was the first he'd heard of the strength of his client's hand; the look on his face said, We're talking a big pot here, a big one.

Diane knew Harley would get his deal.

Peter Symes had three teenagers dead and one missing on his patch; he wanted them off, just as he wanted to hang on to his job; the two concerns were related. His enquiries so far had led nowhere. This was the opening he'd been looking for. Harley would plead to murder two and be walking the streets ten years from now.

If he delivered.

'I'm listening,' Ed said.

'So we have a deal?' the lawyer asked, too eagerly.

'We don't have any deal. I'll listen to what your client has to say, take it upstairs and then they'll come back and tell us if we have a deal.'

'Oh, come on, Detective!'

Ed spread his hands, as if to say, Don't shoot the pianist, I didn't write this stuff. The lawyer stood up. 'We talk to the deal-maker,' he said.

'Suit yourself.' Ed, too, rose. 'I'll see the DA. Can tell you now, I don't think he'll buy.'

'Why not?' the lawyer sneered.

'He's worried about more than Carl. There's two other bodies unaccounted for. Did your client ice them? Will Batman return? To find out the answer to these and other questions, tune in next – '

'Very funny. I'm thinking of reporting you to internal affairs, Detective.'

'As is your privilege.'

'It was Tobes,' said Harley. 'Tobes Gascoign. He killed Carl.'

For a moment, no one associated these lucid words with Mr Rivera, derelict and has-been. Ed and the lawyer were both busy preparing their respective next shots: Diane could almost see their minds working. Then everybody clicked in and Mr Rivera had an audience.

'Tell me more,' Ed said.

'I advise you to say nothing.' The lawyer stood over Harley, wagging a finger, which his client ignored.

'Came to me the next day . . . Said he needed an alibi, like, y'know, real bad? *Real* bad . . . Said he was in the cemetery when Carl got his. Him being in therapy, with a rap-sheet long as your arm . . . didn't want to answer any questions about all of that. So I gave him an alibi, like he wanted. No reason Tobes Gascoign couldn't have killed Carl. No reason at all.'

'Is that it?' Ed sounded bored.

'No,' Harley said. 'That is not it.'

Ed yawned.

'All them corpses were burned, yes? Scorch marks?'

Ed's eyes narrowed, and Diane knew why. That was another detail they'd kept out of the papers (although one out-of-town journal had run it as a flier, and never mentioned it again when no one bit).

'What if they were?'

'Tobes liked to burn. He used to play dare games with the gas-burners. One of the guys got badly scorched. Had to go to hospital.'

'The Down's syndrome boy?'

'Kitu, yes, that one.'

Ed was remembering the burn marks on Kitu's arms, as was Diane.

'Tobes didn't give shit. He laughed when Kitu burned.'

Ed stayed silent for a long time. Diane tried to imagine what was going through his mind. None of her suggestions came anywhere near the truth, for now he said, 'Tobes likes classical music, doesn't he?'

Harley nodded.

'As do you.'

For a moment Diane was flummoxed; then she remembered the radio softly playing Beethoven in Harley's office that Saturday she and Ed had gone there together. So Ed had noticed it, too.

'Me? I'm a Mahler fanatic.' And Harley laughed, the dry choking laugh of a man who needs that sixtieth tube to finish the day. 'Bruckner, too. They say you can't love Mahler and Bruckner both, but don't you believe it! 'Course, I have to give the customers something altogether else.' His face sagged, the momentary light dimmed. 'Wouldn't mind some Mahler right now, yes. Second movement of the Fifth . . .'

'And Tobes? Remember what music he liked?'

Diane held her breath.

'Oh. Wagner.'

And then Ed surprised her. He started to hum. He sang Gilbert and Sullivan for pleasure, so what he hummed was recognizable as the tune they'd heard on the car-radio, the studio re-mix tape. Harley's eyes brightened. He began to conduct Ed with both forefingers, giggling like a child.

'Yeah,' he said, 'yeah. Great. Should play the Forum.'

'What is it?' Ed asked.

'Flying Dutchman. *Der Fliegende Holländer*. Me, I'm a Ring man myself.' Harley threw back his head. He opened his mouth. Out of it floated this gorgeously rich baritone voice, a jewel of great beauty mounted in cracked pottery.

> '*Soll finden ich nach qualenvollem Leben*
> *in deiner Treu' die langersehnte Ruh?*'

He lowered his head and regarded Ed sheepishly. 'That was the Dutchman. It means, uh, can I find the rest I

418

long for in your love? After hell on earth. That kind of shit.' His eyes brightened again. 'It's beautiful? Isn't it?'

Diane rose. 'Daniel,' she said, 'I have to get out of here.'

'What's wrong?'

'I know the worst now. The Flying Dutchman: a man doomed to roam the earth for all eternity until he finds a woman who loves him enough to die for him and set his soul free.'

'So?'

'So Tobes has found his saviour in Johnny. And he's just ten years old. Daniel, where's the nearest phone?'

*   *   *

September 30

> *Dear Mr Detective Hersey,*
>
> *I've decided what must happen. We only get one shot at this life and mine's fast slipping away. Cut a long story short: I'm slipping away, too.*
>
> *I'm going down to police HQ now. I'll leave this at the desk in an envelope with your name on it, and after that you decide. Probably you'll trash it: after all, I accused Dr Diane before, and blew it then, so why pay any attention now?*
>
> *I'll go to Johnny's and say goodbye. It has to be that way. So, a long farewell. And the last. Ever.*
>
> *You want to know what I'm doing? I'm in my room, listening to my music, as usual, and tonight I'm burning incense. Don't know why. Just feels right. There's a lot of fresh flowers here. I'll be sorry to leave them. Paradise Bay, no: I've outstayed my welcome. But the flowers of Southern California will remain with me till I die.*

419

I'm sorry if I troubled you. You never gave me any trouble. Well, not too much. But I'm disturbed in my mind. I'm afraid of Dr Diane. She's no good for me, not now, not since she got her hooks into Johnny.

One last thing. It's about Johnny. Couldn't bring myself to tell Diane any of this, or even the kid, but somebody has to know. He's the only real friend I ever had and I love him. I wouldn't harm him in any way. I know lots of people, maybe you included, think I just want to get in his pants. Untrue. The thought of that makes me sick to my stomach. But . . . things happened to me when I was young. Some very, very bad things happened. I know it's in me, all that sick stuff. The queer stuff. And it's going to muddle up my life, always. Another reason for leaving now.

Tell Diane goodbye from
Tobes

*   *   *

Diane dialled; the line was busy. How could they be talking with strangers when their son was in mortal peril? What kind of parents were they? But then, they did not know Johnny stood on the threshold of the dark valley.

Diane dialled and dialled. At last Nicole picked up.

'Nicole . . . Diane Cheung. Johnny's in danger. Don't let him out of your sight, have you got that?'

'Yes, but . . . oh, Jesus – '

'Listen. Go upstairs. Make sure Johnny's in his room.'

'But I can't – '

'*Now!*'

Down the line she heard footsteps that changed note as Nicole ran up the stairs. Something prompted Diane to look at her watch. Perhaps it would be important in court . . . Nine thirty-eight. Nine thirty-eight and forty seconds when she heard the scream.

*　　　*　　　*

Johnny saw him standing there at nine thirty, their 'time', and went out to him, no second thoughts, like all the trash had never happened. And he said, 'Hi, I've missed you,' and Tobes said the same. He gave Johnny a hug. He wanted to let go quickly, but the boy hung in there. Nobody hugged him much. Dad didn't like that kind of goo. So Johnny hugged Tobes tight and said, 'Why'd you wait so long to come back?'

'Things, y'know?'

'Yes,' said Johnny, though he didn't. He knew you had to lie for adults, though, or they got jumpy.

'I need a favour.'

'What kind of favour? Anything.'

'Like the one you did earlier. An alibi.'

'Sure. No problem. I'll say you were here, with me. I mean, you *are* here with me, right?'

'Right. Kind of.'

'What kind of kind of?'

'I want you to say I was here at four o'clock this morning.'

'Four o'clock this morning. Wonderful, *not*.'

'Will you do it?'

'Sure I will.'

'You don't look too happy.'

'Gee, me happy? Come on, you're confusing me with Wayne Campbell. Why?'

'Why lie?'

'Yeah. If I'm going to do ten years in jail on account of you, I'd like to know what you did.'

Tobes broke away from him then, with his hands in his pockets *real* deep, like he wanted to punch his way out through them, and he wouldn't look at Johnny. After a while he said, 'Last night I went up to Diane's place and made a fool of myself. So I need a little juggling with the time.'

'What kind of fool?'

'What kind of fool am I?' Tobes warbled. 'You know that song? Do you? I love that song.'

'Tobes. What did you do?'

'Um. I cut loose. A bit.'

'Did she see you?'

'Did who see me?'

'Tobes . . .'

'Yeah, all right. She saw me.'

'So how can I say you were with me?'

'Maybe she was hysterical and can't identify me.'

'Tobes,' Johmmy said, very serious. 'Don't ask me to do this. It's just going to make things worse.'

'Harley didn't say that. My friend Harley lied for me, once before.'

'So go ask him.'

'I can't. He's under arrest.'

Johnny remembered the name Harley from somewhere, and, yes! The news prog! They'd got somebody for those murders . . .

'But nobody's going to take the word of a child against Dr Diane.'

'I'll be saying the same thing as you.'

And that was the moment Johnny finally faced it: Tobes wasn't quite all there. He didn't see things like other people. Only a little side-slip. Enough, though.

Johnny wanted to tell him straight out that 1 Child + 1 Weirdo didn't = proof, but how could he? He loved Tobes.

Johnny put a hand on his arm and pulled and pulled until Tobes couldn't go on resisting any longer and their eyes finally met.

'Tobes,' Johnny said. 'I want you to listen. Hard.'

He gathered his thoughts together and opened his mouth, and this scream rose out and up like a vampire's death-cry. For a second Johnny thought it must be some sicko with a knife behind him; then he realized: it was Nicole. The diary-stealer. The by now fully reinstated nosey-parker Wicked Witch of the West.

'Johnny!' she hollered. 'Stay away from that man! Get back in the house!'

Mike Anderson came thundering down the path like the Fifth Cavalry, and he was screaming too, and Johnny couldn't understand one word. Yes, one, he could: DAMN.

They had seconds left. Tobes gripped Johnny's arm. 'I can be your father, a better father,' he babbled. 'I can save you.'

And all that was so much crap. What mattered was that he, Johnny, should save Tobes, the one guy who'd ever loved him and taken his love in return. So he started to run. Tobes was clutching him, but it was Johnny doing the driving as they hared down that path, into the cemetery. He wanted to yell, 'Shut up!', partly to Tobes (so he'd save breath) and partly to Mike Anderson, who was busy telling the world what he'd do to Johnny when he caught him.

Mike's voice faded. Johnny found time to turn. He mouthed, 'Goodbye.' The darkness swallowed them.

*   *   *

423

By the time Nicole returned to the phone she'd assumed a wondrous mantle of authority. She gave Diane the picture, calmly and without embellishment.

She'd gone upstairs to find Johnny's bed tousled but empty. She'd looked out of the bedroom window and seen her stepson underneath the light at the back gate, talking with someone. Then she'd recognized Tobes and screamed. Mike had grasped the situation and belted after them. But by the time he'd charged through the gate they were long gone.

Diane advised her to call the police and sit tight until they arrived. She put down the phone. She went to stand by the window of the office they'd temporarily assigned to Daniel Krozgrow, looking out into the night. No point in rushing. Time taken now would pay dividends later.

'What you're planning is wrong,' said a voice, and Diane turned, half expecting to see Daniel beside her. There was no one there. No one tangible.

'I do what I must, *Ma-ma*. I have to save that poor little boy.'

Diane waited, patiently, but the presence had taken leave of her as quickly as it came. She checked her purse. The gun was there.

The drive up to Court Ridge seemed to take no time, perhaps because Diane's mind was running through her plan over and again. The house was all lit up like the Lincoln Memorial and looked much as it did the day they'd discovered Randy Delmar sleeping nose to toe with Alice Mornay. As Diane made her way under the police incident streamer she allocated herself twenty minutes here, no more, for first aid and the gathering of information.

There were squad cars in the driveway, their lights

revolving; there were the usual press people; radios squawked at one another; and here was Edwin Hersey, Detective First Grade, walking towards her, looking haggard.

'Tobes has to be the killer,' she said, and Ed nodded. 'Where's he gone?' he asked. 'Where's he likely to have taken the boy?'

'God knows.'

They went in. Mike Anderson bore down on her like a tank. 'It's all thanks to you we gave that freak a toehold here,' he yelled in Diane's face. 'I'm going to sue you for every cent you've ever made or are ever likely to . . .' and there was much, much more in similar vein, but she cut through it and collected Nicole, taking her into the kitchen, where Nicole locked Mike out. She was pale, but astonishingly calm. The notion that she'd been expecting this to happen flitted through Diane's mind; no time to dwell on that.

'Nicole, I want you to think back and see if Johnny gave any clue about where he might go if ever he did.'

Not Diane's best-ever sentence, but Nicole got the point. 'He was fond of the cemetery, always, in a strange kind of way,' she said slowly. 'My guess is, they're still hiding there.'

'Did Johnny know where Tobes lived?'

'Not unless Tobes told him. Diane, you asked Johnny to keep a diary. I . . . I've, well, I've read some of it. I know I shouldn't have, but . . . they're very close. I mean . . . *very* close.'

'Ah! He never let me see all of what he wrote. That worried me.'

'They met in the cemetery again the other night. I saw them.'

'Yes, I know. I want to see this diary.'

'It's in his room.'

When Nicole unlocked the door they walked into the arms of Mike Anderson, a force no longer to be denied. Diane stood there, pretending to listen for a minute and a half; when he paused for breath she said, 'Mr Anderson, you have single-handedly wrecked your son's future. You have denied him love, affection, friendship and simple physical contact; I have watched most of that and Johnny has told me the rest with surprising ease. If you want ever to see him again, let me pass.'

People were staring at them: tough cookies, policemen, women special agents, homicide detectives. Nobody spoke. Mike's face was redder than a tomato. Suddenly he raised his hands to his eyes, his shoulders began to shake, tears flooded through his splayed fingers. Diane stepped around this desolate father and, with Nicole by her side, ascended the stairs.

There were no clues in Johnny's bedroom; Diane had not seriously thought there would be, but tonight was not one for slapdash procedures. She took his diary. Downstairs again, Ed met her with the news that a cordon had been thrown around the cemetery. Nicole looked pleased. Diane, however, did not accept her theory, and in any case all Ed meant was that blues were stationed by every exit, whereas Tobes knew better than to use an obvious way out.

Outside, her own resolve cracked. 'How could I have missed it?' she wailed, raising two reproachful hands to heaven. 'It was all there for me to see, and I was blind, wilfully blind.'

Ed put a hand on her shoulder, and even in the depths of her trouble Diane felt there a crumb of comfort: the hand of a healer. 'You can't know everything about your patients,' he said. 'You're not to blame, Diane. *You're not to blame.*'

Diane shook her head. 'The Flying Dutchman,' she murmured. 'It would have to be that.'

'So what does it mean?'

'The Flying Dutchman was cursed to wander the earth until the day of judgement, or until he found a woman who would love him beyond death. He found one; her name was Senta. She killed herself. The Dutchman's soul was set free; they were united in death. Oh dear God, please help that poor little boy . . .'

'Wait a minute, wait a minute. This Senta, she wanted to sacrifice herself? Maybe Johnny doesn't.'

'Tobes has been working on that, my dear. That's *all* he's been working on, don't you see? And now, if Johnny falters, there'll be such a fine line in Tobes's mind between self-sacrifice and *exacting* sacrifice. I must go.'

'Where?'

'To get my Wagner research.'

Ed's hand dropped from her shoulder. 'Diane,' he said, 'you know I love you, with all my heart I do. And because I love you I'm going to repeat something I've said before: you've got to beware of hunches. You cannot base an investigation on a Wagner opera. And what else have we got on Tobes? Not much, only tonight's abduction. From what the parents have said already, it may not have *been* an abduction, the boy may have gone willingly.'

'I'm sure he did.'

'You're *what*?'

'That's what I was saying earlier, about sacrifice. Johnny loves Tobes.' Diane managed a pathetic smile. 'He loves him to death.'

'Diane!'

'Well, what do you expect me to say? I should have pushed Symes. But I couldn't betray a patient, could I, even if it meant he got his teeth into Johnny's neck? Doing the right thing is always impossible. Leave me alone. No, I don't mean that, I love you, I – '

She pushed past him and got into her car.

'Is it always going to be like this?' Ed said through the window. 'Is it?'

Diane didn't know. So she drove away. The dash clock told her she'd overstayed her allotted time by eight minutes.

The area where Tobes lived seemed different by night. During the day there'd been a sense of neighbourhood vitality, albeit not terribly healthy. The dark hours drained everything, leaving the streets deserted, windows unlit, plus the dangerous knowledge that someone, somewhere, had decreed curfew. The street-lighting here didn't work. A glance up at the nearest standard merely revealed shards of glass, their crinkle-cut edges shining in the glow from an upper window. Diane hurried towards Tobes's door, glad to be off the street. She felt her way up the stairs, listening. Apart from things that slithered behind plaster and boards, the house was still.

His door was still as she remembered it: a joke. Two shoulder-shoves had no effect, but then she recalled what cops did in movies and belted it with her foot. Pow! In she went. Either nobody heard her felonious entry, or nobody cared.

From far away, down the street, came the slow, sad strains of 'When I Fall in Love'. Diane couldn't make out the singer. Beautiful, though; and so far off that she experienced it as a gentle pulse rather than heard it as a ballad.

She groped for the light-switch. To her surprise, it worked. The room boasted only a single bulb, but that was enough to show her where to begin her search.

The cardboard boxes . . . She went straight to the one marked with her name and up-ended it on the floor. So that's where her lipstick had gone. There was a collection of erotica – no, why dignify it thus? – of hard pornography: stomach-churning, the sick product of a disordered mind. A smell rose off these drawings, a stench of corruption.

Diane had encouraged Tobes to let his feelings flood out onto paper, graphically. He'd never shown her the results. Here they were.

The room was in such a mess; where to look next? How about the heaps of books, mostly stolen from libraries, and defaced? So many books about China and the Chinese . . .

There were also notebooks, tiny things bought in a Seven-Eleven, filled with page after page of scrawl, with some sentences descending the page vertically, Chinese fashion. Diane read a little of what looked like the methodical record of Johnny Anderson's seduction. She stuffed the books into her purse. Then something else caught her eye.

There was a gun under his pillow. He hadn't concealed it completely. All the breath rushed out of her in a hiss. She reached down to pick up the gun.

That's when she heard footsteps on the stairs.

Whoever was there made no attempt to dissemble. He came on relentlessly, full of weight and assurance. And why not? – no householder ever returned like a thief in the night.

Tobes had her trapped.

Diane fumbled in her purse for her own gun, only to realize that this was stupid. *Don't let Tobes see the gun, don't alarm him, he's got Johnny and if you treat him the wrong way, Johnny's history.*

In her state of near-hysteria she managed to drop her gun. The footsteps had almost reached the top of the stairs. Not taking her eyes off the door, she shoved everything back in the box, while simultaneously grappling with two weapons.

The door started to swing open. Diane thrust one gun in her purse, the other under the pillow. Tobes stood outside, looking at her, his fingers caressing the broken handle. Diane backed up against the window, shaking. *Crazy not to have kept the gun out. Mistake. Fatal mistake.*

'Diane, what the fuck do you think you're doing?'

Diane heard Tobes's voice because that's what she was expecting to hear; and even when Detective Edwin Hersey of the Third Precinct strode into the room to take this stuttering, shivering wreck of a once-dignified woman in his arms she did not fully recognize him.

'I ducked out,' he explained, once she was in a state to listen and understand. 'I saw you were crumbling, so I came after you.'

'I told you I was going home,' she protested weakly.

'You're not a good liar. I asked myself why you might be holding out on me, what I would have done in your place. And here I am.'

'Oh, Ed . . . how did I ever get by before I met you?'

'Just tell me one thing. One, okay? What would you have done if he'd been here?'

'Talked to him. Found out where he was hiding Johnny.'

Ed let silence complete her condemnation. Then he said, 'Let's get out of here.'

He helped her down the stairs, into the street, where his car was roughly parked almost against the fender of Diane's.

'Actually, I knew Tobes wouldn't be there,' she said.

'How?'

'Because I'm pretty sure I know where he is. Harley's Diner. Tobes used to talk to me about that place a lot, in therapy. It was his safe place, his bolt-hole. Where he'd go when things got too tough. He'll have taken Johnny there, too.'

'Thanks, Diane.' Ed took her hand. This was what he expected from her, this was what the Juvenile Crimes Unit should have been all about, right from the beginning: cooperation. 'Thank you.'

Another car rounded the corner and sped towards them. Diane feared attack: only drug barons drove that way. But . . . 'Here's Leo,' Ed said. 'I told him where I was going, got him to cover for me.'

The car squealed to a halt. Leo jumped out and ran across to them. 'Hey, pal,' he hailed Ed cheerily, 'you're dead. Know that? Symes wants you, everybody, at HQ, yesterday. Plus you left your radio unanswered for more than the statutory ten. Evening, Diane, how are you doing?'

'I'm fine, Leo.'

'Really? You look like you've seen a ghost.'

'I can't leave Diane,' Ed said.

'I'll be all right,' she said. 'This time I really am going home.'

'Diane . . .'

'Go.' She give Ed a little push. 'Call you tomorrow. That's a promise.'

'Get in your car,' Leo advised Ed, 'drive like the wind. Oh. Some guy left this at the desk, Marty said to give it to you.'

He handed to Ed a large brown envelope with writing on the front; it was too dark for Diane to make out the words.

'Diane, are you sure?' Ed fidgeted with the envelope. He had only this one career, it was going down the tubes, he must go. She waved, putting her soul into it, and said, 'Fly, big bird.'

'Love you,' he whispered.

They all got into their cars. Seconds later, the street was as empty as it had been when Diane cruised down it twenty minutes ago. With luck, she reflected, much of the Paradise Bay police force would even now be diverting its energies in the direction of Harley's Diner, up the coast; which left her free to deal with Tobes. At last.

*   *   *

Tobes heard a car and shoved Johnny into a doorway. It stank. Someone must have peed over it. Johnny didn't like the neighbourhood, but being with Tobes made him feel safe. Kind of. This cop car raced by, followed by another car. Then, maybe half a minute later, a third. Tobes listened.

'Move,' he said. 'Move fast.'

They walked hand in hand down this wide street. It was almost totally dark, and it smelled of garbage. Johnny kept thinking some huge guy was going to jump out from behind a trashcan with his Uzi and he wanted to run. Tobes wouldn't run, though. Suddenly Tobes pushed on a door and they were in this yukkysmelling place where Johnny couldn't see anything. They batted up the stairs. Tobes stopped dead and said, 'Oi!', or something. A door was open, a light was on inside this crummy dump of a room. A horror museum. House of Wax.

'Welcome,' Tobes said, in this thoughtful kind of way. And it clicked: he *lived* here!

Tobes had a gun.

There he was, in the middle of the room, holding a gun. Johnny said, 'Is that real?' And Tobes said, 'It shouldn't be.'

Now that was no great answer, as far as Johnny was concerned. But when he tried to take a closer look, Tobes snatched it away. 'Somebody,' he said, pocketing it, 'is giving us grief, Johnny. Let's split.'

On the street again, Johnny asked, 'Are we going to take another cab?' (Which was how they'd come.)

'No.'

'Because they'll be looking for us, right?'

'Smart cookie.'

'So what's our next move, wiseguy?'

'We borrow some wheels,' said Tobes

He found what he wanted three blocks south. Tobes penetrated a neat little Subaru DL, and they were mobile.

'Where are we headed?' Johnny asked.

'A place no one will think of looking for us.'

Johnny brooded about that, and while he brooded, Tobes drove. Badly. Johnny got the feeling he hadn't done a lot of this. Maybe someone would notice. Maybe the Subaru's owner was already phoning the cops. But more than anything, he brooded about where all this would end. He could not see an ending that he liked.

They drove out towards the coast. Soon there were no more city lights, and traffic got thin. The road climbed, it twisted and it turned. This was not anywhere Johnny knew. Then they were parking deep in a thicket of bushes, and Tobes got out. Johnny did too. He could smell the sea, and hear it. There was this big house on a hill; they crossed a field to get to it. All the windows were dark, nobody home; but Tobes hammered on the big metal knocker like he wanted to raise Dracula at midday.

No answer. He was getting angry, Johnny could *feel* his anger fizzing away beside him, but really, there was nobody in this house. So now they padded around the deck until they came to some sliding windows. Tobes got out his knife and fiddled with them, which took a long time. Then he disappeared for a while, crawling on all fours, as if tracking something.

'Johnny.' The boy jumped out of his skin: Tobes just came back without telling him. 'Get ready to run. If there's a noise, run, hit the car, wait for me.'

Tobes took a deep breath, leaned against the glass, and gently shifted it sideways. The sliding doors were opening. There was no noise. 'You knocked out the alarm?' Johnny said, and the Big T nodded.

They went in. It was dark, yes, but then Johnny realized that the grey bits were furniture, and the longer he waited the more he could see. Tobes was drawing the drapes. He went over to an inner doorway and turned on the lights.

The boy blinked, and looked around. This was one great property. It had a cosy feel to it. Plenty of books, and flowers every place you looked. Red flowers, mostly, mixed in with white. There was a fireplace, and he just adored that. Also, glass bowls full of scent, with tapers floating inside: many of them, each on a different table, no two the same height. Johnny realized he'd been feeling cold but now was warm, and not just his skin. He *liked* this place!

'Who lives here?' he breathed.

'The person who most truly understands me,' Tobes said. He was over by windows they'd come in through, locking them tight. 'A friend. Someone who lives in a temple of peace and harmony.'

Tobes looked at Johnny as he said this, his eyes very bright, so the boy figured maybe he was trying to tell him something, only he couldn't figure out what. Tobes found it funny, though. He laughed that truly revolting laugh of his. His ghost laugh.

'Tobes, you're not a ghost. Stop that.'

'What?'

'Your ghost laugh. I told you before, I truly, truly hate it. Why won't you understand? You don't *have* to be a ghost, you're a fabulous human being.' He walked towards him. 'You're the greatest. I love you.'

But Tobes fended him off. 'What are you saying? I don't understand what you're saying.'

'What's to understand, for God's sake?'

'You mean you think I'm a pervert? Is that it?' Tobes shoved him in the chest. Johnny nearly fell over.

'What's a pervert?'

Tobes stared at him for a long time; then he did this angry kind of shrug and turned his back, like Johnny was dirt or something.

'I'm hungry,' Tobes said in a sulky voice. 'You?'

'Could eat.'

Funny thing was, Johnny didn't feel hurt by Tobes's attitude: it wasn't like when Mike Anderson rejected him because he was too busy doing something else.

Tobes went into the kitchen and Johnny followed. Whoever lived here certainly had a thing about white.

'Not a darn thing. Champagne . . . ' Tobes rooted around in the ice-box. 'This milk is sour, whew!'

He poured it down the sink and started in on the cupboards. He came up with a chopstick. One. He held it up, and that grin was back now. 'What are we supposed to do with this, d'you think?'

Johnny didn't remind him that *they* were not supposed to be here at all, therefore they should do nothing with it. Now was not the time.

'Let's explore.'

Tobes ran out of the kitchen. Johnny heard his feet thudding on the stairs and followed him up. Tobes raced from room to room, closing the drapes, shrouding them from prying outside eyes. The last room was not a room at all, more a kind of alcove, with a big round window.

'Wow!' Tobes cried. He skidded to a halt. There were scatter-cushions in red and yellow and orange and blue and you name it. The floor was bare board. Johnny noticed more of those glass bowls with wax tapers floating inside. There was this mighty stereo outfit, too, with speakers and two sets of phones and the works. The Big Mac of stereos.

Tobes seemed puzzled. 'She's moved it,' he murmured. 'Now why would she move it upstairs . . . ? But it's better this way, *much* better.' His puzzlement vanished. He approached the stereo with confidence, seemed to know exactly what he was doing. When his fingers played over the black fascia, lights glowed, things hummed.

In the corner stood one of those tower-racks for CDs, designer-elegant. Tobes turned to it, and whistled.

'Wagner,' he breathed. 'The canon. The entire it. All . . . of . . . it.'

He went up to the rack like a Catholic approaching the altar and picked out a disc, which he slotted into the machine. Next minute, incredible music filled the house. To Johnny, it sounded as if the musicians had opened a window somewhere and let in a sea-storm. He could feel the wind blow, the ocean churn, the wave-caps toss and break. Tobes was conducting the music, his eyes shut; the chopstick could come in useful there, so Johnny raced downstairs to get it. Tobes burst out laughing when the boy shoved it into his right hand, but he kept right on conducting, perfectly relaxed now.

After a while Johnny slipped down on one of the cushions, which was *really* comfortable, and his eyes began to droop. The music became quieter. Somebody was singing. Tobes stuck the chopstick in a breast pocket of his shirt and flopped onto the cushion next to Johnny's. The boy leaned against him, letting his head rest on Tobes's chest. He could tell Tobes didn't like it. Johnny didn't care. He was happy.

Tobes fidgeted, though. After a bit Johnny had to sit up, because he knew Tobes really wasn't into this touching stuff and must be feeling gruzzled. 'I won't leave you,' he said. 'Not as long as you need me.'

Tobes's face twisted, as if he'd got an aching tooth. 'You don't understand,' he moaned.

'Try me.'

After a few false starts, Tobes began talking about himself. Johnny couldn't follow most of it. He sensed Tobes kept some things back because he was afraid of hurting him. That made Johnny mad. He tried to tell him so, but Tobes just went on about the age-difference

437

between them, and how he was normal and hated perverts, especially when they went in for kids like Johnny. Which would have been fine if only Johnny had known what a pervert was.

At last Tobes said something the boy could understand. 'I do love you, Johnny. You're a rebel, like me, yeah! You're so like me. Like I *could* have been. And you're the only good thing in my life.'

But while Johnny was riding high on that, he added, 'Pity it doesn't lead anywhere. It never will.'

Tobes heaved a big long sigh. Johnny was about to speak again when without warning his companion jumped up and rushed along the hallway to one of the bedrooms. Johnny ran after him, meaning to protest, only to find him rummaging through a walk-in closet. As the boy came in, Tobes pulled something down off a rack and put it around his shoulders. A blue sailor-jacket! With rings around the lower arms, and tiny anchors on the collar.

Johnny had seen this jacket somewhere before. *Where?*

Tobes rummaged some more. A cream skirt came out. He stepped into it, found the clasp-thingy-whatever. Johnny burst out giggling. Tobes put a hand to his hip and strutted his stuff in front of a mirror. He pranced around so much that the chopstick fell out of his shirt-pocket and lay, unnoticed, on the floor beside the bed.

'Say, you look really cute,' Johnny told him, 'be my date.'

Arm in arm, they hoofed it down the stairway, by now both giggling fit to die. There was a long mirror at the foot of the stairs: they caught sight of themselves in the same moment and collapsed. They had to sit on the bottom step to get their breaths.

What sobered them up was the noise of a door opening.

They turned. Johnny caught a glimpse of a garage, a door connected this lovely house to its garage and the door was open, someone stood on the threshold, and Click! he knew where he'd seen that sailor-jacket before.

'Hi, Diane!' he crowed.

PART THREE

So Diane leaves Tobes's place and drives straight home. Tobes and Johnny aren't there. She knows a moment's surprise, then feels pleased. Their tardiness gives her an opportunity to set up aromatic candles and light a log fire, her first, for the autumn night has conjured up a mist floating in off the channel and a chill in the air, scented with wet fallen leaves. Johnny may be hungry when he arrives: check the refrigerator, then start in on his diary.

As she puts her still-open purse down on the kitchen sideboard, however, Tobes's weeny notebooks catch her eye and she succumbs to that temptation instead. There are six of them. It's hard to fix the right order, but she finds one that begins with these words:

> *Hi there!*
> *I'm Tobes.*
> *My given name is Tobias, but you may call me Tobes.*
> *Everyone does.*

She stands by the sink, preparing to fill the kettle. But she reads, and she reads, and the kettle is soon forgotten.

When someone bangs on the front door, Diane does not panic, even though she is not yet ready to receive her visitors. She gathers up the notebooks, grabs her purse, flicks out the light and silently goes through to the garage. She gets into her car, leaving the door ajar so that the clunk of it closing won't give her away, and listens. All is quiet outside. She continues to read. Ten, fifteen minutes go by, then she hears a noise. The noise is inside the house.

She listens hard, trying to decipher words, but without success. There is no point in rushing. Let them settle, become comfortable . . .

Music. Loud, Wagnerian (she by now has learned to recognize) opera.

There's a gun in her purse, she's not just another defenceless woman at the mercy of some mad intruder. She will go in and confront Tobes: have done with this thing, finish it. All six senses are crisp and alert, more so than ever before. Her blood has diluted and cooled itself to a crystalline, life-giving wine.

She gets out of that car knowing herself now as well as she knows Tobes, almost, and lines of poetry, memorized so long ago, surface for the first time in years . . .

> . . . *Like one, that on a lonesome road*
> *Doth walk in fear and dread,*
> *And having once turned round walks on,*
> *And turns no more his head;*
> *Because he knows a frightful fiend*
> *Doth close behind him tread . . .*

Johnny registers her entrance at once. 'Hi, Diane!' he cries, and starts forward. But Tobes puts a hand on his shoulder and drags him back. In his other hand he holds a short, pointed stick. Diane's lonely chopstick. He brings it around in front of him, holding it out like one of Hitler's field-marshals with his staff of office. Somehow it's more lethal than any stiletto.

444

He is wearing some of her clothes. Diane is aware of Johnny's puzzled face turning between the two grown-ups, but dares not look at him.

Tobes says, 'Put down your purse.'

Diane sees the telephone on a nearby dresser and moves slowly towards it. Tobes does not object. She lays her purse beside the instrument and turns to rest the small of her back against the dresser.

The phone rings.

She half turns and lifts the receiver.

'*No!*' Tobes yells.

'Diane,' says a familiar voice in her ear, 'are you alone, I can hear . . . ?'

Tobes is running.

' . . . Diane, are you okay? What's happening? *Diane!*'

'I'm fine. Can't talk now, I'm fine.'

Tobes wrestles Diane to the floor. Their struggle is short. He weighs her down, the stink of Marlboros in her nostrils, there is a snapping sound, she wrenches her head to the left and sees he has torn the phone from its jack. Bare wire glitters in the light, beyond repair.

'Who was that?' Tobes gets off her and stands up. She also stands, more slowly. Johnny is against the far wall, one hand held to his mouth, eyes open wide. *'Who was it?'*

'A friend.'

'Ed Hersey?'

'A friend.'

Tobes beckons Johnny. The boy goes to him at once. Tobes puts an arm around his shoulder and says, 'Shut your ears, don't listen to a thing she says.'

'Why?'

445

'Because she's mad. And bad, all bad.'

Johnny twists around to look up at Tobes, his face a mask of bewilderment.

'We're going to talk,' Tobes says.

Diane nods.

It's misty outside; now something of the same atmosphere pervades her home. Johnny is wearing only a T-shirt, jeans and sneakers. He's pale as moonlight. A ship's siren sounds mournfully across the channel and he shivers.

'Tobes,' says Diane, 'why don't we light the fire? Yes?'

He takes his time considering it. Meanwhile, Diane wonders what Ed will do. Where was he calling from? Headquarters? That's a forty-five-minute drive.

Tobes puts the chopstick down on the coffee-table for long enough to take off Diane's jacket and skirt. He tosses them onto the sofa, next to his old, weather-beaten jerkin. After an uncertain pause, he pulls on the jerkin, settling it over his shoulders again and again, like a nervous reaction. For a wild second it crosses her mind that he's getting ready to leave. But . . . 'Sure,' he says slowly. 'A fire.'

Diane moves across to the fireplace. Some logs are already piled in the grate. What to light them with?

Tobes knows. With an evil grin he takes one hand from his jerkin-pocket, holding a pack of cards, fanned out. He extends them towards her until she recognizes her own name-cards. Using his other hand he extracts a pack of cigarettes and a lighter. He drops both onto the sofa; then, without removing his eyes from hers, he crouches slightly to pick up the lighter and use it to ignite her cards.

Diane knows that by burning her cards, her name, he is burning her. This is but a prelude to Armageddon, this is foreplay.

At last Tobes touches the cards to the paper beneath the logs, which blaze up quickly. 'I had to throw out your milk,' he says, rising to his feet. 'Maybe we could down that Champagne?'

She starts towards the kitchen.

'Wait.'

Diane stops. 'Yes?'

'The lights. Turn them out. All of them. Light those candles. And please remember, oh healer, that I shall watch everything you do, everywhere you go.'

'You and Sting both? Sure . . . the lights.'

The fire is blazing away now, so when Diane extinguishes the lights the house remains suffused with a pleasant glow. But for some reason this does not satisfy Tobes. He goes to the cupboard beneath the stairs and wrenches it open. Inside is a big fuse-box. He does something, and the music dies. With a scowl he dives back inside her fuse-box, and a moment later Wagner resumes his funereal beat, but the lights stay out.

Diane does the rounds, lighting candles, six of them in all. Scents of mimosa, and lavender, and wild rose, start to pervade the house. The glass bowls, full of oil, look beautiful by firelight.

Tobes says, 'Shall we take cocktails?'

Fire and candlelight illuminate the kitchen enough to let Diane see what she's doing. Her two guests follow her but keep their distance; perhaps they apprehend some awesome display of *kung-fu* histrionics? Johnny looks at Diane as if she has traded places with Nicole, becoming the Wicked Witch of his nightmares.

447

The ice-box is bare. Diane remembers hiding some Doritos on a top shelf during one of her diet phases. They're still there. She hands them down to Johnny, then pours two glasses of Laurent-Perrier. Tobes watches her every move, as promised, but anyway and alas! she has no Mickey Finns.

'Let's go back to the fire,' Johnny says. His voice has shrunk to the size of a pea. Everybody troops back in the living-room. Johnny runs across to the fireplace and kneels, holding his hands out to the blaze. Tobes stands next to him.

'Sit down, Diane,' he says.

She does so. Shadows dance in time to the flames, sometimes letting her see Tobes's eyes, sometimes not. He raises his glass. 'To us.'

Diane drinks.

'I was crazy for you,' Tobes says, tilting the glass to savour the wine's colour. His voice is comfortable, reminiscent. 'I thought you were going to save me.' He shrugs, takes another sip of wine. 'We could have been something wonderful together, wonderful as this wine.' Another sip. 'But you chose to betray me. Hey, this is good, *really*. You live well, don't you?'

The sadness of Laurent-Perrier begins to weave its spell around Diane like a hauntingly beautiful chant heard in a near-empty cathedral on a sunny afternoon. She takes another sip, remembering her old tutor and his never-to-be-fulfilled desire for tenure. Her own tenure on life had never felt so strong, so pure . . .

Through the silence a car can be heard mounting the drive.

Three heads move as one. Three pairs of eyes stare through the gloom at the drapes that conceal the window next to the front door. Sure enough, headlight beams sweep across it, briefly hemming the material with gold . . . Footsteps in Diane's driveway, on her steps, the porch . . . A discreet rat-a-tat-tat, neither timid nor indicative of a desire to beat down the door. Diane gets up, pauses. Still no reaction from Tobes. She walks towards the front door. When she is halfway to it, a cold hand closes around her upper arm. Tobes's face swims into view. His lips are very close to hers.

'Get him in here,' he breathes. *'Do it.'*

Diane stares at the floor. The rat-a-tat is repeated. She looks up, but Tobes and Johnny have vanished. She wheels around. No sign of them. *Where are they?* She pulls herself together and opens the door. Ed has one hand half raised as if to knock a third time. Seeing her, he smiles. 'Hi,' he says. 'How are you?'

Something is wrong.

He should come in – she has stood aside to let him pass – and assume command here. He does not move. Diane looks at him. His face is intense, his eyes strive to send her a message.

'I happened to be passing,' he says. 'Thought I'd drop by.'

'Come in.'

And still he does not move. 'Kind of late. I won't stay.'

His eyes roam over her living-room. He sees the fire, the candles . . . a homicide dick casing the crime-scene.

'Come in,' Diane says. 'Do.' When Ed just continues to stare at and around her, she rambles on, 'Was just finishing up some research. Wagner. You know? You remember . . . ?'

Ed wants her to *do* something. Tobes wants her to *do* something. But what more can she do than she's doing

449

already? 'Ed,' she says, putting some beef into it, 'come in, it's cold, there's a fire, I have wine.'

'Thanks,' he replies, turning away, 'but I'm on duty tonight.'

'*Ed!*'

Ed goes down the steps, down the path; he gets into his car, waves out the open window, starts the engine, and then he drives away.

Diane shuts the door and leans back against it, her eyes closed. But then she hears rustling sounds, and knows she can't stay blind for ever, so she opens her eyes. And there, on the coffee-table, are two glasses, both half full of wine, both twinkling in the flames, calling attention to themselves.

Ed saw the glasses. *Must have done!*

Tobes unravels himself around her kitchen-door, Johnny clutched firmly in the crook of his arm. In his free hand he holds a pistol, aimed at the ceiling. Now he lowers it until it's pointing at Diane. 'Why didn't you get him in? Uh? *Uh?*'

'You heard,' Diane says dully. 'He wouldn't.'

'Yeah, because you were signalling to him, let me guess.' His voice is one long sneer. 'Hey, what do you think of this? Neat, huh?'

He is holding out the gun for her inspection, still holding it by the butt, though. Perhaps twenty feet separate them; she cannot see the gun clearly.

'I found this in my room earlier this evening,' Tobes says to Johnny. 'Kind of unexpected. You see, it's not mine. Three guesses whose it is.'

Diane walks over to the sofa and sits down, yes, even though he keeps his gun pointing at her, connected to her forehead by an invisible wire, so that as she walks it stays aimed at the same spot, somehow she manages that. Johnny's eyes flicker from side to side; Diane assesses him and concludes that her little patient's mind is going back over past landmarks, seeking clues to what is happening.

Those landmarks should not be hard to find, not if she does her job right.

'I don't know what you're talking about,' Diane says. 'Do you know, Johnny?'

'Don't talk to the kid. Don't you dare talk to the kid. You're not fit to wipe his ass!' Tobes has taken two or three steps towards her sofa. 'You want him, but you're not going to have him.'

'Because he's all yours, yes, I know.'

'*No!* Because he's nobody's. He's his own guy.' Tobes's hand, his gun-hand, is shaking. Diane holds her breath and mentally says goodbye to *Ma-ma*, for she's about to die. 'Your policeman friend . . . he's realized the truth.'

The gun has drooped. She is still alive. And Tobes has released Johnny.

'That's why he wouldn't come in.' Tobes's face has taken on a look of calculating satisfaction. 'He got my envelope.'

'Your what?'

'My envelope. I kept records. I wrote up my records and sent a report to Detective Hersey. Plus Júlia's thank-you note for San Diego. I stole it off you. He knows you iced those kids.'

Diane thinks about that. 'Tobes,' she says, 'does Johnny know about your past?' Tobes looks away, silent. 'Does he know you were molested by your father? And that you yourself were into fire-setting? And blackmail?'

Tobes's face turns livid. 'Shut all that shit.'

451

'Johnny,' she says, braving Tobes's wrath, 'there are things about this man you'll have to discover some time, and I think this is the right time.'

'Don't listen to her, Johnny.'

But now Johnny takes an independent line. He says, 'What's a pervert?'

In the silence that follows, Tobes turns away and rests his forehead against her mantelpiece. The gun dangles tantalizingly, but still too far away for Diane to risk a dive at it.

'A pervert,' she says carefully, 'means someone who's taken a wrong road when it comes to sex. You know about sex, Johnny, we've discussed it. Well, a male pervert enjoys making love to another man, instead of a woman. There's more to it, but that's enough to be going on with, don't you think?'

Throughout all this Johnny looks at her with unwavering seriousness, a boy determined to learn. 'You're saying Tobes is a pervert?' he says, once she is done.

'I believe so.'

'Why?'

'Because of some things that happened to him when he was younger.'

Johnny turns to look at Tobes, who ignores him. 'Why not tell me about it?' the boy says softly.

'What's to tell?' Tobes says to the fireplace. He raises his head to look at Diane. 'The police will be here to take you away soon,' he says. 'Until then, shut your mouth.'

He points the gun at her. 'Tobes,' says Johnny, 'don't do that. Please.'

'But she's telling lies about me!'

'Maybe she is.' Johnny turns back to Diane. 'I want to hear anyway.'

He is wavering. He can be made to understand. All Diane has to do is choose each word with care.

Dear God, that's all.

She steels herself to the task, and begins. She tells Johnny about her meeting with Baker, the school assistant principal. It's a fine line when it comes down to physical detail: she must give Johnny enough horrors to lure him to her side, without alienating him. She tells him what Tobes's father said to her. She reminds Johnny, gently, that Tobes was wearing her clothes a moment ago, that he likes wearing women's clothes, that he wore female garments the night he lured Joel Hagen into a basement before setting fire to it, and in the cemetery when masquerading as Alice Mornay . . .

'You're so smart.'

Tobes interrupts her monologue, but in an unexpected manner, without violence. He throws himself down on her sofa, with the gun hanging between his splayed legs, and he says again, 'You're so smart.'

Behind him, through the kitchen-door, Diane can see the corner of a window overlooking the deck. There are no drapes for that window, which is but a glittery black segment. Something, someone, has just moved across it, without a sound.

Who is out there and for whom have they come?

For Tobes?

For her?

She sits forward a little, aiming for sincerity, and says, 'No one blames you, Tobes. There was nothing you could have done to prevent any of it.'

He remains silent. His eyes are level with hers. They waver slightly with the movement of his head as he eases it from side to side. He is worn out. He hates her with a passion, but because he is exhausted the passion lies dormant. Only she can see that hatred. She *feels* his loathing and his rage.

'Maybe you'd better take some more treatment with Diane.'

For Tobes and Diane, locked into their own little world, this comes as an intrusion: their eyes tell each other how much they resent Johnny's interference. Then Tobes says bitterly, '*Et tu, Brute?*'

He pronounces the last word to rhyme with loot; Diane knows that reading in the library with a kitten tucked in your sweater doesn't teach you how to pronounce dead languages. 'Don't blame Johnny,' she says. 'He's not just another traitor. You told me that.'

'I know.'

Tobes stands up (and still the gun dangles, unaimed *but never close enough*) and he says, 'I thought he was different, you see. I realized the safe thing was to turn my back and walk away. But I liked him. Then I loved him. Then . . .'

'Then,' Diane quietly intervenes, 'came a day you wanted to buy him flowers, because that's what you do for your lover, for the love of your life. His betrayal over Alice. The withdrawals, the misunderstandings, the officer's uniform . . . the end.'

For a second Tobes doesn't register. Then he jerks his head up and the murder is back in his heart.

'You read my notebooks. You did. You fucking did that.'

'All of them,' she says, rising from her chair. 'I know you covered your desire for Johnny with guilt-transference, putting your evil thoughts on to me. I know you would have killed him, as you killed all the rest.'

'*Killed* him.' Tobes looks at Diane in astonishment. 'No, you can't believe that. I love him!' He wheels

454

around to where Johnny stands in the corner by the fireplace, forcing himself into the angle of the two walls, trying to magic himself away. 'Tell her I love you,' Tobes shouts. Johnny trembles. He shakes his head, unable to speak.

'You must have known,' Diane says, advancing on Tobes (the gun nearer and nearer now), 'in your deepest heart, that Johnny was only attracted to you because he didn't see the real Tobes.'

'No! You're so wrong, wrong!'

'In his eyes, you were what you always yearned to be.'

'Oh, yes? Which was?'

'Somebody else. That's why you went in for play-acting, dressing up, escaping.'

'But you *told* me to do those things! You were even going to introduce me to the Orcutt drama society, you said you were, you did say that! I'm sure . . . I'm . . . '

Suddenly Tobes's vacant eyes light on Johnny. The boy has stopped trembling. His pale face is blotchy with red spots: a plague-victim. His wide-open eyes keep their dilated pupils upon Tobes – but not in idolatry or adulation. Now he is watching a beast lest it strike him down unawares.

Tobes takes a few steps towards the boy. He holds out his arms, meaning to show love and warmth; but by now Johnny sees only Frankenstein's creation bearing down. He ducks under Tobes's left elbow and sprints for the front door. Tobes reaches it ahead of him. He stands before it with arms outstretched, cruciform; but no saviour, he. His right arm, the gun-hand, swings inwards. 'Back off,' Tobes hisses. 'You know what happened to the women who promised they'd save the Dutchman and cheated? They were damned for all time! *Back off.*'

Johnny spins around and heads for the stairs as fast as his feet can carry him. Tobes charges after him. Diane makes a clumsy effort to trip him up, missing by inches. She knows that once Johnny's upstairs he will swiftly be cornered. Light's the next essential. The fuse-box. She wastes valuable seconds trying to undo whatever damage Tobes did in the cupboard beneath the stairs, but her house refuses to power up no matter what she does, and time is eating away at Johnny.

One hope. Diane races back into her living-room and seizes a log from the hearth. Glowing ash drops on her wrist and she yelps. Nine inches from the flame end, the wood is hotter than she would have imagined possible. She drops the brand onto a table, upsetting an oil-candle. The bowl shatters, oil spills. She snatches a cloth from the sideboard and wraps it around the brand. Then she grabs the gun from her purse and rushes for the stairs, light in one hand, death in the other.

Part of her mind knows she has made a mistake. When she pulled that brand from the fire she dislodged others, sending them in a fiery cascade over her hearth-rug. She should run back and replace them. She should wipe up the oil from the broken candle. No time.

She hits the bottom step and the music reaches a mighty crescendo. At the same second, million-watt beams criss-cross her windows. A voice hails through a bullhorn: *'Gascoign, I know you can hear me. This is Chief of Patrol Sean McShea. We have the house surrounded. Send the boy out first, along with Dr Cheung, and you won't be harmed.'*

Glass smashes on the upper floor. Diane bounds up the last dozen stairs and hares towards her bedroom. On the threshold, she pauses. Tobes has Johnny around the neck and is standing beside her shattered window, looking out. '*Back off!*' he screams, half to her, half to the crowd outside: a big crowd, for many voices now rise and fall on the cool breeze that sweeps in from the channel.

Diane rushes at Tobes, holding her blazing log in front of her. He senses it coming. Next moment, he's holding the boy out in front of him like a shield. Diane pulls back, can smell the singe in Johnny's hair. Another half-second and she'd have scorched out his eyes.

She can smell something else, too. Downstairs, things are burning. Not logs: but cloth, materials, dyestuffs. The logs she pulled from the hearth, the oil-candle . . .

Tobes raises his hand. Metal gleams dully. 'You planted this gun on me, you bitch,' he howls. He shakes it at her; she parries with her log, but that is almost spent now. 'Match the ballistics of this with the weapon that killed Douggan! And Jensen, and Delmar! They'll fucking match. What does that make you, Diane?'

'On the contrary,' she ripostes, 'what does it make *you*?' His gun trembles. Somehow he manages to keep it aimed at her head. 'Your fingerprints are on it,' she continues quietly. 'Not mine. My gun was reported stolen a long time ago. And you confessed to me, remember? You told me that you were the killer. *You* told me about Alice Mornay, you told me about the place where they found Delmar's body.'

Johnny has gone limp in Tobes's grasp. But suddenly he hears a voice he knows, his father's voice, and he dances like an epileptic. '*Johnny,*' Mike croaks through the bullhorn. '*Can you hear me, son?*'

'*Tobes . . .* ' Mike Anderson's voice reverberates through her house. '*Don't hurt my boy. I've got no anger for you, Tobes . . .*'

But Tobes is not listening. His arm around Johnny's neck, gun held out towards Diane, he locks her into a bitter dialogue, a duel unto death. 'You know I only said I was the killer to scare you.'

Diane shakes her head with a smile.

'You know that!' Johnny trembles in his grasp like a soft toy being hugged to extinction. 'Shit . . . ' Tobes looks wildly from window to her and back again. By now, many searchlights are parked on her lawn. It's high noon out there. 'Shit,' Tobes breathes again. 'No one'll ever believe me.'

'That's right. In fact, since you accused me of committing those murders, you've lacked cred. And think of all the evidence against you – cross-dressing, the pornography I found in your room, childhood abuse, your familiarity with the cemetery, your confession to me, your prints on that gun.'

For a moment she fears she has pushed Tobes beyond his limits. His gun-hand stops shaking, she is looking down the barrel . . .

'If you don't kill me,' Diane says, 'I'll still put you away for life. But if you do kill me, they'll give you the chair. And with me dead, your last ally, your white knight, goes down the pipe. Choose, Tobes. Tough one to call, isn't it?'

Flames. The crackling that has nagged at her consciousness ever since she reached this room becomes louder. Her house is on fire; they are trapped. *Keep talking.* That's all she has to do if she wants to pass Go and collect two hundred bucks. Don't stammer, don't stop for breath. 'Put down the gun, Tobes. And let Johnny go. This instant.' Tobes does nothing. *'Now!'*

To reinforce her command, she raises her own gun. And Tobes laughs. 'That gun,' he says, in a hiccuppy kind of voice. 'It's a toy.'

'Oh, really?' Diane says. 'Let's play.'

For all in the same second Johnny bites Tobes's hand, Tobes releases him, his own gun flies upwards. And Diane fires.

Nothing happens. Just a click.

Tobes laughs. 'A toy,' he repeats. He pulls the trigger of his own gun. The world explodes in a volcano of light and sound. Johnny has reached the doorway. Chips of wood fly out, grazing his head. He stops.

'Come back,' Tobes grates. 'Come back here, Johnny. You're a shadow in the firelight, clean as a cut-out target at the fair.'

Diane's mouth is dry as hickory chips. She can't swallow. Johnny comes back. He goes over to her bed, close to Tobes, and sits on it.

Outside, a new note has penetrated the perturbed murmur of the crowd. 'Fire!' someone shouts, quickly echoed by others. 'Get a hose . . . water, quickly!' A woman screams. Nicole.

Tobes is looking at Diane with a wild, triumphant grin. 'It's a toy,' he repeats softly. 'I rented it from Maxine, along with my officer's uniform. A replica. And you managed to pick it up, somehow. But I've got the murder weapon, Diane.'

There is saliva on his chin. On Diane's, too.

'I've got the gun that killed the boys, and it's real, Diane, it fires real bullets, and it's got your prints on it, hasn't it, Dr Cheung . . . *Stand back!*'

For she has taken a step towards him. But then she stops, aware of a change in Tobes. He's staring fixedly over her shoulder. He can see something, someone, on the landing.

There is somebody behind Diane and Tobes knows it.

459

'If you tell me everything,' he shouts, 'I'll let the boy go.'

Intolerable heat is building up. The stairs are on fire. Diane dare not look behind her, dare not take her eyes off Tobes. She has to do something to save Johnny and there is only one thing left to be done.

'Tobes,' she says, 'yes. If you let Johnny go now, I'll tell you everything.'

'Johnny stays. As a witness. I want him to hear this.' And he confirms this by moving a step sideways, so that he can grip Johnny's arm.

'Don't hurt him.' But Tobes's hand tightens on Johnny's flesh, making the boy wince, and, 'All right, *all right*,' Diane shrieks. 'This is the way it happened.'

'Louder. I want Johnny to hear.'

She knows he doesn't mean Johnny, not *only* Johnny. 'Tobes, the house is on fire, you'll kill us, all of us!' But he is once more holding Johnny across his chest, and so Diane takes a deep breath.

'I reported my gun as stolen, when it wasn't, because I wanted a murder weapon that couldn't be connected with me if ever it was found. I had access to CHIPP, so I knew who the offenders were, the men. They'd all been in trouble for illicit sex with younger siblings, cousins; no police records, only CHIPP. I rented a car, different rental-company each time, and I picked them up late at night, or they picked me up, sometimes I dressed in male clothes to confuse anyone who might see me. Men who won't grow up to molest children, like my stepfather molested me, like Terry raped you, I killed those kind of men, you should be glad.'

Tobes and Johnny are staring at her. They breathe heavily. Johnny coughs. Smoke weaves its sickening way around them.

'I fabricated an alibi for Carl's death by pretending to go to San Diego, and sent Julia Page instead, using my name.'

'The name-card, *tell me about the fucking cards*!'

'I . . . I planted my name-card by Carl's body because I knew it was so obvious a clue no one would ever buy it; the cops would suspect my court-referrals instead.'

'Why did it have to be me?'

'From early on I wanted you gone. You'd been staking out this house – after a while I felt sure it was you from your jeans and your Marlboros, you dropped a butt in my garage – and that scared me.'

'So why didn't you just kill me? *Huh?*'

'I planned to.'

They stare at each other, these two antagonists, and for them there is no Earth outside this room, there is no Johnny, no fire, no after-life. This moment is all.

'I planned to . . . you were on my CHIPP list, I knew you'd been abused as a kid, I – '

'How?'

Diane laughed. 'It takes one to know one, isn't that what they say?' She sobered quickly. 'With my experience? clinical and otherwise? I knew. And then I saw how you could be useful to me, that maybe you could be the perfect fall-guy. You came from out of town, with no history, no friends; whereas Jesse, Ramon and Billy were local kids. Except the first time I always killed in the cemetery, and I knew you went there and the police would find that out; and after you told me about Alice Mornay, under hypnosis, I killed Delmar there. And even then, I wasn't sure . . . But then I found Baker and he asked me if the murders involved fire, and sex . . . And after that it was so easy, because until then I'd been fighting your corner, and when I stopped, when even *I* stopped defending you, the effect was crushing, it finished you. I knew about profiling, knew how to point the finger at you in subtle ways; knew how to write up my case-notes to make it all look so fine, and tonight I planted my gun, the one I'd used to kill the boys, in your room, though I didn't think you'd go back and find it, I thought you'd come straight here, and I took yours because I needed a weapon and I thought it was real . . . that's how it happened, now free the boy.'

For a long moment Tobes says nothing. Diane is fighting back a spasm in the back of her throat, for she knows that once she lets it out she won't be able to stop coughing, the cough will become a retch, she will vomit and faint and fall . . .

Tobes pushes Johnny forward. The boy darts past her, onto the landing, which is filled with black smoke. She hears him cry out, 'You!', something like that, and her heart stops. *Who was behind her, what did he hear?* Not 'Dad!' but 'You!' . . . She hears footsteps on the stairs, running, more than one person, Johnny can only have said 'You!' because he recognized whoever it was, must be Ed Hersey, *must be* . . .

Diane hurls the brand against her bed. With its last, dying embers it ignites the sheet: at first the flimsy material only smoulders, then, even as Tobes falls upon it in a desperate attempt to extinguish this new conflagration, it goes up in a whoosh of flame. Tobes's hair catches light. He runs crazily around in a circle, holding both hands to his head, screaming. Suddenly he trips over something, the single chopstick, long forgotten, and falls. Diane, too, falls, knowing that the smoke will be thinner near the floor. Her hands make contact with the chopstick. Tobes's blazing head has come to rest near her hands. He is gurgling, his mouth is open. She closes both her hands around the chopstick and raises herself up, into the smoke, lifting the chopstick as high above her head as she can reach. She falls forward, forcing herself home like a pile driver.

The chopstick encounters resistance, but it is soft resistance. It penetrates and keeps going down, through his tongue, his larynx, his throat, until she has finished it. What she has to do.

Someone is hauling on her shoulders. She is being dragged backwards, away from the excrescence that despoils her bedroom floor, onto the landing. Rough hands lift her upright. Through the whirling smoke she can just make out a face in the firelight: Ed.

His rage-filled eyes dazzle her. Of course, he heard her 'confession'. That, and Tobes's letter . . . not since Judas placed his lips to Jesus's cheek has a man suffered such depths of betrayal.

Ed tries to pick her up. She struggles. 'I can walk,' she screams.

He takes her by the hand and begins to tug her along the landing, towards the remains of the stairs. He wants to rescue her, yes, but this is an arrest also. What matter? For her house is now a fireball, a blazing apogee of heat about to achieve its final moment of glory; and anyway what is justice, if not a kind of peace?

She can't breathe. Smoke fills her nostrils, and it is such evil smoke: no bonfire, this. Plastics, polythenes, poisons, all combine in a lethal witch's brew.

Now the heat has grown intolerable. It scalds her skin. For the first time, she succumbs to the lure of panic. Sparks spit through the floorboards, she can feel the fire-demon's power rising through the soles of her feet.

The stairs go with a crackling clatter of yellows and oranges and a shower of rubies. They collapse with immense majesty, as if the director has decreed slo-mo for this, the final scene.

No way out.

Ed and Diane absorb their fate. Ed stands three feet ahead of her, looking into the inferno. He holds his right arm up to his eyes, shading them, while with his left hand he clutches a handkerchief to his mouth. Because of the way he does that, she can see the top of a brown envelope tucked into the inside pocket of his jacket. She recognizes it as the one Leo had given him in the street earlier. *'I wrote up my records and sent a report to Detective Hersey.'*

Ed begins to turn. She knows what he has decided: there is no way out through the house, they must find a window and jump. But a lick of flame snatches at his heels. He yells something. His trouser cuff is on fire. He stamps up and down and pushes her away, indicating that she is to run for it.

How could she leave him?

He glances over his shoulder, monitoring the progress of the fire. Ed reaches out for her, but somehow, despite her valiant efforts, their hands fail to meet. Their fingers almost brush, almost, almost . . . but then, desperate to extinguish his burning cuffs, Ed slips, teeters, falls . . .

The last view she has of Ed is of him plummeting through bright yellow space, arms and legs outspread so that he is like a star shooting across the firmament, a dark star with stark white edges. Then he is gone.

She turns away from the remains of her staircase, thinking to find an exit clear ahead, only to be faced with a black, moving wall. Smoke has risen through cracks in the floorboards, it fills each molecule of breathable atmosphere. Her face is drenched in sweat, the heat is not to be borne. She cannot see to find her way. She falls on hands and knees. Her head swims. Her lungs burn, her stomach knots in agony. She lifts her hands from the boards, unable to bear the heat. The roar of flames is closer than ever.

Throughout all this death and destruction, Wagner has never ceased to fill her house; Diane can hear him somewhere ahead, pounding away. She starts to crawl towards the noise, moving fast in order to minimize contact with the floor, which feels red-hot. And then Wagner dies on her. One moment, blaring drums and trumpets; the next, silence, except for the roar of the fire-demon at her heels.

Diane feels herself sinking, and it is terrible. Death is not kind. It strips the lining of her chest away, each gasp brings her nearer the edge of oblivion, her eyes are boiling in their sockets. She is lying down now, her head on the boards, and the stench she can smell is flesh. Her own.

She is in the plane.

The plane is on fire, and falling. She fights her way forward along the aisle, striving to reach the cockpit. Coils of poisonous black smoke slither inside her lungs, making her retch. 'Mother,' she cries, 'Mother, help me!' She has to fight her way uphill (strange, because the plane is diving), every inch feels like a mile, her heart pounds, her eyes dim. Through the smoke she can just see the flight-deck door opening. Someone is coming out, someone scary. She falls on her back. The someone comes to stand over her. She – definitely a she – is Diane's end and her beginning.

Diane is outside herself, looking down. Her body is naked and pure white, arms crossed over her breast like a figure on a medieval tomb. Her eyes are closed. She sits up, that dreadful, dead face, *her* face, coming closer and closer, coming upright, coming upright . . .

Shards of glass howl all around. Glass shreds her lips, settles in her hair; when she moves her hands, they bleed.

'Diane! *Diane!*'

The voice comes at her down a long, twisty corridor. She recognizes it. 'Leo,' she croaks, 'here . . .'

He has climbed up to her big round window, the one next to where she keeps her stereo, and he has hammered his way inside and now he is slinging her over his shoulder. They are on a ladder, with Diane upside down: this is pain writ large, bump, bump, bump. Leo nearly drops her as they reach the ground; then he is running. There is a crash, followed by an indescribable sound: Whoomph! They are sprawling, Leo on top of Diane, her face in mud, unable to breathe, but alive.

Diane is alive.

I could have made it with Ed, that was my first conscious thought as Leo rolled off me. Ed Hersey might have been the man to redeem me, to have faced the horrors that beset me and fought them by my side. I will never know; but this I do know: I wanted so much to save him from the fire that I did not even care about the consequences for myself, and that is love. I am capable of real love. Soon I must recall that bitter, betrayed face and cry for him. Not now. Now nothing matters at all. Unless it be Johnny.

Johnny came rushing over to where I lay and told me I was so brave and he wished I could be his mother. He took my hand while they came to cover me with a blanket and he said, 'Oh, Diane, I'm so glad, so glad you're safe. Thank you for saving me, thank you!'

I reached up, and my fingers brushed his cheek, and we started shaking, and then we burst into tears.

'Ed got me out,' Johnny said, when he could speak again. 'He was at the top of the stairs. He ran me down, out the door, and then he went back in again. They tried to stop him, but he said he had to get you.'

I wanted to say, 'Ed didn't make it,' something like that, but Johnny said it for me, and that gave me the courage to tell him, 'Tobes didn't make it either.' Johnny stroked my cheek and whispered, 'No.'

'Tobes was mad, wasn't he?' Johnny went on, after a while. 'I mean, all those bad things he said about you, killing people.'

'He was mad, yes.'

'And you had to pretend to go along with him, or he'd never have let me go.'

He hugged me, forgetting I'd been hurt, and I screamed. Once things had quietened down again I caught sight of something over Johnny's shoulder and smiled. Mike and Nicole stood there, arm in arm. Mike kissed Nicole's cheek, but never taking his eyes off Johnny, and in that moment I knew the boy was loved.

'Diane,' said Johnny, and his voice had turned all wistful, 'Will you be my friend?'

And I said, 'Yes. I'll see you grow up right.'

'Really?'

'Oh, yes. You see, Johnny, it's like I wrote in my book: if you don't grow up right . . . you won't get to grow up at all.'

And he laughed, but not as much as I did.

They came to put me in the ambulance, then. As they loaded me up, I suddenly knew my task was over; I had cleansed the world enough, done what I had to, and now it was time to make a new life. Quite naturally: no pain or grief of any kind. Ma-ma just came and stood there, smiling at me. I said, 'I'm sorry I burned our house, Mother.' And then, 'The flight-deck door opened, but no one came out.' I knew why no one came out, of course: Larry had driven her to a premature death, she'd died of sorrow, had Ma-ma, but I'd got her some revenge, I surely had, and now her ghost could rest.

Just before they closed the door of the ambulance, my house went. I turned my head to see it collapse in upon itself like one of those black holes in space. It all seemed to be over so suddenly, after such Sturm und Drang. One minute it was standing by the ocean, a beautiful, angry firework; the next it had slithered into a heap of charred beams, and doorframes that miraculously kept their shape, and unrecognizable heaps *of what I once owned and thought of as mine. My lovely house had gone. My home had gone.*

Along with it went the following:

Ed Hersey.

Tobes Gascoign.

Tobes's notebooks.

The envelope he sent to Ed.

Two guns, one of them real.

Truth.

I will rebuild the house, better than before. And in the far corner of my meadow I shall plant a sequoia sapling that will grow up straight and clean and true. Hal Lawson would like to think of a sequoia shading his final resting place. The night I picked him up and took him home, he told me how much he loved trees, and I said, 'That's nice.'

The Tiger of Desire
John Trenhaile

In 1973 Iain Forward was framed for murder. After seventeen
years in prison he's finally getting out, obsessed with the
desire to find out who was responsible.

The world outside has changed beyond recognition and the
strain of adjusting to it takes him by surprise – yet there
waiting for him is his wife Alison. Throughout the years,
Alison has loyally stood by him, looking forward to the day
when they can once again plan a future together.

But Iain can think only of the past – of the mysterious events
in Singapore that led to his arrest. As he struggles towards the
real story behind his imprisonment, he discovers disturbing
connections between his employers there, Harchem Pharma-
ceuticals, and current events in the Gulf, where Iraq has just
invaded Kuwait.

When the trail leads him back to Singapore, the dark secrets
he unearths about his former colleagues are equalled only by
the truths he must learn about himself . . . and there are a lot
of dangerous people who are determined that those secrets
should remain hidden.

'The heir apparent to le Carré.'   *Today*

ISBN 0 00 647313 X

Acts of Betrayal
John Trenhaile

THE PENALTY FOR TREASON IS DEATH

When an IRA plot to assassinate the Queen is foiled, an outraged public demands vengeance. Before long Frank Thornton, barrister, businessman, finds himself standing trial for treason. If found guilty, he will hang.

Driven by a long-standing emotional debt, Roz Forbes, deputy editor of *The Times*, launches an impassioned campaign to prevent a miscarriage of justice. As she struggles to clear his name, she unearths shocking links with a shady underworld of drugs and terrorism.

But before she can act on her discovery, Roz herself becomes a pawn in the terrifying world of international politics. While she remains a helpless hostage, time is running out for the condemned man . . .

'This is a novel full of lies and moments of truth: none of the truths is palatable and all of the lies are deadly'

Evening Standard

'Shocking . . . the suspense, woven by a British writer hailed as the heir apparent to le Carré, is killing'   *Today*

ISBN 0 00 617989 4

Krysalis
John Trenhaile

Successful barrister or long-term neurotic? Faithful wife or scheming traitor? Who – and where – is Anna Lescombe?

Krysalis, a highly sensitive NATO file, has gone missing from the home of civil servant David Lescombe. His wife, Anna, has also disappeared. In view of David's position and the importance of the Krysalis file, international security services are quick to accuse Anna of treason.

Convinced of her innocence, David begins a dangerous race to find her – and discovers just how little he really knew about his wife.

From Anna's past emerges the shadowy figure of psycho-analyst Gerhard Kleist. Are he and Anna merely doctor and patient? Or lovers? Or is Kleist's role something more sinister?

'Tense . . . moves forward smartly all the way. Most impressive.'   *Independent*

'A tightly-paced tale of manipulation and deception.' *Today*

ISBN 0 00 617877 4

The Mahjong Spies
John Trenhaile

In 1997 China will repossess Hong Kong. But the KGB is determined to undermine Hong Kong's precarious financial stability, ensuring that the Chinese will inherit only an empty, worthless shell.

The elite of Chinese Intelligence – the Mahjong Brigade – have chosen Simon Young, an influential *tai-pan* in Hong Kong, as their instrument to sabotage the Russian plans. But Young is a novice in the hostile world of international espionage and if he is to survive at all he must secure his own allies in this deadly game.

'Intricate, tense, rich in characters and incidents . . . Trenhaile will please the most ardent fans of spy fare with this gripping story.' *Publishers Weekly*

'Powerful financial thriller . . . a grim, tense and violent slice of the action.' *Liverpool Daily Post*

'A rattling good read.' *Financial Times*

ISBN 0 00 617380 2

The Gates of
Exquisite View
John Trenhaile

Bestselling author of *The Mahjong Spies*

'I WELCOME YOU THROUGH THE GATES OF EXQUISITE VIEW'
– a phrase carved above the entrance to the torture-
chamber of executioner Lai Chun-Ch'en.

To save his life Mat Young must tell his inquisitors the
secret of Apogee – a fifth generation supercomputer.
But it is a secret he does not possess.

Mat has been caught in Red China's deadly ambitions
to take back Taiwan by force. As has Simon Young his
tai-pan father, and Mat's lover, one of Taiwan's most
glamorous actresses . . .

'Rarely a moment to pause for breath between the
agonizingly suspenseful events in a thriller that is
worthy of its genre.'   *Publishers Weekly*

ISBN 0 00 617602 X

☐	TELLING THE PICTURES Frank Delaney	0-00-647924-3	£4.99
☐	VIOLENT WARD Len Deighton	0-00-647901-4	£4.99
☐	WITHOUT REMORSE Tom Clancy	0-00-647641-4	£5.99
☐	PROVO Gordon Stevens	0-00-647632-5	£4.99
☐	NAME OF THE BEAST Daniel Easterman	0-586-21088-1	£4.99

All these books are available from your local bookseller or can be ordered direct from the publishers.

To order direct just tick the titles you want and fill in the form below:

Name: _____

Address: _____

_____

Postcode: _____

Send to: HarperCollins Mail Order, Dept 8, HarperCollins *Publishers*, Westerhill Road, Bishopbriggs, Glasgow G64 2QT.

Please enclose a cheque or postal order or your authority to debit your Visa/Access account –

Credit card no: _____

Expiry date: _____

Signature: _____

– to the value of the cover price plus:

UK & BFPO: Add £1.00 for the first and 25p for each additional book ordered.

Overseas orders including Eire, please add £2.95 service charge.

Books will be sent by surface mail but quotes for airmail despatches will be given on request.

24 HOUR TELEPHONE ORDERING SERVICE FOR ACCESS/VISA CARDHOLDERS –

TEL: GLASGOW 041-772 2281 or LONDON 081-307 4052